THE PIKE BOYS

Book 1

Danny Cherry, Jr.

BIG EASY PRESS
Est. 2023

The Pike Boys
Copyright © 2024 by Danny Cherry, Jr.

For information contact :
Bigeasypress@gmail.com
http://www.bigeasypress.com
Instagram/Tiktok/BlueSky/Twitter (X): @Deecherrywriter

Book and Cover design by Chris Rychter
ISBN: **979-8-9888038-1-2**

First Edition: January 2024

10 9 8 7 6 5 4 3 2 1

Acknowledgements

I want to thank my mother and father for allowing me to explore my creativity in my youth, and for always listening to my rambling stories. I also want to thank my uncle Lawrence for telling me at a young age to always be curious, and for reminding me how, when I was a kid, I constantly talked about wanting to be a writer when I grew up. Thanks to my beta readers, Kassandra Majesky, Matt Donnellon, and Sebastian Richards for reading my book when it was a work-in-progress.

Lastly, I want to thank my wife. She is the person who got me back into writing after I had abandoned it in my teens, and she dragged me to the finish line in the moments where I *really* didn't want to finish this book. I couldn't have accomplished all that I have in my writing career without her.

You all have helped me in more ways than I could ever express, and even when I don't say it, I am forever grateful.

Thank you

Preface

I came up with this book when I was about 20 years old, and finished it about 4 years ago. I was in college when I started, and the nation at the time seemed to be preparing to boil over in ways a 20-year-old had never fathomed. Racial tension seemed (at that point) to be the highest I'd seen in my young life. It was hard to sit down at a keyboard when mounting anxiety from tests and figuring out who I was, along with feelings of existential dread, got in the way. It got hard trying to reconcile that I lived in a nation that sometimes felt hostile to my existence. It was all made harder by the fact I had no words in my lexicon to describe what I felt. (Writers like James Baldwin would later clear this up for me).

So I instead generated an idea so far removed from myself—something I wanted to use to hide away from any existential dread—and invented a comic book character called Jesse "Quick Draw" Pike, a gun-slinging cowboy, and

Claude (he would later become Clyde), a random 1920s gangster.

That's where this book started: an attempt by a 20-year-old who wanted to escape and get transported into a world different from his. And how different can I be from two white men from the 1920s? Then over time, the two characters became brothers, and then I added a brother, a sister, and a childhood best friend. Then I realized I invented a gang.

I had always loved crime fiction, whether it be prose or television. Everything from Sons of Anarchy and Breaking Bad to Don Winslow's Cartel Series lived rent-free in my mind. Also, when visiting my parents, my dad would sometimes have on a true crime show of some form, which deepened my interest in wanting to explore the criminal element. So, I took this family that I was so different from and created the Pike Boys.

Writing this book was beyond daunting. So daunting to the point that I asked a friend to help me write it because I didn't think I could do it alone. Once he said no, I figured I'd use the novel as a chance to improve my writing skills, and not a venture to take seriously. I had read that all first books are bad, so when you're done your first one, you should throw it in a trunk and work on the next. But along the way... I fell in love with the characters. I couldn't abandon it.

Hours upon hours were spent at my dorm room's uncomfortable ass desk and in the school library, where I'd sit by the window and watch my peers congregate while I wrote and rewrote this damn book. Then later, once I got to grad school, I'd sit in my apartment, attempting to build the world within this book, all while stressing over classes like finance or statistics. Once I was done with the book, I was about 24 or 25 or so, and I told myself I'd submit it to agents to see what happened.

But life happened.

Some bouts with depression, namely because I struggled to find work after graduate school despite promises from teachers that the more education I got, the easier finding a job would be. I worked some temp jobs and even drove Uber and Lyft. All throughout these incidents in my life, I tried to keep my mind on this book, but I got distracted. It's hard to focus on writing about fake people when you got real shit going on.

I took a break from this book for a time to see if I was skilled enough to write for large publications. I honed my skills through blogging, but I would eventually end up in national outlets like Buzzfeed News (RIP), The Daily Beast, and Politico, where I wrote stories with racial and socio-political commentary. I've also written for award-winning fiction magazines, like Fiyah Literary Magazine and Apex Magazine. (I've also had a few stories go viral and semi-viral, as well as one story end up on multiple "end of year" best stories lists, but who's keeping track?)

No matter what happened in my life, the Pike family was always there, over my shoulder, reminding me where this dream of mine all got started: with them, right in that small ass dorm room at Southeastern Louisiana University.

Why do I tell you this?

I tell you this because I want you to know that this book means so much to me in ways that I'll never be able to explore within this preface. I tell you this because I want you to know that for me, this ain't just a book, but a testament to the fact that I was able to make it through all of my worst days, and stayed focused on a promise I made to myself nearly a decade ago.

When I recently read through this book, I remember writing some of these chapters at both my lowest and highest moments, including writing and revising some chapters in spare moments before I went pregame with my college friends for a night out in Downtown Hammond, or while sitting in my car while waiting for my next Uber ride.

This book was written by a younger me that was raw and finding his voice and exploring big themes I didn't have words for yet, and it's the messiness of it and its imperfections that make me love it all the more. Whether this book sells 5 or 500 copies, or gets 0 or 5 stars, I am profoundly proud of it, and I want you to know I appreciate you reading it, even if you don't finish. (But please do finish it.)

Now without further ado, I'd like to introduce you to the Pike Boys.

PART I

"No man for any considerable period can wear one face to himself and another to the multitude, without finally getting bewildered as to which may be the true."- Scarlet Letter

Prologue

The Heist

Mid-summer, 1920

Jesse leaned against the base of a mossy oak tree and rapped his fingers against his sawed-off shotgun. Dirt was caked under his nails and flies buzzed around his ears; the humidity and sweat made his long sleeve cotton button-up feel like a straitjacket. But he closed his eyes and relaxed nonetheless, allowing the sound of his timepiece and nature to drift his imagination to someplace distant. He mumbled under his breath: *Cooks, food, food suppliers, storage.*

The sound of chirping crickets and low-flying mosquitoes turned into clattering plates and happy conversation. The grass and marsh his boots sunk into became solid ballroom floors. People scooted their tables back and danced. The strong scent of the swamp shifted into Creole aromas wafting in from a kitchen, and in his mind, he was actually in a restaurant. His restaurant, if this job goes well.

Annoyed grumbles and snapped branches broke his focus. His eyes shot open, and the restaurant décor descended into darkness, while the sight of shit, flies, and animal carcass-infested marshlands returned to him.

His younger brother, Rory, paced back-and-forth and crunched every twig and stick along the way. He continued to fuss to himself. Jesse rubbed his temples and stood. "Do you wanna calm down?"

Rory looked at his watch. "How much longer do we have to be out here?" Rory's eyes were tiny black beads.

Jesse glared at him. Rory was coked-up out of his mind. But Jesse didn't have the energy to argue, so he said, "The job takes as long as it takes."

Rory snorted and wiped his nose and continued to pace back-and-forth at a near-manic rate. Jesse tried to go back to daydreaming before the trucks came, but at this point, he couldn't even envision a single table, let alone a whole restaurant. Rory sat next to Twitch, the brothers' long-time close friend. Twitch sat against a tree and looked expressionless at the dirt road through the bushes and marsh. He clutched a pistol in one hand and pocket watch in the other.

Rory asked him, "So if there were any girl you could take to town at the brothel, who would it be?"

Twitch had a stutter, so he fumbled the first letter for a bit but said, "I'm married."

"Yeah, yeah I know that. I'm just sayin' if you could get

with any dame at the brothel—" Rory rapid-fired off a round of girls' names. He stopped at one and took his fingers and traced a figure 8 in the air and shot his arms out to mimic big breasts. Jesse choked down a laugh. "Rory, please, leave Twitch alone and shut up for Pete's sake."

Rory waved it away. "Good thing Pete ain't here."

Before Jesse could even respond the sound of tires crunching over dirt and gravel approached them, getting louder and closer as the seconds ticked on. He stood and pulled the sack-mask over his head. He looked at Rory and Twitch. They did the same. Jesse heard the clicking sounds of gun chambers being checked and decided to check his sawed-off. He ducked down so he could be flush with the bushes. The crunching grew closer and closer, prompting Jesse to put three fingers in the air.

Then two.

Then one.

His fingers dropped to a fist and the trio sprinted out from the bushes into the middle of the road. Jesse shot a round into the air and watched as the convoy in front of him shook, rattled, and slammed to a stop and caused a mushroom cloud of dirt to cover the trucks.

Jesse pointed his gun directly at the first truck and inched forward heel to toe. He held the warm steel tight, but not too tight. His palms were sweaty and the humidity could cause the gun to slip. He made a swirl in the air with his pointer finger. Twitch and Rory made wide turns on both sides of him.

One by one, Twitch, Rory, and Jesse snatched the

drivers out of their seats and dragged them into the middle of the road. Jesse stood in the middle, Twitch and Rory flanked him. He looked at the three drivers kneeling in front of him and singled out the lead driver, an older man with three threads of hair matted to the back.

"Get up," Jesse said. The convoy leader stammered. Twitch stepped in and cracked the driver's skull with the bottom of his pistol. Rory stepped in closer with his rifle and placed it right under the man's nose.

"I think you want to get up now," said Jesse. The man wiped the blood from his face and Jesse yanked him by his collar to the back end of the first truck. "Come on, you old fuck."

The man moaned and grumbled, but once around the back, Jesse loosened up his grip.

"What the hell was that for?" asked the driver.

"Got to make it look convincing," said Jesse.

The man peeled up an edge of the tarps and flashed the Thompson Distilling Co. emblem on one of the boxes. "I better get the rest of my money I'm owed. It wasn't easy to convince the other guys to not bring guns."

"Yeah, you'll get the remainder of your money. Then you'll go on an extended vacation."

The driver smiled then winced from the bruise on his head. The driver stepped up on the tailgate to produce a bottle for Jesse to examine. Jesse opened the top and the whiff ruptured through his nostrils and strangled his sense of smell. It was the real deal. His retirement plan. His start-up capital for his new legitimate business: 100% pure federally bonded medical alcohol. Before Prohibition, it was worth a lot. It helped cure coughing fits, insomnia, and Moon Madness. Since the start of Prohibition, the shit was worth more than gold. Jesse's smile turned devilish.

Jesse went through the rest of the trucks and made sure the cargo was all there. He then pushed the lead driver back into his spot on the ground and held the gun right where they could all see it.

"Everyone on their bellies with their hands behind their back," Rory said. The men did as told and laid flat and pressed their faces into the ground. Jesse and the gang back-peddled toward the trucks, keeping their eyes on the drivers, then they each got into a truck and kicked up dust down the empty dirt road. After 15 minutes Jesse took his mask off, squeezed the steering wheel until his knuckles turned white, and laughed. He stuck a thumbs-up out the window and Twitch responded in turn by firing two rounds into the air outside his truck.

Jesse looked straight down the road, and the marshes and trees zoomed by outside his window in one thin green blur. The bottles rattling in the back would become real cash, enough cash to change the state of the Pike name. Enough cash to move Jesse into the upper crust of society, where there were cocktail parties and galas and shit his family could never afford to do growing up. It would take some time—he knew that—but he'd have enough cash to finally buy that old, abandoned restaurant outright in the French Quarter with no loans or credit needed.

In the sky, the copper that peeked behind the clouds

made its evolution into a deep yellow with undertones of rustic orange. Jesse took out a cigarette and blew thick smoke out the window and kept the cigarette clasped tightly between the fingers of his driving hand. A new day was upon him. He was heading back to New Orleans a much richer man, and in turn, he would become a much better man.

Chapter 1

The Prince and His Kingdom

Late September, 1920

Jesse's dreams were interrupted every night by the memory of his father's dead body at the family dinner table. It was propped up in a chair, blood and brain matter sprayed against the wall, a slow stream of crimson flowing from its head like molten lava from a volcano. Jesse was a boy then. He still had kernels stuck in his teeth from the popcorn at the silent picture show he, his mother, and his brothers saw. His mother cried on her knees while trying to uncurl the corpse's rigor-mortised finger from around the trigger. His baby sister's cries echoed up the hall.

The night terror made Jesse tremble in his sleep. He twisted into Cindy and woke her up. She tapped him. His body was damp and sticky and he muttered in his sleep over the sight of his father's milky eyes giving him an accusatory glare.

No. No. No, Jesse pled in his sleep.

Cindy tapped his shoulder. It merited nothing. He was captive in a nightmare no person should have to endure as much as he did. She shoved him this time. He shot up like a piston.

Cindy held him. "You okay?"

Jesse took rapid, shallow breaths and hooked his fingers into the blankets like he could be dragged back to the night terror any moment. He stared into the dark abyss of his room and could almost see the silhouette of his father's body in the corner, sitting there, mocking him from the shadows, saying in a near whisper, "Why'd you do this, Jesse?" Jesse, still in a hazy state, heard the voice ask again, "Why?"

Jesse yanked his lamp on. The shadow was gone.

"The same dream again?" asked Cindy. She draped him with her bare body. He lay down, grabbed her hand, and kissed it. "Yes. What time is it?"

She pointed at the slit of yellow through his drapes. Jesse rubbed the rest of the sleep from his eyes and untangled himself from Cindy. She sighed. Jesse was only twenty-six but set in his ways. He thrived on being up before the sun—before the streets of New Orleans whirred with streetcars and tourists and two-bit hustlers trying to make a quick dime.

"Guess I'll get up too," said Cindy. Her milky southern drawl displaced what was once a northern accent. She pulled the covers off of her body slowly, teasing him with every stray second, making him hang in there for the moment he could see her naked body again. He was attentive. He watched her full hips, her long legs, and her ample behind until she made it to his bathroom. She cracked the door and his mind played back a hazy compilation of last night, when a few drinks at his brothel turned to tangled bodies in his bed and bunched-up clothes on the floor. He reminisced on how her body felt soft and warm in his hands—how her thighs, ass, and breasts almost melted between his fingers as he caressed her. Jesse whistled, then got out of bed.

Jesse slipped on clothes and shuffled around his room looking for his cigarettes. He checked the nightstand drawer. Old wrinkled academic honor roll certificates rested uncomfortably under a pistol and green bills dotted with blood. The money wasn't a lot, but he squirreled cash away in case one day he wanted to move far, far away. Arms wrapped him from behind. Cindy pointed at the certificates. "You should hang those up." Jesse was a tall man, so her head rested perfectly in the middle of his back.

He shrugged. "I'd rather have a bonfire with them." Jesse slammed the drawer shut.

Cindy let out an animated sigh and let her arms fall to her side. She ambled over to a box on his floor filled with office supplies. "You might as well throw them in the box with the rest of this junk."

Jesse continued to rummage around the room for his smokes. "I'll think about it."

Cindy put her hands up in resignation. She finished dressing and headed for the door. It took every bit of self-control to keep Jesse from running behind her like a dog when its owner was leaving the house. Big Sal, Jesse's mentor, once told him, "Every man needs a woman. You just can't let them know that." So Jesse locked his knees and winked instead.

She turned before closing the door and reminded him to not get so caught up in work that he'd miss his own brother's surprise party. He told her not to worry; he'd leave the restaurant in time. She blew a kiss his way and left. After finding his smokes, he opened his blinds and flooded his room with the New Orleans sunlight.

New Orleans: the jewel of the South; a city with as much personality as its people and just as colorful. Jesse could see from his condo window, over the buildings of Canal St., a tight cluster of buildings; a compilation of blues, greens, reds, with brick, wooden, and stucco facades nestled together shoulder-to-shoulder. The architecture was all sharp edges and bright colors, with wrought iron railings or thick wooden columns running around the balconies. And right below was Canal St., the Broadway of the South. The street was the main artery of the city, and the thoroughfare separated the old side of the city from the new; the rich from the poor; the immigrant from the American. Canal was dense with buildings half a block high and numerous shops, cafes, theaters, and art galleries, and despite it being morning, the sidewalks were already lively. Jesse had a bird's eye view of small dots moving in between each other to start their day. Bright baubles walked into boutiques and coffee shops, and bland business suits walked to the street cars with suitcases gripped tight. Cars zipped by and yellow taxis let out eager tourists who he figured got out with wide-eyed wonder, knowing that they were in one of the best cities in the country. The best, if you asked Jesse.

During Jesse's childhood, any bit of savings their family accrued was siphoned off by his father's drinking habit. They never had the money to come out to the heart of the city, so he and his brothers would sneak out to see the bright lights, beautiful people, and fancy outfits, and prayed to hear just one loose note from the many music halls. Now Jesse could see the city from one of the top floors in one of the tallest buildings on the street, and catch a stray note floating over to his window from a club below. The fact that he now lived in the heart of all that he ever loved is something he hoped he would never get used to. He loved every moment of it.

Jesse's cigarette's cherry burned bright and fizzled out into a smoky nub, signaling that it was time to head to work.

***

Jesse walked up to his restaurant, The Magnolia, and felt instant pride. It had a "**Coming Soon!**" sign plastered on its doors, and after the renovations, after cleaning more money and hiring more contractors, it would be the hottest place in town. His business partner, Mel, stood under a street light right in front of the restaurant-to-be talking to three gentlemen, who were all either in their late twenties or early thirties.

Mel said, "Hiya there, Jesse."

Jesse shifted his box in his hands. "What's news, Mel?"

Mel was a short man with bug-eyes magnified by the thickest glasses Jesse had ever seen in his life. His demeanor was of a man constantly on the precipice of severe anxiety and he was old-money with a family net worth higher than the wealth of some small countries. He was the complete opposite in every way from Jesse, but Jesse liked the guy. He was an ex-Tulane classmate, and one of the few people there that didn't look at Jesse as less-than.

Mel introduced Jesse to his friends. "Jesse, this is Albert, William, nicknamed Bill, and Kenneth." The men were courteous and welcoming, but in a pretentious way that only meant one thing to Jesse: they're rich too. Not regular rich but fuck-you rich. The type of guys who were born on third base but think they hit a triple. But Jesse smiled, placed his box of office supplies at his feet, and tried his best to be cordial. He learned what the group dynamics were after minutes: Bill was the quiet one. He did whatever the other two wanted because he was too soft to speak up. Kenneth was on the shorter side and felt the need to overcompensate with constant jokes. And Albert, well, he was an ass and by default the alpha of the group.

"So, Jesse, we've heard so much about you from our old friend here," said Albert. "Mel says you went to Tulane with him. So you finished in '16?"

Jesse had a tight smile. "No. A semester earlier actually."

Albert looked impressed. "Advanced classes?"

"Nope, never finished." Jesse's attempt at a punch-line

landed like a brick. Mel's friends looked at Jesse like he'd said something crude. Jesse cleared his throat. "Yea, uh, I had to leave early to start my own business. There was a tragedy in my family."

"Well," Albert said. "I'm sorry to hear that. I was a Yale man myself."

Jesse said, "Impressive." What he thought was, *don't break ya fucking arm patting yourself on the back.* Eventually Mel told his buddies to scram so he and Jesse could go inside and get some work done.

Jesse grabbed his box and walked into the restaurant. He darted past contractors zigzagging back-and-forth with ladders in their hands and tool boxes and tarps to cover the tables so stucco and dust didn't dirty them. Butterflies filled Jesse's stomach with the mere thought of what this place could be. Mel scampered behind him. "I'm sorry about that, Jess. My friends, well, they can be a bit much sometimes. Spoiled brats, you know?"

Jesse shrugged. "It's fine. I'm used to the stuffy types. No offense."

"None taken. You know, you should come with us to the Chateau one day." Mel smiled like he did Jesse a big favor and wanted a thank you.

But it piqued Jesse's interest. The Chateau Social Club was where the elites of New Orleans spent their time, namely, the ruling political machine, the ORD. Those old fucks wouldn't have let him sniff the outside air of that place years back. He always told himself he would never go there. But... that was then. If he wanted to be accepted by high society, he needed to start playing the part. Starting with schmoozing up to Mel and his friends.

Jesse said, "Sure, pal. That'd be nice."

In his office, Jesse put away his favorite books on his shelf, hung a few pictures on the wall, and sat behind his brand-new desk to sort through the business ledgers. Going through the accounting book for the restaurant made him smile. He loved the thought of how the numbers on the page could one day become dollars in his wallet, or paintings on his wall, or cars parked on the sidewalk in front of his condo. All he needed to do was infuse some more of the liquor heist money into the next round of contracting hires and the restaurant would be open in no time. He put that ledger away and pulled a book from behind his shelf. It was a ledger for his brothel, the Rising Sun.

He locked his door and carefully scanned the ledger's columns. Dates, names, room numbers, all inflated or fabricated to hide the source of the building's income. He made up patrons in his ledger one scribble at a time like it was muscle memory. It was a headache, but necessary. On paper, the Rising Sun was an inn. In reality, it was the most popular brothel in the French Quarter, owned and operated by the Pike Boys, under the authority of their acting leader, Jesse Pike.

Being the leader of a gang that owned a brothel wasn't all shattered kneecaps, bruised knuckles, and street fights. It was greasing palms and shaking hands and kissing the asses of his powerful clientele. Knowing which beat cop got how much, which bellhops and taxi drivers got referral fees. It wasn't easy being the Prince of the French Quarter, as some people jokingly, and others seriously, called him. But Jesse was the Prince. His land was the corner of Royal St and Toulouse, and his castle was the Rising Sun. Only reason he wasn't the king was because Big Sal wasn't dead yet. But after Clyde's surprise homecoming party tonight, Jesse wouldn't have to hold the crown anymore. He grew weary of carrying it.

Jesse's head jerked up at the sound of his phone. He'd left Rory in charge of the Rising Sun last night, so his imagination ran through options: Rory sliced a guy's face with a broken beer bottle; he tried to hit on someone's wife; or some combination of the two. He snatched up the phone and out came a harsh Italian accent. It was Big Sal. "You got the papers?"

"Yea."

"Turn to page ten."

Jesse flipped through the pages and saw the bold lettered headline: **"CAMERON MULLIGAN, YOUNG DA AND GOLDEN BOY OF NEW ORLEANS, VOWS TO TAKE ON CRIME; EYES ENDING CORRUPTION AS MAYORAL PLATFORM."**

Jesse raised an eyebrow. "Is this an issue?"

Sal rattled off curse words in Italian loud enough to make Jesse's head jerk away from the phone. Jesse read further. "He's looking into the liquor heist. 'Thompson Distilling CO., a branch of Thompson Limited, had three truckloads of federally bonded, pharmaceutical liquor stolen three months ago. Baby faced Mulligan, DA and the son of a powerful philanthropist and political advocate, says the heist was a slap in the face to the justice system of New Orleans, and he promises to do all he can to make sure due process is completed on this investigation.'" Jesse paused. "So, he's reopening the case on the municipal level."

Sal let out an annoyed groan like his back was sore. Jesse said, "They're calling it the biggest hijacking, money-wise, since Prohibition started."

"Don't sound too fucking impressed."

Jesse's next words were cut off by deep, wheezing coughs from Sal. "You ok, old man?"

"My heart still beats and my dick still works. I think I'm fine. But look, you, your crew, and Pencil-Dick-Thompson told me this would go away after two months. Mr. Councilman Thompson was supposed to collect the insurance, and it would be done. It's been fucking more than two months, Jesse. Why ain't it done?"

Jesse raised his shoulders in confusion. "There's no mention of you here."

"A man could slip, fall, and crack his own skull and I'd get blamed by these Bible-thumping pricks. If a man gets caught with his dick in another woman it was my hands that put it there. I can't catch a break."

Sal was old and frail. Jesse could hear the years of cigar smoke and heavy drinking taking its toll. The paranoia wasn't helping with Sal's condition, either. But Jesse understood it. Salvatore "Big Sal" Bianchi, a feared gangster and respected businessman, ran the Italian underbelly of New Orleans with impunity. His money created a shield of lawyers and politicians and cops, and when there were raids on his gambling dens and cocaine safe-houses, he was tipped off and never spent a single night in jail. He never even sniffed the air outside of a prison. In return for protection, he made sure Italians voted the right way and stayed away from places they weren't wanted. Now he's worried about a city investigation when he's this close to retirement, if not death. Jesse told Sal to relax; it's a publicity stunt for the upcoming election.

Sal sighed. "Ok, Jesse-boy, I'll trust you. I always do."

Jesse eyed the clock. "We'll talk about this more at the party tonight. Ok?" There was silence. The old man had probably fallen asleep on the phone again. Jesse hung up, hid away the brothel's ledger, and went back to unpacking. Once he got down to the last remaining objects (some pencils, a book, and an old photo), he noticed his Tulane honor roll certificate folded into his favorite book. Cindy must've stuffed it in there when he wasn't paying attention. He fought a losing battle against a wide grin. He smoothed out the wrinkles on his desk and contemplated what to do with it.

He pulled out the old photo next. It was a half-faded picture, grainy like torn film footage, of five kids; four boys dressed as outlaws holding wooden guns, and one girl, head full of dark curls, kissing a young Jesse on his dimpled cheek. The picture was dated on the back as 1906. It stated the names of the children as well: Twitch, Clyde, Jesse, Rory, and Rose.

That star-filled night was clear in Jesse's mind.

Whistling cold air stripped the trees' branches bare, and winter's frigid fingers slipped between Jesse and his brothers' poorly patched clothes.

That night, he, Twitch, Rory, and Clyde had seen a cowboy show under the big tent at the Parish Carnival. That night, they jokingly formed their "outlaw gang." Jesse made the boys scrape their change together for the photo. Rory, who was eight, screamed it was supposed to be boys only, but Rose hopped in anyway and planted a kiss on Jesse's cheek.

The photo filled him with pride and sadness. Pride because he wasn't that kid anymore, sadness because Rose wasn't here to see it. He held the picture up next to the Tulane certificate and weighed which one meant more to him now. He tossed the photo back in the box and kicked the box under his desk, so he could remember to toss it in the trash later. He wouldn't need it anymore. He was moving forward with his life. He grabbed his Tulane certificate and nailed it up on the wall, so whenever people needed to come speak to the manager and co-owner, they'd see his accomplishment. He didn't finish, sure. But a kid like him wasn't supposed to get in in the first place.

Later that work day, before turning off the lights, he stopped by the threshold of his office door with the box of trash in his hands and looked around at all of his possessions, wishing he could tell the 12-year-old Jesse from the picture that one day, he wouldn't have to pickpocket anymore. One day, he and his brothers would make enough money to survive after Papa killed himself.

One day, he'd be able to look at the world of crime with disdain, because he'd no longer need the quick and easy money. One day, he would be able to say the words that few gangsters ever say: "I quit."

Chapter 2

Homecoming

Jesse stood outside of Clyde's motel room and listened to his brother's snores roll out through the cracked door. Jesse pushed the door open and was bombarded by a rolling cloud of sweat, piss, and bathtub hooch. Clyde had stuff everywhere: his clothes thrown into piles, the remnants of food unfinished from the diner across the street on the floor, half empty mason jars scattered around the room. And there was Clyde—draped over his bed in a drunken coma, his snoring sounding like a saw grinding through wood, heaving out toxic fumes from his two-day bender with each exhalation.

"Clyde," Jesse said through pinched nostrils.

Jesse stepped forward and clattered two bottles together. "Fucking animal." He side-stepped the remaining trash and stood over Clyde. Clyde had a whiskey bottle gripped tight in his hands, and Jesse tried to pry it from him, but even in his sleep, Clyde's fingers held on like metal coils.

He got the bottle un-suctioned from Clyde's paw and used it to poke him in his side—right where a puckered knife scar ran down his ribs—and jabbed him again, and again, and once more for good measure. Clyde's eyes burst open, and in one smooth motion he swung his legs to the floor, exploded up, and grabbed Jesse by the collar. His eyes were vacant and inhuman enough for the typically calm and cool Jesse to have a slight waver in his voice when he said, "It's me, it's me. It's fucking Jesse."

The veins in Clyde's neck swelled. Jesse looked into his brother's eyes. He looked through the mask of rage to see what four years of living in fear could do to someone. Four years of rattling chains and shank stabbings in the showers and guard towers where an unseen officer massaged his rifle trigger and waited for someone to attempt to run—just to have a reason to punch a bullet in someone's cranium and see the shrapnel of his skull explode in a bloody flurry.

Jesse slapped Clyde across the face and his head snapped back and the vacancy in his eyes dissipated. He released the collar and sat on the bed. Jesse stared at him confused as shit. Clyde said nothing; instead, he stroked his reddish-brown beard and looked at the ground. Jesse snapped his fingers at him. Clyde's head perked up. Jesse gestured in confusion. "What the fuck?"

Clyde stood. "Sorry."

Jesse scratched his head. He knew going to the toughest

jail in the South could fuck up anyone, but dear God, Clyde was a shell of himself. Clyde scavenged through the piles of shit on the floor, picking up pants, dropping them down, sniffing them. It was like he and Clyde occupied the same physical space, but Clyde was a million miles away. Jesse turned his back. "Guess I'll give you a moment."

Jesse looked around and was dumbstruck over the juxtaposition of the mounds of trash on the floor and the tidiness of the countertop. Clyde had taken all of the silverware from the drawer and laid them out in neat rows. Jesse pushed the silverware crooked. Clyde charged over behind him, still in only his underwear and exhaling last night's booze, and pushed the forks and knives back in place. He glared at Jesse. Jesse perked his eyebrows up and tried to hide a smile. "Good to have you back, big brother."

***

Jesse and Clyde made their way to the heart of the city. The skyline was beautiful; lines of molten copper snuck through the swath of purple, gold, and orange skylight. Pretty soon those colors would melt together into a black backdrop with scattered stars and moonlight piercing the New Orleans sky, bathing the French Quarter, summoning the harlots and sinners toward its glow. It would be a signal to the city that it was her time to awaken; a beacon to flappers, drinkers, and gamblers; whoremongers, scammers, and lowlifes, that it was their time. The neon lights outside of the row of shops, theaters, and opera houses started to flicker on. Canal St. was coming alive.

"It's beautiful, isn't it?" Jesse asked Clyde. Clyde stared

out the window. He looked at who filed on and off the streetcars. Groups of women in short-cut, shimmering dresses walked arm and arm with men in suits into the music halls with their heads cocked back in laughter. The stuffy "respectable" folks strolled to the streetcars with their dresses past their knees, along with their husbands who looked like they'd climax at the look of a woman's shoulder. The streetcar hummed down the street. Jesse stopped to let pedestrians cross the thoroughfare. A street vendor was selling lotto tickets while illuminated under the corner streetlight, and did his best impression of a circus ring leader and bellowed to everyone passing him. "Five cents gets ya $500." Jesse waved him off.

"It's like the first time again," Clyde said.

Jesse split his attention between the road and Clyde. "What you mean?"

"The first time we laid eyes on this place." Clyde put his hand out the window and allowed his fingers to cut through the brisk September air.

That was Clyde's first full sentence the whole day, and the second time he'd talked in hours, the last time being when he asked about their little sister, Catherine.

"I remember," Jesse said. He pulled the Packard to a halt on the sidewalk next to a row of tiny shack homes. He twiddled his fingers on the steering wheel and turned in his seat.

"What's this?" Clyde asked.

They were parked outside a row of cribs; a row of tiny homes with dark shutters where you could contract gonorrhea for fifty cents. Homely prostitutes would stick their hands or knickers out of the window to let men know they were open for shop. The only things inside were a tiny cot and lanterns dim enough to make the women look twenty years younger, but just bright enough to reveal track marks and inflamed red genital warts. Outside the car window, a crib prostitute stood in the doorway with her nightgown half off her shoulder. She tried to summon Jesse and Clyde to her with a finger motion. She had droopy eyes and held onto the doorway for balance.

Clyde tensed up. "Please don't tell me this is the place I've heard so much about."

Jesse shook his head, feigned laughter, then prepared himself for his speech. "You holed yourself up for two days in a roach motel outside the city, you don't talk to anyone, see anyone, not even Cath. Are you doing ok?"

"I'm fine."

Jesse nodded. "How did you even stay sane in there?"

Clyde stroked his beard and stared into the distance. "Church."

Jesse snickered. Clyde wouldn't know a chapter in the Bible from a page torn out of a stag book. "Church?"

"Yea, fucking church."

Jesse stared in disbelief. Clyde returned the stare. "What else was there for me to do?"

Jesse let the question roll off of him.

Clyde wrung his hands. "And I thought about Catherine. And Mama. And our family. I want us all to be close again. I wasn't around much before... before I went away. I want to change that."

Jesse tried to read Clyde. He looked nervous, jumpy, but somehow still had undertones of his menacing calmness. He was much more docile than before he was arrested, but at the same time, twice as explosive. The episode in the motel was evidence to the latter.

"Ok. We can find time for that," Jesse said. "But I'm just saying, if you need some more time off, or, I don't know, to see a head-shrinker or get back on the lithium…"

Clyde straightened in his seat. Jesse flashed his palms. "Alright, no head-shrinker or head dope. I hear ya."

Clyde was born with a fire only a high dose of lithium could douse. If the lithium didn't work, their father would beat the demon out of him, spouting scriptures while doing so. It wasn't uncommon for a young Clyde to stare at the wall in their childhood room, murmuring to himself with a string of drool running down his face. But he got older. Bigger. He had stopped eating his grits after realizing what that bitter taste was. The space underneath his mattress became a black hole for his pharmaceuticals, and their mother could no longer force him to take them after their father died.

Clyde eventually relaxed in his seat. "I just need to get back to work. Nothing else."

"I understand. And trust me, I'm eager for you to take my place. I just want to stay on long enough to show you the ropes. I still want my monthly points on the booze, of course, until we're out of stock. But other than that, the brothel will be yours to lead at your discretion; like we talked about."

Clyde smirked. "Yea, like we talked about. You did good. Better than I expected. But it can't be that hard to sell pussy and booze, is it?"

Jesse blanketed his offense with a laugh.

The car's engine roared to life. Clyde rubbed his knuckles for a while, a nervous gesture he'd had since childhood. "I—I know I asked of you something that was hard, Jesse. All those years ago. But you stepped up. You really did. I hope to one day repay you for your sacrifices in perpetuity."

"In perpetuity?" Jesse laughed as they drove off. "Learned that in church too?"

"From a book."

"Shit, when'd you learn to read?"

Clyde tried and failed to hide a soft smile, and eventually, he gave in. The two brothers laughed the whole way up the street.

***

The Packard jerked to a stop right outside of a two-floor red brick building that took up the majority of the corner of Royal Street. Clyde hopped out before the car was fully parked, and ran his hand up and down the thick iron beams connected from the ground to the second-floor balconies. He tried to take it all in, but couldn't turn his head far enough to see the cast iron rail that wrapped around the exterior of the Creole Townhouse.

"Shit," Clyde said.

Jesse shivered from the nighttime breeze that tumbled

from over by the river some blocks away. "'Shit' is right." They walked around to the front. Jesse stood side by side with Clyde. He put his hand up and swiped in the air from left to right. "This is the palace built by Pike, big brother."

"The Rising Sun," Clyde said. The front looked like the face of a monster, the two corner room windows on the balcony making up the illuminated eyes and the double green doors the mouth.

Jesse lit up. "Rolls off the tongue don't it? I did all this myself." He wanted those words back before he said them. Clyde walked toward the door. Jesse sprinted ahead of him. "Alright, wait right here."

He trotted up the three steps and gave two light raps on the front door. A doorman stuck his head out. Jesse whispered, then looked over his shoulder to make sure Clyde wasn't close enough to hear. The doorman nodded and shut the door.

"The fuck is going on here? We going in or not?" Clyde asked.

"We're going, we're going."

Jesse checked the time and knocked at the door again. Clyde, now visibly agitated, said, "What in the hell are you—"

The doors swung open and a sea of smiling faces in masquerade masks and glimmering dresses and finely stitched suits all screamed "Surprise!"

Jesse waited for Clyde's smile. And waited. Waited some more. Clyde stood frozen in place, with the only movement being the slight tremble of his hand and quiver of his lip.

The people's smiles turned to confusion. Rory parted the crowd with two women on each arm. He had a kazoo pursed in his lips and a cone party hat resting on his head. Jesse tried to shake his head subtly to warn him away, but Rory let out a hard squawk and shouted, "Surprise, you bastard."

Rory's eyes darted between Jesse awkwardly scratching an invisible itch on his temple and Clyde standing like a statue. Rory released the women. He turned his finger in a circle and everyone went back to the parlor and the piano music started back up like nothing happened.

Jesse looked at Clyde. "You alright?"

"Fine. I—I just wasn't expecting..." Clyde stared at the ground to search for his words. Jesse immediately regretted not telling Clyde ahead of time.

"I'm sorry," Jesse said.

Clyde said nothing. Rory removed the hat. Rory grabbed both sides of Clyde's face. "Welcome home." He hugged Clyde, wrapping his arms around his wide frame. Clyde was still statuesque. But Rory didn't relent. He squeezed tighter. Clyde moved Rory back and placed his hands on his shoulder. "I can't believe it. My baby brother; a man now." Clyde slapped him on the arm and rubbed the spot where he hit him. Clyde looked back-and-forth at his brothers and the uncertainty slowly melted away. He unbuttoned his coat. "Well, I guess I have a party to attend."

Jesse and Rory smiled. The brothers walked side-by-side up the steps and followed the noise of booming music and happy chatter right into the Rising Sun.

Chapter 3

Wolves At the Door

The Rising Sun was a fortress of fantasies, a palace of pleasure; a place where any man, whether poor, rich, gangster, or blue-collar, could come to be treated like a king. Chandeliers and old paintings classed up the place and allowed Jesse to up-charge on every single thing. The spiral staircase that split the large building in half was like a conveyor belt. Jesse would see a woman go up empty-handed with a john in tow and come down minutes later fifty dollars heavier. And at Clyde's homecoming party, that belt was moving in swift rotation.

Jesse walked through the party and cut through the sea of dark suits and colorful party dresses and was greeted with a myriad of handshakes and conversations. He got some pats on the back and had to feign interest in conversations he wished he was never in, but it came with the territory.

He made it to a cluster of chairs and tables where the working girls sat talking to johns. Those women were more effective than sirens. He'd see the smartest, wealthiest men throw away their lives over a wet slit between two legs.

"Quite the establishment," one man said to Jesse. He sat in a chair with two brunettes flanking him. They were young, early-to-mid-twenties, with smooth skin and dresses hugging their bodies. The man between them was the antithesis, wrinkled and liver-spotted, with a beaked nose. But the money folds hanging from his pockets and gold trim around his glasses distracted from the gut spilling over his waistband and the toupee perched on his scalp. Jesse saluted the man with a raise of the glass and shot a wink at the girls.

Jesse walked up to a group of men; some big whales with big wallets. "What's going on, fellas?" he said. They greeted him like a celebrity, which he was, if only in the vice circles of the city.

"Isn't it crazy what's going on around this country? Some places up north have no booze," one of the men said.

Jesse smirked. "Yea, good thing you aren't up there. Because then you'd actually have to survive on food and water." The men tossed their heads back and laughed.

"How about this one," said Jesse. "A man says to a preacher, 'That was an excellent sermon, but it was not original.' The preacher was taken aback. The man said he had a book at home containing every word the preacher used. The next day, the man brought the preacher a dictionary." The men almost keeled over laughing at Jesse.

He told the gentlemen to go get some drinks on the house and left them to bask in his greatness.

Jesse strode toward the bar, but was stopped by a logjam of people. Without a word, people parted and made an alley to his stool—the spot where he always sat. He rested his elbow on the smooth wooden bartop, and like clockwork, a towel came down to wipe away spillage near him, a fresh drink appeared without his need to ask, but he waved it away. He held up his watered-down whiskey. "I'm good, thank you." The barkeep nodded and roamed toward the end of the bar. Jesse turned in his chair and looked to the dance floor.

People talked and danced. The jazz band's trumpets' wild squawks went on and on, becoming wilder and wilder without a loss in rhythm, but seeming to go nowhere in particular. The music made the crowd cheer louder and dance harder. Cigar smoke hung above everyone's heads and almost dimmed the brothel's crystal lights with a thick fog. The party was packed. And between the full eighteen rooms upstairs and the girls working the floor and the people buying marked-up drinks at the bar, the brothel was going to make more money tonight than Jesse could ever launder in a month. Why was this not enough for him, though? He couldn't explain this odd need he had for validation from the people who made him feel less than. It wasn't these exact people, but kids he'd run into in his childhood who had affluent parents; those who didn't live in a shotgun home or have to share clothes with their siblings.

Jesse pushed the thought from his mind and took a sip of whiskey. He chalked it up to it being some form of vindication for all those years he didn't have money. Now he had a lot of it. When he was little, that's all he'd wanted. Now he needed power. That's all this brothel was for him: a stepping stone to power. Part of the reason he quit crime the first time was because of the risk street-level jobs carried. That's why when he was forced to take over the crew, he pooled all the money they ever made and bought into a brothel.

When he found this place, there was no live music, only the same strained tune emanating from a funky phonograph, and working girls who were drugged up and beat down by patrons and dope peddlers who got too rough. Four years and several minor turf wars later, and here it was, his baby, his once pride and joy, and his stepping stone to the upper-class and legit business. His run with this place was done. He'd made the connections he needed. Now he could comfortably live the life of a common man, and he'd finally prove to all those people years ago that he was more than a street rat.

Jesse caught glimpses of Rory and Clyde through the barrage of moving bodies. They sat at a table in the far corner, where Clyde made liberal whiskey pours into a row of shot glasses. The amber liquid spilled over the glasses, pooled on the table, and spread until it dripped onto the floor. Clyde took all of the shots for himself, and Rory and the three women with them laughed like it was the funniest shit they'd ever seen. The drips on the ground turned into a small puddle at Clyde's feet. Jesse pressed his palm to his forehead.

Jesse turned and whistled to the bar-back, Mickey, who dropped empty glasses into a bin and hustled over like an attention-deprived animal. He slung the towel over his shoulder and stood at attention. "Need something, boss?"

"Go over there and clean that up, will ya?"

Mickey's shoulders dropped.

Jesse extended his pointer finger toward the table. "Now, please." Mickey rushed over with his arms pumping at his side. Mickey was as loyal as a dog. He was the bag boy for the crew and made sure every parcel of money got where it needed to be. His big eyes and baby face were a paradox next to his crooked nose and clipped ear from his days on the street.

Jesse watched Rory jostle Mickey's hair while he attempted to wipe the floor. Clyde was dramatic and made a show of lifting his feet so Mickey could clean under the table. Jesse turned back around and waved the barkeep over. "I'll take that drink, actually."

Jesse left the bar and walked along the outside of the dance floor where people were doing The Charleston. He saw Twitch straight ahead in the corner on a stool. Amidst the chaos and debauchery around him, Twitch was by himself reading a book. Twitch's head jerked up when Jesse approached.

Jesse turned his head sideways to better read the title: *How to Speak Publicly*. Twitch hopped to his feet and stuffed the book in his coat.

"It's fine," Jesse said. Twitch eased up. He had a face branded with the same expression at all times. Not happy, not sad, just pure apathy and indifference.

Jesse's index knuckle rapped against the book in Twitch's coat pocket. "It's good you're learning, though." Twitch curled his lips, which for him, was like someone grinning from ear to ear. Twitch stuttered and stumbled over his words, pausing to pick the right ones, but Jesse was patient. Twitch suffered from fits of stutters since they were children and always got shit for it, and at one point, he used to shake and sputter like a car breaking down. But as he got older, the shakes went away. But the nickname never did.

"The kids," Twitch said. "I want to be able to read to them at night. Sometimes."

Jesse gave a nod of approval. "You're getting better every day." He pulled his pack of smokes from his jacket and offered it up.

Twitch shook his head. "My wife can smell that on me."

Jesse put them back.

Twitch's calm demeanor hid his capacity for violence. He never sought it out, but when it came, he was ready and willing to lay a motherfucker on their ass or take things to a level that gave most people nightmares. He didn't have a broad, bulky chest like Clyde but instead an athletic frame of an ex-MLB prodigy. His arms and legs looked like engorged pythons crawled under his skin whenever he flexed. His frame came from years of being called retarded by the neighborhood kids. Every time a kid called him retarded, he went home teary-eyed and did push-ups. Then dumbbell curls. Eventually, no kid called him retarded again.

Twitch jutted his head toward Clyde and Rory. They were still at their table throwing back drinks. Twitch shook his head and spoke slowly. "Things can't go back to the way they used to be."

Clyde had slammed his hand down on the table, knocking over the glasses, which prompted liquor-induced laughter from Rory and their girls. Twitch held up his wedding band. The light glinted from the silver ring, the smooth circle snug near callused knuckles.

"They won't," Jesse said.

"G-g-good."

Jesse leaned against the wall. "I'll keep him on a leash for a while. It may take Clyde some time, but he will see the brothel business is more fruitful than any heist or odd job he could come up with. I'll be around until he gets acclimated."

Twitch fastened his black tie and stared at Clyde. Jesse put a hand on Twitch's shoulder. "I promise. I won't let anything get out of hand. After we get rid of all of that booze, only thing you'll have to worry about is what you're going to spend all of your of money on." Jesse rubbed his thumb against his pointer and middle fingers. Twitch jutted his eyebrows up and down and gave another corner-of-the-mouth smirk.

Jesse checked his watch. Big Sal and his other special guests would be there soon. Around the room, the brothel's security stuck close to the walls on the perimeter of the party. They all had a uniform look—big heads and wide jaws and thick shoulders, with gun bulges hidden under their jackets. Jesse's eyes scanned the crowd but got snagged by the way Cindy's dress hugged her just right. Her graceful walk and her long dress made it look like she levitated around the room. He smiled at her. She returned it. He stepped toward her, but a man stepped into frame and made him rock back on his heels. The man embraced Cindy and she placed a kiss on his cheek.

The music became slow and somber—a tune that was meant to lull people into intimacy. Everyone stopped moving around and drifted to the dance floor with their partners. Cindy nestled her head into the john's neck. They swayed side to side, her hand on his back and his hands slowly making their way down hers. She playfully raised them back up. He leaned down to whisper something in her ear. She blushed. She returned the favor by leaning in close to whisper something back. Jesse imagined she told the man something sweet and sensual, arousing yet calming, like she did for him last night, and every other night.

Jesse hoped Twitch didn't see his near embarrassment. He did. Twitch looked at Jesse with a knowing look. The look asked, *that's still going on?*

Jesse read his friend's mind and said out loud, "Oh shut the fuck up." Twitch chuckled, then went back to reading his book.

Over the horizon of the dance floor, Jesse saw the first of his guests arrive: Davy Perrilloux. Davy walked around the edges of the party and straight to Jesse. Jesse embraced

Davy with a handshake.

"What's going on, Pike?" Davy asked.

Jesse replied cordially.

Davy was a sharp-dressed colored man with a southern drawl smooth like honey and a joyful demeanor to match. Many of the guests turned to stare. Black men weren't allowed most places in New Orleans, especially not in brothels. But Davy was a friend, business associate, and probably the most important part of Jesse's liquor operation. The guests would have to get over it.

Jesse pointed and gave directions to where their meeting would take place. After Davy walked off, Twitch jumped to his feet. Jesse ordered Twitch to make sure the security was locked and loaded. He waved over Mickey and ordered him to run and get the bag of money from the safe. Mickey nodded and cut straight down the dance floor, bumping into couples who swayed left to right in one another's arms.

Jesse pushed through people and waved his hands to shoo away the girls next to his brothers. Clyde's face glistened from a thin layer of sweat and burned red with drink.

"It's time," Jesse said.

Rory and Clyde both shot up from their seats and swayed back-and-forth and bobbed up and down like buoys in the river. Jesse said a quick prayer under his breath. The Pike brothers cut through the party and Mickey met them at the threshold of the foyer with a duffel bag. Twitch caught up to them. He took the bag and its weight pulled his arm to the earth.

Jesse turned to Mickey. "Tell the band to switch to up-tempo music for a while."

Jesse wanted to make sure if things got loud, they'd at least have some noise blanketing their conversation. The music and chatter lowered from a ruckus to faint noises as they approached the east parlor threshold. A bouncer guarded the doorway with his arms crossed and a scowl on his face.

The Pike Boys walked into the east parlor where several men waited for their arrival. Jesse greeted everyone with "Fellas" and made the rounds to shake hands, starting first with the man leaning against the wall by the fireplace, Hymie.

"Took you long enough," Hymie said. Jesse forced a smile.

Hymie had yellowish teeth and big, clammy hands Jesse couldn't wait to let go of. It wasn't a secret Jesse hated Hymie. He was Big Sal's longtime partner, preferred hitman, and personal attack dog. Hymie had gray, thin hair spread on his head, along with a pot belly developed after years as a baker stretching his cheap suit to its limits. He also always had a toothpick dangling from his mouth. He used the picks to tell if the centers of cupcakes and other delicacies were done baking. The joke around the city was that his fat ass kept the picks there so he could constantly have the flavors on his tongue. No one ever said it to his face though. Hymie picked at his nails and cursed under his breath in Yiddish as Jesse and the rest walked past. Jesse ignored him and walked over to Davy, who sat at a table by himself.

Jesse patted Davy on the shoulder and introduced him to Clyde, who hesitated to take Davy's hand, looking him up and down. "He's an associate I met after you went in," Jesse said, sensing Clyde's hesitance. "He's a good man."

Clyde loosened up some and took Davy's hand. Davy took the suspicion in stride and introduced himself.

Next was Sal Jr. AKA Junior. Junior sat at a table with two of the Bianchi gunmen next to him. Their names were Donny or Luca or some other Sicilian shit Jesse could never remember. He acknowledged them, then went to Junior. Jesse reached out his hand. Junior did everything in his power to make Jesse's hand hang for a while before he ever acknowledged it. He sat back against the table, his elbows resting firmly against it, with his wrist up in the air like he was interested in the time on his watch. Junior had the attitude of a scorned cat; a level of passive aggression toward Jesse that no woman could ever parallel. His face was almost in a permanent pout like a little boy who'd been told no one too many times. Which—Jesse knew—Junior was lucky if he was told no, and not beat over the head by his father altogether.

Jesse gritted his teeth and kept his hand in Junior's face. Junior eventually huffed and gave Jesse a dead fish handshake, something you'd do to a child so that you wouldn't crush their hand. Last but not least, sitting opposite Junior on the other side of the table, was Salvatore "Big Sal" Bianchi.

Jesse smiled wide. He walked toward him while Clyde, Rory, and Twitch completed small talk behind him. His surrogate father had a jovial smile. Sal placed his frail, veiny hands on the top of his cane and tried to stand up, but Jesse put his hands out to tell him to stay sitting.

"No, no, no," Sal said. "I'm old, not an imbecile. I can stand up on my own."

Jesse stood back and watched the man who used to scare him shitless struggle to stand up unaided. His knees buckled and he let out strained groans like needles were stabbing him in his joints. He hobbled over, his cane clicking the ground in stride with his steps.

"Come here, come here," Sal said.

Jesse embraced him with a hug and felt the bones under the thick layers of coats. Jesse couldn't believe how bad he was getting. He'd dropped at least eight pounds in the month since they'd seen each other.

"Good to see you too," Jesse said.

Jesse made small talk with Sal for a little, asking how Mrs. Bianchi was, how the doctors' visits had been, all while the sound of the music from the party drifted into the middle of their conversation. The small talk dissipated. The men moved to tables in the middle of the room.

"Welcome home, boy," Sal said to Clyde.

Clyde responded with a whiskey hiccup and a nod. Clyde, Twitch, and Rory sat at a circular table by themselves while the other men split up amongst the other two nearest tables.

"So, other than this party," Davy said. "Any other reason

we here?"

Jesse grinned. He motioned toward Twitch to open the duffle bag. The handle strained at its ends as Twitch flipped the bag over and caused an avalanche of money, 5 figures total, to slide out and shake the unleveled table. College funds, retirement funds, investment capital, all right there on that table. Davy's jaw dropped. Hymie sat at the edge of his seat. Big Sal stood and walked over to the table. He gave Jesse a kiss on both cheeks. Junior rolled his eyes.

"This is from the second shipment," Jesse said.

Sal went back to his seat. "The out of state contacts really bought that much?"

"Yes. And we have more. Way more."

The Volstead Act was meant to stop the "evils" of drinking—or so the bigwigs in D.C. thought. All it did was make a fifty-cent bottle of wine worth $2 and a nickel drink worth a quarter. And with the large shipment of stolen liquor Jesse had in storage, he'd make 7 times the money as someone who made booze themselves or got it imported. Rory divided the money into portions equivalent to everyone's stake in the job and handed it out.

Davy got a portion for providing the out of state contacts and logistics. Big Sal got a portion for providing the capital for both Rudy Thompson's payoff and for access to transportation of the booze out of the state. Big Sal then divvied the money up amongst Hymie and Junior, then Junior to his gunmen. Sal asked Jesse, "Where's the honorable Councilman Thompson?"

"He didn't think it would be best to be seen with us."

"It's probably smart—what about what we talked about earlier?"

"The 'Golden Boy'? He's a non-issue."

"How you know that?"

Jesse rubbed his nose. "He's a reformer. They never win."

"Until they do," snapped Junior.

Hymie chuckled to himself. "I can always just..." Hymie turned his fingers into gun barrels and laughed hard enough to make everyone in the room feel uncomfortable.

Jesse knew it was no joke though. Everyone knew one thing about Hymie: he'd go to the hospice and put a fucking pillow over his own mother's face if he thought she'd snitch.

Sal slapped Hymie on the shoulder. "Now, now. Enough of that."

Jesse sighed. "Fine. I'll go check in with Rudy tomorrow and see what he has on the guy."

Jesse felt like it was a moot point. But if looking into the guy would make Sal get off his back and free him up to work on his restaurant, he'd do it. Jesse composed himself and looked to Clyde for this next part. "There is another announcement." Everyone's eyes came from their money stacks and straight to him. "As of tonight, I'm out. I'll stay on in an advisory capacity for the time being, and continue to take my cuts of these shipments, but Clyde will be taking over from here on out."

Time froze. No breathing, movement, or signs of life could be seen or heard.

Sal fidgeted. "Why?"

"Clyde's capable," Jesse said. He pointed his hand toward Clyde, regretting the decision after seeing Clyde was still drunk. "And I just think it's time."

Junior responded with a dismissive snicker. His father barked, "You shut the hell up." Junior shrunk back in his seat. "What is it time for?"

Jesse shrugged. "Something else."

Clyde stood and cleared his throat. "I didn't know I needed permission from any of you."

Clyde eyed daggers at every person in the room. Sal's brows furrowed. Jesse saw Hymie's hand move near the bulge in his coat. The gunmen alongside Junior took his cue to do the same. Twitch eyed Jesse, looking for any indication the situation would grow dire.

Sal let out a hefty laugh. A laugh strong enough to force the men around him to move their hands from their coats and join in.

Sal pointed at Clyde. "You're grown. You don't need my permission for anything."

Jesse could see through Sal's laugh and saw he was pissed. Under Jesse's control, the Pike Boys went from stickup men and hijackers to business owners. The liquor scheme wasn't the first time Jesse's connections netted those men money and serious work. Jesse created an environment where businessmen and gangsters could cohabitate, which meant big things for everyone in that room, which meant if Jesse left then their connections did too. Jesse also knew Sal wanted him to be a consultant to the Bianchi family one day. He never said it outright, but he alluded to it every chance he got at their once frequent cafe meetings. Sal wasn't getting any younger, and he needed to make sure the New Orleans faction of the Bianchi family thrived after him. Jesse looked at Junior. Junior smirked— because when Big Sal died now, he would be the sole leader of the Bianchi family, and his father's little pet would have no involvement.

Jesse played it cool. "Like I said, I'll see this venture through to the end the best I can. After that, Clyde's your man."

The men gave reluctant nods of approval. Everyone stood. Davy was the first to leave. Sal walked over and stopped to place a hand on Clyde's shoulder. "Why don't y'all come by the shop sometime, eh? We'll have dinner like old days."

Clyde nodded noncommittally.

Sal walked out and his men followed behind. Junior glared at Jesse the whole time he walked past. Hymie followed last and stopped at the threshold, turning with a confused look on his face, like he was trying to remember something on the tip of his tongue. He snapped his fingers and turned to the Pikes. "Remember when you guys used to shine our shoes?"

He looked around and nodded with a grin at the paintings on the wall, the piano in the corner, and the foreign décor. Hymie chuckled, then said, "I remember."

Jesse bit his tongue. "We've come a long way since then."

"That's all I was saying, kid," Hymie said. "But my shoes sure miss ya." He cackled all the way out the parlor and down the outside steps. The Pikes were alone in the room now.

"Fuck him," said Rory with his fist at his side. "We're not children anymore."

Twitch nodded in agreement. Clyde stood at the table with a dejected, annoyed look on his face.

"It doesn't help that y'all couldn't even wait until after the meeting to get sauced," said Jesse.

Rory grew defensive. "You were fucking drinking too." Jesse put up two fingers to indicate the number of drinks he had. Clyde looked at the ground.

"What's eating you?" Jesse asked.

Clyde left the room without a word.

Jesse followed him back into the party and tried to chase him down, but before he could reach him, Cindy stepped in his way, and she had tears in her eyes.

"We need you," she said. "And now."

Jesse decided to leave the Clyde situation for later.

Jesse walked over to an area sequestered from the rest of the party with a cigarette pursed in his lips, where Mickey, Madam Eve, and Cindy huddled around a girl sitting on a plush bench with her hands clasped to her face. Jesse asked her to move her hands, and his stomach turned in knots. She was bruised, black and blue spots stretched across her face, her eye completely shut and swollen, with webs of pulsating veins spreading across the eyelid.

Madam Eve stepped up to Jesse and shoved his shoulder. "You and your boys are supposed to stop this type of stuff from happening."

The words cut through Jesse like a blade. He rubbed the wounded girl's cheek and told Mickey to get her to a doctor, then to home.

Jesse stood, rubbed the back of his head, and blew thick plumes of smoke in the air. "I'll fix it."

***

The room was dim and bare, nothing more than a loose hanging light bulb swinging free from a fixture and years of caked burgundy stains soaked into the wood floor. A man sat in an old chair in the middle of the room, his head low and tears rolling out his eyes and his face a mask of fear and anxiety. Rory and Twitch flanked him. The man's forehead had a wide gaping scar that yawned open each time he moved. Blood poured from his busted lip and left a bib of red around his shirt's collar. Jesse stood cool and casual in front of the man with a cigarette pinched in between his fingers. Jesse took a stiff toke, mushroomed out a cloud, then laid a light smack on the man's face. "Get yourself together."

"I've learned my lesson," the man said. His words came out like he was speaking with a mouth full of peanut butter; like he accidentally bit his tongue while getting worked over by the bouncers in the alley.

"Did you really?" Jesse asked.

The man nodded. He sniffed up some loose snot then ran his sleeve against his nose. A streak of blood soaked into his shirt. "My uncle, he's—he's O'Grady; might know him as 'The Greek.' Ever heard of him?"

Jesse had. The Greek was a dope-dealing scumbag with

no huge connections. He ran a crew known as "The Riverfront Clubbers." But Jesse shrugged and told the man, "No." The Greek had nothing Jesse wanted.

Jesse looked at Twitch, then back at the man. Twitch's body moved in Jesse's peripheral, a big blob shifting further from Jesse's view into the corner of the room.

"Ok," Jesse shrugged. "Well if you say you learned your lesson, I guess I believe you."

Jesse reached out his hand, letting the man know everything was fine. The man hesitated, but he finally took Jesse's hand and stood. Jesse smiled. The man strained through the pain to grin. Jesse's smile shifted to a frown.

A rope looped over the man's head and wrapped around his neck. Jesse clamped down on his wrist with both hands. The man flailed around, unsure whether he should relieve the pressure being applied to his throat or the pressure being applied to his wrist. They dragged the man, gurgling, kicking, unable to scream, to a table, and forced his right hand flat.

"Come on," Jesse said. "Just put your fucking hand on the table. Come on."

Jesse put all his weight into holding the man down. Rory pulled on the rope tighter, twisting his wrist and turning his body to keep a scream from escaping the man's throat.

Twitch came over with a mallet and handed it to Jesse. Twitch took a towel from his pocket and stuffed it in the man's mouth with three fingers, making sure it got right in the back of his throat. Jesse raised the mallet, took a deep breath, and swung it down.

He hammered until the man's fingers plunged backward at the joints, bending them in the opposite direction and forcing them to make a wet, snapping noise. Jesse swung until the legs of the table wobbled; until veins in the man's neck swelled; until animalistic groans from his throat were hardly drowned out by the loud music from the party outside. The man twisted and writhed, groaned and trembled, but Jesse wouldn't stop. He kept swinging until he hyperventilated and until his adrenaline hit a point where he no longer felt in control. When Jesse was done, the man's hand was a bag of shrapnel. Jesse loosened his grasp and the mallet slid from his hand and clattered to the floor. The man fainted. Rory and Twitch held the man up and took him toward a back door to an alley behind the brothel.

Jesse went to a mirror to fasten his suit. His face was hard and angry. He fastened his tie, but never removed his gaze from his reflection. His mother always said he had his father's eyes. They were capable of holding such gentleness, until they turned hard. Those eyes stared back at him right now. But no, he wasn't his father, he told himself. He wasn't a thug, not anymore. He pulled the knot closed and meditated on what Big Sal once taught him: "As soon as the wolves come to your door, they bring the whole pack with them." He wasn't a monster. He was keeping the other beasts away.

Jesse opened the door. A hallway separated the makeshift torture room from the rest of the establishment. It made it easier to put distance between who he was to his guests, and who he was when in that room. He made sure to take short, measured steps to compose himself, catch his breath, and slip on his prize-winning charm. He stopped at the door, placed his hand on the knob, took several deep breaths, and walked back into the party with a smile on his face. He walked past a man going to town with his saxophone and shot him a thumbs-up. He winked at a customer or two along his route to reach Clyde.

Jesse spread his hands. "You A-OK?"

Clyde stared down at his glass like he'd find an answer in it. Jesse opened his mouth to apologize, but Cindy called for him. She was a few tables over, with well-dressed men who Jesse could only assume were of the white-collar variety. Cindy waved repeatedly for him to come over, and he put up one finger to let her know he'd be a moment.

Clyde took big gulps of his drink and stared into nothingness. "Just go ahead."

"You can come, you know," Jesse said.

Clyde shook his head. Jesse, who felt at a loss, turned away from his brother, and decided he'd try again later.

Clyde's vice-like grip clamped Jesse's wrist. "Your friends over there know the real you, Mr. Businessman?"

Jesse's eyes followed Clyde's gaze to his cuffs. There were specks of blood around them. Tiny dots that were supposed to remain in the backroom, and not follow him into this part of his life. Jesse snatched his hand away from Clyde and walked away.

Jesse took a seat at the round table right next to Cindy and joined in a conversation he inferred was comical in nature. Cindy made the effort of introducing Jesse to her new friends, some out-of-towners in New Orleans on business. One of the men leaned over to shake Jesse's hand. Jesse slowly lifted his arm, but the specks of blood caught his eye. He tucked his shirt cuff deep into his jacket sleeve. After all introductions were done, Jesse slipped on a wide, good-humored, politician-like smile, and began his routine. "So, a man says to a pastor..."

Chapter 4

The Golden Boy of New Orleans

Rudy just *had* to make Jesse meet him in the Financial District; Jesse hated it there. It was a place with monochromatic high-rise buildings of steel and granite and glass that ascended too high for the eyes to follow. The entire area had no personality, no defining features. It was bland and soulless and devoid of culture and beauty, much like most of the boring assholes who worked there. Rudy didn't feel comfortable inviting him to City Hall, so instead, Rudy summoned him to one of his office buildings in the District, much to Jesse's annoyance. But that's what Rudy did to Jesse: annoy the ever-loving shit out of him.

Jesse entered a three-story building, made his way up to the top floor, and walked down the hall until he reached a door with **THOMPSON CO. LIMITED** etched on the frosted glass. The office space was cluttered and furnished with chairs, a bookcase, and a table untidied by old newspapers and magazines. And if that wasn't enough, there was an empty receptionist desk littered with receipts, papers, and stained coffee mugs. Jesse decided to amble past the desk, but a man materialized from a room and blocked his path. "Can I help you?"

Jesse jumped back. The guy looked barely younger than Jesse. He wore too-big glasses, too-big a suit, and too-big a sense of importance.

"I'm here to see Rudy," Jesse said. Jesse sidestepped him. His path got blocked again. Jesse sighed. Apparently, the kid had too-big balls as well.

"I'm his intern, Bobby," he said. "Mr. Rudolph is on the phone handling City Hall business right now." Bobby brushed past Jesse and added even more papers to the mound on his desk.

"There's these things called file cabinets, you know," Jesse said.

Bobby spun around like he'd been told his mother was a whore. "Mr. Rudolph stated he will get me the proper tools I need at a time suitable for him. He is a very busy man." Bobby spoke with enough venom to get Jesse to back off.

"When will 'Mr. Rudolph' be done?" Jesse asked. "He was the one who told me to come at this time."

"He'll be done when he's done, Mr...?"

"That's not important. You know, I'm not sure what he's paying you, but I heard the President could use a new bodyguard."

Jesse took one of the three empty seats, then eyed the stacks of magazines on the table in front of him, which were dog-eared covers of the Sears catalog, the New York Times, and the latest edition of the Times-Picayune. His attention got snared by a picture over on the bookshelf. He walked over to see a grainy photo of Wardolf S. Thompson, the founder of Thompson Co. Limited and Rudy's father.

Wardolf sat on what appeared to be a cheaply made throne. He was flanked by his wife, or who Jesse assumed was the wife. She had the dejected look all disappointed wives had: a face worn and withered from years of dealing with too much infidelity and not enough good sex. To Wardolf's left was a young Rudy Thompson. He wore a schoolboy uniform and knee-high socks. The entire setup almost made Jesse grateful for his abusive father and mentally unstable mother.

"That's Mr. Rudolph's father," Bobby said.

Jesse turned. "Yea, I read the papers."

"Then you know that he died of a stroke," Bobby said. He licked envelopes and stuffed them with papers like he was more machine than man.

Jesse sat. "Yep. Tragedy."

Tragedy and complete bullshit. Wardolf had died naked on top of his 20-year-old mistress, a girl in Jesse's employ. Less than a year ago, a bellhop at a hotel Wardolf loved to visit with his lovers had heard the blood-curdling screams of a young woman come from down the hall. He ran toward the noise and pleaded with the woman to open the door, eventually kicking it off its hinges, and entered the threshold to save the day. He had gotten an eye full.

By the time Jesse, Twitch, and Rory had arrived, Wardolf was sprawled out on the floor like he'd died making a snow angel. His mistress was next to him, dry-heaving into her knees with the force of someone who'd had the wind knocked out of them. They questioned the girl and found out Wardolf had done an excess of coke before they fucked. The vials were emptied out on the nightstand, and had only specks of residue left. The bellhop was standing guard still.

"You didn't tell anyone yet, did you?" Jesse asked the bellhop.

He shook his head. "As soon as she said that she worked with the Pikes, I knew immediately to call you first." He also told Jesse how the girl was, well, stuck under Wardolf's, um... rather large mass, and had needed help rolling Wardolf over. Jesse cringed. He tipped the bellhop extra for almost blowing his back out.

They got the girl cleaned up and out of there. Jesse had an epiphany on the ride home. Wardolf had interests in railroads, distilleries, and land development. He was a heavy financial backer in politics, mainly those who catered to state legislation favoring him, and was one of seventeen members of the city's ruling political machine, The Old Row Democratic Party. He also had a son. If there was one thing Jesse knew about this city, it was that their politics ran on nepotism.

Jesse had gone to Wardolf's funeral. He walked in to see pews full of people with salt and pepper hair. He assumed they were all businessmen and politicians. Jesse squeezed past people's knees and got the perfect angle of the widow and the heir to Wardolf's throne. They had been the only ones not crying.

A baby swaddled in the arms of a young woman had whined, and Jesse turned to see tears running down the young woman's cheeks. The girl tried to calm the baby while muffling her own sobs and staring at Wardolf's casket in a fashion reserved for widows. The pain in her face wasn't from a niece or a daughter... no, this was something else. It was the face of someone who would trade places with Wardolf in a heartbeat if it meant he got to live. Jesse raised his eyebrows. Then he noticed another young girl. Then another one. Then he realized the girl Wardolf almost suffocated probably wasn't his only mistress.

After the corpse was wheeled out, Jesse ran to catch up with Rudy. He had introduced himself and Rudy said he knew of him from various circles.

Jesse took the opening. "You might have some competition for your dad's will."

Rudy turned to see the young women who stuck out amongst the crowd of the old, wrinkled, and grey. Jesse offered to handle his problem for him.

Jesse had made the girls disappear. He got one a good job in another state in return for getting her to sign a contract stating she would never speak about the kid or Wardolf ever again.

Tears had streamed down her face. Jesse calmed her best he could, but she loved Wardolf. They all fucking loved him. Jesse had to negotiate at least three more NDAs and payoffs. All of them with girls who were younger than him, damn near the same age as his sister; all of them poor and sold a dream by a man who promised to leave his wife and take them away from their broken homes where they had no indoor plumbing and broken light fixtures and creaky porches worn from years of neglect.

One negotiation had bothered him the most. The girl was in a type of pain that rolled off of her in waves that Jesse could feel across the table, all while her father negotiated for more money and bonds and interest in Wardolf's companies. Night terrors came at Jesse hard that night.

Rudy had no more impending scandals blocking him from taking his seat as the 5th Ward's boss. He couldn't say no when Jesse suggested he let him steal a shipment of legal booze from his father's distilling company. Rudy collected the insurance money and got paid upfront for turning a blind eye. It was all so easy. Jesse found it ironic his position in life right now was all due to Wardolf getting coked up and fucked out until his heart exploded. But then again, if the coke hadn't done it, then a regular plate of salty food might've eventually done the trick.

Jesse snapped out of his daydream to see Rudy craning his neck out of his office. "Jesse!" he said with one of those phony photo-ready smiles. He then looked at Bobby. "Why didn't you tell me he was out here?"

Bobby stammered for an answer, but Jesse covered him. "He said you were on the phone."

Rudy nodded absentmindedly. "Oh yea. Come in."

Jesse walked past the receptionist's desk and saw a picture of what looked like Bobby and his family. A wife and kid. That explained why someone would ever take this shit job.

Rudy's office was as pristine as a cathedral, and a monument to a rich and spoiled life. It was filled with books and tiny figurines from his travels around the country, and on his walls hung framed degrees in business and finance from universities abroad and domestic.

"How ya doing today?" asked Rudy. Rudy had this aura about him that made it seem like others should be fortunate to be in his presence. His smile bugged Jesse the most. It was like he practiced it; like he was only capable of feigning cordiality instead of being able to just do it.

Jesse took a seat and plopped his feet on Rudy's desk, causing a tremor to shake the figurines Rudy had laid about. Jesse grinned. He wanted to remind Rudy he wasn't one of his employees or aides.

"What do you know about Cameron Mulligan?" Jesse asked. "Who is he connected to?"

Rudy cleared his throat and moved Jesse's feet a quarter inch to the left. "A lot of people. If you haven't seen, he's being endorsed by the Governor now. The fucking Governor, Jesse." Rudy stood and paced behind his desk, then went to the window to look out the blinds.

"Expecting someone?" asked Jesse.

"Hardy-har. This is bad, ok?"

"I know. The Governor caught you guys," Jesse threw up air quotes. "'allegedly,' trying to get one of your own into the Governor's Mansion. Of course he would want you out."

"I'm happy to see you pay attention to politics." Rudy sat, then gently pushed Jesse's feet off his desk.

Jesse wanted to take Rudy's figurines and cram them up his tight ass, but he inhaled, and crossed his right leg over the left. "So, Cameron has some serious power, and you're scared."

"Of course he does. And yes, I am. His power is stifled by Mayor Beckman, but if Cameron wins, no one will be able to stop him."

"What do you have on him?"

Cameron counted on his fingers. "His father was a big philanthropist, a part of the old guard that tried to keep vice out of New Orleans. Sick now. Or dead. Don't really know. His mommy's dead. He doesn't drink, doesn't smoke, and from what we know, he doesn't date." Rudy slammed the desk. "It's like trying to blackmail a fucking nun."

Rudy looked like he could hurl. He loosened his tie and fidgeted the knot every few seconds. Up and down and up and down, adjusting it like it would soothe the situation. Sweat pooled around his neck despite the cool flow of air coming through a cracked window.

Jesse grew impatient. He leaned up at the edge of his seat. "Relax. People that get nervous tend to rat. People who rat get taken for rides by Big Sal. Plus, you have someone out there. Right fucking there," Jesse pointed in the general direction of Bobby. "So please, watch what you say."

"Fine. I'm fine. You can go check out Mulligan at the nigger church in Treme. But somebody has to do something. Because if he wins..." Rudy slid a finger across his neck. "Our money train is gone. I mean, no vice? There is no New Orleans without vice."

Jesse stood. "I'll check him out." He shook Rudy's hand. It was clammy and cold.

Jesse headed out of Rudy's office and walked past the receptionist's desk. He saw Bobby's bright-eyed and determined look had diminished. Jesse's momentum carried him to the door, but his curiosity froze him. "What's eating you?"

"Oh, it's nothing. I, uh, I got a call about my son. He's back in the hospital again."

Jesse winced. "I'm sorry to hear that," Jesse spoke low and pointed down the hall. "Ask Rudy to let you leave."

Bobby shook his head. "I can't do that. There's so much to do here, and well, who else will pay the hospital bill?"

Jesse figured the millionaire fuck down the hall could, for starters, but kept his comment to himself. "Sorry about earlier. I hope everything goes well."

"Yea," Bobby said. "Me too, mister."

***

Treme was the oldest colored neighborhood in the country and was once Jesse's favorite place to go. He'd heard rumblings some years back about some type of music called "jazz," and asked Davy about it. He ended up inviting Jesse out with him one night and Jesse fell in love with the women; the culture; the music. He loved the area because he felt like this was a part of the real New Orleans he loved so much; another one of her many sides. Being that Treme is just on the western outskirts of the French Quarter, jazz eventually made its rounds through the city and onto white, upper-class New Orleanians. Those who didn't call it devil music, anyway. But it wasn't the same.

Jesse wasn't shocked when he received unwelcome looks as he walked through the neighborhood. White men, especially those in nice suits, didn't come to their side of town as of late. None meaning well, anyway. Ever since a string of lynchings decades earlier, the already rocky relationship between Blacks and whites had been irrevocably fractured, and would likely only get worse over time.

Jesse walked calm and collected. He tried to keep a smile on his face and a loose stride in his step to let people know he meant no harm, but people sat in front of their beige and bright blue California-style bungalows and stared daggers at him. Old folks stopped rocking in their chairs and children stopped running in their yards.

Jesse walked up to the front of the Baptist church and got a few looks, but was welcomed by the women who wore beautiful church hats and fanned their slightly damp faces. The church was packed, and it was all to see the man up front: Cameron Mulligan. Cameron looked exactly like Jesse figured, well dressed and lanky, wearing a blue jacket over a white shirt with brown pants and shoes. When Cameron took his jacket off it revealed sweat stains and a rod-thin frame.

Cameron also seemed genuine. He shook everyone's hands, not like he only saw them as potential votes, but because he genuinely wanted to help them. He asked everyone within reaching distance their names and in turn introduced himself. Jesse couldn't help but admire the guy. If this guy was like Rudy or any other person he had ever met, they would've given these people a pat on the back and said "Vote Democrat" then sped out of there like a bat out of hell.

Cameron got up in front of the congregation, two other members of his team next to him. There was an anxious buzz in the crowd, an energy of distrust and weariness that Jesse could feel in the air. The church's pastor stood in front and spoke to steady the storm, which made the aggravated murmurs and untrusting glares cease. For now.

Cameron was introduced, shook the pastor's hand, and flashed an organic, inviting smile. Then his voice boomed from the pulpit to the back of the church. He spoke with vigor and pride and power, but he didn't speak at them, he spoke with them. He wasn't coming to them as a Great White Shepherd for Negros, but as a friend who wanted to help.

Jesse scrubbed the sweat from his brow with his coat sleeve and noticed some of the folded arms got looser and a few people's ears perked up. Jesse got lost in his words like the rest of them. Cameron spoke of a radically different city, a utopia where everyone could exist as relative equals. He spoke of protecting colored wages and colored rights. Within reason, that is. Jesse noticed he never spoke of desegregating the city; the guy was a politician, not a magician. He'd get strung up right next to them if he got too far out of line.

One part in particular caught Jesse's attention: "Your frustrations are fair; your anger is fair. Over the past few years, hell, decades, corruption and lies have ruled this city. Citizens of our city have fallen to the wayside, while the upper-crust thrives in their social clubs. They look down upon the city from their Ivory Towers. They constantly fill their pockets, along with the pockets of their followers and friends, while hard-working New Orleanians like you barely scrape by. I say today is the day it stops. If we wait until Election Day, it'll be too late. They would have made their backroom deals with the Devil by then. They will be there, waiting with bribe money to get you to vote for them, or worse, they'd use brutes like they have before to sway the election. But if we take a stand together, we can change this city's government. Some of you see me as maybe too young for this position. Or maybe too rich. But I've used my money to make this city stronger the best way I can. And lest you forget, it was my father who rid the city of the redlight district, Storyville. As for a question of my youth, I say maybe it's time for a youthful perspective.

"A vote for the Reform Party is a vote to drain this swamp. To push our city closer toward peace and God. I can't promise that I'll rid the city of all corruption, all vice, or all prostitution, because as we know, the Devil is always working. But I will work to limit his evils. I will work to get officers who actually care enough to stop his evils. I come here not promising anything; you've all been given empty promises before. But I come here to show you I care. I care because you are all New Orleanians, just as much as they are. The evil, vile, monsters in the current administration don't see you as such, but I do. So, in closing, a vote for the Reform Party is a vote for your own humanity; a vote for the Reform Party is a vote for a better New Orleans."

The crowd rose and roared and blocked Jesse's view of the stage. Their claps sounded like heavy rain thundering down on top of a tin roof.

After another fifteen minutes of sitting in the church, Jesse came to a conclusion: Cameron was young, energetic, and dynamic. He had fresh, radical views on the city, and genuinely cared. When he spoke, even Jesse felt invigorated. But the ORD would eat him alive. People, the ones who matter at least, don't want change. The city was stabilized by pussy, booze, drugs, and gambling. Yea, there's the importing and exporting business, but those aren't just fruits and vegetables coming into the city. If vice is restricted, you might as well kill the economy. So Cameron would likely be a dud. But, as Jesse shuffled out of the pews with the flow of people, he figured he'd need a plan to offload the booze quicker, just in case Mulligan became an issue.

A bottleneck of people held up the exit, all in hopes of speaking to the "Golden Boy of New Orleans." Jesse was close to the exit when a man stopped Cameron in his tracks to shake his hand. Jesse sighed. But through the barrage of heads and shoulders, he saw a speck of red hair. He froze. People grumbled and moved around him. When Cameron turned to shake hands, Jesse got a better view. It was there.

Right past his shoulder. A glimpse of a ghost of his past. A face from a bygone time, when it was all picnics and strolls across campus to class. Jesse exhaled her name. "Rose?"

Her head turned enough for him to see the corner of her eyes, and he fought through the people, nudging shoulders and stepping on feet, ushering people out of his way like they were children, all in hopes of seeing her. His heart raced; his thoughts were tangled in knots. When he made it to the front, he saw Mulligan, a group of his admirers, but no Rose. He exited the church. He saw cars and bushes and constituents talking to McCabe, Cameron's choice for Deputy Mayor. But yet again, no Rose. He rubbed his eyes. He hadn't been sleeping well lately. It was probably just one of his ghosts; one of the many specters who visited him on nights when his conscience was at its weakest and his resolve at its lowest. Like the impression of his father that appeared in the shadows some nights and mocked him from the corner of his room. He strode out of the neighborhood and toward his condo.

Jesse lay in bed and listened to the white noise of people moving about out on the street below and thought of fond memories from the love affair he'd had with Rose. It made him smile. But it couldn't have been her that he'd seen. She wouldn't be back in town without looking him up. Or would she?

She had a right to want to avoid him, and the more Jesse thought about how they ended, the more he realized it. So he tried to push her out of his mind the best he could so he wouldn't do anything stupid—like getting his hopes up that she'd come back to him. But it was no use. He was at the point of exhaustion where his mental resolve was low and his mind was tired, so as he drifted to sleep, he found himself praying that if Rose really was avoiding him in real life, she'd at least do him the courtesy of visiting him in his dreams.

Chapter 5

Absolution

It was Rose. It had to be. Jesse could lose his memory, but never forget that face. He could lose his sight, but still know when she entered the room: it was like an angel had entered; everyone was happier and birds chirped and time stopped and her peaceful glowing aura smacked you with the force of violent winds. Just being in her vicinity filled people with the urge to be better, to do better, and the thought of her touch made the cold parts of Jesse's heart melt.

Those cold nights in his dorm room bed were bolted to the front of his mind like a bow on the front of a ship not even God could knock off. But she'd left him. Or, well, he left her. At least he got to take the memories when he left.

Sal snapped his fingers. "You want to play or not?" He gestured to the chessboard between them.

Jesse jumped to attention. "Sorry. Not much sleep last night," he said. The floorboards of Sal's front porch whined when he leaned forward to move his piece.

Sal waved away the statement and jumped it. "You're young. Pretty soon you'll be wishing you could stay up without passing out on the couch."

Jesse laughed.

Sal's home was in the Uptown Garden District, where pink flowers and white magnolias lined the pristine sidewalks with explosive color; where winding oak trees protruded from manicured lawns outside of homes; and where those homes looked like either castles from fairy tales or the plantations of yesteryear. The sun's heat was weakened by thick clouds in the sky, but the thin sliver of sun that snuck through still had a bite to it. It nipped at Jesse's neck. Sweat pooled around his collar.

Jesse told Sal about his Mulligan findings: the guy's a straight arrow, religious, don't smoke, don't drink.

"So, in other words, a problem," Sal said.

"Only if he wins."

Sal's several layers of clothing made Jesse sweat just looking at him. And the old man still shivered like a chip of ice had been thrown down his shirt.

"So, any ideas?" Sal asked.

"Not yet. But nothing we can do until we see how things shake out."

"I'm more of a 'pre-emptive measures' kind of guy."

"Well," Jesse slid his piece, "Can't take out the DA."

"I know, I know. I'm just sayin'."

They sat quietly for a moment, allowing the sound of chess pieces clicking against the board to fill the void. Jesse could sense they both had the same topic at the edge of their tongues that they up until then avoided like a landmine: him quitting. With every chess move, Jesse could see the disappointment perforate Sal's veiled happiness, and awaited the inevitable conversation. They both went through several turns when Jesse decided to ask, "You ever, I don't know, think about the past?"

"In what regard?"

"I don't know...the things you've done."

Sal's chess piece dangled in his fingers. "Every now and again."

Jesse rocked back in the chair. "I been having these fucking dreams. These nightmares. I feel like I see all of them."

"All of who?"

"Every single fuck I screwed over one time or another. I see my father –"

Sal silenced Jesse with a flash of the palm. "You didn't put no gun to his head."

Jesse felt like he did. Always sneaking out, doing terrible, terrible things, then showing up with wads of money, making his dad feel inferior and neutered. You can't clip a man's balls like that and not expect him to wanna put a gun in his mouth. Jesse cleared his throat. "Last night, I thought I seen Rose."

Sal sat back as much as his bundles of clothing allowed and eyed Jesse with suspicion. "You ain't quitting because of that girl again, are you?"

Jesse shook his head.

"Because you already quit once because of her. That broad is the reason I wasted thousands on you to go to Tulane. Just don't fucking tell me it's for her, again."

Jesse bit his lip and shook his head. "Never mind. Shouldn't've said anything."

He was halfway up to leave before Sal's arm shot across the board and gripped his wrist. "Well, is she the reason, Jesse?"

Jesse swatted his arm away.

Mrs. Bianchi came to the threshold and looked out the screen door and asked what all the ruckus was about. Jesse and Sal looked at each other and said nothing. She went back in. The flames between Jesse and Sal settled to a calm ember.

Sal smirked, then moved his rook. "Checkmate."

Jesse was stunned at how Sal's anger sparked up and dissipated quicker than anyone he knew. "Alright, guess I'll get out of here," Jesse said.

"One more, yeah?" Sal asked with his eyes perked up and his doughy wrinkled face shaped into a grin.

Jesse stood. "Can't. Got somewhere to be."

The steps creaked and groaned as he trotted down toward the wide horseshoe driveway. Sal called his name. He spun around.

"I know you want to quit," Sal said. "But I need you to stay on this Mulligan guy for a little. As a favor to me." He paused to hack out a cough. "I always told you—"

"'Finish what you start.' Yea, I remember." He looked at the sky, then back at Sal. "I'll do what I can. Sooner we're out of liquor, sooner we're done with this." And the sooner Jesse would have money to infuse into his restaurant.

Sal put on his proud-papa face. "Ok, Jesse-boy. Do what you can."

***

But all Jesse could do was think about the woman he saw last night at the rally in Treme. Red hair, 5'4, impeccably dressed like Rose always was. After losing sight of her, Jesse asked some of the women at the church if they'd ever seen that redhead before. They had. She'd come down to the church before and talked about women's rights, and how important it was for the female voice to be a part of politics.

That's how he ended up sitting in his car, staring out of his passenger window at a meeting hall. He was across the street, parked on the curb in front of a patio cafe and a father-son newsstand. The father shouted "Times-Picayune! Times-Picayune!" while people walked by without acknowledging him. The son did the same in his high falsetto but got the same result.

Jesse started to get out the car and walk into the hall but hesitated; he could just be going nuts. From time to time, he felt like the ghosts of his past haunted him. He saw victims and collateral damage everywhere. When he saw a taxi, he thought about the taxi driver he and Clyde ripped off in their teens. When he drove through a nice neighborhood and saw a four-door Touring, he thought about the same car he boosted a decade ago. Even with the father-son newsstand ahead, he couldn't help but think about the newsstands he'd set ablaze during the height of the "Newspaper Wars." He was about sixteen at the time, and he loved how the wood shifted from brown to charred black and caused the fire's embers to flicker toward the black sky like fireflies in the night. At the time, he knew doing those things meant he and his siblings would eat for at least a week. Now, it all stained his soul. Jesse started up his car to leave.

There was motion across the street. He paused. Women filed out of the meeting hall one by one—old, young, and at the end, the redheaded woman. She waved a farewell to all the women as they left. It couldn't be her. It couldn't. She was on the move now. Jesse hopped out of his car and ran into the street, causing a car to slam on its brakes at the last minute and the driver to flash his middle finger.

Jesse sprinted to her and her bouncing set of red curls, reached out his hand, and touched her shoulder. "Rose?"

She froze.

She turned around with a placid pale face. It was Rose. His Rose. He smiled and babbled like an idiot. "Oh God, I can't... it's you. It's really you."

Rose frowned, then screamed, "No!" She screamed it loud enough to make people across the street stare. She stormed away.

He ran around in front of her. He flashed his palms. "Wait, wait, please, I just want to talk for a moment." Rose twisted and shifted in discomfort. Every step she made; he got there first. When she went left, he stepped to his right.

She resigned and folded her arms, letting her purse fall to her elbow crook.

"We have nothing to speak of," she said.

The smile on his face slowly slipped into a frown.

She sighed. "What do you want, Jesse?"

"I don't know."

He froze. *I miss you* hung on the tip of his tongue; *I always think of you* wasn't far behind. But *I love you* almost roared from his throat, nearly propelled out by the force of his longing. He kept his mouth shut instead and assessed her. He settled with, "I guess I wanted some closure."

Rose snickered. It was humorless and cold. "You can't find any with me."

That was a gut punch that knocked the wind out of him.

"Look," she said. "If you must know, I graduated, taught for a while like my father always wanted, then realized that's not what I wanted. I got into women's rights. I moved away for a bit, came back, and now I'm organizing women's political movements here." She looked at him matter-of-factly. "Is that enough for you?"

It was more than enough. All those years wondering how she was, making up stories about what she was doing, and now he knew; she did everything she ever dreamed of. "That's enough. Why didn't you look me up when you got back?"

She exhaled. "Look, let's cut this short. I'm seeing someone right now."

Another gut punch.

"And, it's early days yet, but I'm sure this one won't

leave me to be a gangster."

Jesse said through gritted teeth, "You know that's not—Clyde went to prison, ok? You knew my family situation. But I'm different now."

Rose touched the side of Jesse's face. It was gentle and endearing, pitying and resentful. "I believe you."

He stared up the sidewalk over her shoulder, right toward the houses up ahead, which appeared to have their roofs decapitated by the glare of the beaming sun.

Her eyes went soft. "I didn't mean to call you a gangster, but don't pop up like this again, Jesse. I'll be praying for you. I truly will. I know there's good in you, I've seen it, but just because you feel bad about the bad things you do and have done, doesn't make them go away. You want absolution, fine, but it won't be with me."

She walked away and out of his life again. He stayed where he was. He played those words through his mind over and over and over, until he realized... he deserved all of that. He walked across the street with what was left of his pride.

The newsstand father-son duo shouted to his right, and the café up ahead was abuzz with people. The patio was surrounded by a wrought iron fence with a myriad of colorful flowers hanging over the railings. People tossed back their coffee mugs so fast that servers tripped over one another to give refills. Jesse caught a whiff of something rank and familiar that made his face sour. There was a phantom taste on the tip of his tongue. He took another close look at the smiling faces. Whiskey. This café was serving whiskey out in the open—in the daytime—like its coffee. He smiled. He knew how to offload the liquor sooner.

"Times-Picayune!" the little boy still shouted behind him.

Jesse walked over to the newsstand. The little boy had on tattered clothes and shoes with holes in them. The father had a five o'clock shadow and a worn face.

"Newspaper, mister?" asked the little boy.

Jesse took one. Today's story was about the political climate in New Orleans and of course, "The Golden Boy of New Orleans."

Jesse rolled up the paper and squatted to eye-level with the boy. "I'll take this."

Jesse took a clump of bills from his pocket and put it in the little boy's hand then headed back to his car. The little boy's squeaky voice turned shrill behind him. "Woah, Daddy! Daddy!"

The newspaperman screamed at Jesse and trotted up the sidewalk. "Sir! Sir! It was only but a few cents!" The man fanned the bills in his hands.

Jesse drove off and in his rearview mirror, could see the father and son hugging. One good deed wouldn't erase the bad he'd done, but if his new scheme went off without a hitch, he'd have a lot more money to do a lot more good with. But first, he had to do just a little more bad.

Chapter 6

No Rest for the Wicked

Prohibition Agent Watkins was a Rising Sun regular. Mid-thirties, slack-jawed, with a face only a mama could love, he came from a small town in Who-gives-a-fucks-ville, Mississippi and spent his days tethered to his desk at the New Orleans Customhouse. He was called an agent, but paper-bitch was what the fellas around the water cooler called him. He'd never fired his gun, but he could lick five hundred envelopes in a shift faster than anyone else. Every time he walked toward the water cooler, his fellow agents dispersed like roaches when the lights came on, snickering to themselves and acting like he wasn't there. But at the Rising Sun, he was a god.

Every day he stepped into the building, loosened the noose-like tie around his neck, took off his smothering suit jacket, and allowed himself to be greeted by one of the many beautiful women of the Rising Sun. They would all be waiting for him. Sure, other men went there. But he was the only one who was a lawman. Women loved men in uniform.

The ladies of the Rising Sun were like the sirens from Greek mythology, and every time he entered the building, he'd understand more and more why sailors in those stories would throw themselves overboard. Redheads, brunettes, Creoles, blondes; his taste was expansive. He'd be led up the winding stairs while sweet-nothings were whispered in his ear, and once he was in the room, he'd toss his badge on the dresser, and tell them stories of how he was the man at the bureau. He'd tell them lies about his career so tantalizing and vivid that he almost believed them himself.

He sometimes told the truth though. He'd say how many crates they'd confiscated and destroyed each day, where the raids were led, how rum-runners used the Bywater area to hide under the cover of night; how they used the marshlands to hide their speed boats and the crates of liquor floating to shore; and how stressful it was that there were only a dozen federal agents for all of New Orleans and its bodies of water.

"The God damned bureaucrats won't give us any more resources," he'd say while having his neck kissed and body caressed.

During foreplay, his words were often bracketed by deep, powerful exhalations. "They're too busy with... Chicago, Atlantic City... oh fuck... they don't understand we're drowning here."

Then they would ride him off into the sunset, rocking the headboards and screaming his name loud and proud for everyone to hear. And afterward, when energy was spent— when the last recesses of his mental fortitude and commonsense were melted away by the raw pleasure and unfettered ecstasy—he would tell them more and more, with the woman-for-the-day's legs laced between his, her finger tracing delicate lines up his hairless chest, and an ear-to-ear grin on his face.

He knew he could get in trouble if someone knew he told confidential secrets. He didn't care. He just wanted to feel like a man for once. Like he was important, and not expendable. He'd leave with a wide grin, empty balls, and a short-lived dopamine hit that'd go away once he walked into his empty apartment. Then he'd fall asleep and start the shitty workday all over again. All his secrets always ended up in the hands of the Pikes.

Jesse had known a Prohie came from time to time, because he would overhear Cindy and the girls talking about him. They made him sound like a weak little lamb that had to go into a wolf's den every day. Jesse made sure the girls always made him feel good. Watkins was never without a drink in his hand or a woman on his lap. If there's one thing Jesse learned, there's no one that gabs more than an affection-starved drunk man trying desperately to get just a crumb of sex out of a woman he knows is out of his league. Men, especially unhappy men, pillow-talked to prostitutes like they were shrinks in lace brassieres.

Jesse pieced together the info he got from Watkins'

favorite girls, pooled it with his knowledge of the local rackets, and formulated a plan.

***

Twitch swayed in a rocking chair with his two little girls nestled against his arms. "The little... dog. Ran across the— the yard."

They were young, three and four, and small enough to sit on his lap. He held a book in between them, some children's book about some dog who wanted a ball from across the yard or something. It was stupid. But Twitch read it every night, less he'd hear ear-numbing screams from the curly-haired little monsters resting on him. Plus, it made him happy to see them smile. They never even noticed their daddy stumbled over certain words. At that moment, he took his time rolling the syllables off his tongue, even though he felt like Sisyphus rolling that boulder up a hill, but he pushed through it despite the jerks and pauses in his speech. He stopped once he felt the girls' dead weight against his arms.

The bedroom door whined. It was his wife, Donna. Donna mouthed "sorry" once she realized the girls were asleep.

"It's ok," Twitch whispered.

He tucked his girls in, rubbed a thumb across their soft cheeks, and placed a single kiss on their foreheads. Twitch was happy. Happier than most men who did what he did for a living. He had two beautiful girls and a beautiful wife, one of those homes with a front yard and back yard to host people in, and a job he really liked. Every morning his wife cooked him steak and eggs or bacon and eggs, and on Saturdays he'd do the cooking, or make sandwiches and take the family down to City Park and take his girls to feed the ducks. The family would sit on a patterned blanket, and he'd hold hands with his wife, who was his teenage sweetheart, and they'd watch their girls walk and attempt to catch unsuspecting squirrels. Those days were his happy place.

But, he didn't have time to reminisce on those moments. He checked his watch. It was time for work. He looked up at his wife and her smile was gone. He put a finger to her lips and pointed to the kids, then submerged the room into darkness with the tug of the lamp cord. In their living room, Donna put both her hands on her hips and paced back-and-forth in front of Twitch. Her face was emotionless, but he knew it would boil over in a moment. "Are you going out again tonight?"

Twitch nodded. Donna stopped pacing. "Maybe it's time for normal work."

Twitch plopped down on the couch and decided to get comfortable for the onslaught. He shrugged and told her this was what he did for a living. She looked exhausted. "I know it is. I know it is, ok? But I thought the late nights at the inn would stop by now." She counted on her fingers, her voice on the edge of pleading. "You know, there's the port, um, there's – there's...." She stopped once she realized there weren't many spaces meant for people with Twitch's unique challenge.

Twitch laced his fingers and looked at their blue rug

under the living room table. His wife didn't know the whole story about everything he did for a living. She knew there was some escorting going on at the inn, she knew he and his childhood friends weren't on the up-and-up, but she didn't know the scope. She didn't know about the torture room in the inn. Or about the dead bodies Twitch was responsible for. How Clyde would loan Twitch's "skills" out to out-of-state racketeers for a fee back in the day. Twitch could shoot a man and be back home hours later playing in the yard with his girls like it was nothing. That was a skill that paid in abundance. Whenever he had to speak to cops, they'd hear his speech, he'd play dumb, they'd call him a retard or stupid or laugh at him, he'd pretend he didn't want to crack their fucking heads under his feet, and he'd be out and ready to accept another job.

Twitch looked at his wife. Her eyes were on the verge of tears, her hands on the cusp of trembling. He stood and took her face in his hands. And he promised her, someday, sometime soon, no matter what, he wouldn't have to work odd hours again. She closed her eyes, took his wrist in her hand and pressed his palm more into her cheek. She looked up at him like she could never be mad at him, no matter how much she tried. He closed his eyes and kissed her, leaning in to breathe her in, holding her close so that he could say with his body what he couldn't express with his words. A car's honk broke through their moment. Orbs of light glowed through the strands of fabric of their curtains. She wiped away stray tears.

"I need to go," he said. He kissed her forehead and

promised tomorrow morning, he'd take her somewhere nice for breakfast. She giggled and said she'd hold him to it. He gave a wide awkward smile with too many teeth showing, only because he knew she'd find it funny. She did, and he left.

***

Twitch walked hunched over and heel-to-toe through the woods with his sawed-off shotgun gripped tight in his hands, allowing the moonlight to guide his way up to the approaching cabin. It was dark; the long, black tendrils of tree branches stretched out across to one another like the limbs of a kraken.

Twitch led a team of five masked men. One of them was Rory, and the other three men were local small-time crooks Twitch contracted. They moved smoothly and subtly to avoid clotheslining on branches or tripping on pieces of fallen wood as the night air whistled between the trees and rustled the leaves.

They reached the cabin, and Twitch pressed his body against it. The rest of the men fell in line. They moved low and tight against the side of the cabin, angling their bodies around the corner to the front door. A bronze glow burned brightly behind the blinds. The thick smoke from the chimney eclipsed the starry sky above them. Twitch pointed to both of these signs to indicate people were inside.

They flanked the front door. Twitch to the right with one man, Rory and the other two to the left. Twitch put up five fingers. Then four. Then three, and after two, Rory kicked in the front door and fanned his pistol from left to right. Inside, two moonshiners were huddled near barrels of 'shine while a third sat in a chair, taking sips of liquor from a mason jar. Their eyes went wide.

Rory screamed for them not to move, but one of the moonshiners rushed him. Rory froze. Twitch stepped around him and brought the broad end of his shotgun down on the charging man's nose, dropping him to the floor and making him writhe in pain at Twitch's feet. The man crawled back toward his cohorts, dots of blood lining his path. Twitch fanned his sawed-off left to right while looking at Rory, out of breath, nervous that he almost lost his dearest friend's little brother. He barked at Rory, "Watch yourself." Rory looked like a deer in headlights.

One of the masked men with Twitch and Rory had an ax slung over his shoulder. Twitch grabbed the ax and proceeded to chop down the homemade still until it was nothing more than hoses and tin and broken beakers scattered on the floor. He threw one chop into the side of each barrel of moonshine next, clear liquid gushing out and spreading across the floor. The ethanol smell could've burned a hole in their sack masks and seared paint from a wall.

"Let's go," Twitch said. The five men high-stepped it all the way back to the getaway vehicle.

Rory drove as fast as the headlights would allow. The car jerked and shook up a barely visible path; the trees were illuminated by headlights and the long dark forms of tree silhouettes in the distance.

Twitch shook his head at Rory. "Pay attention, or-or-or go fucking home."

Rory gripped the steering wheel, embarrassed.

"Where to next?" Rory asked.

Twitch read from a list, then placed a checkmark near the address they'd just left. "Gretna."

The plan was simple: if the Pike Gang could get the amount of alcohol entering the city lower, they could step in and fill the demand. As Jesse told them in the brothel, "When supply goes down, and demand stays the same, price goes up."

The information Agent Watkins inadvertently gave Jesse was enough info to draft up a list of people bringing booze into New Orleans. Jesse wanted Twitch to hit them all.

Throughout five nights, the Pike Gang ransacked another seven distilleries and hijacked two trucks headed for New Orleans. By the end of the week, they were able to make their way into the New Orleans liquor scene. They got a few trusted guys who needed extra work to mix the booze from the Thompson CO. heist with water and rebottle it. Their bottles ended up in a handful of bars, restaurants, and speaks. No one ever found out they were the ones who shorted out the bulk of the supply heading into the city. Jesse's anxiety dissipated from watching the illegal inventory in the warehouse dwindle away.

***

Clyde's jaw dropped when he entered the warehouse. He took his hat off and kneaded it in his hands; walked around, amazed at the operation that Jesse had thrown together. A few dozen sweaty men moved back-and-forth from trucks to stacks of opened crates as other men loaded the crates onto the trucks. A man stood with a notepad and paper, keeping track of what went where and to whom.

Jesse walked up behind Clyde and left a hand on his shoulder. "This is where we keep the booze." He pointed to three trucks parked next to each other. "That's where the stuff for out of state goes." He turned to the right, where another row of trucks were. "That's where the stuff headed for the city goes."

While Twitch and Rory had been knocking over the competition, Jesse was giving Clyde a masterclass of the operation he'd set up. It was simple: Jesse kept the booze in a warehouse outside of New Orleans' jurisdiction in Jefferson Parish and paid a few cops from the local Sheriff's department to keep their mouths shut. He'd meet them by a refuel station with a fat envelope on every morning he needed to move the liquor, then ride through the marsh on down to the gravel road to the warehouse, where he'd watch as the workers loaded the trucks. He checked the list of locations the trucks were headed to, compared how much was loaded to what was on his written inventory, and checked the crates to make sure none of the drivers got too bold and stole. When the booze got where it was going, the money from the drop-offs would be handed to the drivers, who would then hand the money off to Rory or Twitch, who would then bring it to Jesse so he could start the process of cleaning the money and divvying it out.

Clyde pointed to the drivers. "Seems like way too many people to trust."

Jesse rattled off the names of all the drivers and their home addresses. Where their kids went to school. How long they've been married to their wives. The color of the inside of their homes. Clyde nodded and lifted his eyebrows. Jesse shrugged. "Twitch was very thorough with checking into these people."

No one ever stole from them. Not out of fear, even though they had every reason to fear Twitch, but because they were getting ten times the amount of money they'd get doing anything else. The jobs in the city were plentiful, but relied on nepotism and an inside connection. Jesse filled the void.

The lessons carried on through the day. Back at Jesse's office, they went over the books. Jesse taught him about laundering and the etiquette of running a brothel. Who to pay when and what to do if they ever got raided, which would never happen. And even if it did, the guy that owned the brothel? He didn't exist. Feds would spend years looking for someone Jesse fabricated on paper. By day two of the on-job training, Clyde was over the talks of numbers and figures. He wanted to get out on the street.

In the Rising Sun's office, Clyde slammed shut a book on Jesse's desk and shot up from his chair. "To hell with this."

Jesse got up and beat him to the door, putting his hand out to block his path. "We aren't finished here."

He gave a stern look to his brother, who was unfazed

and unbothered. Clyde sighed, then backed away from the door. "You know I've been running rackets as long as you, right?"

Jesse nodded. "I'm aware."

"Then you're aware that I can handle things without an orientation."

Jesse moved away from his office door and moved closer to Clyde. "I want to help. I want to make sure I'm leaving this place in good hands."

"You think you know better than me?"

"With this? Yes."

Clyde stuffed his hand in Jesse's coat pocket, pulled out his pack of cigarettes and lit one. His head jerked like he'd inhaled vaporous acid. "The jailhouse smokes were better." He patted Jesse on the face playfully. "Loosen up—your big brother's back home." A trail of smoke followed Clyde out of the office.

***

Jesse stayed away for some time after that. The restaurant needed his attention more than the brothel, and Twitch and Rory would be wrapping up their last raid, so they'd be able to keep an eye on the liquor distribution. His dream was coming together. He watched the workers paint, hammer up paintings, and turn his vision into something tangible. He'd even found the time to take Melvin up on his offer to go with him to The Chateau Club.

The Chateau Club was a world all its own. Hardwood interior design, warm colors like burgundy, brown, and charcoal on the decor, and a cloud of thick cigar smoke making the main dining area look like a foggy night on the port. And it was all men. Jesse had his own gentlemen's club of sorts, but the lack of women startled him. Plus, he didn't feel near rich enough to be around any of the men in that room.

He and Mel looked for an open table. A server darted toward him with a tray of, well, Jesse didn't know what the hell he was looking at, but figured he'd give it a try. "How much will it be?"

The server's customer service smile shifted to confusion. Melvin took two of the finger-sized foods. "Sorry, my friend here is new."

He gave one to Jesse, who ate whatever ritzy snack it was in one bite. It was like an explosion of flavor in his mouth, an amalgamation of spicy and sweet and tangy. It defied the laws of physics or cooking or whatever the fuck; Jesse just knew it was good.

Mel snickered. "Everything here is free, buddy. You're with a member. Well, the son of a member."

Jesse asked how much a membership was. The number made him choke. He felt like the brown, crispy, flaky treat he swallowed was a brick of gold.

Jesse said, "That's more than most people's cars. Or homes."

Melvin snorted and fidgeted with his glasses. "It's worth it. You meet a lot of swell people."

Jesse looked at all the bourgeois men around him. All their eyes were on him, as well. People like this could sniff out an outsider from a hundred yards away and have their security escorting the peasant from the premises before they even entered the threshold. Jesse felt like a little boy again, walking home from school in wrinkled clothes, when all the other little boys on the sidewalk assessed his value and decided he wasn't enough. That feeling would only deepen whenever Albert, Bill, and Kenneth arrived.

They sat in a booth and chatted about things Jesse would never understand. Things like summer homes and winter homes; investment portfolios and inheritances; breakfast rooms and supper rooms; and butlers with hoity-toity accents. They might as well have talked about putting a man on the moon. He stared at his glass of water the entire time, watching the condensation roll down and hoping his immature feelings of inadequacy would fade away like the melting ice cubes in his drink. When everyone else laughed around the table, Jesse laughed as well, despite not having a fucking clue what was said.

"So," said Bill, "what was your father's line of work?"

Jesse snapped to attention when he realized Bill was speaking to him, then took several sips of water in order to buy himself time before answering. Jesse fumbled his words. "Uh, well, my father was a bit of an entrepreneur."

They laughed. Bill asked, "Ok, but with what?"

Jesse's fingers tapped against the table. "None of his ideas ever got off the ground. He lived and died a laborer." The words slid off his tongue weakly, like if he'd said it low enough, maybe they'd think he said something else and cease to ask questions. But they heard him. They definitely heard him.

"Oh," said Bill.

Albert fiddled with his nose and leaned forward, eyes focused. "So, how'd you get into Tulane, exactly?"

Jesse gripped the glass in his hands like it was Albert's head and contemplated cracking him over the cranium with it. He calmed himself. He couldn't be the poor, violent brute they probably already thought he was. He wasn't afforded the right to have a chip on his shoulder. He wasn't allowed to show genuine emotion. Those were privileges for the wealthy. Jesse set the glass down. "Good grades. And a family friend who subsidized the tuition for me."

Mel chimed in. "I would've never made it through economics or finance without his help. Oh, boy, you should've seen him go whenever the teacher tried to sneak a trick question in on him." Mel took a sip of his water. "He's a real wiz."

"Is that so?" asked Albert.

Jesse nodded. The three men seemed to accept Mel's seal of approval. They went on to talk amongst themselves about something else. Jesse shot a glance at Mel. Mel winked.

***

The workload at the restaurant stopped being fun after a few days. The paperwork mounted and he kept getting calls from the brothel. Apparently, Clyde kept being either totally abrasive to staff and customers, or altogether not leaving his room. He'd been allowing some "riffraff," as the barkeep put it, to enter the brothel and stir up trouble. On the last call, Jesse asked to speak to Clyde. He told him he couldn't be coarse with people, and of course, Clyde didn't listen.

Rory called another day. Jesse was at his desk in the restaurant trying to tune out the sound of hammers beating outside of his office when his phone rang.

"Hello?" Jesse pressed one finger in his ear. "Rory?"

"Yea," Rory took a long pause. "I don't know if Clyde's alright."

Jesse continued to go through the rising cost of the restaurant renovations on the ledger. "What do you want me to do about it? He doesn't want my help."

Rory's voice got tense. "No, Jess. I think Clyde needs to go back to a shrink. He ain't right in the head."

Jesse slouched in his chair. "I'll stop by when I can."

Rory continued to talk, when Melvin stepped in the room with that nervous energy he was so good at emitting. Jesse mouthed "one second" while he continued to feign interest in Rory's bitching.

Melvin shook his head. "No, this is really important."

Jesse took a deep breath and rolled his eyes into the back of his head. "Tomorrow, Rory. I'll come by tomorrow." Jesse slammed the phone down. "What's wrong?"

Melvin spoke in a gasp. "A plumber busted a pipe what should we do what should we do?"

Jesse rested his head in his hands.

***

Jesse entered the Rising Sun for the first time in a week and pulled up a seat at the bar to watch over the patrons. It was the midday crowd, so the room was sparse and the customers were scattered around in their own clusters of conversation. Smooth piano music created a relaxed tone and lowered people's inhibitions.

Jesse turned to the barkeep. "Where's Clyde?"

The barkeep twisted his toweled-hand in a moist glass and jutted his head up to the ceiling. He told Jesse that Clyde was upstairs in one of the rooms nursing a lethal hangover. Jesse's anger sent jolts through his body and made his foot tap in time with his fingers, a rapid pitter-patter that could've doubled as a woodpecker hitting against a tree. The pianist's music stopped and a faint round of claps filled the void. Jesse turned to get up but stopped in his tracks at the sound of a shout. He snapped his head around and saw the man it came from.

"Encore," shouted the man. His hands thundered together as he goaded the pianist to play again. His accent was thick; his words dripped with booze. He sounded like a fresh-off-the-boat Irishman. Jesse saw the uncomfortable faces in the crowd. He asked the bartender, "Is that one of the guys who's been coming around from time to time?"

The bartender nodded. Jesse eyed the man and the friend with him, and they both kept on with their drunken shouting and guffawing while patrons grew more and more uncomfortable by the second.

Jesse inhaled, exhaled, and pushed his anger deep down to a manageable level, attempting to tame it, to force it back into the subconscious box where it rested most of the time, hanging at the edges of his mind like a car dangling over the edge of a cliff.

Jesse walked over to the two drunken Irishmen with a managerial smile on his face and motioned to the pianist to keep playing.

"How are you doing today, fellas?" he asked.

The men's faces burned red with drink, but their eyes were sunken and dead from something much stronger, too. One of the men spoke in what sounded like incoherent jibber-jabber, like he had a mouth full of food. The other hopped in. "Sorry 'bout my frien'. He had a wee bit too much and his accents a li'l thick when he's riled up."

Both of the men's faces were round, but not fat. Just an excess of flesh. The differences between them were in the eyes. The one that spoke gibberish and couldn't keep his eyes open was thinner. He looked younger. He had a full head of hair and he seemed to be the jumpier one. He sat at the edge of his seat the whole time Jesse stood there, like he wanted to propel himself straight into Jesse's body, like it took everything in him to not attack. Jesse kept an eye on him and talked to the calm one.

"Why's he riled up?" he asked, as if the younger man was invisible.

"Probably because you're standing in front of him," the calm one said. The two men coughed out laughs. Their laughter made everyone's attention turn toward the table again. Jesse kept his hands behind his back and squeezed his right fist into his left palm and strained to keep a smile on his face. He bobbed up and down on his tippy toes.

"You gentlemen can stay, but only if you can behave

yourselves," he told them.

The older man tossed back his drink and stood. "Word from your brother is you don't e'en run this place anymore."

"Is that right?"

The man shrugged off Jesse's question. The younger one gazed at Jesse like he wanted to crack his head open. Jesse licked his lips. "Gentlemen, I'm going to have to ask you to leave."

The youngest one shot up. "Make us."

Both men were in Jesse's face. He nodded his head and turned to look for security.

The oldest man started to pick his belongings off the table. "Aye. He's foolin' with ya. I guess it's our time to—"

Jesse spun on his heel and stuffed his knuckles deep into the younger man's gut. The man's neck strained, causing him to release a series of coughs and ropes of saliva. He doubled over to the ground. Jesse grabbed the other man by the collar. His knuckles collided with teeth and jawbone. The man's head propelled to the right, spritzing out flecks of blood with it, making him rock back on his heels and sway side to side until he bumped into a table and fell to the floor. Security came behind Jesse.

The two men were on the ground groaning from pain while security, three men in white shirts with black slacks and suspenders, dragged the two Irishmen to the stairs and booted them out head-over-ass. Jesse's eyes bulged from his head. His vision went foggy from rage and he looked around for someone, anyone, who had an issue with him.

"Do I have to do every fucking thing?" he asked no one in particular.

The patrons who'd stayed stared in slack jaw awe. He calmed down and walked to the front by the piano and spread out his palms. "Drinks on the house." His proclamation was enough for the midday party to start back up.

While the party raged on behind him, he galloped up the winding stairs past customers and women with his fist clenched at his side. He swiveled his head back and forth. He sidestepped people up the hallway, his teeth gritting and his eyes giving an accusatory glance to each closed door. He busted into one room where a man was busy with two courtesans at once. Jesse backed out and apologized. The next room was the right one. Clyde laid nude, face-up on top of the bedspread. The room was muggier than any other part of the house and smelled of sweat and booze, a musty odor that seemed to make the air thicker.

Jesse strode over to the dresser where a cup of water rested under the lamp. He raised the glass above Clyde's head and titled it until Clyde's face and beard were smacked with the downpour. Clyde jerked up and wiped the water from his eyes. Jesse gave him a moment; he wanted Clyde to be fully alert when he said what he needed to say. He stepped back into the doorway. His shadow stretched across the floor and wrapped itself up the bedside and across Clyde's body, submerging one half of his body in dark and the other in hallway light. Clyde spun his legs around to the side of the bed. "What the hell?"

Jesse's eyes locked on Clyde. Jesse fidgeted his fingers at his side and let out one simple sentence: "You're going to learn to fucking respect me."

Clyde met Jesse's gaze with a stare of his own. Something sinister and otherworldly was behind it. Jesse turned to slam the door behind him and left Clyde to stew in his self-loathing and despair.

He stormed down the stairs and shut himself in his office. Or Clyde's office. He didn't feel like he'd ever really gotten to leave. He rubbed his temples and exhaled in rapid succession like he'd run a race up the side of a hill. He stormed in circles around his office and thought about the past four years and all he'd ever done for Clyde. The ungrateful bastard. Jesse gave up years of his life to keep the family afloat—four years—and Clyde marched back in there like it was easy. Like it was something Jesse wanted to do. All Jesse ever wanted was normalcy. All he wanted was reparations for giving up a life, education, and love for the sake of his family.

Clyde was the one who'd come to *him* in his dorm room four years ago and asked him to take his mantle while he was gone. Jesse was the one who had to sever his relationship with Rose. He traded quiet and peaceful for loud, chaotic, hectic. Because that's what men did—or were supposed to do, unlike Jesse's father, who drowned in his own self-hate until he dragged his family under with him. Jesse wouldn't do that. He'd give up three or four Roses for his family. For his brothers. He did Clyde a favor, and now he strolled around there like he didn't care, or like he resented Jesse. What the fuck did Clyde ever sacrifice for the family? Jesse picked up a paperweight and hurled it across the room. It hit the wall, landing on the floor with a loud thud, satiating the remainder of his anger. He took a seat. Closed his eyes. His breathing steadied. He realized that was the problem—his loyalty to his family. He'd burn the world for them, come to their every beck-and-call, and that was a problem.

"Nothing else can go wrong today", he said to himself. "Nothing."

While Jesse still had his eyes close, the door whined open and somebody stormed in, all while Jesse imagined he was somewhere else other than there, other than New Orleans. Maybe a farm with a wraparound porch and nothing but open pastures and clear skies that met at the horizon, like a beautiful painting. He could go somewhere like that. He had the money.

"Where—where's Clyde at?"

It was Rory's voice. Jesse opened his eyes.

Rory stood there with a black-eye and slanted tear in his wool shirt. The black and red stains on his clothes made him look like he'd gotten about five boot kicks to the ribs and three punches to the face while crawling on the ground. In between shallow breaths and broken words, Jesse pieced together Rory's message: "The Riverfront Clubbers jumped me."

Jesse sighed, and pulled a cigarette from his pocket. He hesitated before lighting it and stared at the pure white like it could save him from the inevitability of Rory's gripe being a setback for him. He thought back to when Rose was the only thing keeping him from going through a carton a day. Those were simple times. He struck a match. Jesse broke away from the stolen moment and set the cig ablaze. Like the flame would burn away the anger he lived with, or the chaos of his life. Smoke trickled out from his nose and his mouth as he looked his baby brother in his eyes. "Tell me what happened."

Chapter 7

Haunted

"Don't you fucking move you piece of shit," Rory said with one eye closed and his Colt held up to an imaginary robber. He steadied his right hand with his left and bit his lip. He concealed the gun in his imaginary holster and started the exercise over again. He focused on the chair against the wall in the bedroom. "What? You talking to me?"

He walked back two steps and laughed. Rory couldn't believe the shit this fucking chair was talking. He turned to the bed next to him like it was an associate who'd been watching this transgression go down, then whipped his Colt out and filled the imaginary-gangster-chair with three shots. He imitated the sounds of gunfire. *Bang, bang, bang.*

He wanted to begin the exercise over again, but a woman's voice rang out from the other side of the door. He told her to wait up; he'd be out in a second. She came in anyway. "You need to leave. My husband will be home sometime soon."

He yelled at her to get out, got dressed in slacks and a woolen shirt, and tucked the gun in his waistband like he saw Jesse, Clyde, and Twitch do all the time. He smiled at the cracked dresser mirror.

He'd woken up early that morning, the dew from the nighttime chill still clinging to his girl-for-the-night's bedroom window as the sun peered over the horizon of the raggedy shotgun homes across the street, and he practiced pulling his gun for about an hour. He figured with his promotion and all, he'd have to use it one day.

The teapot's whistle made a duet with the nagging woman's shouts for him to leave. "Please, you need to go; now."

But Rory took his time.

He gulped down two, then three, then four mugs of the bitter tea in rapid succession until his heartbeat thudded out of rhythm and his eyes felt like they'd pop out of his head. She didn't get it; he was a big man now, a factor in the Pike Boys machine, so he didn't need to rush for no-fucking-body. For years he was an underling to his brothers, treated as if he wasn't competent enough to be a decision-maker. Even Twitch got more of a vote in matters than he did. All he ever heard was, *No, Rory. Do this, Rory. Stop sleeping with the girls at the brothel, Rory.* It was unbearable.

It was even worse as kids. They'd sneak to the heart of the city and leave him clutching his blankie and sucking on his thumb. But now, as the bag man for the liquor operation, he had power. He had responsibility. And he was going to bask in it, and prove to himself and his brothers that he could be just like them.

He fished around in his pockets for the woman's wedding ring and flung it on the table. He slapped her on the ass then strolled out of the woman's house and into the early morning day.

**

He got in a car with a nameless goon and they went around the French Quarter taking orders and picking up money. He scribbled down bottle amounts, times of drop-offs, and when the shipment would be expected to be in by. This went on for hours until the sun reached its apex in the sky and the day became steadily more and more humid—the sweat on his back making the metal in his waistband stick to his skin.

He and the nameless goon pulled up on the curb outside of a duplex. The speakeasy was in a residential neighborhood on the edges of the French Quarter, hidden amongst other duplexes with a uniform look: two floors with no driveway, hugging the sidewalk, a wraparound porch with white railings, and wrought iron fencing blocking the entrance to the backyard.

Rory got out of the car and heard the driver begin to get up behind him. He waved him off. That was the last stop for the morning. He hated feeling like he was being baby-sat all the damn time. When he had started out washing beer mugs at the brothel, the bartender was over his shoulder.

When he used to return back to the brothel after dropping off bribe money to beat cops, Jesse always questioned him on what he had said and how he had said it, like he was an invalid who couldn't think for himself.

The mouth-breathing gun-monkey with him made him feel like Jesse and Clyde didn't trust him with his new job title either, like driving around and collecting money required adult supervision. If he wanted his brothers' respect, he had to take matters into his own hands and show them what he could do. He took a deep breath, and entered the building on his own.

The makeshift bar was packed. There were people in wooden chairs at tiny tables scattered around the room. Big burly men leaned on the bar with drinks in hand and made the plywood bartop give under their collective weight. Rory looked around the room. He saw a man with a bandaged hand sitting near the window, and couldn't put a finger on why he looked familiar. Rory waited for the bartender to run up and grab the owner, some immigrant guy with a funny accent and ambiguous skin color Rory couldn't figure out. Rory took his order, wrote down the amount he needed, and took the money in an inconspicuous bag.

Rory felt satisfied when he checked off the last address on the piece of paper he kept folded in his coat's breast pocket. He tucked the paper away and signaled the bartender for a bourbon neat. He deserved to treat himself for another job well done. He took conservative sips, allowing the liquor to barely touch his lips, and continued to stare at the man by the window through the smudged bottom of his drinking glass. He tried to place his face with the names of various characters around the city.

Lefty Louie? No.

Homo Harry? No.

Greg "Cutter" Connors? No.

He couldn't figure it out. As the drink further clouded his mind, the names became more jumbled and mixed up. He heard the men laughing and talking out loud, loud enough for their conversation to be heard over the chatter of the other people in the room.

He took one last sip, then he heard it. He heard the man say a name: "The Greek."

The man with the fucked-up hand and raised scars on his face was the guy Jesse had worked over real bad not too far back, The Greek's nephew. Rory grinned. This was his chance to show Jesse and Clyde he could do more, be more. Rory stood, cracked his knuckles, eyed the man, and went over the logistics in his head: push through the crowd, whip the gun around, and hold it to the man's head; watch as the guy wept while piss stains darkened in his blue pants then proceed to kick his ass up and down the room; show him and everyone else the Pike Gang weren't to be fucked with.

Rory pushed through people, shoving one person completely out of the way when they continued to sway in his walking path. Rory towered over the table where the rival gangster sat and poked his chest out. The man placed his drink down slowly, and looked at his friends across from him with confusion. "Do I know you, kid?"

Rory chuckled. He put his hand on his hip. He said,

"You should. I'm Rory Pike." Rory then pointed to the man's heavily bandaged hand.

The man's amused smile faded. Rory held a stern look with a devilish grin. Rory went over a plan in his head once more: the man would lunge for him; Rory would then whip out his gun; and beat him out of the bar and down the stairs. Then he would go back and tell Clyde and Jesse he wasn't some little boy. He would prove to them that he was as much of a tough guy as they were.

The man asked Rory to repeat what he said. Rory did. The man nodded slowly and looked across to his friends who were at full attention now. Rory reached for his gun and—

***

Rory's story blurred after the "reaching for the gun" part. He remembered he ended up on the ground somehow then things went dark, and when he came to, feet landed on his ribs, his innards exploded with pain, and a hail storm of fists thundered down on him. The ringing in his ear went from a one to a ten, and the blows to his face fractured his senses punch by punch by face-numbing punch. It was somewhere between the first and third time he blacked out that he woke up and stumbled to the car, where the nameless goon sped him to the brothel.

"And that's it," Rory said.

Jesse's fists rested on the desk, balled up to the point his nails dug into his palms' flesh. His posture in the chair was rigid and tense; his muscles stiffened from attempting not to strangle Rory. His eyes were closed and he meditated on the one key factor Rory had yet to mention. "Where's the money, Rory?"

Rory fiddled with his shirt sleeve and looked at the ground like a child trying to avoid his father's disappointed gaze. His head turned when the door opened. Cindy walked in with a towel full of ice and pressed it to Rory's face.

"Thanks," Jesse said to Cindy. She smiled, then left.

Rory fidgeted and stammered. Jesse answered for him. "They fucking robbed you."

Rory's voice weakened. "I'm... I'm sorry, Jess."

Jesse flung a handkerchief at Rory to sop up the blood running down his nose. "Alright. Leave."

Rory walked out with his head hung low.

Jesse knew what this meant. They'd have to respond to the transgression with equal force. People had seen a Pike bagman get his ass stomped out by a bunch of low-life street thugs with no notoriety or standing in the city. Jesse grabbed the phone and got the operator to patch him over to Twitch's home. He dropped it before even saying hello. This wasn't his job anymore. He had to remind himself that. He called Clyde down instead to see how he wanted to handle it.

***

"We gut them. We absolutely fucking gut them." Clyde sat across from Jesse. "We need to gut those sons of bitches, every one of them."

Jesse rolled his eyes. "No. We're not doing that." He leaned forward in the chair and laced his fingers across the desk. It didn't even occur to him — maybe Clyde should be on this side and he on the other.

"I met people in prison. They could help," Clyde said.

"The drunk Irishmen you've been bringing around?"

Clyde glared. "You been keeping tabs on me?"

"I've gotten a few calls of concern."

Clyde turned toward Twitch, who sat in the back of the room and pre-emptively shook his head. Clyde brushed away the offense and continued with the matter at hand. "This can't go ignored."

"I agree. But I don't think we should respond in a way that starts a war," Jesse said.

Clyde dropped a fist on the desk and shot out of his chair. "I don't even know why you get a say." Clyde's eyes grew hard and angry and rage seeped through his pores and infested the room. His chest rose and fell with each heavy breath. He spun around to Twitch. "You've gone soft, both of you." He walked over to him. "I get it, you have a wife. Kids. I can appreciate that. But what's to stop the Clubbers from coming into your home and..."

Twitch put a finger up in Clyde's face. "Watch it."

Clyde backed off and turned to Jesse. "And you, you're the worst one in here. You know better. We should go claim that bar as our territory, but you want to play politics. 'Talk. Talk. Talk.' Sometimes it takes force. I would expect this soft response from Rory. But you? You been hanging around the upper-crust a little too much."

Jesse found it hard to sit comfortably now, but he never averted his eyes from Clyde. "You know what? You've been out the loop for a while, so you may not know. But not everything requires blunt force. I've called the shots for the past four years, and until you get used to how I like things done around here, I may have to continue to. I did all of this for us. I created this business for us."

Clyde chuckled. "'Us'? You created this brothel for us? No. You created this place for you. So you could stroke your own ego, make yourself feel important."

Jesse stood. "I'm sorry I didn't want to be a back alley, mask wearing, car hijacking gangster forever and end up in prison like you."

The room grew silent under the weight of Jesse's words. Twitch looked at the ground and rubbed his neck. Clyde's face was unreadable, a mask of apathy and nothingness.

"I created this brothel, I set up the booze network, all as ways to the next thing: peace. We'll be rich before thirty if you follow my plans. But if not, fine by me, Clyde. If you want to run the streets forever, have shootouts with cops and gangs for the rest of your life, fine. But the world's changing, and soon you'll be a relic."

Jesse could see the subtle shift from defiance to compliance in Clyde's face. "Alright, 'boss.' You want to talk to them? Fine." Clyde threw his hands up in submission. "I know someone who can set up a meeting. You can go off and play with your rich friends. I'll handle logistics." He walked out the door.

***

Two days went by and the meeting was set. O'Grady, AKA The Greek, agreed to meet on his territory. No weapons and no extra men. Jesse, Clyde, Rory, and Twitch pulled in front of "The Greek Palace," a tenement building with green shutters, a dozen windows, and a wraparound wrought iron balcony located in one of the worst parts of Uptown three blocks from the riverfront. It was the home of The Riverfront Clubbers and O'Grady's personal drug den.

Jesse beat on the door until it opened up to a lounging area. The oddest mixture of people was inside. Some slouched in chairs, or lay on top of each other on blankets on the floor, while sharing tokes from long bamboo pipes filled with sweet scented opium smoke. Everyone moved as if time was slowed down and like they were trying to swim through syrup. Jesse felt as if he'd been granted access to a perverse afterlife. He turned to the person who opened the door. It was a short woman, about twenty-three maybe, but looked thirty-five, worn and wrinkled in the face but wearing the finest Oriental garb. She was one of O'Grady's drug slaves. The room was filled with O'Grady's drug slaves; people who would fuck and kill for sweet magical opium smoke down their lungs. The woman pointed down the long hallway. Before they got any further, three men stepped out from the dim parts of the room and made Jesse and the others stop in their stride.

The men patted the Pikes down. Firm grips around the ankles, legs, arms, and sacks.

"You having fun down there?" Rory asked one man.

The three O'Grady goons jutted their heads down the hall and the Pikes continued their trek. Jesse turned to look behind him and saw Twitch leaning forward as the woman whispered something close to his ear.

Opened doors on both sides of the narrow hallway were portals into hedonistic dimensions Jesse couldn't look away from. In one room, two men and one woman pleased one another in bed, the two men kissing the woman up and down her naked body, then meeting in the middle to touch one another. There was another room with a teenage girl. She walked over to shut the door. Jesse could see the emptiness in her eyes through the closing crack of the door, along with the fat bastard waiting in bed in the background.

"Was that a kid?" Jesse asked the men walking ahead of him. They said nothing.

They all walked into a room where a middle-aged man sat behind a table. Jesse figured that this was O'Grady.

"Hello," O'Grady said. He had a meaty face and teeth stained from a lifetime of drug abuse, and next to him was his nephew, the guy whose hand was destroyed by Jesse. He stared daggers at Jesse.

"O'Grady," Jesse said. The room was beyond odd. O'Grady looked like he took the layout of the room straight from a Chinese catalog. With all the different oriental symbols, rugs, ruby red, as well as a canopy bed in the corner of the room, it looked less like a huge office and more like some child's perverted fantasy. Clyde, Twitch, Rory, and Jesse were given chairs, and O'Grady's men sat on the opposite side. The woman who followed them down the hall took a position in the background, like a servant in waiting.

O'Grady said, "So, let's get to talking." He cleared his throat. "Where do you get the balls to do the shit you do?

First, my nephew, which I get it, he's a fucking moron." He jostled the back of his nephew's head. "But then you send a kid to shoot him?"

Jesse scooted up in his chair. "What happened the other day was a misunderstanding. Just an overzealous young man with too much to prove." Rory folded his arms.

O'Grady let out a hearty chuckle that jiggled his jowls. "Well, that overzealousness got him torn to shreds, from the looks of it."

Jesse's eyes twitched. He composed himself. But Clyde's simmering rage rolled off of him in waves like heat.

"He was beaten half to death," Jesse said. "But not just that. Your guys took some cash. Our money. Now if you wanted to argue that beating up Rory was payback for him," Jesse motioned to the nephew. "Then fine. But that was a step too far."

O'Grady took a cigarette from his pocket and pinched it between two fingers. He held it behind his head and the woman produced a flame within seconds. O'Grady puffed out cloud after cloud after cloud, playing the suspense game, trying to show his dominance.

"Alright," O'Grady said. "Here it goes. You get your money back, in full. But you give me the boy."

Jesse laughed. "No deal."

O'Grady wiped his hands. The nephew smirked with his cracked lips and warped face.

"We're at an impasse here," O'Grady said.

Jesse chuckled nervously. Clyde began to speak, something crass and argumentative, Jesse was sure, but

Jesse cut him off. "I'll cut you in for some points on the liquor, in exchange for the cash you took today and no future quarrels."

O'Grady looked to his nephew and then to his men. He took the deal. Jesse didn't have to look at Clyde to know he was enraged. He heard the way his breathing grew heavier, the way his menacing silence said everything it needed to say. Jesse and O'Grady worked out the particulars to both of their likings.

"How about you fellas stay for a nightcap? Maybe a little something extra?" O'Grady waved his fingers and was brought a pouch. He stuffed his fingers in and pulled out a bag full of brown powder.

Jesse shuddered at the thought. "I appreciate the offer, but I think—"

"We got time," Clyde said.

O'Grady smiled. "Oh, look. He speaks. Bring my friends some scotch, why don't you?"

The drink did little to ease Jesse. O'Grady guzzled down shot after shot, and eventually brought in some of his drug bimbos. Rory got up to entertain two of them at a time, which Jesse expected, but what he didn't expect was Twitch joining. The woman that opened the door for them escorted him to the corner with the canopy bed—pushed him onto the mattress—then closed the curtain around it so no one could see.

Jesse raised an eyebrow. Twitch was the most devoted family man he knew, and there he was with the woman, two blobs tossing and turning behind a thin red curtain.

Jesse and Clyde drank with O'Grady, his three men, and his nephew. The awkward uneasy peace was palpable and made Jesse's chest tight. Then he noticed Clyde was barely even sipping his drink. He'd been touching the glass to his lips and tilting it back, but kept his mouth shut while keeping his eyes on O'Grady the whole time.

Clyde cleared his throat. "Hey, O'Grady, I got a question for you." O'Grady scooted in with a smile on his face. "So, your last name, you Irish or something?"

O'Grady nodded.

"The hell's with the nickname then? 'The Greek.'"

"Yeah, so?"

Clyde rested his elbows on the table. "Your name's O'Grady. That's a fucking mick name. Why would you call yourself something like 'The Greek'?" The mood at the table shifted when the ethnic slur left his lips. Everyone at the table clammed up.

Jesse touched Clyde's shoulder. "Clyde..."

The woman who'd escorted them down the hall strode out from behind the red curtain, leaving Twitch behind, and motioned for the other women to follow her out the door. Twitch stayed in the bed, seeming to be fumbling with his belt loop.

O'Grady's brows furrowed. "You boys are so fucking stupid. You come into my place and offend me?"

Clyde stood in a manner so calm and measured that it was almost unnerving, like he was about to give a speech at a friend's wedding. He polished off his drink, ran his fingers down the lining of his jacket, and smiled. "I don't want to offend you, but how about this: we'll keep 100% of the liquor points, and your nephew can go fuck himself."

Before anyone could speak, a sharp whistle followed by a heavy plop filled the void of silence, and a spatter of red dots landed against the side of O'Grady's face and hands and sleeves. He turned slowly to look at his nephew, and his eyes widened when he saw the near-crater in the back of his head. His nephew wobbled and bobbed up and down, eyes jutting back-and-forth rapidly, until he finally collapsed across the table loose and languid like his spine had disappeared.

O'Grady stammered. "No, no, no..."

Jesse watched what happened next as if it was in slow motion: the three gunmen spun out of their seats toward the source of the shot but Twitch was already moving toward them with a silenced pistol aimed in their direction and both hands on the grip. One more whistle, then a man's head exploded like a hammer dropped on a watermelon; two more whistles, then the remaining two each took one to the chest and fell downward like they'd been chopped at the knees. Blood spatter seemed to hang in the air. Smoke trailed from the barrel of Twitch's gun, and in O'Grady's baggy eyes, Jesse could see a realization: he knew he was going to die. All of the bravado and narcissism were gone and replaced by the primal desire to just live.

O'Grady's fat, flabby neck throbbed up and down. His eyes went gentle and sad. "Wait, wait, wait," His arms were held out in front of him. Then his throat ruptured open and he was choking on his own blood. The heavyset man clutched at his throat with two hands, only to have his blood seep through the cracks of his fingers. He collapsed to the floor with his feet flailing around. Jesse fumbled back out of his chair as Twitch power-walked toward O'Grady on the floor. Clyde's face was straight the entire time.

Clyde walked over to O'Grady and stood over him, stepping on the man's hands when he tried to grasp at his ankles. "You shouldn't have touched my brother." Clyde took Twitch's gun and pumped two bullets into O'Grady's skull.

Jesse stopped breathing. He looked over at Rory and saw horror in his eyes. Jesse had seen death and destruction on this scale before, but not Rory. Not like this. Clyde's face was chilling. He maneuvered over the blood and bodies and took a still-lit cigarette from the ashtray on the table and took a deep toke until he blew out thick plumes of smoke. He moved closer to Jesse and pushed his finger into his chest. "You can either be a gangster or a businessman. You absolutely can't do both."

Before realizing what he was doing, Jesse ran for the exit. The hallway seemed to lengthen the harder he ran and that anxiety-fueled expanse gave him enough time to be alone with his thoughts. Too much time. All the times he stole and lied and did whatever he needed to do to gain power came back to him in waves of adrenaline. He thought of his father, Rose, those girls who he forced to sign NDAs so Wardolf's dalliances would stay secret. He tried to outrun the nightmares that refused to leave him and the darkness of the life that was thrust upon him but couldn't escape.

Later that night he curled into bed and was unable to forget all the blood he'd seen earlier. The intruding thoughts grew more aggressive, so he drank until he passed out. But there was no reprieve waiting for him in his sleep. Waiting for him was a new addition to his night terrors: O'Grady. He was just another one of the many ghosts that followed Jesse everywhere he went.

Chapter 8

What Follows You Home

"You know God?" That was the first question the warden asked Clyde four years ago upon his arrival to prison, and his response was yes; he was well acquainted with God. He pled for God often in his youth, especially when his father would ash cigarettes on his skin in attempts to burn the Devil out of him. Little ol' Clyde would curl up in the corner of the living room and bite down on his shirt until his jaw grew sore and his teeth turned sensitive, and he couldn't cry; oh lord, he could never do that. Because when he cried, he was sure to get a tail-whooping that'd make it hard to sit for weeks; a beating that'd make a grown man flinch in his sleep. Clyde was a victim of human duality, the moral grey area, a concept never spoken of in the Pike household. In the Pike household, there was only the rigid black-and-white text of the Christian Bible. Clyde had a scar for every verse; a bruise for every Psalm; he could never forget his Bible lessons because they were written all over his body. So Clyde, on that day in the warden's office responded, "Yes, I know God. I'm not so sure if he knows me."

He thought about that day while in his room in the brothel as cries of sexual satisfaction came from Madam Eve's mouth. He was on top of her, thrusting and grunting and breathing hard and heavy into the crook of her neck, begging her to dig her nails harder and harder into his back until he couldn't take it anymore. She tried, but was reluctant.

Clyde sighed. "Fucking harder, I said."

Before Eve could protest, he propped himself up with one smooth push and took her by the throat. Her pupils eclipsed and her head flung back as his hands enclosed on her neck.

He thrust as hard as he could. Her eyes rolled back. He focused on the rocks of the headboard and near-bleeding back lacerations and hoped they'd drown out the noises in his head. *O'Grady had to die,* he repeated in his head, in the same tone he'd tell his father *I just forgot to clean my room.* The pinching sensation shifted into a piercing burn and ran down the middle of his spine. The physical pain and repetitive thought processes couldn't drown out the noises in his head for too long.

It was the noise of prison bars sliding shut and toothbrush shanks breaking flesh; the howls from race riots in the yard; the chatter of guards taking wagers on whether the "nigs," "spics," or "micks" would kill each other first. The noise of the cell-block Nance paying off his cigarette debt, one pump at a time, right next door to Clyde's cell. The high-pitched, pseudo-feminine groans had been muffled through the pillows Clyde sandwiched his head in, but had been loud enough to leave an impression.

Eve finally dug deep enough to give Clyde the release he needed. Endorphins flooded his body and sent a shockwave hard enough to cause his eyes to roll back in euphoria like he hadn't felt in years. Approximately four. His body clenched up, he gave one final thrust, then he finally released her. The prison went away. Any semblance of shame over O'Grady's death went away. She released her talons from his back and let her fingers ride down his shoulders, his biceps, his chest, a trickle of blood underneath her nails.

Eve had a million-dollar smile on her face. "It's been a long time for you, huh?"

Clyde got off her and pushed his back against the headboard. "You can go now."

Eve, being the professional she was, put her clothes back on and left.

Clyde yanked the lamp's cord to plunge the room into darkness. No matter how much he tried, he could never get any room as dark as the dark in the isolation cells in prison. That's what the punishments were for any infraction at Orleans Parish Prison: the isolation cells. The darkness in those cells couldn't be found anywhere on the mortal plane, not in caves, under the sea, or even under one's own eyelids. It was the type of darkness that siphoned off someone's sanity, making someone question if they were in purgatory or hell.

Clyde got in fights in his first few months in prison, and on his third one, the warden had Clyde dragged kicking and screaming to the isolation cell. The warden followed behind spouting off fire and brimstone Bible quotes, letting Clyde know if he didn't change his ways, he'd spend eternity in damnation. Clyde got tossed in, his last bit of light receding to a thin line when the door shut.

One day went by, then two, and on day nine, the isolation had Clyde rocking back-and-forth in the corner of the dark cell, convinced someone was in the room with him. On day eleven, Clyde cried for the first time since he was a child. He was remorseful for so much. He'd wished he'd been a better brother, a better son. After a while, he'd wished to not be alive anymore. The warden had gone by on day twelve or fifteen to check on Clyde, asking him if he was ready to repent for his sins against man and change his ways. Clyde talked under the slit between the floor and the door, and told the warden, "Yes, yes, please fucking yes." The warden sighed, chastised Clyde for his potty mouth, then walked away from the door.

Day thirty, the darkness began to talk to Clyde in a voice he hadn't heard in years but was unmistakable. It was the second man Clyde had ever killed. A ship captain. Clyde didn't remember his name, but he remembered the night he'd entered the Captain's home. The man had family portraits everywhere; toys, a baby crib, clothes pressed and cleaned in his closet, all the signs he was cared for. The voice of the Captain stayed with Clyde the remainder of the time he had left in the hole.

On the day he was released, it was maybe fifty or eighty, or hell, one hundred twenty days later, the warden had a sermon in the chapel. He asked all the men around him one simple question: "What makes someone a good man?" Clyde didn't know. None of them knew. The warden answered: a good man takes care of his family, forgives others for their wrongdoings, and makes right with their own wrongdoings. A good man is someone who heals as much as they protect. So later, when he was in his cell, he got his hands on a piece of paper and pen and wrote down everything he'd make right once he was out:

Teach Rory how to be a man.

Reignite relationship with Cath.

Reunite family.

Make amends for the Captain.

That list had never left Clyde's presence, no matter where he went.

And he'd looked at it right after Madam Eve left his room in the brothel, reminding himself that he needed to stay on course, and couldn't run from rectifying the things he'd done wrong. He got out of bed, got dressed, stuffed the worn piece of paper in his pocket, and headed downstairs to check on how things were going.

Downstairs was overwhelming. With the lights, the music, and the smell of liquor, Clyde had to fight the urge to run to his room. He walked around the floor and people smiled and waved, but all he could do was give a slight nod.

It didn't help that people kept asking where Jesse went. His least favorite part of the gig was the old fucks walking up to him with a wide smiles on their face, only to get close and realize he wasn't Jesse at all. He was, in fact, three inches taller, two years older, and a whole lot meaner. He sat at the bar and whistled for the bartender. The bartender jumped to attention. "Oh, well, hello there, Mr. Pike."

"Whiskey neat. Please."

The bartender raised an eyebrow. "Hitting it hard early, aren't we, Mr. Pike?"

Clyde glared with unrepentant disdain. The bartender promptly scurried away to make the drink. Clyde tossed the drink back, then got another and another, but the anxiety never went away, so he decided he had to get out of there. When he stood, the tables in his vision tilted on their axis, his knees quivered, his chest tightened.

Two hands came to steady him. "Easy there," said Rory. "You ok?"

Clyde took a while, but said, "Yea."

Rory looked unsure.

Clyde straightened. "I'm fine."

Rory slung his arm around his shoulder. "Come on, let's get out of here."

They stood in the foyer area by the front door, and Rory fidgeted with his fingers and moved around in place like a scared child. Clyde told him to just say what he wanted to say. Rory brought up O'Grady, and how he couldn't get the sound of gunshots hitting human flesh out of his head. Clyde stroked his trimmed beard and exhaled.

"It'll pass."

Rory scoffed and looked around to make sure they were alone. "Clyde, you had a guy's head blown off yesterday. How is that something you just get over and forget about?"

Rory had seen a little less than Jesse and Clyde. As teens, Jesse and Clyde walked in on Hymie and Sal shoving a guy's head into a vice. The fucker's skull turned from an orb to a flapjack in minutes; that shit stuck with you. But Clyde understood why the baby of the boys could see what went down with O'Grady as being a big deal.

Clyde grabbed Rory's face so that when he said his next words, he would know Rory heard him loud and clear.

Clyde said calmly, "Some people deserve to fucking die, Rory. Ok?" Rory's head strained in Clyde's hands, but Clyde wouldn't let him look away. "No, no. You need to hear this. Some people don't deserve to be on this fucking planet. That's the truth of it. You—you know, when I was in prison, when I wasn't holed up, and I did what I was supposed to do, the warden let us read. I'd picked up these medical journal shits or whatever. They talked about how white blood cells healed the body. Attacked the things that didn't belong there, like infections."

Rory stared at Clyde.

"O'Grady was an infection; we're the fucking white blood cells."

Rory's mouth hung open in tamed awe at what he'd just heard.

Clyde got the shakes again as panic rose up his body. "I need to get out of here."

Rory stopped Clyde before he was able to walk out. "Clyde? You said it gets easier after a while." Clyde nodded. "Well, what happens before then?"

Clyde looked over Rory's head and into the crowd in the West Parlor. In between the moving heads was a tall man with bruises around his neck and accusatory eyes staring through Clyde's soul. Clyde rubbed his eyes. The man was gone. "You learn to live with it; you have no choice but to."

Clyde walked out the door and left Rory standing in the foyer, and went on his way to go see someone special.

***

Clyde stood in front of his childhood home twisting the stems of a bouquet in his hands. He hoped she liked it. He shuffled around in his brain the types of flowers she'd always liked: roses, baby's breath, carnations, and lilies. He had added those to the bunch, along with some other flowers he never knew existed until the florist had told him about them. He knocked several times at the door, each knock making him regret popping up without calling. The door swung open to a young woman grumbling under her breath. Her eyes widened after a few seconds. "Clyde?"

Her voice was filled with both excitement and surprise. Clyde's smile widened to a length only ever reserved for her, his little sister, Catherine. "Hi, Cath."

She practically leaped into his arms and squeezed him like she'd never wanted to let him go. He did the same. When they let each other go, he handed her the flowers. Catherine's smile could light up any room, and right then it was the brightest it'd ever been.

"Thank you," she said.

When she was a kid, Clyde would take her to fields on the outskirts of the city and allow her to pick up all the exotic flowers she could hold in her little arms. She'd run up to him with a bag full of colorful plants—blues and yellows and reds with white spots, and he'd try to guess what they were. She'd flash her chubby dimples at his grossly wrong answers, and they'd laugh about it the whole walk home. As he got older and more involved in crime, his visits tapered off. He still hung out with Catherine as often as he could, but it wasn't as much as it used to be. Then he went to prison and left her all alone.

Catherine welcomed Clyde into the home and the first thing he did was look down the hallway. The Pike home had a long hallway leading to their parents' room. Now it was a place their mother holed herself up, so she could go on drug-induced benders. It was her personal prison isolation room.

"She's ok. I checked on her a little while ago," Catherine said glumly after noticing where his gaze fell.

Clyde nodded and took his hat off.

The living room hadn't changed at all. It was still bare, save for the two couches, a fireplace, one table, and several white stucco spots on the walls left from drunken rages past.

"Tea?" she asked.

He declined, but followed her into the kitchen. They took seats at the dinner table.

"You're a woman now," he said.

Catherine's eyes fluttered. "That tends to happen over time. But I don't feel like one. I'm still getting an allowance from my big brothers and can't find work."

"Jesse kept up with the drops?"

She hesitated. "He did, he did. You know how he is, though. He doesn't like coming here, and when he did come, he'd stay outside and ask the same fucking questions: 'how's mother? You doing ok? You need more?' and it's just like get over that spat already."

Clyde jerked his head back at his baby sister's language. She was a tiny girl, 5'4 and petite with the looks of a starlet, but had the traditional Pike Potty Mouth with crassness to match.

He scolded her and she flipped up the middle finger and stuck her tongue out. Clyde chuckled. "Not very ladylike."

Catherine smiled, but slowly, it faded away and her eyes watered, then a tear rolled down her cheek.

Clyde inched his hands toward her like she could detonate. He hadn't consoled her since she was a little girl scraping her knees on the pavement. Now she was grown; he wasn't sure if he should let her be or touch her. "What's eating you?"

"Sorry," she said. "It was so odd without you around. I still saw Rory and Jesse from time to time, sure. But they weren't as... you know, close to me as you were."

He laid his hand on her forearm. "I'm home now. You don't have to be alone anymore."

She wiped the tears away with the back of her hand. She

put her hand on top of his.

He feigned a smile but was annoyed. He'd left Jesse in charge to take care of the family, but he apparently didn't know Catherine as well as he did. Catherine was always headstrong. She'd probably told him she didn't need for anything, but never once mentioned she needed someone there. Clyde would've been there to help her, protect her, shield her from the embodiment of toxicity that was their mother.

Catherine wiped her face with a towel. "So embarrassing."

Clyde waved away the comment. "Hardly."

A cough boomed down the hall from their mother's room. Catherine and Clyde's eyes met. Clyde walked down the creaky hallway and pushed the door open. "Ma?"

The room was dark; the light behind the blinds was muted. The room smelled of trapped old air and dust. He moved toward the silhouette of her bed and lamp, swung the blinds open, and flooded the room in light. "Mother?"

His mother was physically there, eyes cracked open, a pleased smirk, hair spread over part of her face and pillow and shoulder like reddish tentacles coiling around her body. But no one was home. He tapped her to get a response. She flung her body over and groaned child-like. He looked down at her nightstand and saw open bottles of Laudanum. The doctor had given her a prescription for her "hysteria" after their father died, and she never stopped taking it. He picked up one tincture and swirled it under the window light. Near empty. The others were still full. He pocketed them. He touched his mother's pale shoulder and tried to wake her one last time.

The smile on her face and the glossed-over look in her eyes showed she was off in a fantasy world, somewhere peaceful and full of joy. At least Clyde hoped so. He could've used a tincture of this in prison. Clyde closed the blinds and strode down the hall.

"I'm taking this," Clyde said, holding up the tinctures.

"She'll get more," Catherine said.

Clyde retrieved his hat. "She won't."

Catherine didn't pry into what that meant. He gave a little raise of the hand to indicate he was leaving. Catherine grabbed him before he jetted out the door and hugged him tight like it would be the last time she'd ever see him. Clyde embraced her back, the tinctures pressing into his side from her body pressing against his.

"I'm glad to have you back," she said.

"I'm glad to be back. Also, if you need a job, I may be able to help with that."

She nodded with a shy smile. She listened to his offer.

***

Clyde walked into a bar in the Irish Channel and eyes fell upon him and stuck to his back like lint. He kept his shooting arm loose and ready, his mind going through cycles of different ways to maim someone who attempted to accost him. The place had a dark brown wooden interior and smelled of stale beer and whiskey, and the misery and loathing oozed from the patrons like noxious gas filling both of his nostrils and dampening his own mood. Clyde sat with his back to the other patrons, but stayed alerted to every step and creak around him. The barkeep walked over to him. "Eatin'?"

"No."

"We got no booze here, boy, if that's what ye're looking for."

"Did I ask for that? Where's Joe?"

The bartender pointed to the other side of the room.

Moments later, Joe sat next to Clyde with a wide, devilish grin trained on his friend. "Hello, there, old sport." Clyde wore his paranoia on his face. Joe asked, with a slight Irish lilt, "Don't feel comfortable amongst your people?"

"I ain't Irish."

"The tint of red in your hair says otherwise."

Joe had dark red hair, a slender face, and eyes as blue as a clear sky to go along with a smile that could fill anyone with unease. Clyde wasn't scared of anyone. But even Joe's smile made him squirm and question if the bastard could read his thoughts. Because that's how Joe looked: like he knew your deep, personal secrets. Clyde reached in his coat pocket and pulled out an envelope. Joe flipped through the cash within and whistled. "Setting up that meeting with O'Grady was hard. Planting that gun was even harder."

Clyde shrugged. "I'd imagine so. All I could give you right now, though."

Joe waved his fingers and the bartender hustled over. Joe tossed the money at him. "Put it where it belongs."

Clyde got up to leave. Joe's bony fingers snatched Clyde's wrist. "I mention the difficulty I went through because I wanted you to know you owe me a favor. Not monetary."

Clyde peeled Joe's fingers loose.

"I still want to meet your brother. Jesse."

"For what?"

Joe shrugged. "Oh, nothing of importance to you."

Clyde pretended like the jab didn't bother him. "I'll see what I can do."

Joe stood on his tippy toes to get close to Clyde's ear, close enough for his goatee bristles to rub against Clyde's neck. "Protecting you in prison didn't come cheap, my boy."

Clyde's chest tightened. Clyde's second year in jail was filled with attempts on his life; in the shower, in his cell while he slept, while walking the yard. He became afraid to sneeze in fear of closing his eyes for too long. Combine that with the harassment of officers, and Clyde had slowly been going mad. Joe had approached Clyde, told him he'd heard of Big Sal and his old errand boys, the Pikes. He promised he could make all of Clyde's issues go away. Clyde ignored him. The attacks continued. Then one day, Clyde's old cellmate got switched out with someone new: Joe. Clyde knew it was a show of how much power Joe had in the prison, and how little Clyde had. So, with a handshake and a promise to introduce Joe to Jesse when he was out, the deal was done. The main guy who'd been harassing Clyde wound up dead at the bottom of a stairwell with a shiv in his neck and his pants pulled down below his bare ass. The co-conspirators of the attacks on Clyde were never seen again. The guards who harassed Clyde had started kissing his ass.

Despite feeling like decades ago, all the things Joe had done for him while they were inside weighed on Clyde's mind and made it hard for him to ignore his request to speak with Jesse. Clyde stowed away his pride and said, "I'll try my best. Can't promise Jesse will want to talk though."

Joe rubbed Clyde's beard and nodded. "You know, being in the hole can do something strange to a man." Joe pulled a folded handkerchief from his pocket and placed it on the bar. "But then, being back outside could be even worse. I got mates, back home in Ireland, who are part of The Cause. They've seen men's legs blown off, heads cracked open, buildings collapse on babies. After that shite, they come back, mutterin' on about things that aren't there. We could be the only two in the room and me lad could be on about some bloke he shot coming for him, or how he could hear the bombs exploding around him still," Joe shook his head. "Shell shock; it follows everywhere."

Clyde balled his hands into fist and dug his nails into his palm until his fingers turned red. "Your point?"

"I've seen people leave prison the same way. Isolation; it rots ya to the core." Joe scooted the folded handkerchief to Clyde. Clyde's hand hovered over the handkerchief like a force field repelled him. He finally opened it up. Inside was a bag of heroin and a syringe. Clyde closed it back. "I don't need that."

Joe grinned. "So, you haven't brought anything back with you? No sounds? Flashes? Faces? Nothing?"

Clyde saw the dead eyes of the Captain whenever he closed his eyes. "No."

Joe shrugged. "Well, alright then. Let me know when that meeting is, ok?"

Clyde agreed then left.

***

Clyde ventured to Mid-City. The land was once majority swamp, but now it was mostly manicured grass and colorful double-cottage houses with white picket fences bordering around the lawns and cars lining the sidewalks. Clyde held his list in his hand and stared at the two-story house across the street. It still looked the same as the night he'd walked up those steps, gun in his pocket, heart pounding against his chest. He tried to work up the courage to walk across the street and knock on the door. He couldn't. What would he say? What could he say? Then came a creak from the screen door followed by a kid of about eight running out, and a woman trailing behind him.

The kid hopped and skipped down each step like it was part of an obstacle course. Clyde smiled. Then the child and his mama picked weeds from the garden in front of the house. Well, the kid tried. The lumps of dark dirt inevitably ended up on his white shirt, and his pants looked like he'd rolled in mud, and his mother spent more time chiding him than actually picking weeds. Clyde felt the woman's frustration from where he stood. She swiped at the boy's clothes as best as she could but he twisted and turned and bitched and moaned. She grabbed both of his arms. "Edward," she shouted. "Please."

An echo bounced around Clyde's mind. *Oh, that photo is of my son, Edward.* Clyde pressed the heels of his hands into his eyes until the intruding voice from a bygone time went away.

When he stopped rubbing his eyes, he noticed that Edward was pointing toward him. The woman turned around, squinted her eyes, and looked in Clyde's direction. He strode down the street.

This idea was stupid. Fucking stupid. He left the neighborhood in haste, turned into the first store he found, and burst into the bathroom. He kicked open every stall to make sure he was alone and locked the door to make sure no one else entered. He cut off all the lights in an attempt to get it as dark as the isolation room in prison but it didn't work. He slid down against the door and closed his eyes. He felt the Captain's gaze on him in the dark, right next to his face, judging him, telling him he'll never make things right, reminding him he should just do like his daddy did and end his miserable life. Clyde rocked back-and-forth with his knees tucked to his chest like he would as a child and spoke to himself, as well as the Captain.

"I'm so sorry..." he said, his words laced with suppressed fear and sadness. "I'll make things right; I promise. I'll make things right."

Chapter 9

A New Day

Jesse flipped through page after page of the morning papers looking for any mention of O'Grady's body being found. After two weeks of searching, he never found a single drop of ink dedicated to the body being discovered. Not a single black word about an investigation being launched. All Jesse could find were crude drawings of the incumbent Mayor and his cronies, ads for new devices, and fluff pieces on the city's various services.

Jesse flung the newspaper across the room and watched the unattached pages flutter in the air and land in odd angles on the floor. He rubbed his temples and tried his best to calm himself. He knew the deal; knew how this city worked. O'Grady was a scumbag. A dope peddler. And as rumor had it, and from what he saw, a fucking pedophile. The cops probably found him, took whatever money they found, then threw his body in a ditch. Or better yet, in the swamp, that way the gators could have him. But either way, it wasn't his issue anymore.

After the hit on O'Grady, Jesse and Clyde had exchanged words and grappled with each other in the east parlor of the brothel. They knocked over tables, chairs, and lamps, slammed each other into walls, and all Twitch and Rory could do was stand on the sideline while the tumbling mass of men crashed around them. At one point, Clyde got on top of Jesse and pounded on his chest like a mad ape. Jesse had got the upper hand moments later, when he punched Clyde in the gut and made him roll side-to-side on the ground. They had to be separated by Rory and Twitch, with Twitch having to handle the burden of taming a wild Clyde. Jesse had thrown his hands up in resignation then smoothed his suit out. He left without a single word and headed to his condo.

Jesse decided he would no longer step in with issues at the brothel or with the booze operation. Clyde could be the brains of the operation if he wanted to, and Jesse would collect his dividends until the job was done. He'd been preoccupied the last few weeks, anyway.

Footsteps approached behind him, then thin, soft hands went under his shirt, lightly touched every tense spot and pressure point along his back and shoulders, then ended up caressing the nape of his neck until his hairs stood on end.

"What's the matter, baby?" Cindy asked, standing behind him.

He grabbed her hand and kissed it. "Nothing."

He turned to press her against the counter. "Anymore, at least."

Cindy and Jesse's relationship was indefinable; there was the sex, but then there was something else bubbling up under that. Something that ignited their passion beyond that of the flesh, something that transcended the desire for an orgasm and fulfilled them both in an emotionally substantial way. Night terrors plagued Jesse the first night he and Cindy had ever slept together. He woke up devastated she'd seen him in such a weak state. He made up excuse after excuse after inadequate excuse, but instead of Cindy leaving and shunning him forever—as he'd expected—she had laid her own scars to bear. She had shown him her weaknesses, brokenness, and vulnerabilities in hopes he'd help her carry the baggage, the same way she silently promised to carry his. From then on they fucked like they were both trying to exorcise demons.

Having her in his condo the past two weeks put him at ease. His night terrors tried to come for him, but she was there to awaken him, hold him, and tell him they weren't real. He didn't think he loved her. He only ever felt that for one woman. But the image he once had in his mind of what his future looked like was shifting. Originally, his image was him on his patio with a dog on his lap and Rose to his right. His kids sprinting around the yard and the breeze whistling through the trees. But that image was acid-washed now, blurred and destroyed. If he was going all the way with the normalcy thing, he was going to need to recreate it.

"So," said Jesse, still pressing her against the counter.

She responded in a mocking tone. "So."

"You've been here for a while…" He meant it as a tease, but wished he could've put the words back instantly.

"You telling me I'm not any good company?"

He put both his hands up like her eyes were a loaded gun. "Hey, hey. Not what I meant. I just mean, uh, well…"

She stared at him with a raised eyebrow. "Did you hit the sauce early this morning and not tell me?"

"We should grab a bite."

Cindy smiled thinly and said, "From where? I'm a little famished myself."

"No, no, no," he said. He rubbed the back of his head. "I mean, tonight. You. Me. Jesus, Cindy…I'm asking you to go on a date with me."

Cindy's eyes widened. Jesse wanted to shrink away. It was a mistake to make things so serious between them. He ruined the unspoken thing amongst them. He—

"Yes," she said.

His ears and eyes perked up and she repeated herself. *Yes.* The answer rang like music from heaven in his ears.

She got up and got dressed. "I guess I'll have to go to my place to see what I can wear tonight."

He felt butterflies in his stomach like a little child. "It's a date."

***

The New Orleans sky rolled over into nighttime, bringing with it a moon engorged with light and a sky speckled with stars. Up and down the street, neon lights buzzed then flickered on, cars lined the sidewalks, and nightlife chatter filled the streets. Jesse loved every bit of it. The people, the chatter, the atmosphere of being around happy people. But what he didn't like was waiting for Cindy. Jesse stood outside of the restaurant where Cindy was supposed to meet him.

He watched the hands of his watch tick, tick, tick until seconds turned into minutes and minutes turned into half an hour. She was going to stand him up, he thought. He put himself out there and he was going to pay for it. A taxi jerked to a stop in front of the restaurant. His annoyance melted away once he saw Cindy. She looked stunning. Her dress made her look both sophisticated and edgy, the long gown flowed down until it pooled around her feet. Her shoulders were uncovered, a row of goosebumps lined up her arm from the cool night air carried over from the riverfront.

She stepped forward on to the sidewalk with her handbag clutched in front of her. "Hi."

Jesse felt a mild tingle in his gut. "Hi."

He'd never seen her so shy and docile. He'd only ever seen her as scandalous, confident, wild. They were both like timid children feeling each other out before deciding to play with one another.

She laced her arm around his. "Shall we?"

He walked them past the line spilling out through the double doors and curving alongside the front of the building, much to the dismay of the disgruntled patrons. Shouts and insults rang out behind them: "Hey" and "stop" and "dumb-shit" and "cake-eater," but Jesse ignored them.

Cindy had a sheepish smirk on her face. "Those people sound miffed."

Jesse shrugged and walked right up to the host's booth.

"Jesse!" said the excited host. He waved a flamboyant hand toward an angry bulldog-looking man and his homely wife, who'd attempted to question Jesse and Cindy's status in line. The host guided them past rows of white-cloth covered tables with candle-light flames dancing smoothly at the end of their wicks. The ambiance was relaxing, calm, the antithesis of their boozy nights at the brothel. Jesse stopped their stride twice to shake hands with people he recognized, and without missing a beat, he introduced Cindy as his date. Every time he said the word "date," he could sense her fighting a blush.

They'd gotten to their seats. Jesse palmed a bill and stuffed it in the host's hand. Jesse ran around the table to pull Cindy's chair out for her. Next, wine glasses appeared in front of them. One server carefully placed silverware down on either side of them and the other poured the red wine into their glasses until they said stop.

Cindy took a sip of her wine. Her eyes and smile widened. Jesse grinned and leaned across the small table toward her. "Knew you'd enjoy it."

Cindy's eyes darted around. "Should we be doing this?" He noticed she was hesitant to take another sip in a place full of the who's who of New Orleans, especially since the dark, intimate setting was the perfect place for undercover Prohibition agents to hide out and watch people.

Jesse nodded. "Trust me; no one's gonna raid this

place." He raised his glass to toast. "We can do whatever we want."

He placed his hand on the table and her hand wasted no time in meeting it. They kept their hands there for a moment, his eyes locked on hers, hers locked on his. They said a lot to each other without saying anything at all.

Time went on, and silence settled over them. It wasn't awkward; Cindy appeared to be taking in the scenery. Her eyes went wide and she reached over and squeezed Jesse's hand until it turned red.

"What? What?" he asked.

Her breath stuttered like she'd had something caught in her windpipe. "That's Cora Witherspoon."

Jesse looked toward the woman Cindy was now pointing at. He raised an eyebrow. "Who's that?"

Cindy tilted her head and folded her arms. "You go to places where people like Cora Witherspoon are patrons but have no idea who they are." She shook her head.

"So... you gonna tell me who she is?"

Cindy leaned forward like an excited child with a secret. "She's a stage actress, damn it. Last I heard, she was still in New York—on Broadway—but I guess she's back."

Jesse turned again but the plain-looking woman didn't stir the same excitement in him. "I'm sorry I didn't know."

"It's a shame," Cindy said with a smirk on her face. "You know New Orleans, but only for the seediness of it. There's so much art and culture and...and...." She spoke with her hands like she was giving an impassioned speech, despite her speaking at a near whisper, and her eyes had a gleam to them as she spoke about this Cora woman that Jesse didn't know existed until that moment.

"I guess I should try to learn," Jesse said.

Cindy grabbed his hand. "I can teach you."

They scarfed down their meals and drowned themselves in more wine and went on home as fast as they could to pounce each other. When they had sex that time, it wasn't just raw and untamed; there was passion there, the act of two people filling one another's emotional voids.

They went on another date the following day. They grabbed coffee at a restaurant near the riverfront, then walked along the railings on the promenade, staring out into the never-ending horizon of the Mississippi River at the steamboats chugging along in the distance. Jesse stepped behind her and held her to breathe her in, then placed a gentle kiss on her cheek.

They never said it out loud, but their bond grew closer day by day. He already knew certain intimacies about her: she had dreams of being a stage actress, she grew up in a broken home, she was from out west. But then he learned new things, like how she had to eat her dessert before her dinner, how she could be so goofy and giggly when touched in the sensitive spot on her arm, how she often—almost always—dreamt about quitting her job at the brothel. It was those new nuances that pushed their relationship in a serious direction.

Days after the riverfront date, Cindy laid on his couch with her legs over the armrest and one of his shirts covering her body. He approached her with his arms behind his back. She badgered him playfully on why he looked like a schoolboy who'd done something wrong. He smirked then produced two tickets to a Canal St play. Her jaw dropped to the floor. She hopped up and snatched the tickets from his hands.

"Want to go?" he asked.

She hesitated to speak, and instead shook her head. Tears rolled down her face.

"What's wrong?" he asked. "Is this too much, too fast?"

"Oh, no, no, no. Not at all." She smiled. "I think—I think I love you."

He wasn't expecting that, so he stammered. She put her fingers to his lips. "I've wanted to say that for a while now. But I don't expect you to say anything back."

She kissed him. She went to the bathroom and he heard her stifle a giddy noise. He took her place on the couch, and tossed those three words around in his mind for a while. *I love you.* It felt good to be loved. He didn't know if he loved her, though. He wasn't sure if that was good or bad, or if it was even possible to love someone else after already having a first love. But he wanted to try.

The night of the show came. Cindy was awestruck over the people in attendance. The politicians, the rich, the famous, the beautiful, all under one roof to watch the same play as her. Jesse and Cindy walked around the wide theater lobby arm in arm. She whispered in his ear while pointing at each person she recognized. "He's a writer. That's an actress. I think I saw her in a picture show once."

Jesse laughed. "It isn't polite to point, you know."

She waved the comment away. "Let me enjoy myself, why don't ya?" As he was walking toward a cluster of men he thought he recognized, he felt her full weight holding him back. She rooted herself to the ground like a tree and pointed toward a man with a thick mustache and comb-over hairstyle. "Is—is that the Mayor?"

"Yea, that's him," he said matter-of-factly.

Martin Beckman: the incumbent Mayoral candidate and the de-facto leader of the Old Row Democratic Party. The ORD was as big a racket as any crew or crime family in the city. They took bribes through donations, took kickbacks, and did nothing to stop the flow of vice through the city. They had family or associates in all the high places in the city government. They were corrupt, but they helped elevate the city's economy. Martin Beckman was never a gangster, but to say he was complicit in the activity would be putting it lightly. The Mayor strode around the lobby swallowing up peoples' hands with his giant paws, his wife following in tow and being treated like the bride of royalty. Cindy kept looking at the older man, Jesse noticed.

"That's your type?" he asked.

Cindy shook her head. "I never seen him up close before is all."

"Guess I'll have to gain a few hundred pounds and lose a little hair."

Cindy slapped his arm.

"Come this way," Jesse said. "We should try and get to our seat before there's a bottleneck at the auditorium entrance." Cindy went dead weight again. He turned to look at her. "Who'd you see now?"

The enjoyment had vanished from her face and was replaced by shame. She fiddled with her fingers and stared at the carpet. Jesse looked around and saw the group of men he thought he recognized ahead of them. Then he realized why he knew them. "Oh," he said. "I see."

Cindy shook her head. "I knew I shouldn't be here." She stormed off.

Jesse followed her outside and they stood under the flickering lights of the theater marquee. "Why'd you leave?"

Cindy snapped. "Why do you think? Huh?"

Jesse said nothing.

Cindy pointed at him and stared with angry eyes. "See, you can't even say it. "

"Say what?"

"I fucked them, Jesse. Those men. All of them. Probably more in the theater."

Jesse and Cindy had never talked about what she did for a living, and he was her employer for years. Her career as a courtesan hung over their heads, and when they were together, they both tried to duck it lest it ruined the illusion they had constructed together. The illusion that people with their lives could ever be in real relationships.

Cindy folded her arms. "These aren't my people, Jesse. I'm not meant to be here. And the way people like this have always made me feel... made you feel, what are we doing here? All you've ever talked about was how horrid it felt growing up poor, and now you want to be like them?"

Jesse shook his head. "No. I want to be better. I want us

to be better." He pulled her in. "Look, what you do for a living is a role, correct? When you're with those men, you fulfill a fantasy, a purpose. You don't actually like doing it, but you do it nonetheless. Because it's a steppingstone to something else."

She stared up at him.

"I've played a role my whole life as well, just the same as you. So, believe me, this is that 'something else' we been waiting for." He pointed up at the glowing marquee. "You're another step closer to being a stage actress. That's how this game works; we go where these ritzy fucks go, we kiss their ass and talk to them and we shake their hands and maybe, just maybe, they can do something for us. We continue to play the roles we're forced into until one day we no longer need to. And as these roles change, it is ok to change with them. You can let go of your past." Once he was done talking, he realized he was speaking more to himself than to her.

Cindy wiped her eyes. "Then what's my new role?"

Jesse grabbed both of her hands. "A beautiful doll that's out with her very successful fella."

Cindy giggled. "My 'fella'?"

Jesse nodded. "Yes. You have nothing to worry about from here on out. I can carry you the rest of the way if you want."

"Yea, I think I want that."

Jesse nodded. "Good. So, you ready to go see this play, or should I try and get a refund?"

She smiled. "Definitely the play."

The play went by in a flash. Cindy's eyes were locked on the stage from the time the velvet curtains slid open to the time the cast came out for the final bow. Jesse was happy she had fun. She was noticeably more energetic on the walk out of the massive auditorium. She tried to recap the whole thing to Jesse like he wasn't there getting the circulation squeezed out of his arm by her with every plot turn, backstab, or betrayal that took place in the story. She also critiqued the women's performances. She said one was too quiet, another was too loud, and another's voice was shrill. She even talked about maybe getting into some acting classes. Jesse supported the notion. They were almost near the double-door exits. Then Rudy stepped out from the moving bodies in the lobby.

"Hey, Jesse," Rudy said. His eyes were burning red.

Jesse hid how surprised he was. "How are you doing, Rudy?"

Rudy gave a thumbs-up, but his face said otherwise. He was red and sweaty; his breath stank of liquor.

Cindy looked back-and-forth between Jesse and Rudy. "How do you two know each other?" She looked in awe to be so close to *the* Rudy Thompson.

Jesse turned to her. "It's a small world."

Rudy grinned awkwardly and swayed left to right like he could tip over any moment. Rudy looked at Cindy. "Mind if I speak to him for a second?"

"Um," Cindy looked at Jesse. "I guess I can go to the powder room."

Jesse held a smile for as long as he could see Cindy over

the horizon of people in the lobby, then he snatched Rudy by the elbow and guided his lumbering body toward a corner where no one was.

"You can't be serious," Jesse said.

"What do you mean?"

"You're three sheets to the wind right now at a high-profile event, and you really want to talk about that other thing right now?" Jesse stepped back and looked Rudy up and down again. "And should an Alderman really be seen entirely sauced?"

"I thought you were working on fixing the Mulligan problem," Rudy said.

Jesse threw his hands up. "I'm not your errand boy. I don't know how to stop a whole fucking investigation. Other than to hide as much evidence as possible, and we've been doing that. We're gonna be out soon."

"I'm starting to regret it, Jesse," Rudy said in a slur. "I haven't been able to sleep."

Jesse grew impatient. "What are you talking about?"

"I ripped off my own legacy. And for what, some extra money? I have money." Rudy's words came out on the edge of a whine. "They keep asking questions. The insurance people and local feds, that is. 'How often did drivers take that route? What happened to the convoy leader? Don't you find it suspicious that he's nowhere to be found now?' I only let you guys do it because I was so mad at my father for treating my mom so bad. I think they've been tailing me, too. I can't—"

Jesse subtly pushed Rudy against the wall and pressed

his finger into his sternum. "I'm done talking about this with you. Don't say another fucking word about it. You hear me? There's nothing to worry about. Stick to your plausible deniability and keep your daddy issues to yourself. What if you run into Mulligan here, for God's sake?"

Rudy was a wreck. His hair was all over the place, his face was blotchy, his suit jacket was wrinkled. *This is why you don't run jobs with amateurs,* Jesse thought.

"Come on," Jesse said. He guided Rudy by the arms, then straightened out his jacket. "Go the fuck home, now. Ok?"

Jesse sent Rudy on his way like a scolded child. Jesse was stupid for thinking a wannabe gangster-politician like Rudy had the stomach for the nitty-gritty stuff. The Prohies and insurance folks were just covering their bases. They had nothing. But Jesse had to ask himself what he was willing to do to protect his happy ending. He closed his eyes and shuddered at the thought. He wouldn't kill Rudy. He wouldn't need to. Because everything would be fine.

Jesse pushed the intrusive thoughts out of his head and turned on his heel to look for Cindy. The crowds rushing out the door blocked his path, but he forced his way through to get to the other side. Someone's head crashed into the center of his chest. Jesse put his hands out to apologize. "I'm so sorry, miss."

The shorter woman apologized as well.

Jesse's eyes ignited. The shorter woman was Rose. They both held a bemused gaze on one another. They were both unsure of what to say, but neither of them moved.

"How've you been?" she said. She tried to hide the reluctance of the question in her voice.

He answered equally obligatorily with, "Good."

Last time they saw each other she'd made it clear she wanted nothing to do with him, so they both nodded and gave fake smiles to calm the rising awkwardness.

"Maybe I should just let you go," said Jesse.

"Yea, I think that's a good idea.

Then Cindy looped her arm around Jesse's. "Hello." She had a hint of territorialism behind her acknowledgment.

Rose sensed it and took a step back. "I'm just an old friend who's waiting on my date. I was just about to leave."

Cindy's shoulders seemed to loosen up. "Well, sorry the introduction was so brief."

Jesse couldn't even hide the way her answer made him feel. "Friend" and "my date" cut through his heart like a blade. At that moment, he realized just how not over her he was. He looked down at Rose and it all came back to him; every ounce of emotion he once felt rose to the forefront of his mind. And he realized something devastating: Cindy was the bandage on his emotional wounds, but Rose was the stitching. She was the "happy" in his "ending."

Before Rose left, she motioned behind Jesse. "This is my date."

Jesse turned around and couldn't wait to see what man had Rose's heart.

"Hello there," the man said in a welcoming tone.

Jesse's neck tightened. He recognized that voice. He couldn't believe he recognized that voice.

"This is him," Rose said, her arm wrapped in her date's now. "You may have seen his name around."

Her date reached out to shake Jesse's hand. "Nice to meet you, Jesse. I'm Cameron Mulligan, New Orleans District Attorney."

Chapter 10

Closure

Sleep came hard after the play, which in turn made it difficult for Jesse to focus behind his desk at The Magnolia, especially with the hammers beating in the background and the repugnant odor of paint sneaking into his office from up the hall. The mound of papers on his desk—resumes and job applications—put him to sleep quicker than a sedative. He rested his head on his fist and felt his eyelids grow heavy; he blinked for a second and felt his head tug toward the desk.

Jesse decided to take the place of one of the contractors. He stood on top of a ladder and hammered away at the wall while trying to hang a painting. He heard someone come up behind him. Jesse turned his torso and looked down at Melvin.

"What the heck are you doing up there?" Melvin asked.

Jesse beat the nail into the wall and hung the picture, then hopped down.

Melvin motioned toward the moving contract workers carrying ladders and cans of paint.

Jesse caught on to Melvin's confusion. "I want to be able to say I helped build this place with my hands." It also gave Jesse an excuse to keep moving and not fall asleep at his desk. Melvin's blank gaze was intense, like the thought of physical labor eluded him. Jesse set the hammer on top of a nearby tarp-covered table and followed behind Melvin as they had their weekly meeting. They talked and walked through an obstacle course of construction tools and sawhorses.

"I think we can open next month," said Jesse.

Mel's bug-eyes popped out his head. "Next month?" He glared around the room. "Why the rush?"

A distraction, Jesse thought. But he said, "I'm just ready to start making money."

Jesse fought a losing battle to keep his eyes open while Mel continued to weigh the pros and cons of opening next month. He leaned against the wall, his vision went in and out, his hearing warped each time he nodded off for a stray second, then he heard whistling.

"Holy smokes," said Mel. "Who's the doll?"

Rose advanced toward Jesse with purpose.

"A friend," said Jesse.

Rose stood in between Jesse and Melvin with her arms folded in an impatient, defensive gesture. Before Jesse could speak, she hushed him with a finger, and pointed toward the front of the restaurant. "Across the street. Now."

Jesse nodded. Mel whistled. "Whew. Spitfire, ain't she?"

Rose's face turned sour as she sighed.

***

Rose sat right across from Jesse with her face chiseled in apathy and her both hands' fingers laced between one another. Her body language revealed little, but Jesse could feel her tracing his facial structure and looking at how much he'd changed, just as he did to her.

The waiter came over with two menus. "Hello, sir," he said. "What will you and the lady be having?"

"The lady will be ordering her own coffee, thank you very much," Rose said. "And the gentlemen can have whatever he'd like."

Jesse chuckled to himself then ordered a coffee as well.

The waiter put the menus back under his arm and walked away, clearly irritated by the clear role reversals. Jesse wasn't irritated by it, though. She'd always been that way. Whether it was arguing with the boys at the park over whether girls should be allowed to play baseball with them, or whether it was in the Tulane quad arguing with men over whether women should have the right to vote, she'd always fought against being put in a box.

She cleared her throat. "I just need to say this, and then I'll be on my way."

Jesse leaned with his elbows on the table.

"You hurt me," she said. Jesse's energy deflated. "You hurt me more than you know, and you made a fool of me. I went against my father for you and never, ever heard the end of it. And when I told them that you'd left me, they just said, 'told you so.'" Rose tensed up. "'Told you so.'"

Jesse knew she was being nice. What her thin-haired, dog-faced preacher father probably actually said was, "I told you so, Rose. He's a street rat raised by a whore and who works for a wop." Jesse had an easy time imagining that because her father had told him to his face when he was sixteen years old. Jesse had shelled out money for a nice suit, ripped off some bright flowers from someone's garden, and stood on their stoop, only to have her father get to the door and throw out words like "she's too good for you" and "whore mother" and "flames of hell." He slammed the door shut in his face, leaving him standing there with a handful of flowers and a fractured sense of self.

"I'm sorry," Jesse said. "I really am."

She scoffed and rolled her eyes. The server walked toward them with two ceramic coffee mugs. The thick steam drifted from the top.

Jesse was so captivated by Rose he didn't even reach for his coffee. He didn't want to miss a single word or expression on her face. Rose stirred her spoon in her coffee slowly. "Is there anything you want to say other than 'sorry'?"

Jesse crossed his legs. "How've you been?"

"Exquisite, actually."

"Is that so?"

"It is." Rose slurped her coffee while keeping an attentive eye on Jesse.

He nervously cracked his knuckles under the table, then

broke the silence. "Look, I'm sorry I left you the way I did; left school and what-not. It was hard to stay there. The classes were tough. Everyone there was worlds different than what I was accustomed to... I mean, what was I supposed to do, be a banker? Buy a small house somewhere outside the city and raise chickens with you?"

"Yes," she hissed. "That was exactly the plan when you proposed to me."

He avoided her gaze.

The night of their proposal was present in his mind: candles, a cake, him on one knee in her cramped dorm room at the Sophie B. Wright girl's wing of the campus. He had been just twenty-one, Clyde hadn't been arrested yet, and it had seemed like he was done with the streets forever. Months later, he had dropped out of school, leaving her crying in the same spot he proposed to her, and left out the door and wouldn't speak to her for a long, long time.

Jesse leaned forward. "I was just playing myself, I guess. I always knew my past would come back for me some way, somehow." He stared into her eyes now. "I just didn't think it would hurt you. The only thing I was ever good at my whole fucking life was screwing people over, doing the type of stuff that gets people locked behind bars. It took me years to find something I'm actually good at, outside of that." Jesse pointed over to the restaurant across the street.

Rose cut in. "You sure made it sound like your brother put a gun to your head and made you quit college." She shook her head and stood. "You're just making excuses. You can't be honest with yourself, let alone me."

153

Jesse snatched her wrist as she turned away. She scowled at him. His face softened. Almost like he wanted to will her back in his chair. Her scowl relented. She sat.

"Ok," Jesse said. "You're right. When things in my life get quiet for too long, I get nervous and self-sabotage."

Rose poured sugar into her coffee and mixed it around with her spoon. "Can I ask a somewhat related question?"

"Go ahead."

"What does happiness look like for you?"

Jesse swiped his arms across the street to the **"Coming Soon!"** sign that hung outside.

Rose bit down on a laugh. "Seriously?"

Jesse jutted up a confused eyebrow. "Yea, what you mean?"

Rose said matter-of-factly, "Physical possessions won't lead to any true fulfillment. Want my honest opinion?"

"Go ahead."

"You've never known what happiness looked like for you. You always run back to your family when you're scared." Rose held up her fingers. "When you were a boy, you were just happy to get new clothes. I could remember the look on your face when you finally had socks that didn't have holes in them." They shared a smile. "But then that wasn't enough. So, then you needed more money." She pointed toward his clothes and watch. "Now you have money, and that isn't enough. Then it was me...." She let the silence carry the weight of the words. "Now you think it's a building? Or a business? What if that's not enough?

Jesse shrugged. "It has to be."

"But what if it's not?"

"Then I'll find something else."

Rose sighed. "If that helps you sleep at night." They paused for a moment, sipped their coffee, then Rose asked, "May I ask why quit now?"

"Can I be honest?"

"We don't date anymore. You can be honest now."

Jesse shifted uncomfortably in his seat. "There's only so much bad someone can witness before it weighs on them."

Rose held a blank gaze on him, reading him, assessing how she felt about his words. Jesse must've passed the test because all she said was, "Ok." Indistinct conversations, silverware clattering against ceramic, and noise from the street filled the vacant space of silence between them.

"Well," Rose said, gathering herself to leave. "This has been fun."

"Wait," Jesse said. "How'd you find me?"

"It's a small-big city. People's names and whereabouts come up sometimes."

Jesse smirked.

She gave a cutting glance. "Don't flatter yourself too much." She reached into her handbag and put money on the table for their coffee, despite Jesse's protest.

He told her where to reach him.

She said, "It's been nice, Jesse. Let's not open any closed doors. I just wanted closure."

"Did you get it?"

"Yes."

She turned away and walked out of his life again. The

conversation wasn't exactly an easy one to have, but at least he knew one thing: he didn't break her. He didn't ruin her. She bounced back better than before. She bounced back with someone better than him: Cameron Mulligan. He kicked himself in the ass for not asking her about him, but he let it go. He didn't care anymore. Ever since the O'Grady hit, he told himself he was done, and he meant it. He stood to leave, then he saw Melvin run across the street waving his arms in the air like a maniac.

Jesse put a hand on Melvin's shoulder while he caught his breath. "Jesse," Mel gasped for air. "Someone is on the phone for you; they say your father fell ill. He's at Charity."

"That ship sailed years ago. Maybe the operator got the wrong—" He sprinted to his car before the words formed in his mind. He needed to get to Charity Hospital before Big Sal died.

Chapter 11

The Offer

Jesse rushed down the white halls of Charity Hospital's private wing with sweat stains spreading across his shirt's collar. He asked every nurse and doctor walking past him where Sal was, but some couldn't understand him since his haste made his words come out jumbled and fragmented. But one doctor jutted his head down the hall. Two men with long black coats and gun bulges around their midsections stood guard in front of the door.

Jesse charged past the men and barreled into the room. "Sal," he said.

In the room were Junior and Hymie. Figures, Jesse thought. The two men at the door must've been a part of Hymie's hit squad.

Sal was under the covers. He looked like a deflated version of himself. Loose skin around his eyes and face, so pale it looked like all the blood in his body had been drained.

He groaned and turned his head toward the door. Jesse had his hat in hand.

"Jesse boy," Sal said with a rasp.

Hymie acknowledged Jesse with a nod. Junior said nothing. He sat in the corner and looked out the window, but Jesse could see the lines of frustration on the side of his face.

"Sit, sit," Sal told Jesse.

Jesse pulled a chair close to his bedside. Sal strained to push himself up. He waved away the three men who were eager to help.

"Junior," Sal said. "Why don't you and Hymie give me and Jesse a moment alone?"

Sal Jr. twisted his body around to protest but was silenced by a glare from his father. Jesse saw a flash go across Junior's face. It was but a moment, but he saw it. It was the flash of fear, a gut reaction from years of backhands and tongue-lashings, and subtle but powerful reminders he was a disappointment. Junior got up and headed outside the door. Jesse couldn't look at him. He honestly always felt sorry for the guy. Hymie closed the door behind them.

Sal grinned. "Happy you could make it."

"Why wouldn't I make it, old man?"

"You're a busy man now, is all."

Jesse sat back and swung his left leg over his right. Jesse thought to ask him about the men at the door, but he knew how Sal was: cautious. Paranoid. He always thought someone would come to kill him one day when he was weak and off his game.

"I call you here, not only because I missed your conversation. But because," Sal paused. He stared deep into the bare white wall ahead of him like he was writing a draft of the words he wanted to say next. "Because I'm not immortal. I'm old. And frail. And I can't do this too much longer."

Jesse's legs uncrossed. He'd known the day would come. "What are you getting at?"

"The Bianchi Family is thin. Many of the people I came up with, started this with, are dead. And the other half of my blood, if still alive, moved out east after the lynching of the Italians years back." Sal made the sign of the cross. In the 1890s, a well-liked police chief was assassinated by a crime family in the streets. It was in the middle of some turf war going on over a noodle factory. Every Italian in sight was arrested, no matter their age, or whether they even lived in the area. Most were let go, but about twenty were rounded up. Half were acquitted, and the other half didn't even have their trial before the town came for them and hanged them from trees in the middle of the city.

"I remember the story," Jesse said.

"If I'm dead, and they're gone, and only Junior and Hymie and his crew of ruffians are left without a brain at the head, my family and legacy will die with me."

Jesse sat close to Sal's bed. He shook his head. He ran his fingers through his hair. He knew what was coming next.

"Jesse, my boy, my second son," Sal's hands trembled

over Jesse's. "I need you to be the right hand to my blood-son. He's the muscle. You're the brains. Your family and mine can merge."

Jesse leaned back in his chair. "I'm not Sicilian."

"Neither is Hymie. But he's an associate to the family. Your brothers will be associates. You'd be my son's counselor... an advisor of sorts."

Jesse couldn't believe the proposition. Big Sal was the de facto face of the Italian criminal underworld in New Orleans. There wasn't a small-time Italian gang or family who didn't kick-up to him. And all the other organizations feared him. They feared his business savvy, political connections, ruthlessness, and he was asking Jesse, a non-Italian, to run the show with his son. Jesse would be powerful. This would be the type of power he'd been in proximity of most of his youth, so close that he could taste it, and now, he'd finally have it.

Jesse twisted his hat in his hands. He had but to say "yes," and his life would change forever. He looked at Sal. Sal strained his whole body to smile at Jesse. Jesse put a hand on the back of Sal's. "No. I can't."

Sal's smile shifted to a frown. "I understand. You don't have the stomach anymore."

Jesse moved around in his seat.

Sal flashed his palms. "No, no. I don't mean to slight. It was just an offer. An idea. I don't want you doing anything you aren't comfortable with, alright?"

Jesse nodded, then neither had words to add so a thick fog of silence filled the room, until both men decided to push through it by feigning cordiality for a bit. Jesse jibed him about his old age and Sal returned a joke of his own. They laughed and caught up. Jesse was tempted to ask for life and love advice from the old man. He sometimes forgot they had that type of closeness. But he decided against it. Sal's answers were always a variation of "marry Italian."

Junior flung the door open. "The nurse wanted to see you."

Big Sal frowned. He chastised him for not knocking. Familiar discomfort came over Jesse.

"I think I should leave," Jesse said.

"Wait," Sal said. "We need to talk more, yea? Over dinner tomorrow night, maybe. Mrs. Bianchi misses you around eating up all our food."

Jesse was between the door's threshold, Junior behind him, close enough for Jesse to feel his angry breath against his back.

Jesse said, "Yea, sure."

Big Sal grinned from ear to ear. Jesse turned toward Junior's gaze and wondered how often Junior had contemplated putting a knife in his back or slitting his throat. His glare said he'd considered it at least once, maybe twice. Jesse never asked to be Big Sal's favorite son. But he didn't turn down the food or trips to the park with him either.

Jesse clapped Junior on the shoulder. "Take care."

Junior's angry eyes bore deep into Jesse's soul. Jesse walked away, fully aware that one day, the passive aggressiveness and subtle flickers of anger that often slid across Junior's face would turn into something much more dangerous. He was aware that Junior probably thought often of all the ways he would kill him, and honestly, Jesse couldn't blame him; he'd probably carry the same type of resentment if roles were reversed. But there were limits to Jesse's kindness and understanding, so if Junior ever decided to come gunning for him, he better not miss.

Chapter 12

Risk taking

Rose walked in circles in front of the tan-brick headquarters of the Mulligan Foundation. She murmured curses to the wind, kicked branches and loose rocks in her path, and wished she could go back in time and lay into Jesse worse than what she'd done earlier that day. It peeved her to think about how he could sit there and smile and smirk while she'd attempted to tell him off.

"Is everything fine?" Cameron asked her.

She turned around to see him looking at her like she'd gone mad. He had his coat draped over his forearm and black circles under his eyes. He removed his glasses and rubbed his eyes until they became adjusted to the outside world.

She nodded. "Why? What makes you ask that?"

He smiled. Cameron had a gentle smile capable of

putting anyone at ease. "Because one of the secretaries said a woman was moving about like a mad person out here." He kissed her cheek. "I assumed it was you."

Cameron was sweet, kind, intelligent, and complimented her endlessly, unlike the men before him. Everyone after Jesse was a stereotypical man who couldn't remove their heads from their own asses long enough to realize the world didn't revolve around them. She'd been on many a date where'd she go into a fancy restaurant with an open mind and open heart, willing to give the men a try, but they all turned out the same carbon copies of each other. Spoiled brats. Apathetic monsters. Worried more about the pleasures of the flesh than what she felt about women's rights to vote or the moral crisis the city was in. And they always took her disinterest as "playing hard to get." Fifteen minutes into dinner, and a warm, clammy hand would grip her thigh under the tablecloth. She ended all the dates the same, too: with a slap to the face or a cup of water tossed on their suits or a scream at the top of her lungs loud enough to cause everyone in the restaurant as much discomfort as she felt.

"Why do you do this?" her father had asked her once. He had wiped the residue of greasy chicken and peas from the side of his lips and tossed his balled-up napkin to the ground.

Rose munched her food and covered her mouth to ask, "What do you mean?" Her father prayed for a second into his laced fingers and asked the Lord for patience with his difficult daughter. Her mother had stared into her plate like she was waiting for permission to speak.

"You have all of these good, fine men who want to court you. Why do you reject them? Why must you be so difficult? Don't you realize you're getting well past marriage age?"

She had dropped her utensils and matched her father's aggression. She had told him about her dreams and ambitions, how she wanted to change the world one day, how the world was waiting for more female leaders to step forth and mold it into a more inhabitable place for all. She said she couldn't be with small-minded men, with over-sized egos and outdated ideas on a woman's place in the world. She refused to be the wife who hid away in her hole until her husband needed something on his arm for galas. She wasn't a piece of jewelry, but a functioning woman with a functioning brain and goals beyond that of being a mother or married. He had laughed. It wasn't a quick laugh, either. It had been long, hard, and from the diaphragm. He had blamed her mother for telling Rose to go to college instead of typist school. Rose had gritted her teeth and looked at her mother. Her mother had said nothing. As she and Cameron stood in front of the building she remembered all those dates and the conversation with her father and thanked God she never had to worry about Cameron being that way. He empowered her.

"Are you ready? Or would you like to continue to terrorize those rocks and leaves?" asked Cameron.

She looped her arm around his. "Yes, I actually would like to continue to kick rocks."

They made their way to the hall where Rose held her weekly meetings on women's rights. Inside, members of Rose's organization sat in scattered islands of conversations. Cameron took the first seat in the back near the entrance, allowing the women to file into the seats ahead and rendering himself a fly on the wall. Rose walked up the middle of the aisle past two sides of tightly lined chairs, ascended three steps, turned to the podium, and asked for everyone to be silent. She read the group's upcoming itinerary while a sea of eyes, wrinkled and smooth, green, blue, brown, and hazel, stared back at her and hung on her every word, sitting at the edges of their seats and nodding along to her suggestions. Rose's eyes scanned further back to the only man in the room, Cameron. He probably couldn't tell, but she looked right at him. Right into those gentle brown eyes and soft facial features that were still masculine, yet not overly gruff. He muttered word for word the speech she had practiced in front of him nights before.

This made a tingle flutter up Roses' body; it was like a jolt of electricity that produced a smile across her face. Her pale cheeks erupted into a blush. Someone raised a hand. She acknowledged them. The woman spoke, but her question slowly lost volume and drifted into the background, like an ocean outside a window creating white noise. Rose's eyes were on the woman, but her mind was on Cameron. And his smile. And his bright white teeth. And gentle hands he liked to rub against her cheeks and her arms and legs and through her hair. And that made a tingle shoot up her legs again—it started at her toes and went past her knees, crawled up her thighs and coiled around the inside toward her pelvis. She imagined it was his hands, his fingers, his lips, his—

"Rose?" The woman with the question looked confused. Rose snapped from her fantasy. "Rose?" the woman asked again.

Rose pretended to cough into her arm to allow the hue of red on her cheeks to fade back to pale white. "Whew, pardon me." She fanned her face and let out an awkward laugh. She peeled her focus from Cameron and put it on the woman with the question. "Can you repeat your question again?"

Cameron's car kicked up gravel and rocks out of the parking lot and shot down the road toward his home. Rose's hand rested in his lap the whole way. Then she gently traced the curve of his jawline with her finger. He turned to her for a split second, revealing the streetlights and moonlight gleaming off his glasses.

They couldn't even make it to the porch before they started to kiss each other. He fumbled with one hand to get his front door open while she pulled and turned his face toward hers, pressing her lips into his, gripping the back of his neck.

"Rose," he said from the side of his mouth.

They stepped inside after he had a moment to get the door open. Rose continued to kiss him, wanting him to take her to his room or bend her over his office desk. But she felt him let up.

He moved his lips from hers. "Uh, Rose."

He adjusted his glasses on his face, looked at the ground, and ran his fingers through his hair. Rose stood there with the tingle of sensuality rushing through her body and her feral mind on high alert. She shuddered in embarrassment and covered her mouth. "My goodness, I'm so sorry." She'd forgotten... he's abstinent.

They stood in the dark foyer for a while and he pretended to stare at the silhouette of his vase and stack of books on the table lined against the wall. She felt terrible.

"We can just relax and talk," she said.

He nodded and took her hand. They sat on the couch and talked. Which was fine. But all they ever did was talk, mainly about law and politics, things that, over time, grew old and took away from the tender moments they shared. Abstinence wasn't a deal breaker for Rose. But dullness was. Rose felt bad thinking it, but it was true. She had to drag him out of the house for that play the other night. If it was up to him, he would've stayed home and stayed up all night under the glow of his desk lamp and planned out his policies for the city of New Orleans. She loved that he wanted to save the city—hell—the world, but she sometimes wanted more.

Now, on his couch, she nodded along with everything he said, his plans for new infrastructure, how he wanted to create the "city manager" position, how he'd approach crime in the city and the surrounding areas, how he wanted to beef up Prohibition enforcement. His talking became dull and hypnotic, like a long stretch of road, and she felt herself losing focus. If he wanted to douse out her fire, he did a great job.

"Sorry if I ruined things," he said.

She snapped to. "It's fine."

"Maybe we should take things slow." He put a friendly hand on hers.

That's not the type of hand you give someone who just tried to grab your penis, but she said with a smile, "We can do that."

His phone rang out like a fire truck siren, and before she could speak, he trotted over and answered it. She slouched into his couch. She looked around his living room and took in all the brown wood and bland colors that made her shudder. Overhead, looking down upon her from a portrait on the wall, was the often-mentioned father of Cameron. His portrait reminded her of the imagery of the saints her father made her learn as a kid, and she thought it was ironic, since people spoke of Cameron's father in the same fashion, like he could heal the sick or walk on water, end a world war with his words and send ships full of men to die in his honor. This made Rose feel sorry for Cameron to a small extent. It had to be hard to grow up in the shadow of a giant.

Cameron was a busy man and a go-getter, all to keep pace with his father's legacy. He'd never made time for women until her, and she was ok with taking it slow. She really was. But her physical urges hadn't been fulfilled since the night before Jesse had quit school, and the thought made her mood sour. She stood and walked toward Cameron to let him know she should probably leave. He whispered low into the phone, looking over his shoulder every so often to acknowledge her existence. He put a finger up, then whispered into the phone, "One second." Cameron cut Rose off before she could speak. "Hey, Rose. This may be longer than I thought. Is it ok if we connect again tomorrow, or maybe the day after? I'd really like to see you again."

She said yes, and before she could even say the word "bye," he'd placed a kiss on her cheek and walked away from her with the phone's candlestick base and cord in hand.

The front door to her parents' home swung open to reveal a familiar picture: her father marking Bible scriptures in pencil, head down and staring deep into the dense words of the Lord, and her mother next to him, weaving threads in and out, in and out, like she always did. Rose figured it was a sweater or another blanket. Rose put her house key down on the table, acknowledged her parents, and tried to dart past them.

"Tonight went well?" Her father asked.

She shuddered. Her father's voice always agitated her to the point of rage. She slid on a happy face and turned toward him. She nodded and laced her fingers in front of her waist. "Yes, father."

"You didn't put out, did you?"

Rose's hands balled into a fist. Her mother's needle and thread slowed at the question. She started up again. For a moment, Rose thought her mother would show some emotion, or a sign she was a functioning woman. "No, Father."

"Good," he said, finally looking up from the Bible and

into her eyes. "Men don't like easy women. Let's not lose this one. And then maybe you can quit that," he paused for a moment and made air quotes, "'job,' of yours. Maybe go back to teaching if you want. But I don't see why you would want to do that, either."

He went back to scratching down notes and making marks and diving even further into the depths of his own moral hypocrisy. Rose said nothing to her father. She looked at her mother once again, an empty, soulless vessel occupying human skin, and turned to go to her room.

Her mother's thread and needle that perpetually moved had become symbolic of her parent's relationship, just the same thing over and over again with little to no deviation from the day before, the minutes and hours and years weaving in and out of one another just to lead to the same point every time. It was even symbolic of how her mother was forever tethered to her father, threaded at his hip and doomed to forever stay at his side.

Memories of secretly wanting her parents to separate as a child came to Rose, but she knew her mother would never do it, because women who left their husbands didn't get the favor of the lord, or whatever the hell her mother believed in

Her mother would secretly tell her stories of an Italian boy she'd loved in her youth, smiling at the mention of his black hair and his olive skin. But her parents would never let her do that—date a WOP, that is—so she chose Rose's father. Her mother was happier talking about a fling from her teens than the current decades-long marriage.

Rose got out of bed and snuck down the hall toward her parents' bedroom, where through the opened door she saw the moon's glow through the window cast a blue-ish tint on her mother's face. Rose tip-toed in and stood in the middle of the wide expanse between her mother's bed and her father's bed, then laid a kiss on her mother's forehead. Rose stood in the kitchen in front of the phone now, contemplating what she should do. Her fingers hovered over the receiver. Should she play it safe, like her father wanted? Or take her mother's silent but painfully loud warnings? She listened to her mother. She got patched through to the number she needed to reach and said, "Good evening. Are you free tomorrow night?"

Chapter 13

Nowhere To Run To

Jesse entered his long walk-in closet with clothes on either side of him, a cascade of colors for various events. He had suits in light browns and dark blues, white woolen and rose-colored sweatshirts for when the humid heat of New Orleans made way for the one week of winter the city got every year. Hangers screeched on the clothes rack when he swept his clothes to the side. He pulled out a dark blue suit jacket. He picked pieces of lint and hair from it, wondering where he wore it last. A piece of hair from within the threading curled in his fingertips. He realized he wore it last with Cindy.

He'd spent yesterday late afternoon at Cindy's place after leaving the hospital. He'd called her from a payphone and asked her to come over whenever he got home, but she instead gave him her address and told him to come spend the night. He went over there and conversation quickly shifted into sex, but it didn't feel right. It was odd for him because he never felt more secure than when he was saturated in Cindy's love, never felt higher than when they were entwined and ascending toward climax, but right then, her legs around his waist, her touch felt like sandpaper against his bare skin; right then, a woman was planted firmly on his brain, and the woman underneath him wasn't her.

It wasn't fair to Cindy. He didn't finish, and claimed he was sick; she'd begged him to let her take care of him, but he insisted on going home. He left the small duplex and returned home for the night and received the best call he'd received in a while. It was from Rose.

Jesse dropped the hair and felt instant guilt. He and Cindy were doing fine and going places. But, it's not like they were officially together. Just dating. Besides, he and Rose weren't going on a date. It was just two old friends who wanted to catch up over a drink or meal or maybe both. The logical gymnastics stuck its landing and eased his guilt. He picked a dark blue suit.

***

Cracked, uneven streets and mile-deep potholes made Jesse's car shake and tremble and sputter. The roads in that part of town had deep divots and splintered concrete like the earth had tried to swallow the neighborhood whole but decided not to halfway through. He had his head on a pivot. The homes in the neighborhood were decent, but not quite up to the level he'd expect to be picking Rose up from since she grew up in a more affluent area. He hooked a left at the end of the street and saw her standing on the corner next to a stop sign. He was dumbstruck by her beauty. Her light blue dress made her usual faint red hair appear to be a deep crimson, and her green eyes a vibrant emerald.

He said, "You look nice."

She sat in his passenger seat with her evening bag in her lap, holding on to it like it could jump out the window. She turned and told him thank you, and gave him a soft smile.

"Why'd you tell me to pick you up here?" Jesse asked.

"Well, my father still hates you, and he's still up right now, so..."

Jesse couldn't help but find that funny.

He couldn't go to his usual haunts. New Orleans was a city of hundreds of thousands, but many people ran in the same circles. Rumors spread quicker than wildfires, and were even harder to get rid of. And there was certainly no need for a night out with an old friend to be made into something more than what it was. He took her to a jazz joint in Treme, Treme Hall, a light-green two-floor camelback shotgun house with white steps and railings.

Rose was suspicious as they walked up to the home. "This is a house. What are we doing here?"

Jesse squinted his eyes. "You really don't get out much, huh? This place? The cat's meow."

She looked unmoved and skeptical. Jesse knocked on the door until a slot in the center opened up and the faint sound of music rolled out. The doorman stared daggers at Jesse and Rose.

Jesse said confidently, "I'm good with Davy."

The door flew open to a doorman who towered over Jesse by at least six inches. The place was a hole in the wall where everyone was packed like sardines but it was ok, because all it did was amplify the music. There was a makeshift bar in the corner and the band was center stage, their instruments squawking out tunes that seemed to be random and unplanned but yet still got peoples' feet to tapping and heads to swaying. Everyone there except for Jesse, Rose, and four other people, was colored. Everyone danced, hopped, and skipped to the music.

Rose squeezed Jesse's arm. "How the hell do they fit all of these people in here?"

Jesse shrugged. "Probably one at a time, if I had to guess."

She slapped his arm playfully.

Davy was by the bar leaning against the wall nursing a bourbon neat. He strode over with a little pep in his step when he saw Jesse. Jesse introduced Rose to Davy. Davy motioned them toward an empty table off to the side, close enough to feel like the trumpets were right in your ear, but not so close that the people kicking their legs up and dancing would hit the back of your chairs.

"Whatever you want," Davy said, pointing at himself, "it's on me."

Jesse shook Davy's hand, then sent him on his way. Jesse pulled out Rose's seat and she reluctantly sat. Rose's head swayed from side to side as she scanned the crowd, her purse still clutched in her hands with a death grip. Jesse put his hand up to order a drink. The waitress walked over with a tray in hand and Jesse ordered a drink for himself then looked over to Rose, regretfully remembering she was a teetotaler.

When Jesse's drink appeared he just stared at it. Rose's hand rested against her chin and she looked at him, then to the drink, back to him, with a smirk on her face. "You know that's illegal, right?"

Jesse stammered.

She shook her head. "I'm kidding. Go ahead."

Jesse smirked and took sips from his glass. He leaned in close to her, almost touching her ear with his lips. "I was shocked when you said you wanted to step out with me."

"Why so?"

"This isn't your crowd."

She looked confused, then he did the sign of the cross and pretended to pray.

She said, "I wanted to try something different for a change."

Jesse rested his hand on hers, her fingers squeezing tighter into her purse. "Then loosen up, why don't you?"

The night went on and they made conversation about anything and everything, flowing smoothly like a river, and eventually, Rose no longer choked the life out of her evening bag. Instead, she clapped and enjoyed the sound of the jazz band and as time went by, Jesse and Rose got a little closer to each other and traded short, reluctant glances, his hand drifting to hers accidentally a few times just for him or her to snatch it back. There was an obvious line between them, and he wanted to see how far he could cross it.

"This is so fun," Rose said.

Jesse smiled.

After another drink Jesse couldn't stop looking at her. The lights were dim but her eyes still twinkled like stars in the nighttime sky. She was at her most charming when she was relaxed and enjoying herself, and she had a half-smile on her face from looking at the people around them. That's what he always loved about her: her ability to be pleased by the simple things in life.

He bit his lips and reached his hand out. "You want to go dance?"

Her eyes widened. She leaned in close enough for him to catch another whiff of her enchanting perfume. She smelled of daisies.

She said shyly in his ear, "I can't dance that fast."

Jesse responded, "I don't think anyone can."

Just like that, the band switched to a song they could sway to. He gradually leaned in closer to her, scooting her hair out of the way. "You have no excuse now."

Her deep dimples carved holes in her cheeks. "Ok."

As she stood with her hand out, Jesse saw the clock over her shoulder. *Fuck.* He had told Sal yesterday that he'd come by for dinner at his house.

Rose turned to follow his gaze. The excitement left her face. "We don't have to."

Jesse shook his head. "No, I'm staying. I don't have anywhere else better to be."

He led her to the dance floor. They got right in the

middle and held each other. He could feel her body tense in his hands, like she was afraid to let herself go. He pulled her in closer; she rested her head on his chest. Shoulders from other people bumped into his back, but with her, it felt like they were all alone. He looked at the clock again and prayed the tick-tick-tick would slow down and allow him to bask in the moment, because for the next few minutes, he would have her in his arms, and for the next few minutes, he would have a genuine smile on his face. An hour turned to two, which turned to three, then Jesse saw how late it was and decided to take the little church girl home before her papa came looking for her.

The energy in the car was more upbeat than before. On the ride up, he could tell Rose was tight, but after dancing for a while and listening to good music, she couldn't stop talking. She talked about the music, the dancing, how she wished she could get that low to the ground or spin in the air. She mimed kicking her leg up and giggled like a schoolgirl.

She grabbed Jesse's wrist with a delicate touch. "I really enjoyed myself, Jesse."

"I'm happy you did."

As they turned out of the residential area and onto the main roads, Jesse couldn't help thinking about the elephant in the room: Cameron. He wanted to know what their deal was, but he didn't want to make things strange between them.

But the question was out of his mouth before he could stop himself. "What's the deal with you and Cameron?"

She tightened up again. "Well, if you must know, I met him working with the campaign on a volunteer basis. And yes, we see each other from time to time."

Jesse feigned excitement. "That's good, that's good."

Rose continued. "He's sweet, and nice, and so smart—"

"Sounds like there's a 'but' coming."

She looked confused.

"As in," Jesse said. "'He's sweet, nice, and smart, but...'"

She giggled. "I guess you got me. He's a busy-bee and a worrywart. He really loves this city, you know. We're not steady, yet. So, I give him time and space to work."

Jesse nodded absentmindedly.

Rose made Jesse creep up slowly to her house. It was nighttime and her father was always out by eight, and the living room light wasn't on, but she wanted to be careful. "Right here is fine," Rose said, pointing at the house next door to hers. Jesse stopped right in front of the neighbors' driveway.

"You don't want me to walk you to the door?" Jesse asked.

"I think I can take care of myself," Rose responded. "But thank you."

Jesse nodded. "I really had fun tonight."

"I had a swell time. And it was good catching up."

Jesse looked longingly into Rose's eyes and the seconds seemed to unfurl slowly like a spool of yarn. He leaned in to kiss her.

A stiff hand pushed his face back. "No, Jesse. I agreed to this for old time's sake. Just because we were friends too at one point. But that's it. Just friends." Rose looked disappointed in the fact he'd even try.

Jesse said, "I didn't mean to get forward with you."

Rose hopped out of the car. "As someone whom I once cared for deeply, in an emotional way, I care for your wellbeing. And I hope you do find that elusive happiness one day. But, hear me when I say this: it won't be with me. I won't be the person you run to whenever things go wrong. Not anymore." Rose slammed the door.

Jesse watched her walk away up the sidewalk, trot up her steps, and walk into her front door. He waited for the porch light to go off. When the porch lights went off, when he was unable to see the mosquitoes and dragonflies swirling in front of the door, he pulled away. He made peace with the fact that this was likely the last time he'd see her again, and she would never be a part of his happy ending.

Chapter 14

The World in His Image

"Hello, Father," Cameron said.

He stood with his hat in hand in the doorway of his father's room in the mental asylum. His father was in bed—unresponsive—with his head hung slightly to the left and his eyes cracked open just enough to see his pupils. He murmured to himself with slight twitches of the lips like he was whispering secrets to the air.

Cameron turned his concerned gaze to the nurse in the room. She shook her head, subtly letting him know things were getting worse. Cameron sighed. The nurse walked off.

His father's room was tiny and only had the essentials: a bed, a mirror, a dresser, and a sink. The only sound was a leaky faucet and his father's labored breathing.

Cameron sat at the foot of the tiny bed, then pulled a wrapped sandwich from the inside of his pocket and said,

"I hope you don't mind if I eat. It's my lunch break."

His father said nothing. That silence percolated between them until it became thick and palatable but Cameron pushed through, as he always did.

"I've heard you've been getting treated well here," Cameron said. "I call from time to time and they say you really respond well when you're wheeled to the garden out back." Cameron continued with the one-sided small talk while eating. "Yea, yea, I know, it can be a bit drafty out there but I always tell the nurses to make sure they bundle you up tight."

He continued like this for several minutes, smiling and laughing, telling stories of humorous things he'd seen recently, cackling to himself with a mouth full of food and reenacting every scenario from that week. Cameron couldn't catch his breath from the laughter of telling his father about a silent film he'd recently seen. One where a man kept tumbling down the stairs over and over and over, seeming to be nowhere near the end of his descent. He brought up current affairs, all with the vigor of someone who was having an actual back-and-forth conversation. He continued to talk as if he were to stop for just a moment, the split second of silence would be a crushing reminder that his father's figurative lights were on, but no one was home.

After a while, Cameron got the wheelchair from the corner of the room, lifted his rail-thin father from the bed and into it, then wheeled him over to the mirror by the sink so he could shave his father's face. Slowly, his smile wavered; the mood he tried to force dissipated into the air like smoke from a candle's wick that had been burned away.

"Dad," Cameron said while holding up his father's chin and applying shaving cream. He took a beat or two to think of what to say and how to say it. "I... I think I might do something bad."

***

Days Ago

Cameron loved feeding the birds. Outside of visiting his father, it was the one thing in the world he enjoyed that left him guilt-free. It gave him time to think; think about his life, his relationship with God, his relationship with Rose, and his relationship with New Orleans. That day in the park was a beautiful day. Clear skies, swift breeze, and the white noise of rustling leaves underscored by the chirping of birds. It was the perfect weather for strolling the streets and seeing the good people of New Orleans. That's the one thing his father taught him years ago: "You can't lead from a distance." So, Cameron walked the streets every morning before work to see the good, hard-working people of the city.

He hummed and whistled as he waved at passersby while walking up the sidewalk. He said, "Swell morning, isn't it?" or "Grand morning, everyone!" to every single person he walked past like they were old friends. He believed good moods were contagious and tried to get as many people sick with happiness as possible.

The French Quarter was busy. People walked around

with groceries; others appeared to still be drunk from the night before. He shook his head at them. It irritated him how people seemed to be at peace with their self-destruction. No matter. People were flawed when left to their own devices and he couldn't judge someone from straying too far from God's light. He had done it more times than he'd love to admit, and there was one point—back in his past life—where he secretly imbibed from time to time. It was a brief moment, a mere drop of water in the vast ocean of his life. He was young and dumb and dealing with the stress of holding up the weight of his father's expectations. Law school was brutal, and his father was slowly slipping into a bad state, often stopping his sentences short in the middle, eyes wide with shock, and appearing as if he'd forgotten not only what he was going to say, but what room he was even in.

Sometimes the pressure of Cameron's mere existence had been enough to make him hide in the bottle. That was something no one ever knew and a shame he was forced to carry all alone, because it would look bad if people knew the city's leading teetotaler's son had been a drunk. But Cameron had worked through that affliction of his. He kept an old bottle of booze in his desk in his office at home as a reminder of that past. Every morning that he stared that bottle down and chose not to imbibe was a reminder that he did have a choice in the matter and did have control over his urges.

Cameron stopped by a street vendor who was hawking fresh produce from a crate on the corner. Mounds of apples, shiny red and green, practically spilled over the top of the crates. He bought two dozen. The vendor placed them in a sack and whistled. "Sure are rail thin for someone who eats so much."

Cameron smiled and left the man with his change and bid him a blessed day.

He made a turn down a side street but froze mid-stride. People were sleeping on the sidewalk. He couldn't believe it. Behind him, the streets were filled with people who bought in excess and purchased things because they wanted to and not because it was needed, while all a few hundred feet away were their fellow men sleeping on the ground like dogs. There were five of them lying along the sidewalk, and their belongings—or maybe it was trash—were clustered together in a heap against an abandoned storefront. Four of them were adult men of undetermined ages, but one of them was a child. A little boy sleeping in tattered clothing and on the bare concrete with no blanket.

Cameron's eyes watered a bit. His father used to sometimes say Cameron was too soft. But he wasn't soft; he was just confused and angered by the mystery known as human nature. Why is it that he was blessed with money while it seemed as though others never had a chance to begin with? How is it that the last time he walked that way, the sidewalks were bare? It was as if the city chewed up and shitted out people overnight. Those people in front of him were a byproduct of a failed system that ran on corruption and graft and people taking more than what they should just to show they could.

Cameron and his father had both tried to make a change in the city via their money, but the corrupt people running the city had just as much as them, plus the political connections to be more effective. Then Cameron tried to fix the city by getting elected to be the District Attorney. But again, if the likes of the Mayor were still at the helm and giving tacit permission to others below him to be corrupt, then what the hell was the point? This often made Cameron feel like his title as DA was meaningless. But as Mayor, if or when he won the election, that would change. Or, that's what he hoped for at least.

Cameron decided to place the apples on the ground next to each person's head, along with an info card for the Mulligan Foundation, being sure not to wake them as he walked past. He stood over the child now. His face was cherubic and smudged with what looked like dirt. Cameron tapped the child. His eyes fluttered awake, then shifted through confusion, shock, then fear.

Cameron put his hands up. "I mean you no harm."

The child didn't buy it. He scooted back into the façade of a shuttered business and was blanketed by the shadow of the awning.

Cameron approached slowly. "Would you like somewhere to sleep and something to eat?"

The child was sheepish, almost hesitant to nod, but eventually he stood and stepped forward. Cameron reached out his hand slowly. "Come on."

Cameron removed his jacket and placed it around the child's shoulders. He held his hand and walked and talked with him up the busy sidewalk. Cameron hailed a taxi and rode with the child to the Mulligan Foundation office. On the steps the child started to hand back Cameron's jacket but Cameron waved it away. He got down on one knee and smiled. "I have far too many as it is. It is yours."

The child hugged Cameron, long and tight, then entered the building where he would be given a meal and a bed and put into the foster system, where he would be eventually placed with a good Godly family. It filled Cameron with joy knowing he was able to help at least one person that day. That mood didn't last long though.

In his office in City Hall, he sat behind his desk and flipped through pages after pages of "opposition information" from his campaign advisors. He exhaled and pinched the bridge of his nose. It was dirt. Everything in the folders in front of him was notes and allegations on the ORD.

Cameron believed in the letter of the law. He was a man of strong convictions, and believed order needed to be maintained. He wouldn't use dirt or cheap tricks to win. He proved earlier that morning that good can drive out evil, light can prosper over darkness, and a man walking the path of righteousness can conquer all.

Walking the path of righteousness wasn't always easy though. Rose had him dead to rights in his foyer the other night, one hand around his neck and the other inching over his belt loop and toward his privates, and he'd wanted to seal the deal. The passion simmering between them was palpable and he wanted nothing more than to feel her skin against his. But the eyes of his dead mother's photograph trailed their movements and their every slight footstep towards the stairs. His promise of abstinence to her and God screamed in his mind. So he had turned Rose down, and he couldn't believe it.

Cameron opened his desk drawer and pulled out his Bible. He prayed to the Lord for forgiveness for his weakness and strength in the face of all challenges: the campaign, the family's foundation, and Rose.

He wanted to ask God for more, then someone knocked at his door. He yelled for them to wait, then put away the campaign dirt and his Bible. He fastened his tie and straightened his glasses. "Come in."

His aide poked her head in the door. "They're here, sir."

Cameron sighed then looked at the clock. The Governor was there. "I'll be right there. Thank you."

Cameron waited for his door to close then pulled his Bible out again. He scanned through it, reading passages on one's inner strength and what can be done when God was on your side. His finger ran under a circled verse: "I can do all things through God who strengthens me." The passage was a family credo. Cameron recited the passage over and over with his eyes pinched shut, pushing away lustful thoughts of Rose, and scornful thoughts toward the Governor.

Cameron walked into the conference room and was greeted with handshakes and smiles from his comrades in The Reform Party: a precinct chief; the local Director of the Prohibition Bureau; Cameron's campaign manager; his pick for Deputy Mayor, Andrew McCabe; and directly across from him, the Governor.

"Hello, young Mulligan," said the Governor.

The Governor had snow white hair and a slender face with a beak nose. He walked around the table and gripped Cameron's hand like a tight vice.

"Good to see you, sir," Cameron said. But it wasn't true. The Governor had called during his and Rose's alone time some nights back and had made things more awkward than they already were after he backed out on sleeping with her. He couldn't even step away for five minutes to walk Rose to the streetcar because the old man kept squawking in his damned ear.

"Now," the Governor walked back to his chair, sat, and crossed his legs. "We all ready?"

Everyone nodded.

The Governor laid out policies he believed would work best for the city of New Orleans and everyone else just nodded along, no pushback, no rebuttals, just an elephant-sized amount of ass-kissing that annoyed Cameron to no end. This "meeting" was a waste of his time. All of the Governor's "policies" were veiled laws and ordinances targeted at screwing over political opponents. Everyone in the room was treated like soldiers in a bureaucratic war none of them wanted to be a part of. But they had to listen. They had to kiss ass. He was the Governor, and he could make their lives a living hell.

"Cameron?" boomed the Governor's voice across the long table.

Cameron snapped to attention. "Yes?"

"Any developments on your end of the investigation?"

"I've tried everything. We can't scratch anything up." Cameron gave an exasperated sigh. "But sir, if I could ask a question: why would Rudy Thompson have his trucks boosted?"

The Governor drummed a pencil lightly against the desk. He stood and turned to look out the slits of the blinds in the office. He walked slowly back-and-forth in a circle, breathing deep and low. "Why does a fly land on shit? Why do dogs bark? Rudy 'boosted' his own product because he's greedy. It's in his nature." He scoffed. "They switch routes one time and all of sudden they get robbed? And now we can't find the driver? It's all too coincidental."

Cameron twisted in his chair and curled his lip without the Governor noticing. The Governor wanted to see what he wanted to see. He was still upset over the attempt to rig the Gubernatorial race and he was grasping at straws.

The Governor stared at Cameron like he was reading his mind. "Alright," the Governor said. He motioned a hand toward the Director of the Prohibition Bureau. "Show them what you got."

The Director pulled papers from his briefcase and started to read detailed briefings from field agents monitoring an associate of Rudy Thompson: a young man named Bobby. Bobby was married, poor, and had a sick child. He was with Thompson everywhere, from his office in the Financial District to his office at City Hall, all the way to the dinners at The Chateau Club.

They looked up his college transcripts, medical records, where he went to church. He had one wife with no mistresses, girlfriends, or even boyfriends. He didn't have much in the way of vices and even when he ran up his credit at the deli, he always paid them back in full. The kid was as clean as could be. However, according to what Cameron was reading, they had engaged him anyway.

They went by his home one night. The report noted that Bobby rented a shotgun home with a free dangling porch light and wood rot eating into the fiber of the exterior. The agents had approached the front door and heard muffled cries from a baby. Bobby answered and the agents had peered into his living room through the door crack over his shoulder and saw the mother and baby were on the floor crying.

They questioned Bobby for some time and he resisted. He said he didn't know anything and stonewalled every question. The whole time they talked, they noted he looked stressed and worn down. Seeing this, they reminded him that withholding info on a crime had the penalty of jail time. And jail time wouldn't be good for him or his sick kid. Bobby panicked and told them everything he knew, whether small or big or relevant to the booze or not. Package drop offs, coffee runs, driving Cameron's car around while he visited "Boys' Town." There were also random visits from a man whose name started with a J. Bobby had said he was ordered to receive a package from a man of Big Sal's—more than once—leading up to the day of the heist. He looked in the package when he wasn't supposed to and it was money. Money that went to a locker at a bank. Bobby even admitted that he knew that not everything that Rudy did was on the up-and-up.

Once the Director stopped speaking Cameron let the silence in the room bubble up as he looked around the table at the men who avoided his gaze. He saw through their loss for words as what it really was: a silent understanding. "You... you all coerced a confession out of this kid by leveraging his child? His sick child?" He shook his head. "What if his statement can't be corroborated? Will there be evidence? He may really not even know anything. You put him on the stand and he'd say anything if it meant he wouldn't go to jail."

"I know," the Governor said.

Cameron stood and shook his head. "I'm done with this. You will not make this man a part of your war with the ORD. I've said again and again I will not play petty political games and I meant it. You didn't ask yet, but I'm assuming you wanted me to call in a few favors from a judge for a warrant, right? Do you mean to mock me by even thinking I'd breach ethics like this?" The men in the room couldn't even look Cameron in the eyes. The Governor, though, did not look away. Cameron continued, "His confession was extorted out of him, and we're wasting public funds on this. As far as I'm concerned, this case is closed on the municipal level. If the feds want to reopen it, fine. But Orleans Parish will have no cooperation in it. If I see anything concerning this farce come across my desk I'll automatically do away with it and have you all brought on charges of coercion."

The others were silent and their eyes darted from Cameron to the Governor, and before the Governor could get a single word out, Cameron walked out of the room and headed back to his office to sit down and stare at his ceiling. He wasn't alone with his thoughts for too long, though. Somebody knocked at his door. Before he could ask who it was, the door opened. It was the Governor.

Cameron sighed. "What do you need, sir?"

"Just checking in, my boy," he walked around the room assessing all of the paintings on the wall and the books on the shelves. "Your head doesn't seem in the game anymore."

Cameron scoffed. "'Game'?"

The Governor raised two placating hands. "You know what I mean."

"Yea, I do. This is a game to you."

The Governor's smile barely hid his disdain for that comment. He cleared his throat. "You know," he said. "Your father's the reason the redlight district in New Orleans doesn't exist anymore. Storyville was a scourge on this city, and your father lobbied to have it eradicated. He used all of his money and power and crushed those whoremonger bastards. That's what made his name."

"Your point, sir?"

"This could be your Storyville. The one that puts you on the map."

"I don't need to be on anyone's map, sir. I just want to help the people of New Orleans."

The Governor took a seat and shrugged. "The two run

adjacent to each other."

"Sir, when you said you would endorse me and help me out with the campaign, you said you would allow me to do things one-hundred percent—not eighty-five, not ninety—but one-hundred percent my way. Are you sure you can remain impartial against a political opponent?"

The Governor scowled. "Of course I can. What do you take me for?"

Vindictive; petty; just as power hungry as the rest, Cameron wanted to say, but didn't. He kept his lips zipped and summoned every ounce of patience he could muster.

"I'm just saying," the Governor said. "You will only win if you get more aggressive." He turned slightly and jutted his thumb toward the door. "Do I need to twist the Louisiana Prohie Director's arm and get someone new down here? I heard your uncle has been doing well in—"

Cameron shot up from his chair and furrowed his brows. "I don't need any more help, sir."

The Governor's eyes widened. "My, my. The boy does have some fire in him, after all."

Cameron adjusted his tie and fidgeted with his glasses. Getting loud made Cameron uncomfortable, so he tapered his anger down to annoyance then down to something resembling regret, but he forced himself to stay steadfast, and not cave to his emotions or apologize for how he felt. "The current Director is just fine, and we've been coordinating together just fine."

"Ok," the Governor said. "I'll leave you be." Before the Governor left the room, he turned around. "Just do me one favor...."

Cameron crossed his legs. "What would that be?"

"Consider how badly you want to win. You may think this is solely about my vendetta with the ORD, which I'll admit, plays a huge factor. It's also about what's good for this city. Almost every leader in this city, to varying degrees, is in bed with the crooks. You give the citizens evidence of this, even if you only catch Rudy, you win. So, you remove me from this situation, and take it as seriously as you would if you knew I wasn't involved in any way, shape, or form."

Cameron stared silently.

"Lastly," the Governor said. "If... I mean, when you win, you'll have a friend in me, able to grant funding to whatever public works projects you have in mind: increased funding for roads, new construction, law enforcement... public psyche wards. Whatever you would love to use the state funding for is yours." The Governor walked out the room and left Cameron to stew in his contemplative silence.

Cameron went home that night and went over his options. He sat at his desk, a glass of warm milk and a scratch pad with "pros" and "cons" on it in front of him. One side had more than the other. The con side simply said "it is unethical." He threw his pen down and reached for his phone. He called the smartest person he knew: Rose. She could give him information. She would set him right on track. The operator patched him over, and her father answered. "She's somewhere else right now. Maybe one of her meetings or something." Cameron said thank you and hung up, but he knew her meetings were never on those nights.

He looked over his scratch pad again. The word "unethical" was singular next to the many reasons why he should prop this young man up as a sacrificial lamb. However, he remembered how he promised himself that he wouldn't use people. He was going to run a good, clean campaign that didn't rely on cheap tactics. Cameron sighed. He pushed the pad away and went for a walk around the city.

He went to his favorite bench, but no birds were out. He walked around the Quarter, but only the drunkards were around. A prostitute stood in the spot where the apple vendor was just earlier that day, and Cameron tried to greet people he walked past, but they practically snarled at him.

When the sun went down another side of the city he loved came out, and he never understood how to cope with that. He walked toward the slum alley, where he'd found all of those homeless people earlier, with his head low and fist stuffed in his pockets and prayed to himself that it wouldn't be worse than last time. He bent the corner onto the street. Only one person was there; a small, fragile body on the sidewalk. Cameron eased his way toward the person.

They were facedown on the concrete and their feet were bare and clothes were torn. He flipped the body over and shuddered. He stumbled backward and tripped over a crack in the ground. It was the child he'd brought to the foundation earlier that day, and he had a syringe stuck in his veins.

His eyes were wide open in horror and his face was pale

as a fresh layer of snow. Cameron hyperventilated at the sight. He shook and trembled and sobbed uncontrollably as he stumbled to his feet toward the child.

He eventually found a phone booth and called the cops. When they arrived he was in a haze; one part anger, another despair. The cops who came nodded absentmindedly as he spoke but there was something in their eyes that let him know they weren't listening. They were going through the motions. As DA, Cameron knew the crimes they were tasked with stopping: murder; prostitution; gang violence. They were stretched thin and tired and this one kid was just a drop in the bucket to them.

One of the cops took notes and others walked around the body looking for any evidence of any form. Cameron knew, though, it was all moot. One of the cops gave his theory in a nonchalant tone. The boy was likely shooting up with others, got a bad batch, then had whatever little belongings he had taken from him while he seized up. Cameron noticed that one of those belongings was likely the coat he had given him.

Cameron listened and could tell it was pointless for him to try and make those officers care more. Nobody forced that needle in the kid's arm. And even if they did, he knew this one incident would get outweighed by all of the other deaths and murders in the city. In the mind of those cops, it was just another low-life kid dead in the street from drugs.

The boy's body was eventually taken away but Cameron stared into the spot where he had found him well after he was gone, trying his best not to feel hopeless, but losing that battle as the seconds ticked on.

***

Present

Cameron stared into the mirror while his father's face was only half-shaved. He'd zoned out while telling that story. The shaving razor shook in his hand as he thought about that dead boy over and over because that was his first time seeing someone just dead in the street like a dog. He cleared his throat and pushed through, and finished shaving his father's face.

He got his father back in bed and kneeled at his side like he was about to say a prayer. He started to cry. He held his father's hands and pleaded for him to tell him what to do. He needed to know if there was such a thing as doing a bad thing for a good deed; if God could forgive him for compromising his morals; for being a hypocrite.

But there was no answer. The facade he built up—pretending like his father could hear him—wavered and shattered into pieces and made him realize how all alone he was. Cameron let his father's hands go, and his father's right arm fell to the side of the bed, limp and lifeless, fingertips just inches from the floor, swaying back-and-forth subtly like a pendulum, until it stopped altogether. He stood and walked toward the door, then stopped at the threshold to tell his father good night, despite remembering his father was just a shell where a mind once was.

He walked out of the infirmary and went to his house, then trotted up the stairs and went to his office, and dug through his drawers, and grabbed the dusty bottle of scotch he'd kept there for a long, long time. He brushed the dust aside and held the amber liquid to his eyes and swished it around as the liquid bubbled up, and thought about all of the preaching he did and how he told people that ethics mattered. He thought about how he always said he'd never play political games to win, and how he was disgusted days ago at the mere thought of using campaign dirt against his opponent. Then he thought about that little boy's body, and decided his ethics could be damned if it meant something good came from it. He'd launch a thousand flimsy witch hunts if it meant he'd take over the city and purge it of corruption for once and for all.

He opened the bottle and chugged the contents until his throat burned and his gag reflex tried to push it up, and after a while, there was no burning, or gagging, but nothing but the sweet feeling of intoxication that sated and numbed his troubled mind for a time. He drank long and hard that night, staring at the pros and cons on that notepad, then threw it in the trash, poured remaining alcohol over it, struck a match, then set it on fire and watched the tiny flames flicker and wave as black smoke slowly built up. He put it out, and when the morning came, made a few calls.

A judge he was close to who didn't ask questions granted him the warrant he needed, and he in turn granted the Prohies and local cops their permission to do what they needed to do, hoping they'd find something incriminating so that none of it was in vain. He told local authorities to prepare somewhere for Bobby and his family to hide out.

Once the calls he needed to make were done, he went to his bathroom and stared in the mirror then fell to his knees; he crawled over to the toilet as his breath began to hitch in his throat, then turned to hyperventilation, and he began to wretch up everything he had drank. He stayed there for close to an hour, praying before the porcelain god, as his body purged itself of the poison he'd consumed the night before.

Chapter 15

Pre-emptive Measures

The skies were cement-gray with thick white clouds engorged like fat ticks. An angry storm plummeted down on the Port of New Orleans and slammed the tides of the Mississippi River violently toward the pier and onto the slick banks. New Orleans Harbor Police stormed across the dock toward the offices of Bianchi-Rizzuto Imports, pushed their way into the building, and demanded every single one of the workers to put down their phones and stand where they were. Junior was in his office. He was on the phone with a chatty client when he saw through his office window the saturated black uniforms of the Harbor Police and his employees standing with their hands raised behind their desks. He sprung from his chair and tried to wrench himself from the talkative client. "Yea, yea, I'll call you back."

He stormed out his door into the main office area, where he ran into a big, burly man holding a piece of paper up for Junior to see. Junior snatched it from his hands. The paper was water-spotted in some areas but the bold letters stating **WARRANT** burst off the page. "Oh, fuck!"

He took long, powerful strides back to his office to call his dad.

But Sal was already aware.

An informant from the police force stopped by Sal's hospital bed hat-in-hand to give the news. Sal's strained breaths made his words come out in gruff, broken syllables. "How... bad is it?"

The officer stammered. Sal mustered the strength to reach out and yank the man's collar. He said in a low, raspy voice. "How bad is it?"

The cop fidgeted. "Officers from multiple precincts launched a full raid of multiple locations. The restaurants, grocery store, even known gambling dens, they all got stormed and trashed. Prohies are hitting warehouses." The cop stumbled over this next part. "Some of the workers were taken in. They were found with drugs. They're being threatened with deportation and questioned about your relationship to local politicians."

A roar like a boom of thunder rolled out of Sal's throat. Sal got dressed and left, much to the protest of the doctor, and got to a payphone in the first-floor lobby. He phoned his lawyer first. Then he phoned Hymie's bakery. "Find out who and what started this raid." He looked out through the glass panes of the phone booth, making sure no one was close. "No loose ends."

A little leg work and a few hundred bucks got Hymie what he wanted within hours. He got the names of the men who were talking to the cops and feds, three men in total. They were fresh off-the-boat immigrants who could barely speak English. The few words they knew, they used to give up whatever they could about Sal. They were in the interrogation rooms singing about whatever could get them protection.

***

Clyde was in the middle of screwing Eve when Rory busted into the dark room and doused the interlocked duo in light from the hallway. Clyde rolled over and threw the covers over himself.

Eve didn't budge. "Either get out or join in."

Clyde squinted at her.

"Clyde," Rory said with his head turned and eyes covered. "You need to come. Now." Rory began to walk away but stepped back into the threshold. "Well, not 'cum'… but yea, cum then come. Like, you know what I mean. Like—"

Clyde hummed a pillow at his head before he could finish talking.

Rory caught Clyde up to speed while they walked. Clyde stopped his stride in the middle of descending the stairs. His fingers stopped moving up his unbuttoned, long sleeve shirt. "What's that got to do with us?"

Jesse spoke from the bottom of the staircase. "Hopefully, nothing."

Rory, Twitch, Jesse, and Clyde all sat in the east parlor and spoke at a whisper so the customers moving around couldn't hear. Clyde was visibly anxious, playing with his fingers, shaking his foot, beginning to speak but saying nothing. When he found the words, he asked, "What's there to be nervous about? How can this blow back on us?"

Jesse looked at Clyde's bobbing foot. "You say that for me, or for yourself?

Clyde folded his arms.

Jesse cleared his throat. "Before I even called here, first thing I did was talk to my contacts in Jefferson. There's been no warrant request for that Parish, and Orleans has no dominion in that regard."

"Meaning?" asked Clyde.

"Meaning, even if the local police did try to pressure Jefferson Parish authorities into assisting, they wouldn't have to listen. But it doesn't matter anyway."

Clyde sat. "Why?"

"We're using Sal's warehouse, but it ain't under his name. And all the Prohies are checking the Orleans Parish warehouses under Sal's name. Whoever launched this didn't even consider checking outside of Orleans. The driver of the convoy is out the state. I don't even know where he is. There's literally nothing that can tie this back to us. We're fine."

Twitch's arms flailed out. "And Rudy?"

Jesse swatted the suggestion away. "He's too chicken shit and too afraid of Sal."

Jesse wasn't entirely sure. He was convincing himself as

much as them. But when Clyde got nervous, he overreacted. He'd waltz into Rudy's office and blast his brains out. So Jesse needed him calm. The brothers had too much product to move at once and not enough men on such short notice to do it. Plus a convoy through a small Parish like Jefferson would make too much noise. The truth of the matter was if feds did raid warehouses in Jefferson, they'd be fucked regardless, and there's nothing they could do.

Twitch scratched his chin. "So. Wh-what happens now?"

Jesse's mouth opened to speak, then his eyes ceded the floor to Clyde.

"I think we just wait," Clyde said.

Jesse asked for what. Clyde gave a knowing look to him. "For Sal to fix it. It's his problem for now. For all we know, Hymie's probably cleaning this up as we speak."

They all sat in silent agreement, and waited in the east parlor with the phone near, just in case they got a call.

The call came several hours later, from Hymie. "Get to the Warehouse District, now."

Within minutes they were on their way there. The quartet drove around the block a few times, just to make sure everything was on the up-and-up. They pulled in front of a tall, red-brick building smushed between two bigger tan buildings.

They parked and entered with Jesse leading the way. Hymie, Big Sal, Rudy, and Junior were in the center of the room surrounded by towers of stacked wooden crates and each man's face told a different story. Hymie's indifference manifested in the form of him picking food out his teeth with his nails. Junior had the usual look of constipation and overall annoyance with the world. Rudy looked like he was about to shit himself. And Sal... Sal looked determined. Like a fire in him had risen that hadn't been sparked in years.

"Fellas," Jesse said.

Clyde moved up to the side of him and Twitch and Rory flanked them. There were no formalities or handshakes. A green, lumpy tarp was in the middle of the two groups.

"I called you all here to let you know the problem has almost been handled," said Big Sal. "I'm going down to speak to the feds, say I have no connection to whatever criminals are working within my business." Sal jutted his head at Hymie. Hymie lifted up the tarp like he was a magician doing a reveal.

The smell caught everyone before the sight did. Jesse recoiled in disgust; acid settled at the back of his throat and he covered his mouth to keep it from spewing out. Sal, Junior, and Hymie covered their faces with handkerchiefs. Rudy stepped backward with body shuddering fear.

In front of them were three dead bodies with incisions across their necks and deep red stains running down the fronts of their shirts.

"These are three men who thought they would speak about me," said Big Sal.

"What did they say?" asked Jesse through his forearm.

Big Sal shrugged. "Enough."

"Nothing related to the liquor heist?" Clyde asked.

"No," Sal said. "They gave what little they had on political dealings, drugs, gambling, things of that nature. Hymie was so kind as to extract the nature of what they gave up before he sent them to their eternal paradise. Their families will be taken care of."

The thought of those men being tortured and then having to suffocate on their own blood made Jesse's stomach churn more than anything.

Sal stretched his cane across the blockade of bodies to poke Jesse in the chest. "But you. This all started from you."

"How?"

"You said this job of yours wouldn't blow back on me. You said it wouldn't cause trouble for my interests. But this all started from an investigation into your misdeeds." He turned to Rudy now. "This is your fault too." He cursed Rudy in Italian. "There's a fox in your henhouse. The name 'Bobby' mean anything to you?"

Rudy's face went pale. Jesse remembered the guy who sat behind the desk in Rudy's office. The one with tears in his eyes. A picture of his family in front of him. The guy with the sick kid.

"Bobby doesn't know anything for sure," Rudy said.

Sal shouted with his hands splayed out in front of him. "It doesn't fucking matter what you know for sure. Not to the feds. Not to the cops. Someone gave them confirmation that their theories were closer to the truth than they initially thought and that is enough for them." Sal's words forced Rudy back. "You allowed him to follow you around everywhere, including when dealing with things with me, and you didn't think the kid was perceptive? You thought he was an invalid? He told them he made a money pickup the day before the shipment went missing."

Rudy's throat bobbed up and down. "I told him not to look."

Everyone in the warehouse sighed.

"He's got to go," Sal said.

Jesse shook his head. "He has a kid—a sick kid—and a wife."

Sal nodded his head. "She can go too." Sal stepped toward Jesse. "And the baby can go on side the road. Or in front of the fire department. I don't care really."

Sal ambled around the carcasses, slow and careful, with his eyes on Jesse. He spoke softly, placing a gentle hand on Jesse's shoulder. "You're going to do it."

Jesse's eyes darted around the room. He calculated if he could get off enough rounds to shoot every fucking body in the room with the exception of his crew. He could shoot Big Sal in the chest, then aim for Hymie, then Junior, then Rudy last. Those monsters could all fucking rot for what they were allowing Sal to consider. But his rage subsided. It wouldn't work. Not like this.

"I've never killed anybody before," said Jesse.

Sal placed a hand on the side of Jesse's face. "You've broken my heart many times, my son. But I'm giving you the chance to piece it back together. This started with you, and it ends with you."

Jesse nodded. "I understand."

Sal smoothed out the sleeves of his coat. "Good. Stay by

your phone."

What Jesse understood, what was hidden under the carefully placed words, was Sal saying he didn't have a choice. Either do this, or Bobby dies anyway and you get buried next to him. Sal always pulled on people's emotional strings to get them to do what he wanted. Jesse had seen it a million times. And this was the first time it happened to him.

They wrapped up their conversation. Hymie threw the tarp back on the bodies and initiated the process of dragging them and stuffing them into nearby empty crates. Sal hobbled over and said one last time to Jesse, "It ends with you." He left Jesse and his group there.

The storm outside of the warehouse tossed swirling gusts of wind against the front of the building, causing the doors to tremble and the rolling gates to shake. Jesse was standing still like a statue.

Clyde walked up to him. "I can do it."

"No, I got it. You and Rory just wait at the brothel until it's done."

Jesse pointed at Twitch. "But you'll come with me." Twitch agreed. They left Hymie to his work of making the bodies fall off the face of the earth.

Jesse sat in the backseat of the car and moved around the imaginary chess pieces. This mission wasn't just to get rid of a witness. No, he could have sent Hymie or any of the street thugs who are indebted to him to do it. He sent Jesse because Jesse rejected his offer to serve at Junior's side. Jesse was close to breaking away from the grips of Sal's manipulation and power, and this was Sal's way of sucking him back in—this was his way of saying *I fucking own you,* except he said it with a pat on the cheek and a stray tear on his eyelids.

Rose was right to reject Jesse's attempt to come back into her life. He was toxic to anything he touched. Just like Rose told him the other day: he didn't have to say yes to his brothers. That same logic extended to Big Sal. Jesse would've probably died, but at least he wouldn't have to live feeling like a monster. The car sped back to the brothel, but Jesse asked to get dropped off at his condo instead. He needed his time to reflect. Because before the end of tomorrow, he would have the blood of two lives on his hands, and he would orphan a child, and his soul would forever be owned by Sal Bianchi.

Chapter 16

Hush, Little Baby

"We need to get our things and leave now," Bobby said to his wife as they crisscrossed one another to throw their shoes, undergarments, and essentials into one suitcase.

She begged and cried for him to explain what was wrong but all he did was repeat "I messed up, I messed up, I really, really messed up," which prompted his wife to stop and ask him, again, to please tell her what he did.

"I'll explain once we're out of here," he said over his shoulder while he leaned down to get his savings from the dresser. He stuck his hand blindly under the dresser and retrieved a sock full of change and a few dollar bills. He turned and tossed the balled-up sock into the suitcase.

His wife moved frantically, on the verge of tears and confusion, then he grabbed her arms, held her wrists. "Look, we're going to be ok, ok? I'm going to get us out of here, then I'll tell you everything." He smiled to reassure her. She wasn't appeased. Then the baby cried.

He turned to go check on the baby, but she beat him to it. He continued to search their room for more loose change while she walked up the hallway humming a lullaby.

Hush little baby, don't say a word.

At the end of Bobby's search, all the money he and his family had in the world could fit into the palm of his hand and this made him feel small. Weak. Less than a man. He wouldn't even be able to get more than one train ticket. He did the right thing though, right? The lawmen made it sound like he would go to jail for a long time, and he couldn't afford that to happen. Not right now. Not with his baby so sick. But he couldn't trust the law to protect him, either. No telling who in the city would tell Rudy what he'd done. He wished he would've considered all of that before snitching.

Bobby stopped his ruminating for a second and noticed how quiet it was. All he could hear were the creaks and thumps of the house settling. Bobby called for his wife but she didn't respond. He slammed their dresser drawer shut; this was not the time for her to ignore him. He picked up the stuffed suitcase and carried it toward the living room but stopped once noticing his baby's window was open.

He heard someone humming. It was lower, deeper. He called his wife's name again while fiddling with the suitcase's zipper. He inched toward the baby's room; the sound of rain pitter-pattering against the ground outside grew closer as he went up the hall. The window curtains waved up and down from the whistling wind rushing through the opening. He stepped in the threshold and called his wife's name. His suitcase fell from his hand and all of his clothes tumbled to the floor.

The rocking chair in the corner whined as a masked man held his child and swayed back and forth, back and forth, humming the lullaby. Another masked man had his hand over his wife's mouth with a gun to her head. The masked man holding his baby spoke in short, awkward phrases. "The window. Shut it."

Bobby moved like he was on a field of landmines. The man with a gun on his wife spoke next. "All five of us are going to go to the car out back. We need to have a little discussion.

Chapter 17

Freedom

Bobby couldn't see. His eyes were open but restricted by a thick blindfold wrapped tightly around his head. He tried to scream, but his tongue was suppressed by something woolen and thick straining his jaw's hinges to their ends. Time and space eroded; he knew they had driven for a while, but he didn't know how long or how far. He only knew that his body was tossed and turned at every hop and skip of the car's tires over uneven roads, then not long afterwards, he was dragged kicking and groaning into a building then bound to a chair, left listening to the creaks and groans of whatever structure they'd brought him into.

Now, he sensed someone lurking on the other side of the black wall created by his blindfold; they orbited him, sized him up like a shark circling a tiny boat. And in all of this, Bobby wanted to tell his wife he loved her one last time. If she was even alive anymore.

The black wall came down, and in front of him was one of the masked men. He sat cross-legged with his gun held across his knee. His eyes were hard, almost monster-like, through the holes cut in his sack-mask, and his aura oozed of unrestrained menace.

"Are you going to scream?" the man asked.

Bobby whimpered and rocked back-and-forth in his chair. He couldn't see his wife or his baby. All he saw was boxes, like they were in a warehouse. The lighting was dim, the towers of boxes casting demonic shadows all over the floor. The masked man uncrossed his legs and pointed over Bobby's shoulder. Bobby's chair was twisted around by the other man to show him his wife and baby were fine. The child was quiet, nestled gently in a basket, and his wife was bound and gagged and couldn't make a sound. Her eyes, though, said everything. Bobby whimpered his apologies into the void of the sock-gag but was turned back toward the other man.

"Don't scream," the man behind him said. He spoke infantile, like every syllable was a leap of faith. Bobby nodded. The infantile one walked into view and loomed over Bobby while he stuffed his hand in his mouth and wrenched out the gag. Then he walked out of focus.

"What did you want to be when you were growing up?" asked the man sitting in front of Bobby.

Bobby stayed silent. The man screamed and repeated his question, making Bobby jerk backward and his wife groan through the mouth-gag. Bobby spoke in a shaky voice. "A... cop. I wanted to be a cop."

The man slouched, like he was relaxed now, like he was having a drink with an old buddy. "Hm. A cop."

His partner moved back into frame with a bag. He dropped it to the floor and it made a metal-on-metal clattering sound. He kneeled over it and took out a bone saw. It glinted against the sparse light. Bobby shuddered.

The masked man sitting in front of him laced his fingers over his head. "Me? I wanted to be a gangster."

His partner pulled a hammer out of his bag next, sized it up, then shook his head subtly when he didn't like it. He pulled out a much larger one instead. He placed it neatly next to the bone saw.

Bobby sobbed. "Please, let us go."

But the man continued with a tone of nostalgia. "Who wouldn't want to be? I mean, growing up I seen these guys with flashy clothes, absolutely gorgeous wives, and cars imported from overseas. The world was a fucking platter, and they feasted on it. Me on the other hand, I had one pair of undergarments, and tattered socks that I would sometimes have to turn inside out when one side got too dirty. So," he spread his hands out. "There it is. It all started because I just simply wanted some un-tattered socks." He paused for a moment and stood. "Cops around here get paid nickels to fight a losing war just to end up like the people they hate so fucking much. Eh, oh well. But hey, I guess in a sense, me and you would've ended up on opposite teams anyway."

His partner laid out all his tools next to each other like

an artist lining up his brushes in preparation for his masterpiece. Bobby began to plead for his life, his wife's life, his baby's life. The masked man in front of him shook his head.

"But please..." Bobby said in a strained tone. Then he screamed for help. He put up a wall of aggression to show these bastards he wasn't afraid, but it quickly crumbled when the infantile man walked over and slapped Bobby across the face hard enough to knock him over. Then he was hoisted back upright.

The masked man with the gun forced his hand into Bobby's mouth and gagged him again. He pressed the gun barrel to the front of Bobby's head. Bobby groveled and rocked back and forth. It was no use. His wife and baby both began to cry behind him. *No, no, no,* he thought to himself. *Not like this. Please.*

The man cocked the hammer on the gun. "I'm sorry, Bobby."

Bobby stopped shaking, closed his eyes, then focused on the happiest moment of his life. The black behind his eyelids became a white room.

Oh, my God, it's a girl!

Then everything went black.

***

The stars and moon were swallowed whole by a whale of a storm, thunder crackling across the great ashen expanse of clouds like a shot from a cannon, purple lightning strikes giving a brief refuge from the abysmal raining dark blotting out the bright spectrum of colors making up New Orleans.

The rain hammered down. And Jesse's body felt heavy. He wasn't sure if it was because his coat took on water from the storm, or just the general weight of the blood that was spilled since the beginning of this ordeal. Either way, he was heavy. His body felt like an empty husk that he had no control over.

The meeting back at Sal's warehouse was a blur. The conversation was one-sided; answers came from Jesse's mouth but his mind was locked away in a state of shock. Sal, Rudy, Clyde, and Twitch stood around him.

Sal asked, "Was it done? Did you do it?"

Jesse's head moved up and down slowly without his prompting. The others talked, but he said nothing. Sal and Rudy were happy though. Sal and Rudy talked about the kid being offed like it was an inconvenience. Like this 21-year-old was a fucked-up meal at a restaurant that had to be returned.

Rudy wiped the sweat off his smug face and said, "I guess that's done with."

Jesse stared at the ground. There were black dots on the pavement, right by Clyde's foot. He figured it was just the blood from the three bodies earlier. Before Clyde turned to leave, he placed a hand on Jesse's shoulder. "It had to be done."

Clyde, Twitch, and Rudy left.

Sal spoke softly. "I knew you didn't go soft on me."

Jesse had no reply.

Jesse rushed home in the blinding rain, showered off his sweat and filth, all the murder and death, then sped down out of the heart of the city to the residential neighborhoods. He wasn't sure where he was going; he allowed the pure adrenaline to carry him like a decrepit ship guided to shore.

There was a feral part of his self-consciousness that wanted to protect him, to take him where he needed to go. Somewhere he'd be safest. His car jerked to a stop in front of a home. The rain was coming down still. He couldn't feel the beads. He was numb. He ran out of his car, trotted up the steps of the porch, then banged on the door until someone, anyone, answered. The door swung open and the person behind it gave a questioning look. "Jesse, what is this?"

It was Rose.

He didn't even realize he was there until he was looking at her. But she was what he needed. Jesse was pale, wet, and shaking. "Are your parents here?"

Rose shook her head. "No. Wednesday night Mass."

He could tell she could see something sad in his eyes. He stepped through the threshold, placed his hands around her head, and kissed her. She feigned reluctance, then allowed their bodies to fall into place like tumblers in a lock, then into her room, where they stripped each other bare and she looked deep into his soul, his eyes covered by damp pieces of hair. They fell into her bed and their hands were still familiar with every contour of each other's body. And in moments, he was washed clean of all the dirt from the day, his soul was replenished.

Bobby and his family were on Jesse's mind still, in particular, the fear in Bobby's eyes when Jesse had squeezed the trigger, over. And over. And over, but there was no bang. There was no death. Just a young man in front of him with piss stains on his trousers and shock in his eyes.

Jesse had kept pressing the trigger. Bobby shook like a hit dog every time he heard the clicking noise, then realized the gun was never loaded. Bobby had rocked back-and-forth in a state of shock. Jesse crouched in front of him. Bobby smelled of urine and sweat.

"That's how easy it is. That's what it feels like to be powerless. Just like that." Jesse snapped his fingers. "I could've ended your entire existence."

Twitch cut the ropes from around his wrists and placed a bag of clothes at Bobby's feet, along with a rubber-banded stack of money to go anywhere they wanted.

"Go be a cop. Or whatever you want to be," Jesse had said. "Just not here. Please. Don't make me beg you."

Bobby rapidly nodded his head and grabbed his family then ran to a car Jesse had waiting for them, where Davy was given instructions and cash to drive them to the train station. Twitch was originally worried their plan to scare Bobby wouldn't work. The piss stains on the warehouse floor had told Jesse otherwise.

Jesse peeled his mask off and put his finger in Twitch's face. "Remember, this stays between us. Just me and you. You owe me after stunt you and Clyde pulled with the Greek." Jesse gritted his teeth. "Don't ever go against me again."

Twitch nodded.

As Jesse lay in Rose's embrace, he knew the ghosts of his

past would haunt his sleeping conscience still. They would try to taunt him, drive him mad with images of all his wrongdoing. But Bobby and his family wouldn't be a part of that movie. For once he had chosen the right thing, even when it was the hard thing. For once, people weren't a means to an end. Freeing Bobby freed Jesse's soul, and now it was his to keep. It wasn't for New Orleans, a vortex that sucked everyone under. Or for his past life of crime, where few people ever successfully moved on to legit means. And certainly, it wasn't for Sal, who thought he could manipulate Jesse like a puppet. Tonight Jesse cut the strings. Tonight, Jesse reclaimed his soul. So when he would sleep later, he would close his eyes peacefully, finally knowing the answer to the question of what truly made him happy; he would sleep well knowing he now had his freedom, and he was not capable of being a monster.

PART II

"No good deed goes unpunished"- Clare Boothe Luce

Chapter 18

Vacation

Jesse and Rose cuddled up under satin sheets and watched the fan spin into a blurred circle. They said nothing to each other. They were worn out from lovemaking, which started when Rose walked through the penthouse doorway, then transitioned to against the wall, and ended with them on top of each other in the bed. So the silence was fine.

Rose was still trying to catch her breath. Jesse liked to listen to her steady breaths while her head rested against his chest. It was funny to him what one grew to miss after they lost someone they loved; he missed the days where they'd curl up on his tiny dorm room bed and talk about their dreams and hopes. Her breathing was always so calming. He missed four years of that. Now he held her tightly to his side, despite the vast amount of bed on either side of them, like her presence could evaporate in between his fingers and billow out like smoke.

She broke the silence first. "Is this wrong?"

"Is what?"

She propped herself up. "Us, Jesse."

It had been a couple weeks since they'd started their illicit affair, and he was surprised it didn't come up sooner. They'd been sneaking around, meeting each other in places where no one would notice them, holding hands then letting go when they thought they saw someone they knew.

Jesse turned to look her square in the eye. He rubbed her cheek. He told her no, it wasn't wrong, because they'd loved each other first. Cameron was just a minor inconvenience, in his mind.

Rose stared off into space. She clutched the blanket around her top like she thought it could hide her shame. "I'll have to end it with him soon."

"You need to do what's best for you."

"I know. It's just—it's complicated."

Jesse ambled across the room to the minibar to pour a glass of water. He spoke over his shoulder. "You can wait until after the election is done to decide. I don't want you to hurt him during an already trying time."

Rose smirked. "You're assuming I'm choosing you. Quite confident."

Jesse turned back to Rose, who was still clutching the covers. She asked, "You don't have anyone you're hurting in this?"

Jesse thought of the dodged calls and cold shoulders towards Cindy, and instead of answering Rose's question, he climbed under the covers with her and they had sex again. After another thirty minutes went by and another brief silence, Rose asked, "When are you going to take me out on a real date?"

Jesse was befuddled.

"It's just that," Rose gathered her thoughts. "The sneaking around, the meeting in hotels, it feels dirty. I feel dirty."

Jesse rolled to his side to look at her. "You know that's not possible. Not right now."

Rose gave a faint smile. "I know."

Moments went by and they decided it was time to leave. Jesse allowed Rose to get dressed first while he sat in bed and smoked a cigarette. The ambient light beamed through the room window. She planted a kiss on him then walked out the door and made her way back into someone else's arms.

***

The headline "DA Mulligan Drops the Ball" was all any citizen could read that morning on the front of about every paper in the city. The story was about how Cameron Mulligan led a raid on the word of an improperly vetted source (left anonymous), causing the arrest of many of the workers in the Bianchi-Rizzuto company employ, and disrupting Mr. Bianchi's businesses.

Mr. Bianchi gave a quote: "It's a shame that a man of my stature, a hardworking, honest businessman who came from nothing, has to be targeted and harassed by the city's judicial system like this. I've been followed, falsely accused, and disrespected throughout this entire process." The betrayal Sal referred to was about the three "criminals" he wasn't aware he had working in his organization. The papers said the three men were on the run. Jesse knew they were in barrels at the bottom of the river, probably gator food at this point.

Cameron ended up having to apologize for what he did, which for Jesse, was pure comedy. The poor bastard was so close, but so outmatched. He underestimated the lengths Sal would go to in order to save his own ass. But, that was none of Jesse's concern anymore.

He sat in The Chateau Club awaiting the company of Mel and his three cohorts, Albert, Bill, and Kenneth, as waiters floated by with drinks, food, napkins, and cigars on their trays. Jesse waved them off each time they roamed over, but made sure to leave a hefty tip nonetheless; he could afford it. The past few weeks for Jesse had been the freest he'd ever felt. He had money rolling in from the liquor business, and the first thing he did, after stuffing some cash away in his drawer and putting some in the restaurant, was buy himself a month-long membership to The Chateau Club. Not killing Bobby freed Jesse in ways he didn't know existed. He was now able to explore the noncriminal side of himself, now that he knew that side existed.

Jesse stopped daydreaming when Mel and the spoiled-brats-three walked up. "Hey there, Mel."

Mel said, "Hey there, old sport!"

Albert, Bill, and Kenneth slid in the booth and

immediately put their hands up to order a drink from a server. Albert made a disgusted face and picked Jesse's paper up like it was a stinky fish. "You read this left-wing vitriol?" He flung it back on the table.

Jesse laughed. After a time hanging around Mel's friends, Jesse figured out that's how the young, rich, and spoiled joked: by making fun of anything contrary to their beliefs. "Yea. I like to stay well-rounded."

Kenneth wiggled his two fingers to summon the waiter and ordered a round of drinks for everyone. "Well," Kenneth patted Jesse's stomach. "Keep coming here as much as the doorman says you have; you'll certainly get well-rounded."

Laughter roared from the table. Jesse even found it hilarious. The lunchtime gathering went on and soon everyone was entirely buzzed and ready to move on to the next place. Except for Jesse. He needed to get to the restaurant.

Bill shook his head at Jesse. "You work way too hard."

Jesse smirked. "Someone has to."

Mel mockingly clutched non-existent pearls. "How dare you!"

"But no," Albert said. "You really need to take a day off. How about this?" He paused to down the remainder of his drink. "The Police Ball is coming up. How about you come?"

Jesse, caught off guard, said, "I'd love to."

"And bring whatever girl you're seeing," Albert winked.

Albert put his hands up to summon over the waiter, whose back was turned, dealing with another table. He let out an exasperated sigh and waved his hand. The waiter turned around, flashed a smile, and put up a finger to let him know he'll be a moment. Albert shook his head. "These fucking smokes working here are lazy." An alcohol-induced fit of hiccups struck him. "I oughta talk to my dad about this."

Mel snickered. "About what? He's busy."

"He can move faster."

Everyone at the table ignored Albert's tirade.

The waiter scampered over with a tray under his arms and a smile on his face. "Yea, sir?"

Albert leaned in close with a shaky, drunken finger wag. "When I call you, boy, you fucking run. You hear?"

The waiter's smile dropped. "Yes. I understand."

Albert sneered. "Good. Now I need to close the tab."

The waiter ran off with a spring in his step.

"See? Now he's getting it!" He patted Jesse on the arm while laughing maniacally to himself, which forced others to laugh.

"Eh, the man was busy, no need to talk to him like that," Jesse said through a forced chuckle.

"It's just a joke." Albert continued to grin. "But no, really, sometimes you got to put people in their place. You remember hearing about that, uh, what was it." Albert snapped his fingers. "That lynching in Thibodaux? Terrible, right? But it's a needed evil." He sat back like he made a good point. "They ain't had trouble out of those niggers since!" He received indifferent smirks from the others but a glare from Jesse.

"So, you saying a whole bunch of coloreds got to get strung up and killed to make a point?" Jesse said as calm and coolly as he could.

Albert raised an eyebrow. "Ay, I said it was terrible."

Jesse glared over at Albert long and hard.

Mel cleared his throat and touched Jesse's shoulder. "You got to excuse him; he went see Birth of a Nation one too many times."

The table erupted again, except for Albert, who pantomimed laughter and picked up the paper Jesse was reading earlier. "Laugh all you want, but half the fucking people in this room are Klan sympathizers." He pointed at Cameron's name on the newspaper. "Including this one's uncle." The political rumor mill had taught Jesse one thing over the past few weeks: the rich and powerful gab about one another more than broads do.

After a while, Jesse's blood cooled and he found Albert tolerable once more, then eventually, the men wrapped up their conversation and got up from the table to head to their next destination. Jesse followed behind them in the parking lot as they talked about real estate. One of the men talked about Grand Isle being a hidden gold mine, to which Mel replied, drunkenly stumbling over his words, that the place was a ghost town. Jesse stopped in his tracks. He had an idea.

***

"Where are we going?" asked Rose as Jesse led them outside of Orleans Parish limits. They drove down a road that cut through miles of overhanging Cypress trees with wispy moss hanging from the branches. Jesse said nothing, only giving her a knowing look and mischievous smile every few seconds just to screw with her. Twenty minutes went by and eventually the woods to the left and right of them disappeared and made way for the wide expanse of the coastline to come into view. The water was still, shiny, and unmoving, looking like a pristine sheet of silver.

She was bewildered. "The beach? In the fall?"

Jesse pulled the car to a stop by the high grass on side of the road. "Grand Isle is beautiful this time of year. What can I say?"

Homes hoisted up by wooden pylons were up the road from where they parked. To the right was the open sea and the shore with green grass sprouting up through the sand, seagulls and pelicans flying about picking at discarded items left behind by recent visitors.

Rose's mouth hung open. "But it's cold!"

Jesse nodded. Then he removed a blanket from his backseat to reveal a basket underneath. She blushed.

"Yea." He animatedly turned from left to right. "At least no one is out here but us."

They ate and relaxed on the blanket, the wind kicking up sand every now and then and temporarily blinding them, but they were still comfortable, still at peace knowing no one would interrupt them. The conversation was absent of talk about politics, business, or other relationships. Their time together was loose and fun, something neither one of them experienced in a long time. Eventually, they walked along the shore and held hands, something they would never have been able to do in New Orleans.

"Isn't the sight beautiful?" she asked.

"Not any more beautiful than you."

"You ever wondered what would have happened, if we had stayed together?" Rose asked.

Jesse moved his head around like he had to think about it for a moment, but really, he had played that scenario in his mind hundreds of times: they'd be somewhere far away from New Orleans, somewhere with pastures maybe and a barn house and a patio with rocking chairs where they could watch their kids, one boy and one girl, run across the field chasing each other. They would grow old and gray together, and Jesse would probably die first—he lived a harder and rougher life—but on his deathbed, he'd have no regrets, none at all, because he'd spent the best years of his life with the beautiful girl with bouncy hair who he met after church all those decades ago. In that hypothetical moment, he'd look up at her, take her hand, kiss it, and die happy knowing he was loved by the most amazing woman in the world. But Jesse didn't say any of that, or any of the stories he'd written in his mind.

He instead said, "We don't have to wonder. We're together now."

They stopped walking and faced each other; the wind blew the hair into her face and made Jesse squint. They kissed long and hard. They untangled their fingers. Rose's arms fell to the side as she looked around to the ocean. "Can you do it?"

Jesse raised an eyebrow. "Do what?"

"Be in New Orleans and be a different person."

"Yes," Jesse said, then he said, "I mean, I think I can. I have already." Jesse said that in a way that made it seem as though he wanted to convince himself.

He'd spent the past week with a gun under his bed, thinking one day Sal would find out about his lie and send Hymie for him. Clyde also didn't know. If he did, Bobby and his wife would be as good as dead. Only other person who knew the truth was Twitch. But after conspiring with Clyde behind Jesse's back to kill the Greek, he would never betray Jesse again. For now, Jesse's secret was safe. But it was the "for now" part that made him sleep with a gun under his pillow.

"What if we left New Orleans?" Jesse asked. Rose chuckled but he grabbed her and held her firmly. "But seriously. We could be like this all of the time." Jesse turned her toward the ocean. The sky was icy grey and the wind tumbled from over the ocean. "We could move down here to Grand Isle." He kissed her cheek. "And hide away from everyone." He kissed her hand. "What do you think?"

"Jesse..." her words trailed off with the wind.

"I understand," Jesse said. He couldn't even be honest with himself about whether he could live in the city and not be a part of it. And he couldn't expect her to up and leave everyone behind.

Jesse rubbed the back of his head. "Let's head back. Yea?"
Rose nodded. "Yes."

They drove back up the path with their hands wrapped in one another's. She leaned her head on his shoulder. He rested his head on top of hers, keeping one hand steady on the wheel. As soon as they crossed the "New Orleans" sign on the side of the road, the emotion in the car dissipated. Their hands and bodies unlatched from each other, and he dropped her off down the street from her parents' home. There wasn't much of a goodbye; they were back in town and they had to assume their public roles again. He stayed parked at the corner while he watched her walk past several houses then turn up the steps of hers.

Jesse dropped his car off in front of the condo on Canal and decided he'd walk to the restaurant. He needed time to think about their conversation. Could he up and move? Would he? He wasn't sure. The restaurant was almost done. And Rose had her local women's movement going. But she could do that shit anywhere, he figured.

The streets weren't busy, not much noise from cafes or shops either along his walk. He'd been zoned out, but after a few blocks, he noticed he was being followed. Or maybe he was being paranoid. He heard a car moving behind him slowly, and every time he turned around, it got marginally closer. Two men were in the vehicle. He tensed up. He saw the cross-section of the street coming up. He figured he would have to take a dash to the right once it came. He instinctively felt for the gun typically tucked in his waistband, but it was missing. He looked over his shoulder again, and the car was closer. He bent the corner in a dash. He ducked off the main street and onto a narrow, cobblestone road and the car sped up behind him.

He pumped his arms as he ran when another vehicle turned the corner and came down the street toward him. It screeched to a stop and turned sideways onto the sidewalk to block his stride. He dug his heel into the ground and turned to sprint but the other car blocked his path. He was sandwiched in. A window rolled down. "Get in."

Jesse panted. "No."

Then a man from the vehicle behind him put a gun to his back. "You should listen to him."

Jesse raised his hands and entered the backseat of the car where he was sandwiched between the gunman and another man, who grinned, with a head full of red hair and his teeth yellowed from cigarette smoke.

"Sorry to meet you this way, Mr. Pike," the devilish grinning man said. He also had a slight Irish accent. "But you're a hard man to reach."

Jesse said, "Fuck you."

He felt the barrel opposite him get pressed into his ribs. The grinning man shooed away the gun.

"Now, now, no need for mean words." He reached out his hand. "How do you do, Mr. Pike? My name is Joe. And I really need to talk to you."

Chapter 19

Sinn Fein

The car Jesse was taken in pulled to a jerking stop in front of a rundown bar in the Irish Channel which wasn't too far from the Mississippi River. The air around the port always had the scent of salt water, and the scent meshed with the smell of cigarette smoke that clung to the coats of the men who'd taken him. The man who held a gun on Jesse hopped out and held the car door open for him. Jesse watched the second car pull behind them and out hopped four men of varying sizes and ages with hardened battle-worn looks on their faces.

Joe put a hand on Jesse's back. "Come now, Mr. Pike. This is my humble abode." He ushered Jesse over to a cluster of tables in the middle of the room and waved away a group of boys that Jesse figured couldn't be older than sixteen. The boys' conversation halted and they scattered without a word from the seats Joe claimed for himself. "Take a seat, Mr. Pike."

Joe had this air about him, this slimy confidence Jesse could tell hid something sinister and evil. Even when he asked those young boys to move away with a smile on his face, it seemed as though the smile was more like a warning.

"May I ask what you kidnapped me for?" Jesse asked.

Jesse was flanked by two men who sat at nearby tables. They seemed disinterested, casual, but every time Jesse shot a glance to the door, he saw one of the men lean on the edges of their seats, ready to spring at him like a lion on a gazelle. He decided against running. If they wanted him dead, they would've shot him already and dropped him in a ditch.

Joe sat across from him. "I've been telling your brother for some time I wanted to meet you."

This is the Irishman, Jesse realized. The guy Clyde buddied up with in prison. "Is that so?"

Joe laced his fingers and nodded.

"What's so special about me?"

"Your contacts."

"My what?"

"Your contacts, Mr. Pike. Or can I just call you Jesse?"

Jesse shook his head. "Mr. Pike is just fine."

Joe shrugged. "You have some very powerful friends."

"Maybe you should've kidnapped them."

Joe slapped the table and laughed maniacally. All the chatter in the room stopped while he let out what was quite possibly the most frightening laugh Jesse had ever heard.

"This isn't a kidnapping, Mr. Pike. Your brother didn't want to pass my messages along to you, so I figured this was a good way to get ahold of you. Being that you're officially not running the brothel anymore." Joe shifted in his chair. "Here's the thing. I have a cause, a purpose."

"Oh, yea," Jesse leaned forward to meet Joe's gaze. "What's that?"

Joe swept his right hand across the air like he was unveiling a marquee. "Freedom."

"Freedom for what?"

One of the voices to the side of Jesse interjected, "Northern Ireland."

Jesse perked up in his chair. "You folks are IRA."

Joe grinned. "You say that with such disdain."

It wasn't disdain; it was shock. He'd read about the Easter Rising four years back, the Irish Nationalist war against the British. The bombings, executions, and murders. He never thought he'd be staring a product of that war right in the face.

Jesse cleared his throat. "Wars take money, money buys guns, and guns win wars. You think you can pull on the heartstrings of some locals, maybe pull the 'Irish blood' card, but you don't have the...," Jesse paused and looked the men up and down, looking at their unkempt clothes. "You don't have the ability to enter into the rooms I can."

Joe's grin turned into a big smile. "See, always knew he was the smart one."

"Well," Jesse said. "I don't get involved in international politics. Can't help you with anything."

Joe's eyes twitched slightly. "Mr. Pike, let me explain to you the phases one goes through when under a regime's boot."

Jesse paid attention.

Joe leaned forward. "So, one day, when you and your people are minding your own business, some people come and say, 'Hey, savages! What's yours is mine, and what's mine is mine.' And you go, 'well, that isn't fair.' And that's the worst thing you can say because now they have to show you the error in that logic. They do something so ghastly to you and your people that for generations you start to think, 'Aye, well maybe mine is theirs. But maybe I should ask for more of it.' So you do, you go to them hat in hand, and your oppressor... they laugh. Then they beat you like a dog for having the audacity."

Jesse shifted in his chair.

Joe picked up a shot glass from the table next to them and squeezed it. "Then you go back and beg, Jesse. Beg. On hands and knees for these foreign gods to take mercy on your weak 'savage' soul. You say, 'Sir, I have no food, no land. Please at least split what you took from me. I'll do anything.' Then you do anything, and maybe even your wife does anything, yet you somehow end up with less than you had before."

Joe's breath started to hitch as his grip around the glass seemed to grow tighter and his eyes grew harder and emptier. "So—so, you go back with picket signs, no longer begging for food, but for them to at least see you as human, and this time, this scares them," Joe stood. "So they beat you down worse than ever before, leaving you and your comrades' corpses right on the ground—right there in the dirt; in the fucking dirt—as a reminder to others that if they ever fucking ask again for the things they took from you then you'll end up just like them." His breathing quickened from barely subdued rage. "They say to you that you are nothing and will have nothing; they own you; your crops; your home; your women; they own your fucking soul and you just can't fucking take it anymore," Joe slammed his fist to the table, and caused the glass to shatter and his hand to bleed.

Jesse and everyone in the bar sat in stunned silenced.

Joe sat and took several deep breaths, in and out, in and out, until he was calm. He took a dirty rag off of a nearby chair and wrapped it around his hand. "But next time when you go back, empty stomach, head wet because you have no roof, you use your last remaining strength to raise a gun and tell them 'You will fucking give us what we need.' And you show them that maybe, just maybe, they were right to call you a savage."

Jesse said nothing as Joe and he locked eyes.

"So, Mr. Pike. When you equate my plight to 'international politics,' I quite take issue with that." Joe exhaled. Within seconds, he was back to grinning, and he drummed his fingers on the table playfully. "Now! Where were we?"

Joe got up and waved Jesse over to follow him. Jesse didn't think he had a choice in the matter. They walked down to a back room, which led to another door, which was thick and heavy like it was meant to protect a castle. It opened slowly. Two men cleaned guns and listened to music from the gramophone. Joe spoke so quickly in his natural accent Jesse couldn't follow the order he gave them. But they stood and slid out thick wooden boxes onto the floor. They cracked them open.

"Dear God," Jesse said. Thompson machine guns lay in the boxes, barely covered by hay, and surrounded by grenades the size of ornaments alongside it. They pulled out another box. It was filled to the brim with pure brown heroin. These guys weren't average street thugs—street thugs' only motivation was money—but something much worse. They were soldiers fueled by idealism. Jesse's mouth turned desert dry. "What are you showing me this for?"

Joe wrapped an arm around his shoulders. "To show you I'm a good person to have on your side. You do me a favor, introduce me to some of your friends, preferably ones who would be sympathizers to the cause, and you'll have me in your corner."

They walked back to the main bar area. Joe leaned against the bar and held out his arms. "So, what do you think?"

Jesse swallowed. "No. I can't do anything for you."

In that moment, Jesse saw the real face of Joe. It was a microsecond, but he saw it: his grin flickered away and his eyes grew heavy and dark, his worser nature coming to the forefront slowly like headlights through the fog. He recovered quickly though and slipped back on his perky face. "It's just a 'no' for now." He reached for a handshake.

Jesse sized it up. Then he shook it. "It's a no."

Joe tightened his grip. "Oh, I'm very persistent."

"I'll bet you are, Mr...?"

"Joe is all you need to know me by. Would you need a ride back to your place?"

Jesse assessed Joe and noticed a tinge of eagerness underscoring the question. Joe didn't know where he lived. They must've just been waiting near the restaurant and didn't actually follow him from his place. "No. I'll make it back myself."

Jesse walked away feeling Joe's beady eyes burning a hole in his back the whole way to the door. He was up the street and around the corner and still felt those damn eyes on him like he was being watched from the shadows.

Jesse walked in his condo and strode to the phone to call the front desk. He urged the doorman to let him know if anyone, and he meant anyone, came around looking for him. Jesse slammed the phone down, then pulled his gun from under his pillow. He poured himself a drink and sat at the edge of his bed for the rest of the night, a gun gripped tight in his left hand, a glass of bourbon in his right, the amber liquid swooshing around as his hand trembled.

Chapter 20

Healing

Louisa Pike had deep red hair and full cheeks with a smile that could light up the darkest cave and looks that could bring sight to a blind man. She once dreamt of dancing or singing, maybe going to New York or seeing somewhere abroad, possibly marrying a rich man and getting to be a luxurious housewife. Instead, she married Jesse Pike Sr. A laborer. A man with many ideas, but no execution. He was filled with more empty promises than a politician, and more lies than the devil. He said he'd pull her out of their small cottage one day. He said his ideas would make them rich and she'd be happy. Instead he went to the pub and Storyville and knocked her up with baby after baby after baby until her arms were too full and eyelids too heavy to see a way out of her life.

She liked to think he tried, though. Maybe when he was

drinking, he was meeting with investors, or someone who could make his various ideas come true. That's what she'd whisper into baby Clyde's ear as she rocked back-and-forth on the couch with him in her arms, his face red from angry tears.

"Daddy's gonna take care of us; just you wait and see," she'd say. But daddy never did. It was always just Clyde and his mama who looked after one another in those early years, and that's why he sat at her bedside today.

He watched her sleep like a child, deep in peace and unconcerned with the world outside. But she wasn't a child. She was an adult who had been on a drug-bender for months, and who rarely left the house. Clyde and Catherine were concerned.

Clyde checked his watch. "We need to try and get her up."

Catherine threw her arms out. "How am I supposed to do that? I could bang pots in here and she'd still be sleeping like a bear in the winter."

Clyde sighed. He couldn't be mad at her. He'd been keeping Catherine at the brothel to help with the books, so she hadn't been there much to keep an eye on their mother. God knows how much Laudanum their mother had put down in the past few days, hell, or weeks. She smelled ripe, like she hadn't moved in forever. Whenever he had been over at the house, which hadn't been much as of late, she was in bed. He wouldn't be shocked if that nightgown turned out to be fused to her body. It was once pearly white but was now a dingy, storm cloud gray.

Clyde scooped her limp body up in his arms and carried her down the hall. She felt like a broken baby bird in his hands whose wings he had to mend.

Catherine followed behind. "What are you doing?"

Clyde lowered her into the tub, and her head and body tilted to the right while her nightgown pooled around her. Louisa began to awaken.

Clyde unbuttoned and rolled up his sleeves. He said to Catherine, "Go heat water."

Catherine was confused but listened nonetheless. Louisa's eyes fluttered every few moments, a slight sign she was amongst the living, but she wasn't there yet. Clyde touched her arm gently. "I'm gonna make you better, Mama. Fit as a fiddle."

A thin smile lengthened across her face, but he knew it wasn't because of his words. She was in a land where no words could reach her, riding the waves of a thick drug-induced haze that clouded her senses. Nothing was going to get through to her. Catherine returned with the hot water. Clyde began to pull Louisa's nightgown up.

Catherine snapped. "What on earth are you doing?"

"She needs to bathe. You're going to do it."

Without much protest, Catherine did it. Catherine poured water on her mother's head while she clutched her knees to her head and groaned. Clyde stood in the hall outside the doorway. He stared at the wall and imagined the days his mother would chase him around this little house of theirs. Jesse and Rory would get mama's attention too, but Clyde was her special boy. She would hold him after he had an angry fit and hum in his ear how everything would get better.

"Mama loves you, my dear," she would say. Those words were a sedative for his fried and frayed nerves. Now it was his turn to help her get better. It was his turn to prove to himself and God that he wasn't a monster, a broken man who was only adept at chaos, but that he could actually heal someone. After Catherine was done with her, Clyde went and grabbed her some more clothes. Something that didn't smell rancid. Catherine dressed her. It was like trying to put clothes on a newborn.

"Clyde," said Catherine. She waved Clyde over to help get their mother on her feet. She was sitting at the edge of the tub, hair still dripping. He pulled her up. She was more conscious now, her feet were moving, but she was still incoherent.

"Cly-Clyde," she said.

"Yea, it's me, Mama." They got her on the couch and she sat without speaking, barely even moving.

"So, what now?" Cath asked.

"We wait."

"For?"

"Her to sober up."

Cath folded her arms. "She'll just go back to the doctor again and get more."

Clyde shook his head, calm and casual. "Won't be happening anymore."

"How in the world do you know that?"

Clyde stared.

"What did you do?"

"I just scared him."

Thirty minutes rolled by, then almost an hour, then Louisa finally was alert enough to look confused. "Clyde?"

"Yea."

"You're home? Is this really you?"

"Yea. It's me, mama."

She stood and drudged forward and put two frigid hands on his face. "You've been gone so long. When'd you get back?"

It'd been slightly over a month. But he said, "Not too long ago."

She hugged him tight and for as long as her frail arms could stand it. Clyde motioned over to Catherine, who was hesitant, clutching her dress at the knees and staring at the ground. But she gave in. They hugged one another, long and hard, like it was a family reunion that was long overdue.

The sickness took Louisa hours later. She rocked and shook in her bed like she was possessed and sweat seeped through her clothes and soaked her sheets. Catherine had to change her again and again to make sure she stayed clean. Clyde didn't leave her side once, and held her hand as tender as possible to let her know she wasn't alone. He made sure he was there for her, as she was always there for him.

Days went by but he was able to run the brothel and booze operations from there. The brothel's business had picked back up significantly in the past few weeks. Not doing it Jesse's way, though. Clyde wasn't one for shaking hands and kissing ass.

One night while he watched his mother sleep on the couch, he asked Twitch over the phone, "You sure they're always busy?"

Twitch said on the other end, "Always."

Clyde sent Twitch on a mission to see where the next popular brothels were in town, and Twitch noticed some of the old Rising Sun clientele moving around the joints. Clyde stared at his mother's unmoving body, watching the slight rise in her chest, making sure she didn't go to the pearly gates in her sleep.

Twitch asked, "Clyde, you st-st-still there?"

Clyde grunted. "Ok, add us in the Blue Book, then light up the place." Twitch opposed for a moment, citing that they never had a listing in a Blue Book; they thrived off word of mouth. Clyde retorted, "Regime change. Now do it."

And he did. The New Orleans skyline burned red from the angry fire that took the fire department a long time to put out. Clyde swore he could see it from the stoop of his childhood home. The next day it was all over New Orleans: an infamous cabaret bar burned to the ground over-night. No one was inside, thank God, but no one was sure how the fire happened.

The next night, Twitch called the house and voila, there was more walk-in traffic in the Rising Sun. Clyde grinned thinking about how he still had it. Jesse wasn't the only one who knew how to run a racket.

In total it was five full days of Louisa vomiting and

speaking gibberish. Then one morning, when Clyde was asleep in his chair at her bedside, she was up and awake. She awoke him with the smell of seasonings wafting from a plate of eggs in her hands and the sing-song tone of her voice, like when he was a child. "Get up sleepy head."

Catherine was already at the table with a sheepish look on her face. Their mother was moving around the kitchen with a buzz and energy Clyde hadn't seen in a while. It was like she hadn't purged her guts for days on end. Catherine's face showed she wasn't impressed; she'd seen this part before. This was the part where it's sun and rainbows, right before the inevitable thunderstorm came and decimated everyone. Clyde sat, then kicked Catherine's shin under the table. Her eyes said, *it won't last.* He ignored her.

"Beautiful morning, isn't it?" asked Louisa.

Clyde promptly said, "Yes."

They sat and ate breakfast. Only their mother talked; they just listened. Even Clyde, who had wanted this, didn't know what to say. His typical nervous demeanor was heightened when he started to go through potential topics of conversation, only to realize there was nothing for him to talk about. Well, unless she wanted to hear about prison, but that was a topic he tried to avoid. He placed a hand on his mother's, which shut her up, and gave a strained grin. "I'm happy to be home, Mother. And to see you're alright."

"Oh, dear," she said. "Look at me flapping your head off when I should be asking you how you're doing."

Catherine mixed her eggs on the plate and pretended to be in a different world.

"It's fine, Mother," he said. "I want to listen."

**

Clyde went for a drive later in the afternoon, close to 3 o'clock, when the school children were being let out for the day. He crept behind a group of eight kids, all in similar outfits, and watched their walking group dwindle down from eight to seven, seven to six, and so on the deeper they got in the neighborhood as each kid filed off once they got to their respective homes. There was an 8-year-old in the bunch walking with what seemed to be maybe two 11- or 12-year-old kids. After following close for a while, he noticed the two older boys shoving and mocking the younger boy. He could see the younger boy growing agitated and curling his hands into fists. Then he let out a high-pitched, "Just leave me alone."

Clyde hammered the gas to catch up and hopped out the car with a scowl. The three kids froze in fear. Clyde eyed the two older boys. "You two want to go fuck off somewhere?" The two children ran down the street.

The younger boy looked up at Clyde with unsure eyes. He stammered, "Thank you, mister."

"No need to mention it." Clyde's fingers fidgeted. "You need a lift back to your place? Those kids might just wait up the street for you."

The little boy bit his lip then looked down the street, eventually nodding. Clyde tried his best to pretend he didn't already know where the boy—Edward, the Captain's son—lived.

Clyde pulled in front of the house and Edward jumped

out the car, turning his head slightly to say, "Thank you!" Edward sat his books in the grass and immediately darted for the ball that'd sat there for a while. He threw it against the wall and played catch with himself. Clyde gripped his steering wheel and tried to talk himself out of doing anything stupid. He told himself he'd done enough. Watching the kid and making sure he got home safe was enough. But the intruding thoughts didn't stop him from getting out of the car, walking over to Edward, and asking the boy if he needed someone to play catch with.

Edward was caught off guard, the ball behind his head in mid-throw, but he spun and tossed a wobbly ball to Clyde, who shook his hand, pretending that the ball was too hot to catch. Clyde wasn't sure what he wanted from this. But it made him feel... good.

A door whined opened, the steps creaked, and a woman was to the right of him with her arms folded. "Who are you?"

Clyde moved toward the woman with his hat in hand. She looked like the pictures he saw all those years ago, more beautiful even. It was like time knew what she'd been through and decided he would leave her skin, eyes, and hair untouched.

He twisted his hat like he wanted to wring it out. "Ma'am," he said in his most pleasant tone. "I didn't mean to overstep my boundaries; I just saw your little boy getting harassed on his way from school and figured I'd do him a favor and give him a lift home."

The woman looked at Edward. "You got in a car with

some strange man?"

"Ma, ma, you should've seen it," Edward said. "He made the bigger boys run off! He said he would stay and play catch with me! Can he? Can he?"

Clyde began to back away. "I'll just be on my way. I really don't want to overstep."

"No," she said. "It's fine. He could use a man to teach him how to throw the ball around, I guess." She still seemed unsure.

Clyde nodded. "Ok."

Clyde squatted down and underhand tossed the ball back-and-forth with Edward for a few turns while the woman stood guard like a sentry. The wind blew and caused one of the window shutters to rattle. She placed the flat of her hand to her head. "Damn it. I thought I fixed that."

The house was big but uncared for. Boards were crooked and the shutters rattled on their frames from the winds. Clyde said the first thing that came to his mind: "I can fix it." The woman said it was fine. Clyde took off his coat and threw it over his arm. "No, really. It would be no problem."

The woman fiddled with her fingers while she contemplated. "Fine." She brought out her husband's old toolbox, and after ten minutes of Clyde working on it, no more squeaks. The woman stood a little looser now, her hands at her side and a slight smile on her face.

"Thank you so much," she said. "It took me a long time to try and fix that."

"It's no issue, ma'am. Anything to help." Through the

window he could see the living room. A bookcase, sofas, lounge chairs. He felt an onset of jitters prickle up his arm like ants. "I should go now."

Clyde put his hat and coat back on and bid the woman and Edward a good day. Edward ran up and touched Clyde's hands. "Can you come back and play catch with me sometime?"

Clyde wanted to say no. His deed with this family felt done. He caught a glimpse over the woman's shoulders, in the window, of two accusatory eyes staring at him. They were gone as soon as he saw them.

"Only if your mother says it's ok," Clyde said.

The boy looked to his mother, who nodded slowly. "But no more rides home from school." She gave a tight smile and played with the pearls around her neck.

Clyde bit back a grin. "Ok then."

Clyde walked into the brothel with a spring in his step. He felt lighter, happier. He felt he was on his way to being a truly good man. His office door was cracked open. He inched down the hall and expected Rory to be in his office. But instead, it was Jesse, who sat in his chair.

"The hell you doing here?" asked Clyde.

Jesse placed a gun on the desk between them. "Who the fuck is Joe?"

Chapter 21

Moving Forward

Jesse and Clyde sat across from one another inside the brothel's office. The gun rested on the desk between them like a silent warning to Clyde. The meeting with Joe had Jesse shaken—how long had he been watched? Even in the safety of the brothel, he felt watched and unsafe. Every shadowy corner hid a possible threat; every creak of the floorboards was oncoming danger.

Clyde stared at the gun. "What's that for?"

"The Irishman you told me about. Joe? He paid me a visit yesterday on my way to work."

Clyde grew angry. "I'll go speak to him."

He pushed himself up, but Jesse called him back to sit. Jesse's fingers pitter-pattered the table like he was using a typewriter. "No. Don't fucking antagonize him."

Clyde sat with an eye still on the gun. "Well. I see you've

seen his charm."

Jesse took a sip of water, then wiped some spillage from his lips. "I don't like surprises."

Jesse thought about those Tommy guns shredding through this fucking building like it was paper, wood chips and body parts flailing around and falling to the earth like snowflakes.

"What did he tell you?" Clyde asked.

Jesse explained everything from yesterday. Shame grew on Clyde's face. Jesse leaned forward. "Did you know he was IRA?"

Clyde rubbed his beard. "I knew he was an ideological fanatic of some form. Didn't think it was that."

"What was he in for?"

"I don't know."

"How many others are in New Orleans with him?"

"I don't know."

Jesse fought the urge to curse his brother's name. "How does he even know about me?"

Clyde scoffed. "Everybody knows Jesse Pike."

Jesse pinched the bridge of his nose. Everyone knows Jesse Pike.

"My first day in prison, he approached me. Said he heard about me and you through the grapevine. Said he liked our work and knew about our time with Sal. He said he thought we'd be 'assets to the cause.'" Clyde shook his head and scoffed. "I told him to fuck off."

"Then what?"

Clyde ran a line down his ribs that mirrored the path of

the knife scar Jesse had seen before. "Then I started getting attacked."

"You think he had something to do with that?"

"I know that the attacks stopped once he started protecting me."

It made sense to Jesse. How else to get someone to see that they need you other than giving them a reason to?

"Well, he has my attention now," Jesse scratched his head. "Anything else you want to say about the pen?"

"No."

Jesse responded, "Rory told me a little ways back that you were talking to yourself."

Clyde shook his head and denied the claim, but Jesse wouldn't back down.

"Alright," Clyde said. "You want to know the truth?"

Jesse nodded and Clyde unleashed everything he could onto him. The isolation room, the fights, the stabbings, drug usage, the waking visions and night terrors.

"So, in these nightmares," Jesse said. "Who do you see?"

Clyde shook his head. "It's like they weren't nightmares, but visions instead. It's like I was back there looking into the Captain's eyes."

Jesse squinted. Then he remembered exactly who the Captain was. It was the only time Clyde had ever looked so shaken in his life. He'd walked all the way to Jesse's dorm afterward and told him everything, slept on his floor face up with no cover, jerked awake every few minutes. "But why is that coming back now?"

Clyde shrugged. "Maybe I'm being punished."

Jesse immediately thought to his own night terrors—
the ghosts of his past that haunted him from time to time.
Then he looked straight ahead to Clyde. He was a version
of what Jesse would've become if he didn't quit the criminal
life. If Jesse believed in heaven, hell, or ghosts, he would
think that he and his family were actually haunted, but as
he watched his brother speaking solemnly about a mild slip
into madness, the truth was evident: the human mind could
only handle doing so much bad before it snapped. Clyde is
what Jesse would be if he had killed Bobby.

"You did what you had to do," Jesse said. He couldn't
help his next question. "Clyde, don't take this the wrong
way. But everything you've done, why is it that you feel so
awful about that one person and nothing else?"

"Because I wanted his life."

Clyde's words sent chills down Jesse's back. His brother
was feared by most men, but it was that answer that made
Jesse finally feel it. "Plus, he was the only person I felt didn't
deserve it. And Dad, he always told me I was possessed. I
believed it, you know. For a while. And prison brought
those thoughts back up. What if Daddy was right? What if I
have some demon in me only capable of hurting?"

"You're not possessed. You are... were, sick. Prison...
what happened to you before and during, it's enough to
drive anyone mad."

Clyde nodded. "I'm better now."

Jesse flashed his palms. "I see that."

Clyde pointed to the sky. "I think I'm making things
right with The Lord. I think sticking to my word and

focusing on re-attaching what I've broken has made things right between me and him." Jesse didn't know what Clyde had been up to, and was scared to ask.

It was silent for a while. Clyde spoke, then stopped then looked stressed out by the words he wanted to say but didn't know how. He looked down and scratched at loose threads on his pants. "I considered offing myself in there. And I thought about it once even before then."

"Why would you even think something like that?"

Clyde shrugged. "It was just a thought. Like how you see a gnat fly past really quickly? It was there, then it was gone."

Overwhelming silent emotion filled the room and loomed over like a storm cloud, like there was much more Clyde could say, but feared to. Jesse didn't know if he wanted to hear anymore. He'd never seen Clyde so soft and vulnerable, two traits his brother didn't wear well. Jesse started to feel like he'd walked in on someone changing, like he shouldn't be there while his brother revealed once hidden layers of himself.

Clyde's words flowed now. "There was another thought I had in there. I wanted my family back. I wanted to be someone who doesn't just hurt, but also heals."

Jesse shook his head slowly. "I—I hear you, I just don't know what to say."

"Me, you, Rory, Catherine," Clyde leaned forward. "And Ma. There was a point where after Dad died, maybe for a month, where we were fine."

Jesse remembered. Before his mother suffered her nervous breakdown and stopped being a parent, they were ok. The suicide of their father was a stain on them for a moment that quickly faded after the smell of booze no longer floated around the house and everyone realized they no longer had to walk on eggshells anymore. But things got worse again. The Pikes were meant to live in chaos the way fish were meant to stay at sea.

"I remember," Jesse said.

"I want us to have a dinner together sometime soon. Me, you, Rory, Catherine. Mother."

Jesse squirmed in his seat.

"Just think about it, please," said Clyde. "Just... put your feelings about Ma to the side for a little."

Jesse closed his eyes. "Alright, alright."

"Ok, then."

Jesse nodded and got up to leave, placing his gun in the holster under his coat. "So," Jesse said. "Is Joe someone I need to be worried about?"

Clyde shook his head. "I'll talk to him. You have other things to worry about."

Jesse accepted the answer and walked toward the door.

Clyde called his name. "Let's meet up for baseball in the park sometime this upcoming week. Would you like that?"

The idea made Jesse happier the longer he thought about it. "I would like that."

Chapter 22

Until Death

Thick plumes of smoke rolled from Jesse's lips as he took his time considering his next chess move. Sal's impatient eyes lingered on him. "You gonna make a move or what?"

Jesse planned on it, but the hangover from last night's gathering at The Chateau Club shrouded his thoughts and further diminished his already low desire to be around Sal. He moved his piece and Sal captured it; he moved again, same result. They started another game; Jesse took another leisure toke of his cig, crossed his legs, and looked off into the distance for a while and watched blackbirds flutter by in the blue sky and kids ride by on bicycles in the street. Sal shifted in his seat, grew impatient, and eventually, he quit altogether, citing being tired as a reason. The quiet settled uncomfortably over them. The same way it had the last few times Jesse had been summoned to Sal's home.

"Beautiful day, isn't it?" asked Sal.

Jesse twisted a chess piece in between his fingers. "It's adequate."

Sal sighed.

Ever since the "hit" on Bobby, Jesse had to play the role of the dutiful but shaken son: he showed up for their weekly meetings, let Sal think he was rocked to his core from having to take a life, when in reality, he was enraged, finished with Sal's manipulative bullshit, and biding his time until the old man finally died. He tried to ignore Sal for a while, but he couldn't; there was some childish part of him that still saw Sal as his father, as someone who took care of him, when in reality he was closer to a prison warden, or Jesse's master, than he ever was a father. For Jesse, each long pause between moves and every slow burn of his cigarette was his way of dragging out the duration that he was the one in control. It got him one second closer to death claiming Sal's soul and freeing their bond for good.

Jesse looked at his watch. "I'm going to need to leave soon; I have business I need to attend to." In reality he had a tee-time with Mel and the fellas, but he didn't have the strength to argue today. "What'd you call me over here so early for anyway?"

Sal scoffed. "I see the art of niceties is no longer a thing with your generation. I guess I'll get to it. I know you're going to the Police Ball and—"

"Are you spying on me now?"

Alarm flashed across Sal's face. "No, no, no, let me restate. I was invited to the Police Ball as well, but due to the

261

recent controversy, I deemed it best not to go. I got a glimpse of the list and saw your name."

Jesse pretended to be at ease, but he wouldn't put it past Sal to have him tailed. Sal was the type of man who liked to keep all of his belongings within arm's reach, especially when those perceived belongings wanted nothing more than to pull away.

Sal said, "I need a favor."

"What is it this time? Am I bombing a train-car with nuns and children on it? Stabbing a priest in the neck?"

Sal stared at Jesse, but let the jabs roll off of him. "I need you to speak to two detectives that'll be there."

"No," said Jesse.

Sal went on to explain how no one else could do it. He couldn't be seen approaching the detectives in public and he'd feared if he sent Junior or anyone else, the situation could turn more serious than what it needed to be. Jesse shook his head again.

Sal sighed. "I thought you were tougher than this, boy. First sign of adversity and you're ready to curl up like a kitten in the corner."

Jesse didn't respond.

"Look, truth? Things are slipping out from under me. That situation we had to clean up hurt some of my favors and goodwill in the city, and I can't let anyone, and I mean anyone, defect right now. Those two cops are on my payroll, and they're important. The house of cards is falling down around me, kid." Sal's hands shook as he spoke. "And I need you to help me prop it up."

"Let it fall then, Sal." Jesse flicked his cigarette over the porch railing and stood to leave, placing a gentle hand on Sal's shoulder, and ambled toward the steps.

Sal said, "You owe me this."

Jesse spun around. "How is that?"

"How many less beatings did you get from your old man because of me? How many more meals, clothes, shoes, good memories, were due to me? Your first Christmas with gifts? Me. I did that for you." Jesse's eyes fluttered at the thought. "I get it, ok. I misjudged you. I thought you had a little more of a soldier in you. I asked you to do something that pushed you too far. But I just need this one last thing, just the one, and I'll let you be." Sal spoke soft and gentle, like he didn't want to harm the already fragile state of his and Jesse's relationship. "I know that's what you really want."

The words had Jesse's feet glued to the patio, the memories pulling at his emotions like the strings on a marionette. His rational mind told him he shouldn't concede any more, but the child in him, the one who once unwrapped those gifts from Sal, said he should do this one last thing.

"Ok," Jesse said. "I can try what I can. But after this, I can't do any more favors for you."

Sal nodded solemnly, then motioned to the chessboard. "Do we still have our weekly games?"

Jesse nodded. "Yes, I'll be here next week and every week after." *Until you die.*

Later at his condo, Cindy was on Jesse's mind and he

couldn't seem to remove her. His conscience had been quiet lately. The night terrors had been null, the stress and anxiety that used to come to him at night was nonexistent. But the one thing he needed to reconcile was the way things ended with Cindy. Or didn't end, he should say. He stopped calling and she stopped visiting. There were some half-hearted attempts by both parties on several occasions, but he figured they'd both come to the mutual conclusion to let things die between them.

But if that was so, he thought to himself as he stood in front of the phone, why was he so nervous to call her? He took a deep breath, closed his eyes, then asked to be wired over to her. She sounded confused when she answered the phone.

He asked, "What are you doing tomorrow night?"

***

Jesse stood outside the women's bathroom in a black tux and bowtie, leaning against the wall and trying his best to not seem like a pervert. When women walked out and saw him standing there he gave an awkward smile and assured them he was waiting on his date. Cindy walked out with a napkin in hand. She dabbed at the sides of her mouth.

"You ok?" Jesse asked. She covered her mouth again like she was about to retch.

"No," she said.

Jesse handed her a hard candy he stole from the hotel lobby so she could mask the smell of puke with that of butterscotch. He held it out like an olive branch.

She hesitantly took it. "Thanks. I think it's something I

ate." She stared at Jesse, moving the candy around in her mouth until it appeared as a small circle outside her cheek. "Any reason you invited me to this special event?"

The question was expected, but still hit Jesse like a brick. It would have been better if they'd rode together to the Police Ball, so that way they could've gotten this done in his car. But she refused to ride with him.

"I—I just really enjoyed... enjoy... spending time with you," he said.

Cindy put her hand up. "You know what, it's fine. You don't owe me anything. We are— we're casual." She sucked on the hard candy. "I complicated things when I said I loved you." She stepped toward him and held his wrist. "Really, it's ok." She smiled. "I'm happy you'd keep me in mind for an event this ritzy."

Jesse rubbed a thumb across the back of her hand. "I'm happy you said yes."

Their eyes locked for a second longer than intended and Cindy pulled away. They walked up the wide hallway toward double-doors where doormen checked off names on a list. A line of people in tuxes and gowns flowed out the doors. Jesse noticed two men with thick black mustaches and comb-overs shaking hands while stepping slowly into the ballroom. Those were the two guys Sal told Jesse to look for.

Inside the ballroom was majestic and bright. Waiters roamed in and out through the crowd smoothly, being everywhere at once while being almost unseen. They carried trays of hors d'oeuvres to the middle of standing conversations—and there were many conversations. People stood in the middle of the ballroom, while tables draped with white cloths and adorned with glass vases were placed staggered on the perimeter.

Cindy had that same wide-eyed look as when Jesse brought her to the play. But this time, she was different: confident, emboldened, moving around the room like she'd belonged there and everyone else didn't. Her elegance emanated from her like warmth from a lamp, and honestly, Jesse almost had a hard time keeping up.

She walked right up into the middle of groups, with Jesse in tow, and held her own in conversations about writers like Joyce and Anderson, and butted into debates about the cubism art movement, and whether or not it was really art or just some bourgeois bullshit Jesse didn't get. After a while, Jesse started to feel like half the reason she came was the display her impressive knowledge of art and culture. He wasn't mad, though. He loved to watch her work.

Next, Jesse networked. He found Bill, Kenneth, and Albert, along with Mel and some other gents in a group standing over by the orchestra.

Albert whistled when Cindy walked up next to Jesse. He took her hand and laid a kiss on top of it. Some mild jealousy tinged the edges of Jesse's cordiality. Mel introduced Jesse to the remainder of the group as his business partner. It was a repeat of last time Jesse met some of Mel's friends:

"Where'd you go?"

"So you didn't graduate?"

"What's your line of work?"

But at this point of deep-diving into the upper-class, Jesse knew how to frame it. "I went to Tulane. No, I didn't finish, but it was because I decided to leave and start my own business in the hospitality industry. I'm branching out to broaden my portfolio."

They nodded and chewed on his words, and apparently liked the taste.

What they heard was that he grew up poor, pulled himself up by his bootstraps, got into Tulane, then learned what he needed to learn to start his own business. The rich loved stories like that, Jesse had figured out. One part of it was the "American Dream" crap. The other part was because it allowed them to feel good about their wealth and ignore the fact that the vast majority of people from Jesse's background could never and would never do what he did. But, for Jesse's purposes of entering into their circle, the tired trope would have to work.

"The Magnolia is actually opening soon," Jesse said. "You boys come on down and we can comp you a steak or something." They loved that even more than his story.

Mel mouthed "What are you doing?" behind everyone.

Jesse walked over to his partner and said, "Getting people in the door."

After leaving the circle, Cindy tried to stifle a giggle.

"What?" Jesse asked.

Cindy added a mocking British accent. "'Broaden your portfolio.'"

Jesse snickered. "You trying to say I'm snooty now or something?"

Cindy shrugged. "Or something, I guess."

Jesse smiled at her, but over her shoulder, a sea of black and white tuxes parted and Cameron came into view. He had a glass of water in his left hand and his right wrapped around Rose's waist. Jesse's face turned sour at the sight. He instinctively pulled Cindy to go into another direction. Cindy anchored him down and looked at what he was staring at. "Aren't those your friends?"

He stammered an excuse, but before he could think of anything he heard that God damned voice call them over. Jesse looked up and Cameron was motioning them over. Rose looked as ill as Jesse did.

"Fancy seeing you two here," Cameron said.

Cameron greeted people like they were long lost friends, and that was something Jesse kind of admired.

"See," Cameron said, looking down at Rose. "I told you it was your friend."

Rose's expression was a portrait of thinly hidden anxiety. "Oh, seems as though I was wrong."

Jesse saw her eyes drift from him to Cindy. Jesse, who was often considered cool and calm under pressure, was falling to pieces trying not to look worried as Cameron held him captive with the conversation. Every thought and every answer was a struggle, and every sentence was a leap of faith that he wouldn't say, "I've been sleeping with your woman." He nodded when he could, and gave short answers where acceptable. Jesse figured this newfound guilt stemmed from Cameron possibly being the kindest, best human being he'd ever met in his life.

"So, what are you doing here?" Jesse asked.

Cameron gave a dopey shrug. "Just to tell the boys in blue how much they are appreciated!"

AKA, free PR spin to rebuild whatever political capital he may have spent on misusing city resources. But Jesse nodded along. Cameron was a good politician, but still a politician.

"You ever get nervous going to speak in front of big crowds like this?" asked Jesse.

Cameron responded, "Ah, geez. To be honest? Every single time." He chuckled. "But you know what makes it easier? I speak from the heart."

Jesse nodded. "That's refreshing to hear."

Cameron smiled. "Thank you. Just know when I say that I want to stop crime and corruption, it's not just talk."

"What's your plan for that?"

"Well, for starters, there's a lot of incentive for a public official to take bribes and steal money, so I'd adjust the laws and legality behind public officials profiting from their positions. There would be in-depth investigations on city contracts and the like. I believe people want to do better, and can do better, when not tempted with reason to do otherwise. Also, I'd get rid of patronage. Only merit-based jobs."

Jesse responded, "That's a start."

He said it in a fashion that made even Cindy and Rose, who were half-listening, half-assessing one another, make a face. Cameron was enthusiastic about the challenge. "You have any suggestions?"

"Your plan is good for upper-class crimes. But what about the street gangs? And the drugs? And the murders? The way I see it, it's a simple economic issue."

"Simple?"

"Yea. It takes less time and earns more profit to distribute drugs or run whores—er, excuse me, run a brothel—than it does to, let's say, be a paperboy or go to college to be an accountant."

Cameron looked intrigued.

"You bring more jobs to the city, pay people a living wage, that gets rid of half the stick-up men and drug dealers in the city, and keeps the jails bare. The biggest route of crime is socioeconomic oppression, my friend. The average person wants to do good but can't afford to. Literally."

Cameron rubbed his chin, then laughed. "I never thought of it that way. You really know your stuff. My upbringing has clouded me in many ways, and the most obvious is how I'd viewed street crime. Thank you for that, Jesse." He touched Jesse's shoulder. "Seriously."

Jesse bashfully responded, "No problem."

Rose stared at the floor.

"If you don't mind," said Cameron. "Would you join us at our table? Maybe I could pick your brain a little more."

Rose cut in. "But sweetheart, your speech is up shortly. And you know you could talk for days."

"Oh, I have time."

Jesse reluctantly agreed.

During his and Cameron's small talk, Jesse could sense the tension beaming from Cindy and Rose. Women had this odd ability to sense one another's feelings, he figured. He could feel Cindy's eyes on the side of his head at one point, then her hand gripped his arm. Rose, who gave an anecdote once or twice, checked out of the conversation altogether. She instead stared toward the orchestra. Over Cameron's shoulder, Jesse saw the two detectives on Sal's payroll get up at the same time and walk toward the double doors.

Jesse removed Cindy's grip from his arm and silenced Cameron with a finger. "Excuse me, I'll be right back. I just have to run to the men's room." He saw the look on both Rose's and Cindy's faces say the same thing: *don't you fucking dare leave me alone.* But he powered on.

Jesse walked into the men's room and pretended to piss at a urinal. He instead stared into the odd-looking, brown floral wallpaper and listened to the two cops he'd tailed have a conversation while washing their hands.

After waiting for the extra men to leave the restroom, Jesse strode toward the door and locked it, then stood in front of it with his arms folded as the two detectives moved toward him.

The taller detective's eyes grew big. "What's the meaning of this?"

"I'm with Sal Bianchi," said Jesse.

The two men back-peddled ever so slightly, like the name repelled them.

Jesse put his hands out. "Relax. Nedley and Rogers I

presume." Jesse knew that the taller man was Nedley, and the shorter, huskier man was Rogers from Sal's description. Jesse rested his back to the door. "You need to start returning his calls."

Rogers folded his arms. "We can't, pal. We refuse to do anything else for him." Jesse craned his neck down low to make sure no feet were under the stalls.

Nedley said, "Yea. After, you know, the failed raids, the missing snitches, the changing political climate, there's a bit of a schism in the Parish-wide police force."

"How?" Jesse asked.

The two men looked at each other.

Nedley said, "It was always a quiet secret. If you want to make extra money, keep your mouth shut to what you see. But people can see the writing on the wall. The old guard's almost out. The ship's sinking. And we're trying to hop on to the next vessel before we get brought down with this one." The man pointed his finger to the ground to make his point.

Rogers continued with their point. The failed raids did nothing to hurt Cameron's polling, apparently. In fact, some people loved that Cameron had the balls to go at someone who was deemed untouchable. And some cops were getting scared.

"You don't say," said Jesse.

"I do," said Rogers, his skin sheened with sweat. "Now can we get out of here?"

Big Sal was losing more support than he initially thought.

Jesse would keep that to himself though. He ignored the knocks at the door and continued to negotiate on the behalf of Big Sal. The two high-ranking officers, who both attempted to play the high and mighty lane, eventually caved. Because they both realized what Jesse realized—it wasn't an option to quit. The two men settled on a number, reluctantly, and shook Jesse's hand. Jesse stayed in front of the door. "I may need you guys for something one day. I can pay you the same amount if it comes to it."

They looked at each other and shrugged. Nedley asked, "How'll you find us?"

Jesse unlocked the door, tiring of the back-and-forth movement behind his back. "Oh, I'll find you. What type of detectives are you two anyway?"

They both said in unison, "Homicide."

Jesse nodded. He sidestepped a man rushing in the bathroom and left the two detectives to stew in what they'd talked about. Jesse was walking down the hall toward the ballroom when he felt someone pull his coat sleeve from behind him. He turned to see Rose. Her eyebrows were furrowed and her lips curled in a sneer. She pushed a broom closet door open and forced him inside.

"What's the meaning of this?" Jesse asked.

The smell of cleaning products swirled around them. A string dangled free from the ceiling. Jesse tugged it. Rose unleashed an incoherent tirade at him. He signaled for her to hush up, fearing someone would hear them. She snatched his fingers from his lips. Tears developed around her eyes.

"Don't you dare tell me to shush. What are you doing here? Who is that girl? You told me you had no one."

Jesse thumbed his eyebrow. "It's—complicated. It's nothing."

"Is it nothing or is it complicated, Jesse?" Rose snarled at him like a predator baring its teeth. "The way she's looking at me, with such contempt. I just can't. You shouldn't be here." Jesse grabbed her wrists and told her to calm down. She hit him in his chest. He backed into a shelf and nudged a broom with his elbow.

He grabbed her again. "It's. Nothing. She's a friend."

A thin tear ran down her cheek, illuminated by the lightbulb in the ceiling. "This is harder than I thought."

"Yes, it is."

They stared at each other, the light bulb's white cord dangling between them. Jesse ducked down to kiss her and she lunged at him. He began to undress her, but she pushed his hands down, instead hiking her dress up her thighs and pulling down her pantyhose, which ripped at the seams from Jesse's excited grasp. He removed his belt, dropped his pants, and thrust himself inside of her, while their hands held onto shelves of paint and nails and brushes and tools that wobbled with each thrust of himself into her.

He covered her open mouth with his left hand to suppress her moans while his free hand held firm to her thighs, gripping flesh, squeezing tighter once he hit that point where ecstasy was around the corner. Once he reached it, he held her closer; she pulled her legs in tighter, both of them holding on like they would float to the heavens on the rising current of their climax alone. Once they both hit the sweet all-consuming feeling of their release, he let out a low sensual grunt, and her moans tapered away, and she placed a gentle kiss on his palm right before he pulled his hand away from her mouth.

When they were done, and the high faded away, they were silent. Only the sound of Jesse's zipper purring when he pulled it up, Rose's dress rustling down, and the light bulb above buzzing with electricity could be heard. Jesse reached for her shoulder and Rose evaded it. She didn't look at him, couldn't, he figured. She walked out. Jesse followed a few minutes later.

Jesse walked back in the ballroom to see Cindy, Cameron, and Rose seated with each other. Cameron and Rose were in conversation. Cindy had her arms crossed and boredom written on her face. Jesse pulled back an empty chair next to Cindy and apologized to her for taking so long.

"My stomach was killing me," he whispered to her.

"It must be going around," she retorted. Letting her eyes linger on Jesse longer than usual.

Jesse turned his gaze to the stage when the speaker called for Cameron. Cameron finished chewing his red beans and washed it down with water. He dabbed at his face with a napkin while half standing.

"Alright," he said to everyone at the table. "Wish me luck."

He leaned down to kiss Rose and she turned her head slightly, just enough for him to barely get the side of her lips. She gave a weak smile. Cameron strode toward the stage with a pep in his step and a piece of paper clutched in his hand.

Rose had her arms folded on the table and her eyes staring at invisible spots on the white linen top. Jesse was gutted over the way Rose was feeling, but there was nothing he could do. He placed a hand on Cindy's knee. It moved away from his touch. He turned to look at her and her eyes quivered in silent anger. The crowd behind them rose to their feet and cheered for Cameron as he took the stage.

Chapter 23

Quiet

Twitch kept knocking the ball out of the fucking park every time it came over the plate. Jesse, not the most athletic but not the worst, tried to turn and chase the ball down, but every time he looked up, he'd see the white ball turn into a black ascending shadow that looked like it got swallowed up by the sweltering sun. Twitch flipped his bat and trotted around the bases like he was going for an evening stroll. He had time; it would take a while for the ball to crash back to earth.

Clyde cursed from third base. Jesse threw his hands up and shouted, "What was I supposed to do?"

He ventured into the woods to retrieve the ball from the bushes and brushed off leaves and grass. He turned around to see his brothers talking to one another, Twitch leaning down to kiss his wife and kids on their foreheads as they sat on the sideline, and the various other people that were invited for the game. His sister sat on the benches next to the makeshift baseball diamond they'd made on the grass field. He wasn't entirely ok with the fact that Clyde hired her to work at a brothel, but it wasn't his business anymore. Plus, she was a grown woman who contained more depth and nuance than he previously considered. Cindy wasn't there. She'd typically be at things like this, but Jesse and Cindy hadn't spoken to each other since the Police Ball. But in all, he was happy. He was with his family and his loved ones. Everything was alright.

He rushed over to the sidelines to meet up with Clyde, Rory, and Twitch. They stood where no one could hear them. "How's the inventory looking?" asked Clyde to Rory.

"Eh, not much." Rory's jaw motioned up and down from a thick gob of gum. "At this rate, we're gonna be out in another few months, maybe less."

Jesse raised his eyebrows. "I knew the envelopes have been getting thicker lately. Didn't realize you all were moving that much, though."

Twitch waved at his kids in the distance, then asked, "We—are we going to continue this?"

He and Rory looked to Clyde, who was stroking his beard. "This was supposed to be a one-time thing, but the money is lucrative. But we can't rip off another truck. That's an easy way to end up in the penitentiary."

Clyde invited Jesse's input.

Jesse said, "Want my opinion? Cash in your chips and get out. Invest your earnings, clean the money, and just keep what you've made as a nest egg. Booze is a hot-button issue right now."

They all agreed.

"Yea, you're right," Clyde said.

Rory lifted his eyebrows. "Did hell just freeze over? Did you two just agree on something?"

They all laughed and then went back to playing the game. After the game, when everyone else left, Clyde and Jesse stuck around on the benches to watch the sun go down. Birds twittered and the wind rustled the leaves of the trees, and the sun receded behind the skyline, giving the sky a molten copper glow.

"This is strange," said Jesse.

"What you mean?"

Jesse shrugged. "It's quiet."

This was the first time in a while that neither of them had anything to do or anywhere to run off to. There were no impending threats. No jobs needed to be pulled. Everything was sailing smoothly and it felt like they were kids again, back when things were simple and they were only brothers and not business partners or competitors.

"You know," said Jesse. "I would really like you all to come to the opening of The Magnolia."

"Really?"

Jesse nodded.

"Even Ma?"

Jesse shook his head, then pressed his palms to his forehead. Clyde turned to face him on the bench. "She wants to see you."

Jesse thought about it. Things between him and Clyde were better now, his life was better now. He was in the middle of releasing all of the baggage he'd carried. This could be another opportunity to let some go. "Fine."

Clyde smiled.

"But," said Jesse. "Don't let her come doped up."

"I think I could swing that."

The sun went in for the night and the boys sat there, like when they were kids, and enjoyed each other's silence. Jesse put a hand on Clyde's shoulder and Jesse could tell Clyde pretended this didn't make him happy, biting down a smile created by pure joy—something he didn't get often.

***

Clyde didn't go straight home after leaving the park—the rage within him spoke to his darker impulses and told him he should go over to the Irish Channel and burn that whole block to the ground. His car pulled in front of Joe's headquarters wanting nothing more but to barge in and strangle that red-haired fuck until his head exploded. But Clyde calmed himself. He was trying to be different now. He thought this over and over again until it drowned out the dark noise in his head. One deep breath in, then two, and after a few moments, he was calm. But he still needed to make a point. He strode into the bar and everyone stopped talking. His eyes darted left to right. He scanned tables and faces until he laid eyes on Joe, who had that typical grin on his face. He raised his hands and waved Clyde over. "Hey, Clyde, pull up a seat—"

Clyde snatched the smaller Joe out of his seat, clattering

the chair to the ground, tossing the skinny man onto the table next to him. He gritted down on his teeth and growled out his next words while staring deep into Joe's eyes. "Stay the fuck away from my family."

The childlike glow never left Joe's eyes. Clyde continued, "I promise, if you don't, I will fucking kill you."

A gaggle of hands and arms reached around Clyde's body and pulled him off Joe. Joe rose and brushed the spilled peanuts and booze from his shirt, an amber stain settled at the left side of his sleeve.

"Well," Joe said. "I see you talked to Jesse."

Four men struggled to hold Clyde back. Joe waved them away. Joe tapped Clyde's shoulder playfully. "Alright, buddy. I hear you. Loud and clear."

Clyde turned and darted for the door.

Chapter 24

Politics, Politics, Politics

The first rule of politics: it doesn't matter what you believe in, only what your constituents believe in. If they thought there was cheese on the moon, then you best bring crackers to your next rally. You gave people what they wanted, and in turn, they let you do what you wanted. Martin Beckman followed that strategy for years, starting from his position as an Alderman, all the way to the mayor's mansion. But tonight, for whatever reason, his typically magnetic charms faltered, and Cameron Mulligan was handing him his ass. Martin stood at the podium and droned on and on as he got tossed questions that he thought he knocked out of the park: "Mayor Beckman, some people believe you are soft on the criminal element in the city. What is your rebuttal to this?"

Beckman gave a light chuckle and smoothed his

mustache with his thumb. "Good people of New Orleans…" He paused dramatically to catch the eye of every man and woman in the hall. "Please do not be fooled by what is said in the right-wing newspaper outlets. The arrest numbers for the city have gone up exponentially since I began my third term. I've empowered the precinct captains to take free reign of their divisions, and arrest any rule breakers and scoundrels roaming the city looking to do harm. Any questions of why there may still be some lagging should be directed to the highest-ranking law official in our city." He motioned to the right toward Cameron. Martin only received a few sparse claps.

Then it was Cameron's turn. He knocked his response out of the park. He was energetic on the stage, charismatic, unstoppable. Martin didn't even hear what the kid said. He let the claps from the crowd tell him that he was losing. At the end, Cameron got a thunderous standing ovation.

The next day, the newspapers were unforgiving. Even the third largest publication in the city, *The Item*, which typically was a propaganda outlet for the ORD, said Beckman got "trounced." The political machine railroaded the competition every single year except this year. The latest polls: Mulligan neck and neck with Beckman (incumbent).

This didn't go over well with the ORD.

The Chateau Club was empty, save for the full membership of the Old Row Democratic machine. All seventeen men, one for each of the seventeen wards of New Orleans, sat together in a tight cluster in the center of the room as Martin paced back and forth with his arms behind his back. They were familiar with this pace; he got like that whenever he was mad or thinking. And he was usually a combination of the two. The sixteen other men chattered amongst themselves, recounting what had gone wrong with the campaign.

He stopped pacing. They stopped talking. He spread his palms. "Gentlemen, this campaign, I dare to say, has been a disaster."

Small hums of hesitant agreement came from the men. A man with a beak nose and a crown of white hair around his wrinkled scalped spoke. "Yes, it certainly has been." His voice was deep and distinguished.

Martin furrowed his eyebrows. "Then may I assume you have a solution to the obvious dilemma?"

The older man snorted. "Now assistance is needed."

Martin let out an exasperated sigh.

"First, you don't take the threat of the DA seriously. Secondly, you lose the newspapers. Thirdly, we fail to get our guy in the Governor's mansion," he pointed his crooked finger toward Rudy. "And lastly, you let this young miscreant run wild too often. You gave the most important ward to the most incompetent person I've ever seen."

Rudy threw his hands up. "How dare you?"

The old man hobbled over. "You're part of the reason the papers are against us." Arguments broke out around the room.

Martin put his hands up and they all fell silent. "Gentlemen, no need to point fingers. We've all made mistakes when we were young. Have we not?"

No one answered. Rudy twisted his glass in his hand. "Alleged mistakes."

Everyone glared at him.

"But," Martin continued. "Let's not forget something. We still have the chips here." Martin rubbed his middle finger and thumb together. The second rule of politics: if you couldn't win an election, you could always buy it.

The plan for the ORD over the next week or two was broken down into three phases.

First phase: control public perception.

In politics, it wasn't about gaining all citizens' approval, just enough to win the vote. Martin called the office of *The Item's* editor-in-chief and asked him to stop running negative stories about him. The editor-in-chief snickered and politely said, "No, but nothing personal."

He waxed poetic about journalistic integrity and being the voice of the people, and, honestly, Martin zoned out after integrity. The truth was the ORD had lost the favor of *The Item* over the Gubernatorial election scandal. They propped up an incompetent crony with no government experience as their choice for Governor. Martin would've been the real Governor; the guy in office would've been a puppet with strings leading back to New Orleans.

The editor-in-chief, after years of taking bribes, finally put his foot down and grew a conscience, it seemed. That conscience eroded after pictures of him and a negro prostitute were in his mailbox one day with two simple words on the cover: "Nothing personal."

The headline of The Item's next issue read, "**MARTIN BECKMAN, CHAMPION OF THE WORKING MAN!**"

Underneath that story was a nice little write-up about the Mulligan family's hefty fortune.

Second: the constituents needed to be rallied.

Every single Alderman threw a rally on the same day to gather support from their ward's constituents. Food and water were passed around, family-friendly carnival games were played, and big red balloons were handed out to the kids. They organized a march of community supporters to walk around the neighborhoods and hand out pamphlets, and convinced small business owners to put Martin's face all over their stores. While that was going on, Martin had men at the cemeteries writing down the names they saw on tombstones. Those names would then be put on voting cards and handed to Italians and Blacks who would go and vote on Election Day, once as themselves, and many times after, each with a new name card.

Third and most important: ridding the city of visible demonstrations.

Anti-ORD protests weren't uncommon in the city. But it wasn't until Mulligan gained momentum did the movements catch fire. People marched the streets in front of City Hall and in front of businesses that supported the ORD with picket signs and soapboxes to stand on.

Martin couldn't outright tell them not to protest. But he could hire thugs to go into the various protests in town with bats and hammers and club the shit out of anyone protesting against him. The men hid in the tightly packed groups of protestors, then swung on anyone near them. The brawls led to lower turnouts for these displays, and many citizens begged the Mayor to do something about the violent protests in the city. Which he was happy to do. He mandated that due to a rise in extreme violence, demonstrations were to be vastly limited.

The Item spun the story as "**Mulligan Supporters Start a Brawl.**"

The ORD's three phase plan, in total, took place over two weeks. Enough time for a new round of polls to come out. Martin sat in The Chateau Club with a grin hidden by his thick mustache. The server brought a steaming cup of robust coffee to Martin, along with that week's paper. He flipped open to the middle, then lost his smile. He screamed. His voice rang out through the entire club, startling people on the golf course, making people eating their meals choke on their food. He'd regained some popularity, but was still projected to defeat Mulligan by only one percent. One measly percent.

He folded the newspaper and tossed it to the other side of the booth. His eyes darted around; his thoughts swam. He was all done. He had nothing else to throw at Cameron. Even with the coloreds and Italians voting multiple times on Election Day, it was still too close to call. Too much can happen before Election Day. Which was in six days. Martin got on the phone with an ORD old-timer and talked out a new plan of action.

***

Cameron Mulligan couldn't believe Mayor Beckman stood at his office threshold with his usual smug look on his face. "Top of the morning to you."

"Mr. Mayor. What can I do you for?"

Martin slinked in and sat without being prompted to. Cameron commented in stifled frustration, "It's typically proper to ask if someone minds before you sit."

"Really? Is that how they do it in the upper-crust?"

Cameron knew what this was; some type of verbal jousting match to rattle his cage so close to Election Day. Cameron stayed calm though. He would never give Beckman the satisfaction of anger. "What can I do for you?"

"I'll be frank," Mayor Beckman leaned forward. "I like your idea for restructuring the government. I think I can restructure it. You know, give you a position as my Deputy Mayor." Mayor Beckman smiled. "Comes with a pay bump."

"I don't need the money."

Beckman nodded. "Of course. But you'd still be in a position to make real change."

"A DA can't make change?"

Martin snickered. "I'm going to cut the double-speak here. You know you can only do so much without the help of the administration. My administration. We're a symbiotic force, one hand that washes the other. I can make your job hard."

Cameron closed the book and glared across the desk.

"But, you bow out now, become my Deputy Mayor, I'll give you free reign over social aid programs. How the money is spent on those programs, all that jazz."

Cameron's hand hammered the desk. "No. You don't get to threaten me, you uncouth..." He noticed his finger was in the Mayor's face trembling with anger. He sat back in his chair and smoothed his tie, embarrassment at his outburst weighing heavy on his shoulders.

Beckman shrugged. "Isn't a threat. You get your social programs; the City Council and I handle the other things."

"Like taking kickbacks from contractors?

Beckman snapped his fingers. "Exactly."

Cameron was in disbelief. Beckman got up and left without saying a word. Cameron rested his head on his desk. Politics to these men—the Governor, the Mayor, the ORD—was a game. A stupid game. They saw people as assets or commodities whose value increased or depreciated depending on what they could use them for. Cameron didn't think any one man should be able to mold the world in their image, but damn it, he felt his image was the fairest one. Why was it so hard to create? He wanted a place where people didn't die in hospitals due to inadequate services, a place where the negro could get their own version of the American dream on their sides of town, a place where people didn't fade away in squalor in a mental institution. A place where children didn't die on a side street twenty feet from one of the most prosperous shopping districts in the city. But that meant nothing to men in power. That meant nothing to Beckman. If he didn't have equity in it, he didn't give a damn.

Cameron went for a walk through the Quarter to clear his head, then stopped at the nearest phone booth to call Rose. Her voice was always calming to him. She was smart, so smart. He needed guidance on how to move forward with this... this moot campaign. This dying attempt at a movement. But she had her own cross to bear. He was with her the other night at dinner, but she didn't seem all that interested in him. Her body was present but her mind was far off someplace outside the restaurant. He put the phone down. He then went to see his father. Sometimes talking to the vessel where his father once resided gave him inspiration, but today it seemed sad and hopeless, and he was in no mood to pretend.

When he was really at his lowest, he thought of Bobby. Bobby hadn't been found, and neither was his family. They could've been in the wind; could've been dead. Either way, he didn't do enough to keep them safe. When he thought of that moment—when he used the law for his own end—he wanted to have a drink. But he couldn't. He couldn't be weak again. No matter how much it would ease his conscious.

As Cameron walked, he grew resentful. The people of the city... they were ok with their masters, the ORD, using drugs and booze and women as a distraction from their evil deeds. He stopped walking and leaned against the outer wall of a store with an outstretched hand. He'd prayed long and hard to avoid this day, the day his resolve would waiver, and the Lord told him he was strong enough to complete this mission. But his morale was low, and he was bitter, angry, and very close to abandoning his mission. He needed an impartial friend to talk to talk to and tell him what he should do, because he felt he could no longer trust himself. Then a lightbulb went off.

***

When Jesse picked up his phone he would've never bet in a thousand years that it would be Cameron Mulligan on the line. But it was. And now they were sitting in a café not far from Jesse's condo.

Cameron flashed a playfully embarrassed smile. "I'm sorry if this is, um, a little odd."

Jesse didn't know what to say. Part of him couldn't help but stare at the entrance over Cameron's shoulder, in case it was an elaborate setup. The other part felt awkward about the whole Rose thing. "It's not odd at all."

Cameron ordered coffees for him and Jesse to break the ice. "I'll get on with why I'm here. In my line of business, to be frank, I don't have many people who can give impartial and intelligent insights to me. And right now, I just need the ear of an impartial and intelligent man."

Jesse nodded. "Well, I'll let you know when I find one and send him your way."

They both laughed.

"So, what can I attempt to help you with?"

Cameron told Jesse everything. On the outside, Jesse

was attentive. On the inside, he thought about how it was the perfect opportunity to make Cameron drop out of the race and make him believe it was all his idea, which would guarantee that the status quo of New Orleans stayed the same. But, Jesse admired Cameron. It made him conflicted about what to say. Or was it that he felt guilty about Rose?

Jesse asked, "What makes you think I have the answer?"

"Oh, don't play coy. You're smart and really caring."

The conflicting sides of Jesse fought. The side of him that's always looking for leg up, and the other that never wanted to kick a man while he's down. His better side won.

Jesse leaned forward. "Honestly? I think he's scared. Beckman is and has always been publicly loud and boisterous. Around this time, he's flapping his gums and talking to the newsies about his victory before it even happens. I honestly think he's scared of you."

Cameron crossed his legs and laced his fingers. "You think so?"

"I know so."

"How?"

"Just a gut feeling."

Cameron nodded. "You know, Jesse. I've only been around you a handful of times, but I feel I can trust that."

This filled Jesse with pride. "Well, that's good to know."

Cameron asked, "Can I be frank?"

"Go ahead."

"I'm in awe by you."

Jesse raised an eyebrow. "What for?"

"I'm familiar with your history. Your criminal past."

Jesse cleared his throat and squirmed in his chair. Cameron stammered and scrambled to regain Jesse's attention. "What I meant was I recognized your last name. In relation to a Clyde Pike. I was an ADA when his name came across my desk for a B-and-E. When I met you, I went and did some digging and realized you two were related. And I also found out about your arrest as a young child." Cameron took a sip of his coffee. "Shoplifting."

Jesse eased up a bit. "Yea, I'm not proud of that."

Cameron put his hand up. "I'm not judging you." He motioned his hand around. "What you came from to be able to transform yourself, it's like alchemy of some sort. That doesn't happen often in this city. There are fellows I've met in my economic class who couldn't do the same with all of the resources in the world. And for that, you have my undying respect."

Jesse nodded. "Thank you."

"Sorry, if that was untoward."

"It's fine."

"As you said at the ball: 'socioeconomic oppression is the root of crime.' Being poor and needing food didn't make you or your brother bad people."

Jesse wondered if Cameron would have the same outlook if he knew of all of the skeletons in his closet. Jesse and Cameron left the café and walked until they reached the streetcar stop. It came up the rails at a leisurely pace.

"One more thing before I go on my way," said Cameron. "Rose. You and she have been long-time acquaintances."

Jesse nodded.

"Has she always been so remarkable?"

Jesse smirked. "Always."

Cameron bit down a smile, then fiddled with his fingers. "I'd figured. We're going through a rough patch right now, you know, with my campaign and all. I really would like a future with her after the smoke clears. Things are just hard right now."

Jesse's stomach tightened. "Yea, I'd imagine so." The streetcar ground to a stop. Something compelled Jesse to say these next words: "She's worth it. All of it. Whatever rough patch you two are going through, it'll be worth it."

Cameron was halfway through the streetcar. "I know it will be. Good day, Mr. Pike." And like that, Cameron Mulligan was still in the race for mayor and Rose's affection, and Jesse was left wondering what the hell he was thinking.

Chapter 25

Opening Night

The line outside The Magnolia winded around the corner and stretched for a block like it was opening day at the Fairgrounds. Jesse wasn't shocked. He'd anticipated this. For weeks he called every socialite he could think of, every friend or associate he'd made over the years. The line was full of a who's who of New Orleans, and he stood outside the closed double doors taking questions, comments, and praises from all of them. It felt good to feel like a minor celebrity for something other than owning a whorehouse. But someone was missing. His family would arrive soon, even Big Sal, but the one person he wanted to come, the one person whose validation he needed, wasn't there. He had invited Rose and didn't care if she brought Cameron. He wanted to be able to give a toast, look across the room, and see her smiling beautiful face looking back at him with pride and admiration. So far she wasn't there. And he wasn't sure if she'd come at all.

Mel stood next to him and rocked on his toes like a nervous child. "This is so exciting. You ready to open?"

Jesse looked at his watch. "Let's give it time."

Time ticked on. The familiar click-click-click of Sal's cane alerted Jesse to his presence. Sal said, "Come here, come here."

Jesse's smile hid his hesitation. He hugged Big Sal.

"I'm so proud of you," said Big Sal. "You know that, right?"

Jesse nodded but said nothing more. It was his special night, and he wouldn't give anyone room to manipulate his emotions.

Time went by and the line grew thicker, longer, and Mel's questioning grew steadier. Jesse felt like a broken record saying "Let's give it a little longer" over and over again. Albert, Bill, and Kenneth lumbered across the street. They walked with the precision of a newborn and screamed when they spoke and didn't attempt to hide the fact they were drunk in public.

"What's going on, old sport?" asked Albert. He pushed Jesse's shoulder in a playful, but rough, manner.

Jesse took it on the chin. "I'm doing fine."

Their breath reeked. Standing in the middle of them was akin to being in the middle of a distillery. Jesse wrinkled his nose. Albert, who rocked back and forth, reached in his coat pocket and pulled out a flask in front of everyone and took a deep pull. Mel pinched the bridge of his nose. Albert,

Bill, and Kenneth laughed and passed the flask back and forth like they weren't standing in front of a line of people. Most people were in their own little clusters of conversation, so no one saw. Jesse took the three men and ushered them off to the side before they could be seen bringing booze into the restaurant. Jesse went back to the front of the line with his hands on his hips. "Dear God, Mel. We can't let them in like that."

Mel put his hands up. "They'll be fine. I vouch for them."

"Yeah. Whatever you say," Jesse pointed in the general direction of Mel's friends. "But if Albert starts flapping his gums all crazy like he usually does, I'm kicking him out."

Mel nodded. "Ok, fair enough."

Eventually Rory, Twitch, Catherine, and Clyde arrived. Louisa Pike was arm-in-arm with Clyde. Jesse's mother was unrecognizable when she was sober and not ranting and raving depraved shit at him.

Louisa Pike had been sufficiently drowned in booze and Laudanum the last time she and Jesse spoke face-to-face. She had called him a disgrace, blamed him for his father's death, then hurled things at his head and told him all he would ever be was a thug and a lowlife. She had told him he would never graduate from Tulane, and well... that prediction came true. That hadn't been the first or second or even tenth time she'd gotten obliterated and said hurtful things to him. But that night hurt beyond words because he had been trying to get his life together. So to hear her say so many vile things to him as he begged her to stop caused him emotional anguish he had never felt before. Later that same night, after his mother berated him, Jesse held her hair while she vomited into the toilet and pleaded for his forgiveness. He never forgave her, and never would.

Even though all of that happened years ago, as Jesse stood in front of The Magnolia, he remembered it like it was yesterday, and struggled to stay calm.

Louisa smiled at Jesse. "Hello, son. You look well."

Her smile agitated him, but he locked away his anger for the sake of Clyde. "Mother, it's been some time."

She hugged him and fully engrossed him in her body like he was a little boy again, and he tried as hard as he could to not nudge her away.

Afterwards, Jesse walked up to Clyde and whispered in his ear. "I'm going to try."

Clyde responded, "That's all I ask."

Mel tapped Jesse and then tapped the face of his watch. Jesse told him to wait and looked over and around the people near him. He thought he could wait maybe five or ten more minutes, but he let that thought go. People were getting restless and hungry.

He cleared his throat. "Everyone, welcome to the opening night of The Magnolia!"

Everyone clapped and roared and hooted like frat boys at a burlesque show. Jesse fanned his hands toward the double doors, the doormen held them open, and within seconds, the main dining area of the restaurant was swamped by patrons. Waiters stood around tables and ushered people to their seats. A band played an upbeat tune to get everyone in an elated mood. Jesse stood at the threshold and took in the sight with immense pride.

Rory whistled as he walked past. "Shit. Didn't know you struck oil."

Jesse laughed. He'd spared no expense on the paintings, tables, cooks, cutlery, lighting, or even the napkins. He felt joy watching people enjoy his hard work.

Jesse and Mel made rounds for half an hour to make sure everything was in tip-top shape. The compliments rained down on Jesse, and he had to go through the motions of saying how he couldn't have done it without Mel, when in fact, he could have.

Once the ass kissing was done, Jesse went to check his family. The Pike Family had a table all to themselves in the far back. Jesse noticed a slight silence, with beads of conversation here and there as everyone at the table tried to chew their food and entertain one another the best they could. "Everything ok over here?" Jesse asked in a managerial tone.

"It's alright. I heard the owner's a fucking asshole though," said Rory.

Louisa stared daggers at Rory. "Now, now, shouldn't speak that way in front of ladies."

Rory responded sheepishly, "Yes, ma'am."

This annoyed Jesse. "Its fine, Rory. I know it was a joke."

That familiar scolding glance flashed across Louisa's face, but she stayed quiet, instead instructing everyone to scoot over a chair so Jesse could sit right next to her. She patted the open chair. "Come, come. We have a lot of catching up to do."

Awkwardness blanketed the table. Eyes darted back and forth between Louisa and Jesse, from her smile, back to his plain expression.

He gritted his teeth, bit his tongue, and simply replied, "I have a little time."

Rory and Catherine tried their best to fill the void of noise, understanding Clyde and Twitch were useless conversationalists, and Jesse was too annoyed to pretend to care to be there.

Jesse tried to be cordial. He truly did. But something about his mother's smug attitude, that smile across her face, irked the hell out of him.

Louisa speared her salad. "Ah, my little children all grown up," she said in an almost sing-song manner. "I'm so proud to see you all doing so well for yourselves." She placed her fork down and looked at Twitch. "And Daniel, you know I always considered you a fourth child."

"Fifth," Jesse said. Everyone looked at him. "You have four children already; he's like a fifth child."

Louisa held her mouth slightly open, like she couldn't believe the math. "Of course, it was an honest mistake." She smiled ear-to-ear and nodded. "Twitch, you're like a fifth child." Louisa pushed on and continued to find things to talk about: the food, the decor, the dress Catherine wore. Everyone nodded and gave non-committal answers, mainly head motions that gave the illusion of acknowledgment without having to actually answer. Jesse was so zoned-out he didn't notice someone stumbling and rocking their way over to the table. If he would've, things may have gone differently. If he wouldn't have been so engulfed in childish resentment at his mother, everything would be ok. But now, Albert stood over him grinning from ear-to-ear with his hand pressed down on Jesse's shoulder with his full weight.

"This must be the lovely Pike Family," said Albert.

Everyone acknowledged his presence half-heartedly. Albert cleared his throat over and over until Jesse got the hint. Jesse sighed. "Family, this is Albert. A new friend of mine."

Albert slapped Jesse on the back. "But we get along just like we're old pals!"

Albert walked around the table to shake everyone's hands. He started with Rory, then Twitch, but he lingered by Catherine for a while. Jesse couldn't hear what was said, but Catherine's blush and the sly smile on Albert's face were enough to make him uncomfortable and enough to make Clyde scowl.

Jesse mouthed to Clyde, "Let it be."

Clyde continued to cut his steak and kept one eye on Albert. Albert made it down to Clyde's side. Clyde rose and towered the man. Albert was 5'8, but looked much smaller next to Clyde's 6'1. Clyde's hand swallowed Albert's, and from the reaction on his face, it must've been a tight squeeze. "Whew," Albert said. "Easy there, slugger."

He held onto Clyde's hand and looked at Jesse. "You didn't tell me your brother was a heavyweight champ!" He busted into laughter at his own joke. Albert ambled over to

Louisa, who ate up the attention like it was a death row meal. Albert grabbed Louisa's hand and stood her up, spun her around to get a good look at her. "Jesse! You certainly didn't tell me your mother was a starlet!"

"Now, Albert," said Jesse. "It was good seeing you, but I think you should head back to your table." Jesse patted the booze in Albert's pocket. "And probably take it easy."

Albert sneered at Jesse. "What? I'm just having fun."

Louisa wasn't quite done with the attention. "Why don't you pull up a seat?"

And that's exactly what Albert did. He grabbed an empty chair from a table over and stuck it right next to Jesse. Even when sitting he had no control over his body. His knees kept bumping Jesse's.

"So," Louisa said. "How do you know my boy?"

Albert responded, "From The Chateau Club." He said it like it was an everyday place where everyday people can go.

"Isn't that an invite only place?" asked Louisa.

Jesse shrunk in his seat. "Yes. Mel invited me."

Albert said, "We actually first met outside this place some time ago, but I really feel like we hit it off that first time at the club."

Louisa stabbed her salad. "Well, that's great for you, honey. Guess you're moving up in life." Her envy spooled out from her with every moment, every breath, even the simple act of using a fork.

Jesse cleared his throat. "It's a nice place, sure. But I'd rather something simpler."

"Simple?" Louisa snapped. "Is that what we little folks

do? Simple things?"

Albert laughed. Jesse didn't. "I didn't mean to imply anything of the sort, Mother."

"You know," interjected Albert, "I never knew much about you, Jesse."

Louisa cut Jesse off. "Well, Jesse Pike Jr., before he was a big man, grew up in a little ol' house on the outskirts of the French Quarter. He used to share a room with his brothers, and actually used to love his mother." Louisa sat back and crunched her lettuce while staring at Jesse.

Albert chided Jesse. "Aw, man. Why don't you visit your mother more?"

Jesse turned around to Albert. "Ok, buddy, knock it off."

"No," Louisa said. "That's a great question. Why don't you?"

She slanted her eyes and declined her head to the side, waiting for him to answer. Jesse squeezed the life out of the roll of silverware in front of him. He said through gritted teeth, "I've been really busy, Mother."

"Several years busy?"

Albert said, "Years? You got to do better than that."

Clyde glared at Albert. "Ok, you need to go."

Albert got defensive. "I was just messin' with my pal here." He slapped Jesse's back again.

"You know, Albert," said Louisa. "My son always did think he was a little better than everyone around him." She chuckled. "I don't know why I'm shocked that he'd join private clubs or make bourgeois restaurants."

"Mother," Clyde said.

"But no matter how much he thinks he's changed, no matter how much he thinks he's better than me," Louisa continued. "He will always be more like his father than he thinks."

Albert laughed.

The restaurant was loud, Jesse noticed. Loud with conversations; from the swinging doors chafing together as it went in and out, in and out; from Rory slurping his water; his mother's loud chewing; and Albert—his incessant fucking need to talk and talk and talk when everyone wanted him to shut the fuck up.

"You alright, pal?" Albert asked.

Jesse's blood rushed through his eardrums, like listening to the ocean through a conch shell. He closed his eyes. Albert placed a gentle hand on Jesse's shoulder again. "You ok?"

Jesse slammed his fist to the table and propelled himself up. "Get your fucking hand off of me."

Jesse's anger caught the attention of a few patrons nearby. Eyes fell upon the table, but he was too blinded to see them. Albert's eyes were wide with shock and awe. Catherine got up and walked toward Jesse. "Ok, maybe we need to settle down now."

Jesse pointed his finger toward his mother. "No, she can antagonize me, sit there and bait me, but I'm the one who needs to settle down?"

She played the broken widow so well—so fucking well—with all of the complexity of a trained stage actress.

Being soft and emotional, and at the same time coarse and toxic. Her words were always like dog whistles; harmless to others but made specifically to screw with him. He built his dream life, or at least was in the process of doing so, when his mother came along and made him feel small again.

Jesse stared at his mother like he wanted to hit her. Everyone stared at their table now. Everyone. Mouths hung in suspension with half-chewed food protruding out. Conversations ceased. The band played still, but it did little to cover Jesse's words. Albert spoke to Jesse, asked him why he talked to his mother in such a way, and placed a hand on Jesse's shoulder again.

Albert stumbled backward with the first punch. He doubled over with the second. Blood shot out of his mouth when Jesse grabbed him by the collar with his left hand and twisted his right fist up into his gut. He crumpled to the ground and moaned. Jesse straddled Albert and threw punch after punch until his face resembled a squashed berry. Hands pulled him up to his feet and from on top of Albert. Jesse's face was red, veins popped from his neck, and every single person in the room looked at him. He exhaled and inhaled until he relaxed and the sobering grief of what he'd done came over him like a tidal wave.

Mel shouted, "Is someone in here a doctor?"

Albert groaned in agony on the floor. People kneeled at his side and put ice balled in napkins to his bruising face. Jesse stepped back inch by inch away from the gaping faces until he bumped into a table behind him. He looked out into the crowd. He saw Rose and Cameron in between peoples' heads. Rose's shock and grief and disappointment stabbed him in the heart.

Jesse stormed off to his office. He paced around in an angry daze. He swept every single item off of his desk and onto the floor. He kicked his bookshelf until all of the books came tumbling down. He reached behind the shelf and grabbed the brothel ledger. He tore the pages from the binding and threw them around the room. He leaned against his desk; his knuckles were covered with Albert's blood still. He grabbed a nearby handkerchief and tried to wipe it all away, but all it did was smear, absorb more into his skin, and spread into every fine line of his hand.

His status was done, over with. He'd never come back from this. Never. Everything he'd done, all of what he built that was supposed to be his and new, was gone. Rose was right. He couldn't be in New Orleans and be a different person. Clyde burst into the room.

Jesse stopped pacing. "I should've never let you bring her here. This place was my chance, my one chance."

"You should've ignored her, and that asshole out there. Mother's better now."

Jesse snickered. "She's not sorry, she's not better. She came here to ruin tonight, to treat this like her own stage, and you let her. I tried, Clyde. I did. But I'll never forgive her. How can you forgive her? The scars on your body are evidence of her being an abysmal mother; she never protected you. She never protected *us*."

Rory tried to walk in, but Clyde pushed him back out and locked the door. Clyde snarled. "But she's still our mother. What is your real problem with her?"

"She reminds me of every part of myself I want to remove." His face was a portrait of anger and disgust and sadness. He'd never said that out loud before. But now it was out.

Clyde shook his head. "You always thought you were so better than us."

Jesse threw his arms up. "Maybe I am."

Clyde got in Jesse's face close enough to nudge him backward on his desk. "Ask Bobby just how much better you are than me."

Jesse laughed. He held his stomach and laughed as hard as he could. "I didn't kill Bobby, you sick fuck." Clyde's shoulders dropped. "I would never do that. Ever. But you would. That's why I didn't let you come with me and Twitch. Because you're fucking sick. You've always been sick, Clyde. You may think you're some 'good man' now, but I'll always be better than you."

Clyde grabbed Jesse's collar and screamed in his face like a wild animal. Something in him, something he'd built up since he'd been home, broke. It broke in him and he wanted to break something in Jesse. He wanted to make him hurt the way he'd always hurt.

"Do it," Jesse said. "Do what you're good at. Hurt me."

Clyde let him go. He stormed out into the ballroom and out of the restaurant and out into the cold New Orleans night.

Jesse looked at his certificate from Tulane. He picked up a paperweight and shattered the frame.

Chapter 26

Broken

Clyde's body lumbered up the street. Headlights on cars and the lights along the sidewalk all looked smudged, as if from behind rain covered glass. He was high. Time didn't exist for him anymore, reality was negotiable, and his body was numb. His mind still spiraled though. The dope he pumped into his system from the Chinamen Uptown was cut to shit, unlike the drugs he'd found in prison. He still had Jesse on his mind. No matter how many things he tried to change, no matter how much he tried to rectify who he was, he would never be enough. He'd never be better than Jesse.

He blinked and awoke in a new drug den. He shared a pipe with a man next to him, even though he thought it was a woman last time, or maybe he was seeing things. He didn't know where he was. Clyde was missing for a full day, but he didn't know that. The drug dens he fell asleep in were all dark, and every time he woke up from a nap, he'd see the same people still sitting in their same spots with the same expressions of serenity across their faces. He was kicked out of one den, though, after threatening to bash a man's face in.

He was back on the street again. It was nighttime. A couple looked at him like he was deranged as he lurched slow and menacingly up the sidewalk. He tried to say "what are you looking at" but it came out as inhuman gibberish. The man grabbed his partner's hand and they ran across the street. Clyde laughed. They ran from him like you were supposed to when you came across a monster.

He made it back to the Rising Sun and headed straight behind the bar to take a bottle. He trotted up the spiral stairs to an empty room and closed the door. His room was quiet, isolated, like it was no longer a part of the brothel but a part of a different dimension. He trotted in circles around the room. The shadows taunted him, the noise from outside beat against the walls of his eardrums, the streetcars cried like banshees, the chatter from downstairs and that damn jazz music made his head split. He cried out for it to stop, please, please stop, but it didn't. He curled up in the corner of the room and further drifted between places, between then and now, sane and hysterical, heaven and hell. He lost track of who or where he was.

He was back in the Captain's house. No, wait, the Captain was in his room in the brothel. He couldn't see his face. The light outside the hall and the darkness inside the room formed a silhouette, but he knew that silhouette anywhere. "Please, just leave me alone to die." The shape came toward him, reached for him, said his name. *Clyde, Clyde, Clyde.*

Fear and anxiety clouded Clyde's drugged brain. He shouted for the shadow to not come any closer. When it did, Clyde lunged and wrapped his hands around its throat. Just like the night he strangled the life from the Captain and shot three rounds into his lifeless chest for being an idiot, for being so stupid as to think he could steal from Big Sal and not get caught. Clyde would have given anything— everything—for a picture-perfect life like the Captain's. He walked in and saw those pictures everywhere, the baby toys, the signs of domestication, and wanted to murder the man for jeopardizing it all. Clyde hated the man for making him into his killer. Clyde choked the shadow and felt the struggle to live drift from its body. Its hands started to release from Clyde's wrists. Its heels stopped knocking against the floor. "Why don't you leave me alone!"

Clyde heard his name again. But it wasn't the shadow below him. He lifted his head up to see Rory rushing toward him. Rory tackled Clyde. Clyde flipped his smaller brother off of him and pointed toward the still shadow below him. Rory slapped Clyde. "What are you doing?"

Clyde was out of breath from his two scuffles. He looked at the shadow.

Underneath Clyde was Catherine. Her eyes were tear filled and she coughed for air. An unquantifiable amount of horror was in her eyes. She held her neck, now red and bruised, and crawled from under Clyde. Clyde stood, knees weak, hands trembling, heightened anxiety taking over his body, and he reached for her slowly. "No, no. I would never hurt you..."

She recoiled from him. Rory ushered her away without a word to Clyde. He didn't even look at him. Clyde walked into the hallway to see Rory explaining to Jesse what happened. Clyde jogged up the hall. "Wait! Catherine, please!"

She rushed down the stairs, weeping.

Jesse threw a punch that knocked Clyde to the floor. His lips quivered in disgust. Clyde was sick to his stomach. "I would never hurt her, Jesse. You know that. You know I wouldn't." His voice sincere but weak, the adrenaline starting to leave his body and allowing the reality of the situation to hit him. Clyde screamed, "You know I wouldn't!" He pleaded for his brother for help.

Jesse stepped back from his reach, looked down at him, and shook his head. "You should've just killed yourself."

Jesse left Clyde on the floor, light from the hallway shining down upon him and forcing him to see the wreckage he'd left in his path.

***

Clyde found more drugs: heroin, coke, opium, whatever he could put in his body to numb his pain. He was at the Captain's house beating on the door, harder and harder and harder, screaming for his wife to come out. She looked through the blinds. She cracked the door with the chain still on it. Clyde was manic, sweaty, pale, and his smile unnerved her. "Tell me I'm a good person, please, tell me I am. You meant that, right?" He nodded in anticipation of an answer. The rain pitter-pattered against the awning.

The woman looked the disheveled Clyde up and down. "I think it's best if you never come here again." She slammed the door and he heard the various locks clicking into place. He walked out into the rain. He turned around and saw Edward at the blinds now. Clyde walked away.

***

Clyde, dripping wet, clothes eviscerated now, lumbered into Hymie's bakery. He muttered to himself. Hymie walked from behind the counter and took off his apron. "The sign says we're closed. You can't just—"

Clyde got to his knees, slow and uncoordinated, and took a gun from his waistband and slid it to Hymie's feet. "Kill me."

Hymie's eyebrow rose. Then he laughed. Clyde rocked back and forth. "Do it." He pulled money from his waistband and let it fall to the floor. It was mangled and soaked. The sweet scents of the lobby mingled with the smell of rain and sweat.

Hymie eyed the money. "What is this?"

"I can't do it myself."

Hymie picked up the money. He walked to the door and locked it. Clyde closed his eyes. He focused on his breathing and waited for it to all come to an end. He heard the drag of the gun against the floor, the slow steps of Hymie moving behind him; felt the barrel pressed against his head, pictured a world where things were different.

Where he wasn't wired for self-destruction, where he wasn't designed to harm himself and others. He realized he didn't know what that looked like. He heard the drop of the hammer. Then there was a click.

Hymie laughed. "It's empty, boy."

Clyde trembled with his eyes shut and tears running down his face. Hymie scoffed at him. "You're not fucking right, boy. Never been right." Hymie tossed the money at Clyde's chest and let the bullets he had removed clatter to the floor. "Whatever problems you have are your own. Call whoever you need to call and leave." Clyde fell backward and groveled on the floor. Hymie sighed and called the line to the brothel.

Twitch arrived moments later. Hymie helped pick Clyde up, who was still talking to himself. He spoke about how Jesse was better than him, will always be better than him. Hymie mock agreed. "Yea, yea."

Twitch pointed Hymie to the backseat where they would lay Clyde down. His words were barely discernible. "Everyone wishes I was dead. I should be dead. Jesse couldn't—Jesse couldn't even do it. But everyone loves him. Fear me, but love him. Why does everyone hate me?" He repeated that over and over again.

Hymie responded, "Yep. Couldn't even do it."

Hymie had a handle on Clyde and told Twitch to go start the car. Clyde blocked Hymie from pushing him in the car. His words slurred. "Jesse can't even kill him. He's gone. I would've done it."

Hymie stopped moving. "What did you say?" Hymie

held Clyde up.

"Jesse—he... he don't have the stomach for this shit. But I do." Clyde pointed at his own chest. "I always did. Why doesn't anyone trust me?"

Twitch looked back to see what was going on, but Hymie put a finger up to tell him to wait. Clyde said, real low and close to Hymie's ear, "Bobby's still alive. Jesse didn't have the stomach for it. I could've done it. Jesse couldn't. Jesse couldn't." Clyde lay across the backseat and Hymie shut the door. The car pulled off and Hymie stood there in the rain still thinking about Clyde's words. *Bobby's still alive. Jesse couldn't do it.*

Chapter 27

Fresh Start

It rained the whole night as Jesse sat at his kitchen table, but he didn't mind it. Clear skies were reserved for happy days, and today was not happy. He drowned himself in booze as he thought about everything he'd been through over the past few months. Hell, over the past four years. His dreams of a different life were done now. No one would deal with him. He was sure of it.

Mel hadn't called him back since opening night. He'd reached out to Albert to apologize, but no response. He was sure a lawsuit was coming his way, but he'd have it settled out of court. He'd learned so much about Albert since their friendship began that could be used against him, so he would give Albert no choice but to settle out of court. Jesse poured another drink. He chuckled at the thought of blackmailing Albert. It didn't take him long to revert to his old ways. Rose hadn't called him, and Clyde, fucking Clyde, almost killed their baby sister. His family was toxic and the city was poison.

Jesse threw the bottle at the wall and watched the whiskey drip slowly to the floor. He stormed over to his stash of money in his top drawer. He had enough left over from what he gave Bobby to leave this place for a while. He sighed. He still had unburned bridges out of state. Maybe he could go to New York or Chicago. He looked around the condo, then out his window over the cloudy, stormy city skyline. Canal St. was empty and the city was lifeless. He needed to leave this place. New Orleans wasn't somewhere he could be who he wanted to be. He started to pack his things.

Chapter 28

No Going Back

Two days before the election and the Women's Temperance Movement base buzzed like a bee's nest. Jesse found Rose next to the stage. She was busy grazing her finger over the itinerary while another woman stood next to her and nodded along. Jesse approached her.

"Hey," he said.

"Hey," she responded, with a hint of suspicion. She finished tasking the woman, then followed Jesse to the corner of the hall. He put his hands on his hips then turned around, looking from the floor to the stage and up to the ceiling, biding his time to gather his thoughts.

"What are you doing here?" Rose said. "You know it isn't proper to stop by like this. What if Cam—"

"Leave with me," he said.

She stammered.

"You were right. I can't be someone different and still stay here. Too many memories, none good, that flood my mind and make it hard. I know too many people. Too many connections. And my family...." he paced back and forth in a tight circle. "I will continue to go through this repetitive cycle if I stay here. Further becoming someone I don't like." Clyde's descent into a hollowed-out shell of himself came to mind. Then Albert's beaten face. "I want to write my own story. One with you in it." Rose was in stunned silence. "So please, say you'll come with me?"

Rose didn't move, didn't blink. She anxiously twisted the itinerary into a cone. "Where—how long? What is your plan?"

An exasperated snicker was all Jesse could muster. "I don't know. Months. Forever. I need to be gone."

Jesse put a finger up before Rose could speak. He wasn't ready to have his heart torn from his chest. "Don't... don't answer right now. I want to give you time to think. A day."

Jesse stormed off and left Rose twisting her itinerary into dust.

Jesse kept his head down when he walked through the doors of the Rising Sun. He couldn't afford to get entranced by its siren song again. He walked through the parlor and on to Clyde's office. He pushed through the door and saw Clyde there, eyes half opened, with a mess of papers on his desk, a glass of whiskey, and a bag resting in the chair across from him. There were no words shared. Jesse knew that had gone right out the window after he'd told his brother he should've killed himself. But Jesse didn't feel much remorse for those words. Catherine could've died. And for that, he'd never forgive Clyde.

The money was all there; a front on the remaining money from Jesse's portion of the liquor job and a buyout of Jesse's portion of the brothel. Jesse zipped the bag back and stared at his brother, taking him all in. "Nothing left to say, I guess."

Clyde shrugged. "I guess not."

Jesse reached out for a handshake, but his arm hung there waiting for Clyde to muster up the strength to reciprocate. His brother looked so drained and depleted, like his body struggled to function, like his hangover had a hangover. Clyde lifted his arm and trail marks were all over it; tiny little holes that danced along his forearm like tribal markings. "Jesus," Jesse said. The trails stumbled and bumbled like the steps of a drunk man in snow; they looked like he got the first plunge right, then struggled to find another vein for the next hits. Each mark was further and further from an actual vein, with one even looking bruised. Clyde was too ashamed to speak.

Jesse pulled Clyde's sleeve down for him. His last favor for his brother would be to help him hide his shame. "I hope you find the peace that you need, brother. I truly do." Jesse walked away, trying his best not to play the role of Clyde's fixer anymore. Clyde would be someone else's problem from now on.

Jesse powered out the office, down the hall, then he opened the door, and almost ran into Cindy. She looked up at him from the step below.

Jesse shut the door behind him. "Hey."

"Hey," she responded. Her eyes went down to the bag, and then back up to him.

"Always up to something, I see." She said it with the imitation of cordiality. He had a tight grin.

She fiddled with her fingers. "I was actually gonna need to talk to you. I called your home and I went by the restaurant, and you were nowhere to be found."

"I'm sorry about that."

Cindy began to speak, but Jesse couldn't contain his anxiety. "I may be leaving." He talked like if he said the words quick enough, it would lessen the blow.

She nodded slowly. "Oh. Where?"

"I don't know."

She squinted and pursed her lips. "You going alone?"

The question made Jesse's tie feel tighter. "I don't know." Her silence cut deep. Deeper than he would've thought. Because he didn't even consider telling her he was leaving. "I just... need to get away for a while."

Cindy looked out into the empty street, then bounced up and down on her tippy-toes, then closed her eyes to take a deep breath.

"Look, Cindy— "

"Don't. You don't have to. I always told you; you don't have to explain anything to me." He dropped the bag at his feet, then rubbed her cheek. He did care about her. He truly, truly did. The feeling of having someone you care about taken from you felt like walking around with one leg; life was off balance. And now he was amputating her, forcing her back into a world of disequilibrium. Their eyes looked longingly into one another's, like neither wanted to forget what the other looked like. Jesse unzipped the bag, pulled up stacks of money and forced it into her hands.

Tears streaked down her cheek. "Jesse, no."

"You always wanted to be an actress. A big star. Get you a ticket. Go out west. Live your dreams." He smiled wide. "I just want you to be happy."

Cindy shook her head in disbelief. Then she hugged him. "I just want you to be happy, as well."

Jesse went on to give his notice-of-leave to his sister, who cried on the steps of their house. He told her to tell their mother for him. Then he went to see Twitch. Twitch was always the strong, silent type. He didn't say much whenever Jesse told him, but Jesse knew the guy for years and knew it would hit him hard after a while. Twitch gave him a handshake and told him not to be a stranger. Rory was nowhere to be found. The hardest conversation, by far, was the one with Big Sal. He took the old man out to his favorite café in hopes this would be enough to stifle the blow. But when he picked Sal up, he was already in a terrible mood. He sat in the passenger seat and refused to look at Jesse before Jesse could even tell him the news.

"What's eating you?" asked Jesse. "I thought you liked this place."

Sal didn't touch the coffee in front of him. He stared at it like it was poisoned, and twisted his cane across his lap. "What do you want, Jesse?"

"I'm leaving."

This derived no emotion from Sal. "For what?"

"A change of pace."

Sal placed his hands on the table in front of him and said nothing, just glared like he was more angry than sad. Jesse said, "I always, always, will be indebted to you for everything you've ever done for me. I wanted to say that to your face."

Still nothing from Sal.

The tenseness was unbearable.

"I understand, Jesse. I do. Do what you must. I'm not feeling well, though. How about I go home, yea?"

"Ok," Jesse said.

He brought Sal back to his house and helped him out of the car and up the steps to his patio. They shook hands, but then Sal pulled Jesse in for a hug. Jesse was hesitant, but he wrapped his arms around the man who raised him up, and taught him how to be a man. The door behind them opened up, and Junior stood in the doorway. He looked as if he was about to rush out the house, but the sight of them hugging stopped him in his tracks. Jesse cleared his throat and let Sal go. Sal turned around. "The hell you looking at, eh?"

Junior walked out. "Not much."

Jesse shook his head. "I'll miss our little pissing matches, Junior." Jesse turned to leave and was on his way to beginning his new life.

Chapter 29

Moving Target

The cloudless day was beautiful; the sun was an engorged ball of light taking the sting off the sharp breeze ripping through the air. The man enjoyed it. He sat in his car and rode slow up Canal St. behind his target. His target: adult, male, probably late 20s, maybe early 30s. He drove a black Packard, so the guy must've done well for himself. And based on the huge, red brick building he came out of, he must have money to blow. The man had gotten the call about this target yesterday morning. He rolled over, wiped the sleep from his eyes, and started taking notes. "I'll need some time."

His contact had snapped. "You get no time. There's a tight window." And his contact went on to lay down the specifics. He'd worked with contact before, and he was guaranteed a large fee upon completion, so he accepted.

Now he wished he wouldn't have. The target in question was always around people, and when he wasn't around people, he was in his car. And when he wasn't in his car, he was safely away inside a large, populated building that he assumed was his target's residence.

The target pulled over to the curb in front of a tight row of storefronts, and pulled down the sleeves of his suit. The man pulled over as well, three cars ahead, holding up a tiny mirror so he could keep an eye on his target. The streets were lively, busy; people bumped shoulders past one another as they entered and exited the boutiques and cafes and bookstores. He got out of his car, and tried to move with intent through the crowd. He kept a tight eye on his target. The man could barely keep up; a plethora of shopkeepers popped out to try and drag him inside their little stores. He put up his right hand and said, "no." He kept his left hand tight on the gun in his coat.

He played it out in his mind: he'd go up behind the target, put the gun on his back, tell him to play along or he'd shoot him right where he stood in broad daylight, which he'd done before, granted it wasn't in a city he actually lived in. Then he'd guide the target back to his car, take him for a ride, then he's upriver and gator food. Simple. The target bent over to tie his shoe. The man sped up his stride. He bumped through people who wouldn't move, ignored the calls and cries for donations from a little boy with a ringing bell and no shoes. He was almost on him. He was so close to the target he could smell his expensive aftershave. Then out came some beat cops from the bakery right next door. *Fuck.*

The man decelerated his stride and let his fingers unlatch from the gun. The target was up and standing now. The man brushed past his target, narrowly hitting him with his shoulder. "Watch it, buddy," said the target. And the man feigned apologies. The target stopped to talk to the beat cops. *This fucking guy knows everybody.*

The man leaned against the wall and made mental notes. The target surely wasn't an actor or the President, but he wasn't some Joe Shmoe either. The man watched from the corner of his eyes as his target dipped off into a store, apparently a flower shop from the looks of the chain-linked sign swaying from the horizontal pole out front, and decided this wasn't the time for the target to die. He'd wait until the night provided cover. Nighttime was the best for a hit, because everyone in this city would be too fucked up to know what they saw. He walked back through the thick crowd, hopped in his car, and waited for a better time. The man pulled out his note pad and scribbled some notes: *Ask for more money and a ride out of town after the job is done.*

He went through his notes once more. *Target: male, about late 20s or early 30s, hardly alone, name... Jesse Pike.*

Chapter 30

God's Will Be Done

The night before the election

Cameron's party was packed. Red, white, and blue streamers hung from the rafters; Mulligan banners were draped everywhere for the eye to see. Yet some people's gazes fell upon Jesse. He snaked through the clusters of people, and many didn't bother to hide their glares or muffle their disdain. Word amongst the elites traveled faster than Chlamydia in a whorehouse, but he didn't care. He was on the hunt for Rose, and, in the morning, he would make haste in heading out to broader pastures. Eventually he spotted her. "Rose, we need to—"

"Jesse!" Cameron's hand appeared in front of him.

Jesse could barely feign niceties. "Howdy."

Cameron chatted up Jesse and told him how happy he

was to see him, how his talk gave him the confidence to stand strong on his convictions. But it was all background noise for Jesse, who was held captive under Rose's gaze. Jesse gave a noncommittal gesture to Cameron, who stopped speaking once he noticed Jesse wasn't paying attention to him. His face went from confused to astonished in mere seconds. Jesse and Rose's affection for one another rolled off them in waves so powerful even Cameron could feel it. And they didn't care. Cameron's campaign manager came over. It was almost his time to make a speech. An absentminded nod was all Cameron could muster.

"I'm happy you could make it," he said to Jesse.

Jesse's eyes didn't move from Rose. "Yea, no problem."

The lights dimmed; the center stage lit up like a single star in a vast canvas of dark sky. The crowd roared when Cameron's name was announced to come to the stage. Jesse leaned in to whisper into Rose's ear. "I need to know what you're thinking."

Her soft voice was muted by the people clapping and chanting *Mul-li-gan, Mul-li-gan*. Jesse cupped his hand around her ear. "I can't understand you." She spread her arms out in frustration. He pointed toward the exit. She put up one finger, letting him know she'd need a moment. He nodded.

He paced outside of the building with his fist tucked tight in his pockets; his thick condensed breaths trailed him like steam from a train and drifted into the cold night air. He needed to leave. With her, without her, it didn't matter anymore. He was silly to think he could be new, different, transformed and still live in a city that turns people into demented, morally fractured humans that'd get over on their own mothers just for a slice of power. This city made people monsters. He would go somewhere for a while, maybe forever, it didn't matter, he simply needed to know if he was making plans for two. The streetlights lining the sidewalk cast a glow, and a shadow appeared next to his on the pavement. Someone stood behind him.

**

The atmosphere in the Rising Sun was fading. Guest trickled in every few minutes, sat at the bar or at a table for a drink, noticed the place was dead, then left. The front door was a revolving door at that point. Clyde wasn't shocked. There were a lot of pre-Election Day events going on. He sent Twitch home and Rory, well, never showed up. He and Catherine were avoiding him. As they should have.

The customer next to Clyde was eyeing him. The guy had been nursing the same drink for about a half-hour or so since the last real customer went upstairs with one of the girls. Her name was Maude or some shit like that. Either way, the guy next to him had been giving Clyde quick glances and trying so hard to pretend like he wasn't that it was made even more obvious. It put Clyde's nerves on high alert.

The bartender went over to the man. "Still working on that?"

The man responded, "Is it not still in my glass?"

Clyde normally would have put the man in check, but this time, he didn't give a shit. His killer instinct was dampened in a fog of the day before yesterday's booze and drugs. The bartender scoffed and walked away.

The phone rang. The bartender answered. "What? Who—Uh, yes, he's right here." He dropped the phone down and turned to Clyde. He said it was the girl Maude and that she needed him to come upstairs.

"What'd she want?"

The bartender shrugged.

Clyde trotted up the stairs and down the hall to look for the room he was summoned to. He found it, the door half-cracked and the light from the hall slicing into the room and illuminating a corner of the bed and Maude's leg.

"You needed something?" Clyde asked. He wiped the bourbon from his lips with the tip of his shirt and took a step forward into the dark of the room. Her eyes twitched. "Yea. Uh, I need you to take a look at something."

"Wanna turn a light on?"

Her voice trembled subtly. Her pupils darted slightly back and forth, she didn't blink, her quivering lips belied the seemingly calm message. "Oh, I think you'd like the dark better." Her eyes darted again. On the floor were her clothes, and a jacket for a man.

He understood. "Ok."

He took a step in, then dropped his shoulder and slammed the partially ajar door into the wall. A man's hand flung out. A gun pitter-pattered across the floor.

"Agh! Fuck," the man yelled. He was sandwiched between the door and the wall. Clyde held him there with his big frame while trying to get the gun on the floor.

Maude screamed and covered herself with the blanket.

"Don't just fucking scream! Get the God damned gun!" Clyde said. The man got free. Maude rolled off to the opposite side of the bed while Clyde and his assailant wrestled each other for the gun on the ground. Both men climbed over each other, groaned, strained, and stretched their fingers out to give themselves the advantage. Clyde dropped an elbow into the man's jaw. He grabbed the gun. He cocked back the hammer and straddled the man. "Who the fuck are you?"

The man's eyes shifted to behind Clyde. A shadow formed on the floor. Pain—cool and sharp—rapidly spread through Clyde's right shoulder, making his arm painful to use. A knife protruded from it. Behind him was the man from the bar.

The man pulled the knife out, and with it came teardrops of blood that dotted the floor. Clyde yelled in an agonizing pain that strained the cords in his neck. The shiny blade came toward Clyde's face, but he flung his entire mass up into the man's swipe, forming a shield with the forearm of his uninjured arm. He rammed the man into the wall in the hallway. A struggle ensued; Clyde attempted to raise his gun to the man's face. The knife got closer to his eye. The gun felt like a thousand tons due to the pain from his stab wound. His wound ruptured further, his laceration tore more, blood ran down his back and to his leg and pooled on the floor and around his shoe.

Clyde heaved and ignored the pain and lifted the gun and pulled the trigger. There was an eruption. His ears whistled. The man's skull exploded like a hammer dropping on a watermelon, crimson chunks and shrapnel of skull stuck to the beige wallpaper. The body slid down the wall leaving a snail trail of gore in its wake. Downstairs the music stopped. The very few people in the building ran out at the sound of gunshots. The other assassin fled down the hall high tailing it like he was late for the night's last streetcar. Clyde's injured arm lay useless at his side. He spun toward the sound of receding footsteps, aimed with his uninjured arm at the man's back, and fired. A bullet snapped through the man's ankle. Clyde shrugged; he wasn't left-handed.

He moved slowly toward the crawling man. Clyde hovered over him with a demonic grin on his face and a look in his eyes that'd strike fear into God. The man put his hands up. Clyde put the gun to his forehead, and squeezed the trigger. The blood misted on to Clyde's white shirt. He leaned against the wall. The pain grew. The girl came out into the hall and shrieked. In between sparse breaths, he said, "Please, go find some bandages." The girl ran naked down the hall with her hands covering her mouth. Clyde shook his head and stumbled to his feet. "Bitch."

He limped and hobbled his way down the stairs. He went behind the bar and took rags out to hold against the bleeding. He dialed up Twitch. "Get over here, right now." His hand smeared blood against the bartop. "And find out where Jesse is."

***

Jesse's guts swirled into a knot. "Cameron?"

Cameron seemed peeved. "Thought you two were just old friends?" His voice broke. "I knew something was going on with someone. She'd been strange and distant lately."

Jesse wanted to lie, but Cameron was smart. He'd had a feeling about this in advance. "It's—Cameron...It's complicated."

Cameron looked at the ground. He raised his glasses ever so slightly to swipe a finger at his eyes. "Are you in love with her?" Jesse's love was an understatement. He craved her, desired her, needed her. But Jesse didn't say that. Instead he stammered for words to say to the sad—bordering on pissed—man in front of him.

"You can't have her," Cameron said. His eyes turned angry. "Please. What will it take? Huh? Money?" Cameron's eyes misted. "I have a lot of money. A lot of it." He clenched his fist, a lone tear streaking down his cheek. "I love her so much."

Cameron was willing to throw away money and time for the woman he loved. Cameron stood in front of Jesse, visibly straddling the line between enraged and saddened, when he was supposed to be on stage giving a speech to a hundred people. A few handlers came to talk to Cameron, tried to tell him he should be on stage. He waved them away.

Jesse said, "I can't—I can't make any decisions for her."

"You two have history, I can't compete with that. And she's her own woman, so I know either way it's a crapshoot that she'll stay with me. But I need her by my side. I don't have anyone else I trust." He moved closer to Jesse. "I need her by my side because it is God's will."

Jesse squinted his eyes. "God's will?"

"Like I said, I don't have anyone else that I trust. My entire life, I've had people trying to tell me what to do, where to go to school... how to run Mayoral campaigns. But with her, I feel good. I feel like there's a reason God brought her into my life, and that reason is because he knew I needed someone like her."

God's will, Jesse thought to himself. A bold stance to take, but Cameron said it so confidently, so wholeheartedly, Jesse believed him. Cameron was a version of Jesse that wasn't corrupted or tainted by nightmares and feelings of insecurity. He wasn't a bad man. Maybe Jesse could've been him if he'd had a better upbringing, or better role models. Maybe God did draw Cameron and Rose together, because he knew Jesse was terrible for a woman like Rose. Maybe Jesse was meant to be alone so that he didn't drag someone down just like his father. She was taken from him once before. He could afford to lose her again. Cameron couldn't.

"I don't need or want money," Jesse said. "I'll back off. Just tell her..." Jesse choked on his words. "Tell her I just want her to be happy." Cameron's eyes closed with subtle elation. Jesse oddly felt happy for him.

More people came out to try and grab Cameron.

"I'll let you go," Jesse said.

Cameron nodded.

Cameron grabbed Jesse's shoulder. "Wait, Jesse, I—" Cameron's speech stopped. His eyes widened. Jesse spun around to see what Cameron saw. A man charged forward.

The glint from a gun muzzle flew out of a coat. A pop rang through the hollows of Jesse's ears and drowned out the sound of screams. He dropped to his knees, the world went off its axis, and the streetlights turned to shapeless blurs in his fuzzy vision. The cool night wind blew against a damp spot on Jesse's shirt. His hand came up. Blood. The assailant ran off with a look of shock on his face. The screams of passersby and the sounds of people gathered behind him. Jesse thought about how these were the last sounds he would hear before his trip to the afterlife. He closed his eyes, and waited for his heart to stop.

***

Jesse opened his eyes. The people who ran outside weren't looking at him. The blood on his shirt wasn't his. His shock heightened to an extent he never felt before.

Cameron was on the ground gargling on his own blood right next to him. A red stream spurted from his chest, and he took hard gasps for air, a failing attempt to claw at breath that wouldn't stay. "I'm right here, buddy. I'm right here. You're going to be alright," Jesse said. Cameron's eyes were wide in shock, his head jerking up and down like a fish on land. He was scared. So, so scared.

"Cameron. Cameron," Jesse said over and over again. Jesse tried to press down on the wound, but more blood came out and stained his hands. Cameron rested his hand on top of Jesse's. He squeezed so tight, like he was hoping Death wouldn't be able to snatch him from this plane. Someone ran to get help. But it was too late. The gurgling stopped. The light in Cameron's eyes went out, and all that was there was the last face he'd ever make, one of confusion, fear, and deep, deep regret. Jesse let Cameron's hand go. It fell to the ground.

Jesse hovered over the body in complete shock. "No, no, no...."

He got up, shaken, blood on his own shirt and hands. Oh, God, his hands. He looked up at the circle of people, clutching pearls, covering their mouths in shock, tears streaming down their faces. Jesse stumbled away. A man stepped in his way and spoke with a shaky voice. "Hey, young man, you need to stay and speak to the police."

Jesse's bloody hands gripped around both sides of the man's collar, a feral, wounded animal look in his eyes. "It should have been me." Jesse looked disturbed and pale, like blood had been drained from his face. "I did this to him." He pushed the man aside and stumbled down to an alley where he lurched, dipped to the side, then threw up against the wall. In the background, he could hear a woman asking to be let through, asking for people to get the hell out of the way. There was nothing, followed by a deep, agonizing yell. It was Rose. Oh, God, oh, God. It was her.

Jesse stumbled in a daze on the four-block walk from the party to the Rising Sun. He saw nothing on the walk home but Cameron's eyes, which were etched into his brain, etched into his soul, vying for room along with all his other memories. His father. Newsstand owners. O'Grady. Cameron. Rose.

Jesse pushed open the front door of the brothel, lurched

around the corner into the east parlor where Rory and Twitch were busy wrapping up Clyde's arm, and froze where he stood.

"Jesse?" said Clyde.

Jesse looked at the ceiling. "It's all my fault. It's all my fault."

Part III

"The most dangerous creation of any society is the man who has nothing to lose." — *James Baldwin*

Chapter 31

Election Day

The news of Cameron's death spread like a fire through a forest. It came through the radios in dives and saloons, it came from men hawking papers for both the *Times* and *The Item.*

Bold big black letters ran across all front pages: **GOLDEN BOY MULLIGAN, SHOT DEAD BY GANGSTER.**

The body: *Cameron Mulligan, heir to the Mulligan family throne, New Orleans District Attorney, and candidate for mayor, was gunned down at 8 PM last night right outside of his own campaign party. The cops are on the hunt for a person of interest. No other information has been given as to whom or what spurred this killing. The election has been scheduled for a later date.*

The picture on the front page of the *Times Picayune* was of uniformed police officers and street clothed detectives standing over Cameron's covered corpse. His arms and feet spilled out from underneath the white sheet.

In public, Mayor Beckman stated he'd find out who'd done this if it was the last thing he did. In private, he got handshakes and pats on the back from his club members. There was no way Reformers' back up choice, Andrew McCabe, an entrepreneur who made his money with coffee and tea, could fill the slot.

Now, Mayor Beckman had his feet kicked up on his desk within City Hall, writing his victory speech and working on walking the tightrope between thanking the people for voting for him, and remorse for Cameron's family and constituents. Then shards of glass sprinkled and glimmered over his shoulders and a rock pattered across his desk. He spun around. Through the jagged-tooth hole in his window, he saw a crowd metastasizing on the steps of City Hall. They all cried for his resignation. Within minutes, uniformed officers were shielding the steps from the roughly thirty or so people, and Beckman was outside doing damage control. "Good people of New Orleans! I—"

Another rock came for his head. The thrower ended up on the ground with a billy club to the ribs and a foot on his back.

While the city spilled into chaos, the west parlor of the Rising Sun was quiet and somber. Twitch, Rory, and Clyde stood near the bar while Jesse sat quietly next to them.

"Jesse," Twitch said. He pulled on his shoulder and snapped in his face. He was out of it. He hadn't moved in the hours. He hadn't moved, spoken, or even blinked. He stared into an abyss of nothingness, his mind frozen in time, on the moment the gun was pointed at him, and he anticipated the bullet shredding through his flesh and out his back, but instead... Cameron's eyes, they were a deep black pit Jesse couldn't escape. Cameron knew the whole time he was dying, and there was nothing he could do about it. He couldn't even give Jesse last words to give to Rose. Just a quiver of the lip, a gasp of strained breath, and eyes that pleaded to stay within the realm of the living.

Jesse moved, finally.

He took his coat off to reveal the swaths of thick red blood still on his shirt. He walked around the bar and grabbed a glass and bottle. "Someone tried to have us killed last night."

Clyde had his arm in a sling made from bar rags. "But what does that have to do with Cameron?"

The whiskey warmed the middle of Jesse's chest. "That bullet was meant for me."

"How-how do you think?" Twitch asked.

Jesse turned to face him. "The gunman, he looked right at me. And Clyde being attacked at the same time? I don't know. I don't know. I think, I think Cameron might've jumped in the way." Jesse exhaled. "I'm supposed to be dead right now." He ran his fingers through his hair. "I'm supposed to be dead."

Clyde shook his head in disbelief. "But why? Could it be one of the out of state booze buyers?"

"No, that wouldn't make sense."

"Revenge for O'Grady?" Clyde asked.

"No, I—I don't know." Jesse's lightbulb went off. "It could've been fucking Joe."

Clyde gritted his teeth. "You really think—"

A knock from the front door echoed around the empty parlor. Everyone's eyes darted back and forth to one another. Twitch inched toward the door with his gun at waist level. Rory, Jesse, and Clyde stood by the bar with their jaws clenched. Twitch walked back into the parlor and waved Jesse over. "It's for you."

***

The interrogation room was cold and cramped, about 8x10, with chipped pastel-white brick walls and a recessed mirror directly to the right of the table. Jesse laced his fingers on the table while the two detectives across from him machine-gun fired questions his way to knock him off balance:

"You were at the party, right?"

"People said you were at the party."

"Why'd you leave the party?"

"Didn't think to change your clothes?"

Jesse didn't make eye contact with either of the cops. The short glimpses he got of them were enough to let him know they were two interchangeable, square-jawed, faceless assholes like most detectives.

"I ran away because I was in shock. The man died in front of me. And as far as the clothes," he looked down at his shirt under his jacket. "I don't know."

Asshole # 1 cleared his throat. "Witnesses said you were

outside talking to Cameron right before the assassin approached."

Asshole # 2 asked, "What were y'all talking about?"

Jesse said, "Business. Politics."

That's when the questions and comments came even quicker, almost to the point he didn't speak, mainly because he could barely keep up with who was talking:

"So, at no point your conversation got emotional or heated?"

"Heated enough to kill?"

"Maybe he mouthed off."

"Yea you seem like a hothead."

"You ever got in a brawl before?"

"You seem like the brawling type."

On and on and fucking on they went. It was like they were playing tennis with thinly veiled accusations, trying their hardest to get him rattled and say something incriminating.

Jesse's head lulled back and he closed his eyes. After a while, the men lost steam, and the monotonous back-and-forth of accusation/answer tapered down. He answered their questions perfectly. They had nothing. He stood to leave. As he opened the door, one of the detectives asked him one last question: "If you really didn't have anything to do with the hit, why did an eyewitness claim you said, 'this is my fault'?"

Jesse paused. He hysterically ran into a man nearest him after Cameron had been shot and said those stupid, stupid words. "I was in shock. I guess... I guess I blamed myself for him even being in a position to be shot." He left the room.

The waiting room was a cacophony of unbridled anger, despair, and anxiety, with a mixture of grieving eyewitnesses waiting to speak to detectives, uniformed officers with notepads trying to forge whole sentences from the muddled words of emotional witnesses, and six angry citizens at the front desk near the entrance pleading their hearts out to be allowed to form a search party. The same happened years ago. That search party ended with six Italians hung from trees in the city square.

Jesse was near the double-doors when he overheard a cop on the phone vetting what sounded like a lead. He inched slowly away from the door. He walked over to the cop, who was young and in uniform and wore his aggravation like a mask. Good. Emotional people are talkative people.

He never lifted his head and pointed toward the hallway Jesse just came from. "Lead detective's over there."

Jesse put on a concerned front. "Just crazy what happened last night, isn't it?"

"You have no idea, sir." He cut Jesse off and picked up the phone to write down another lead. He furrowed his eyebrows, then slammed the phone down. He massaged the middle of his forehead.

"It's so maddening. A crisis happens and people think it's time to play jokes on the phone," Jesse said.

The young cop put down his pencil and paper. "You have no idea. I've been at this all morning, going through calls with crazies, trying to figure out which leads sound plausible."

Jesse feigned concern. "Well, I hope the boys in blue catch him. Any of the leads solid?"

"Some say he is hiding out in the swamp; some say he is in the old Tenderloin, some—"

Bingo. Jesse heard the answer he liked. The guy was on foot. Eyewitnesses saw his face, so he would lay low until he could get out of town. It's not far from where the hit happened. Jesse cut the young man off. "Thanks for the chat, and good luck catching that bastard."

The young cop nodded with pride. "We'll get him, sir."

***

Clyde, Twitch, Rory, and Jesse pulled the car to a stop in front of an abandoned mechanic's garage. The building suffered from wood rot, with weeds growing high around the lower exterior. It was the fifth abandoned building they'd checked out.

Everyone hopped out of the car. Clyde took the lead. He gestured for Rory to follow him around back, and for Jesse and Twitch to walk right to the front door. The gravel crunched under their steps as they took measured, careful steps to the door next to the sliding garage door. Twitch counted down, then kicked in the entrance.

The boom caused a man, sitting in the dark, to stumble from his seat. "Fuck." He gathered himself and ran toward an exit.

Jesse squinted. "That's him."

The man fired off-balance shots as he ran. Twitch and Jesse ducked as the bullets plunked into the walls near their heads. They chased him. The gunman knocked over a tray of tools, then turned to shoot at them one more time. They ducked behind a metal barrel. Jesse looked at Twitch. "We need him alive." They stayed hidden while the bullets dinged against every surface around them.

The man ran for the exit, heaving and pumping his arms. He saw the bright lights of daytime. Then Clyde's fist flew at his face. The lights went out.

***

"Look—looks like he's up," Twitch said.

The man eased from the fog one blink at a time. Then alarm set in. His wrists, arms, and ankles were bound by ropes. Twitch clicked his tongue. "You're not going anywhere."

Jesse leaned against a workstation. Rory sat on a stool. Clyde paced back and forth like a madman. Twitch fumbled through the bags of tools he'd found in the shop, examining each one like a child would a brand-new toy.

Jesse spoke first. "Alright, you can make this easy, or hard." The man's eyes darted toward Twitch every time he heard the metallic clang of tools hitting the concrete. The man shook but said nothing.

Clyde dropped a jaw-shattering punch using his left fist. Jesse forced Clyde back and pointed at the spreading stain underneath his sling. The man spat out blood. Jesse asked him, "Ready to talk?" The man laughed and exposed his crimson coated teeth. Jesse scratched his head. He motioned to Twitch. "Do your thing." Twitch approached the man with pliers. The gunman squirmed in his bindings while Twitch gripped his jaw. "Open up."

The gunman's pursed lips could only resist the pliers for so long. The gunman let out a squeal, then a throaty scream. Twitch strained, then yanked out a bloody tooth. The gunman's chair rocked back and forth in rhythm with his writhing agony.

Rory winced. Clyde cleared his throat. "Now that you see we aren't fucking around... you already know why we're here." Clyde motioned around the room. "Somebody wants us dead. Who?"

The man's expression was still. The wrinkles on his face read like the lifeline of a man who'd seen some hard days on the streets. He had wiry thin hair and trickles of blood running down his lips. He spat blood at Jesse's feet. Twitch slid on brass knuckles and cracked the side of the man's head.

Jesse nodded. "You were sent to shoot me, then freaked the hell out when you realized you shot the wrong man."

The man growled, "He got in the way."

Jesse's emotions boiled over. He moved Twitch out the way and grabbed the man's neck. "You know who you killed? Do you? And it means nothing to you?"

The gunman winced. Crescent-shaped bruises spread across his cheek like spilled water. "Why do you give so much of a shit?"

That was a question Jesse had been wondering about since the night prior. He and Cameron only had a few conversations. When he pondered the notion though, what came up over and over was three things: the bullet was meant for him; Rose was crushed; and Cameron was the best of men in New Orleans. He carried all that guilt with him, and would likely carry it for years to come.

Twitch snatched Jesse's hands away. He ushered him toward Clyde and Rory. He spoke to them in a calm, measured tone. "Give me five minutes."

The three men walked into the other room and left the gunman alone with Twitch and his tools. The screams that came from the next room weren't human. The metallic surfaces and open space around the garage made the screams seem to come from nowhere and everywhere at once. Clyde smoked a cigarette. Jesse leaned against a workstation. Rory looked like he could throw up.

Eventually the screaming stopped. Twitch came out with a bloody hammer and wrench in his hands and called for Jesse. Clyde and Rory tried to follow, but Twitch warned them away in a flat tone. "Just Jesse."

What Twitch told Jesse sent shivers up his spine. Not from fear. No. Rage. Anger. Pure animosity coursing through his body. Jesse returned with a stifled step and pale skin, like all the blood drained from his body. "What is it?" asked Rory, whose foot wouldn't stop shaking.

Jesse didn't answer. Instead he ambled over to a workstation and pressed his palms against the counter and slid his fingers into the chunky black grit. The silent anxiety overtook the room while Jesse gathered his thoughts. Then he spoke. "It was Hymie's man. Sal wants us dead."

Chapter 32

Betrayal

Everyone's expressions were frozen between anger and confusion. Clyde flicked his cigarette. "What's his grief with us?"

Jesse stared daggers at Clyde and dug his fingernails into his palms as his ears rang. He couldn't believe what the hitman had told Twitch, and in turn, Jesse couldn't believe what Twitch had told him. The hitman said that Clyde, who according to Hymie was drugged out of his mind, let it slip out that Jesse didn't take out Bobby. Jesse rejected that notion. He had told Twitch, "Clyde would never. He would fucking never do that." Twitch had agreed... then added, "N-n-not so-ber, at least."

Twitch then revealed he had to pick up Clyde from Hymie's bakery some nights back because he was borderline passed out, and stumbling around while murmuring to himself. Twitch added, "He probably doesn't re-re-member doing it."

That broke Jesse's heart beyond repair. But he would have to address that later though. For the time being, Jesse told Clyde, "I'm not sure."

Rory paced around in a circle. "We're going to need back up, right? We have guys."

Clyde rejected the idea. "Hymie's got a hit squad. Our doormen just throw out horny drunkards; they don't get in gunfights."

Jesse interjected. "Hymie called in eight guys. Two for each of us. They're down to five. If Sal calls in some hitters from the East Coast... things can get ugly fast."

Jesse's mind whirled. They were outmatched, outmanned, and outgunned.

He marched off into the next room, stepping over the puddle of blood running from the moaning and groaning mess of a man tied to a chair, and picked up the phone on the workstation. When nothing came through, he slammed it against the counter until his arms got tired. He slammed it until all of his anger and anxiety wore off. He marched toward the door.

Jesse's car weaved in and out of traffic on his way to the French Quarter. He abruptly jerked to a stop in the middle of the street and left his door wide open. He wouldn't be long. He walked into the café and saw Sal and Hymie sipping coffee at a small table. They saw him. Jesse walked through the packed café slowly but on the inside he wished to unload his gun into their faces right there, right then. He pulled up a seat at their table while they looked at him like he had three heads. It was an awkward silence. A server approached the table and Jesse shooed him away. Now, Jesse just stared across the table, unsure what to even say.

Sal lifted his cup and saucer, and took a slow, appreciative sip of his coffee. "You betrayed me."

Jesse's rage simmered. Hymie pitter-pattered his fingers against the table. He started to inch up to walk away. "I guess I'll leave you two..." A click from under the table stopped him in his tracks. He was in a half-standing, half-sitting posture.

"Think you'd wait for me outside, then follow me to where ever I go, huh?" Jesse rubbed the contours of the trigger under the table. "I don't think so."

Hymie sat back down.

"You won't use that here, Jesse. You're too smart," said Sal.

Jesse shook his head. "You always use to tell me how desperate men did stupid things."

"What you want from this? Huh?" asked Sal.

"A way out."

Hymie almost spoke, but Sal shushed him. "This can be rectified. Turn yourself in, please. You turn yourself in, and I'll leave you and your family alone. Only one of you will have to die. No one else."

"You know my brothers would never let this go."

Sal took a calming breath. Then exhaled, like a doctor preparing to give a terminal diagnosis. "Then I gun them down in the streets. I cut that retard Twitch up and hang him from a tree like a fucking nigger. I throw Rory into the bottom of the river for the gators. And Clyde—I'll shoot him in the head like the dog he is. And your mother. And your sister. And it would take nothing for me to find out where Rose lives." Sal said all of this in the same fatherly tone he'd used thousands of times.

Jesse's gun shook in his hands.

"But, if you turn yourself into Junior, Hymie, or any of my other men, I promise they live."

Jesse closed his eyes. He thought of the moves he had left to make. There were none. Sal had politicians in his pocket, cops, lawyers, power Jesse had no access to. And that's not to mention he could have even more hitmen in New Orleans in less than a day. "I'll need until end of the day. To... to get my affairs in order."

Hymie pointed a nubby finger across the table. "You get five minutes head start." He flashed a gritty grin.

Sal grabbed Hymie's wrist. "You get a couple of hours. I'll give you that much."

Jesse nodded.

Sal reached across the table for Jesse's hand. "Now you're making sense, my boy." Sal gave a forgiving grin. "You're doing the right thing."

Jesse went back to the abandoned garage. Clyde, Twitch, and Rory's faces hung on the edge of suspense. "Where the hell did you go?" asked Clyde.

"To see Sal."

"And?"

"He says if I turn myself in this ends."

They all pled for him not to.

But what was he to do? They had no soldiers. Clyde was injured. Sal had the money, the power. The resources of the city. There was nothing Jesse could do to change that. There was nothing...

A neutered groan came from the gunman. Jesse stared at him. "I have an idea."

***

Big Sal was tired. So, so tired. It was deep, existential exhaustion rooted in the marrow of his bones and nestled deep in his soul. He sat on his couch with his cane across his lap. He gripped and twisted both ends like it was a magical wand capable of turning back the clock. Where did he go wrong? He brought Jesse and his brothers into his life, showed them the finer side, paid them for work, put Jesse through school, gave Clyde freedom to pull whatever jobs he wanted... he even took Jesse to the park to throw the ball around when his father was too drunk to walk, too enraged to love, too stupid to nurture Jesse's burgeoning genius.

He was old, his son was inept, and Jesse would soon die. Clyde would come for him afterwards, then he'd have to die. Then Rory would attempt. And so the pendulum would swing until the entire Pike Clan was gone. Sal closed his eyes. He prayed.

The house was spacious and empty when he was alone. He told his wife he needed some space for a while. He sent away Hymie. He needed the room for his grief.

There was chatter outside his front door. He'd heard something growing incrementally louder over the past half-hour, but he'd hoped it would go away. Then a knock came. His knees ached when he stood; his hands trembled on his cane. He closed his house robe over his pajamas and shuffled off to the door, grumbling under his breath. "Yea, yea. I'm coming."

The door swung open. Chills spread across his body. "Can I help you?"

A man asked, "Mr. Salvatore Bianchi?"

His heart almost stopped. "That's—that's me."

Handcuffs dangled from a detective's thumb. Another one stared at him with contempt. Big Sal shook his head. "What? Wait, no. What is this?"

He tried to back away, tried to fight, but the two younger men's grips felt like straitjackets, and next thing he knew, he was out of his house. "Can I please put some clothes on?" They ignored him. They didn't even bother to shut his door. Outside Sal's house, on his lawn, in his driveway, were journalists from newspapers all over the city.

"Mr. Bianchi! Look this way." A bright camera flash exploded into Sal's vision.

The detectives parted the people like The Red Sea. There was tandem noise coming toward Sal; the sound of the cops reading him his rights, the questions from the intrusive journalists. He screamed his confusion and ignorance at the top of his lungs. A journalist jumped in front of his lumbering stride to the police car. "So, what you're saying is that you had nothing to do with the dead assassin being found in the garbage outside of your restaurant?"

Sal rooted himself to the ground. "What?"

"The man who killed Mulligan. You had a well-publicized feud with Cameron, so, did you hire the assassin to take out Mulligan? Did you kill the assassin afterwards?"

Sal felt dizzy. The detectives barked at the journalists. "All right! All right! Move it, you vultures."

Right before they tucked his head down and threw him in the backseat, he caught a glimpse of a familiar face on the outside of all the madness. Jesse.

Jesse stood under the mighty oak tree at the edge of Sal's lawn. Their eyes met. Jesse held his gaze on Sal, letting him know it was he who called the detectives and left an anonymous tip. Letting him know who called the papers. Letting him know who took his political power. Sal's face hung between hurt and enraged.

Jesse looked at his watch. He only had a few hours, maybe half a dozen at most, before Sal got a lawyer down there to point out the circumstantial nature of the evidence. But it was more time than Jesse would've had previously. Sal got carted away in the back of the cop car, and Jesse set his mental clock. He only had a few hours to figure out how to beat Big Sal.

Chapter 33

One Last Move

Moving a dead body across town in the backseat of the car isn't hard when most of the town was out boycotting the current city administration, Sal figured. It's especially easier to move the body from the car to the street to the dumpster behind the restaurant when it's wrapped up tight like an old throw rug. Plus, it wouldn't be difficult to find the nearest phone booth and phone in an anonymous tip. Sal pieced that much together as the two detectives grilled him and called him slurs like he was some nobody dog. Sal pressed his head into his hands and laughed, and laughed, and laughed. It's all he could do. The detectives asked him what the issue was. He said, "Nothing." He was buying time.

Now the clock started for Jesse. Sal could only be locked up for so long and Jesse and the gang needed to scramble to get their ducks in a row. Twitch was dropped off at his house, where he grabbed his daughters and his wife quickly, not giving the girls a chance to wipe the sleep from their eyes or ask any questions. His wife didn't even bother; she looked at him with restrained anger and got in their family vehicle. It went about the same with Catherine and Louisa. Jesse had the women and children stashed safely away at the top of a penthouse suite, with four armed guards roaming up and down the halls.

***

Davy's pool hall was empty, quiet. If one listened close enough, they'd hear a lone fly buzzing around the room. Davy looked at the four nervous white men leaning against his pool tables with great reservation. "What the hell y'all got into now?"

Jesse told him everything he could, then explained why they asked him to shelter them for a bit. Davy said, "Smart. Hideout here, because a bunch of Jews and Italians would stick out like sore thumbs if they walked around here looking for you."

Jesse nodded.

Jesse moved pieces around the chessboard in his mind. Having Sal brought in for the murder of Cameron and the assassin wasn't permanent, but it diminished his political capital and bought Jesse a little time. Which leaves Hymie in charge for now. Hymie at the helm would be good. He's a soldier, not a thinker. And Junior's a non-factor. He formulated his plan then talked it over with Twitch, Rory, and Clyde.

Clyde shook his head. "This... it's not smart."

Jesse snapped at Clyde. "It's all I got."

"What if this doesn't work out?" asked Rory.

The four men all looked at each other, understanding they might not make it out in one piece.

"Well," said Jesse. "It's been a hell of a run."

***

Jesse stormed into Rudy's office and slammed the door behind him. Rudy jumped at the bang. "What's the meaning of this?"

Jesse hovered over Rudy's desk with his knuckles grinding into the wood. "I need help."

Rudy cleared his throat and fidgeted with his tie, a sign that he was gearing up to bullshit Jesse. "With?"

"How long can you keep Big Sal locked up?"

Rudy feigned ignorance.

Jesse snapped. "Don't toy with me, Rudy. I know you have people who can keep him detained for questioning for a long, long time. Don't you act like you don't know what's going on." Jesse eyed the newspaper on Rudy's desk.

Rudy's thumb slid across the image of Cameron's body splayed on the pavement. "Did—did Sal really do this?"

Jesse chose a half-truth. "Yes."

Rudy got up and ambled over to the bar. He was tense now. The veil of practiced confidence dropped like a tidal wave. He took a swig of whiskey with his back still to Jesse. "No."

"Well, can—can you at least have some police buddies pick up Hymie on bullshit charges?"

"I can't do that, Jesse." He turned and pointed a finger.

"A lot of bad things have happened since I last listened to you. And the ORD had a good working relationship with Sal, who was a respected businessman, and who got the vote out from the Italian community. And we had to lose that, because of the mess you dragged us all into."

Jesse was in Rudy's face in two long strides. "I didn't make you take the money, you greedy asshole." His finger hung inches from Rudy's face. "You're scared because you think Sal will get out, and if he finds out you aided me in any way, your head will be on a pike, you yellow-bellied piece of shit."

Jesse was close enough to see Rudy's fat Adam's apple anxiously bob up and down. Rudy slipped on his famous sleazeball smile. "It's just business."

Jesse stepped backward. "Business. Understood." Rudy Thompson: politician and businessman first, human being second. "Rudy, if I live past the next day or so, I want you to know something: you're gonna wish you took my side."

Rudy toasted Jesse. "We'll see."

Jesse's nerves were on edge the entire ride down the elevator. Every shake or tremble or grind made him think *this is it.* He exhaled when the elevator's operator opened the gate and no one was waiting in the lobby with a Thompson machine gun. But the lobby doors were still far away. Between him and the outside was a wide cavern of possible assassins. Every moving body around him was a threat. Today could be the end of the world for Jesse, but the financial district still buzzed on without a hitch. He moved one leg in front of the other. His eyes darted left to right, from one stranger in a suit to another. His heartbeat thrummed in his ears, his legs wobbled, but he made it across the wide expanse and down the steps to his car.

He sped off from the sidewalk into the busy intersection. The monochrome grey buildings of the financial district blurred by in his peripheral. He was flying by the seat of his pants. Big Sal could only be held up for so long.

In moments, without realizing it, he was in front of Rose's house. Whenever he was nervous or scared or shaken to his core, he always went to her. He watched her through her window. He could see her father and mother holding her while she cried on the couch. Jesse squeezed the steering wheel. He almost had it. He almost had freedom. He almost had the life he'd always wanted. He punched the steering wheel and screamed as he drove up the street. He was so close, closer than he ever would be to true freedom again. But he would mourn his losses later. He had one more plan waiting for him in the Irish Channel.

***

"Tear this place apart." Hymie stood at the threshold of the Pike's childhood home and struck a match to light his cigar. He watched his men turn the mostly bare home apart through the thin film of smoke in front of him. "Ah, nebekh bastardz," he said to himself in Yiddish. *Poor bastards.* The Pikes barely had a home for him and his men to tear apart. But that didn't stop them from tossing the table over in the kitchen, rummaging through the rooms, and breaking the one vase sitting idly next to the worn couch. He pinched the bridge of his nose. "Let's get out of here."

Hymie had gone to sleep the night before with the knowledge that by morning, the Pike Boys would be dead. He'd have a few extra grand in his pocket, enough to get his wife something nice, hell, maybe even enough to get his girlfriend some pearls too, but instead, he woke up to the news he was down a man, maybe three, and someone had killed Cameron Mulligan on accident. The fucking DA. It was a wrap; he was going to make Jesse's death slow and painful.

Next stop, The Magnolia. Jesse's partner almost pissed himself when Hymie strolled into his office with a gun conspicuously poking from his waistband. Hymie opened his mouth to go with the usual speak-or-die rhetoric, but Melvin spoke all on his own: "I don't have any money, but take what you want, what is this about, I don't know anything. I don't even know who you are."

Melvin went on like this for a while until Hymie was no longer amused with his girlish squealing. Hymie put a fat, nubby finger, in Melvin's chest. "If Jesse comes back, let me know, alright?"

Melvin nodded his head like it was on a spring. Hymie walked away slowly, then jab-stepped at him to see the small man flinch. He chuckled.

Cops flowed from every crevice of Sal's restaurant, examining the entrances for blood, warding off aggressive journalists, forming a barrier between the crime scene and passers-by. Hymie pushed through the civilian viewers to get up close. The body had been taken out the dumpster but sat slumped against the wall, like a carelessly thrown garbage bag. His flesh was a Rorschach test of bruises, with gashes of red scattered around. Hymie spotted Junior on the opposite side of the cordoned-off area arguing with a cop. Hymie walked over and snatched Junior by the elbow. He dragged the boy away while he launched expletives toward the officer.

"What are you doing?" Hymie asked.

Junior swiped Hymie's arm away. Junior glared like he wanted a fight. Hymie flashed his tobacco-stained grin. Junior shrunk away.

"This is bullshit. My father would've never," Junior looked around. "He would've never done this like this."

"We're gonna get your dad out, boychik. You can't help by getting tossed in the slammer for assaulting officers, though."

Junior stepped up to Hymie. "I want to be out there. I can fight alongside you."

Hymie gripped both of Junior's shoulders and massaged them. He placed his words as gentle as possible. "This ain't for you, Junior."

Junior, yet again, swiped Hymie's hands away. Hymie scowled. Junior paced around with his hands on his hips, then stopped to pivot toward Hymie. "I have men of my own. We could storm the streets."

Hymie laughed. It was a big, hearty laugh. He held his stomach like it was going to rupture if he let go. "Your dad lets you keep the books for a few of his interests, and you can't even do that. Me and my men, we're going regroup.

I'll be at home, and they'll be at the bar." He patted Junior's face. "Let me know when you're ready to be a man and not a spoiled fucking brat." Hymie brushed past Junior like he wasn't there, leaving him to sit with his anger. Letting him know he wasn't a factor in this war.

***

A cloud of resentment trailed Junior all the way home. His father called Hymie first. Not him. He didn't know his father was even in trouble until he saw the cluster of cops outside the restaurant, picking and probing every crevice, molesting the place that would be his upon his father's death. Hymie's words bounced around his mind: "spoiled fucking brat." He would prove Hymie wrong. The thought of being the first to find Jesse made his nostrils flare and his mouth water.

Junior sifted through his ring of keys while walking up the steps of his stucco two-floor home. His front door whined open an inch with barely a touch. He pushed the door open further. "Hello?"

The agape front door left the living room sliced into diagonal halves of natural sunlight and dark misshapen figures in the far corner of the room. One of the shadows moved. Junior grabbed the gun from the top drawer of the credenza and flung it up toward the shadow. "Don't fucking move." The shadow stepped forward with his hands up. Junior's nerves frayed and snapped. "I said don't..."

Sunlight splashed across part of the shadow's face. "Good morning, Junior," said Jesse. "I'm ready to turn myself in."

Chapter 34

Where It All Began

Junior's gun turned Jesse's mouth desert dry. His weapon was accompanied by a wide smile running across his face like Jesse was a prized buck. They'd been sitting in the sparsely lit room for what felt like hours, waiting for a call from Big Sal. Eventually, the phone chimed. "Dad?" asked Junior.

Low chirping came from the phone. Then Junior said, "I got him, dad. I got him." He smiled. Then it disappeared. He nodded up and down. "Uh huh, ok. Yea, yea I'll call him." Junior set the phone down.

Jesse stowed away his fear. "I'm guessing your father's been bailed out."

"Shut up."

"He wants you to call Hymie, doesn't he?"

Junior was silent. But Jesse kept talking and talking,

doing nothing but filling the silence, hoping anything he had said or promised would land. Eventually, Junior checked his watch, then carted Jesse off to his car.

Jesse's heart thumped out his chest when Junior's car stopped in front of the old Bianchi's grocery store. Junior cut the car off. "Get out."

Jesse moved slowly, making sure Junior saw his hands at all times. He'd rather not get shot in the middle of the street and left to be found like... Cameron. He shuddered at the idea. Junior got behind Jesse and poked the gun in his back and stood close to him like they were two pals having a good conversation, but Jesse was frozen. "Wait."

Junior jabbed a little harder in Jesse's side, but Jesse was struck by how similar today's weather was to the day he and Clyde tried to steal food from the storefront. They were so young, Jesse thought. That was the same day they had met Big Sal. The townhouses on both sides of the grocery store still had the same bright green ferns draped over the black railings, and he bet if he knocked on the doors, the same families would still be living there. Jesse eventually walked inside after getting tired of the barrel touching his back.

Inside the store was naked, but there were once cans stacked on the shelves, produce boxes in front of the store, various lively chatter from Italian gangsters who'd come stop by to shoot the shit while customers shopped in the background. Jesse and Clyde had to work off their attempted theft by sweeping the inside of the store every single day after school. And then they began to skip school.

Jesse rubbed the countertop. A much younger, skinnier,

Hymie would've been leaning against it while picking at his teeth. Junior would be behind the cash register, resentment radiating from his pores. And Sal would be in the back with his feet kicked up reading a newspaper.

"Move it, fucker," Junior said.

Walking up the long hallway to Sal's office felt more ominous and heavier than usual. He stopped right outside the door. As a child, he would push the door open and see Big Sal with that jovial, immense smile on his face. "Hey there, boy." Jesse rubbed a hand against the door.

Junior gave him a push. "Come on."

Jesse's overwhelming nostalgia almost made him expect to be greeted the same way. But instead, Big Sal sat in his chair with his hands stacked on top of his cane. He looked old. Weak. Like a hard wind could make him fall to pieces like a house of cards.

Big Sal struggled to his feet. He grabbed both sides of Junior's face. "You did good, boy." He guided Junior's face down to plant a kiss on his forehead.

Junior's face swelled with compassion and love. "Thank you, father."

Junior moved to the background.

Big Sal motioned Jesse to the seat in front of him, then waved his hand over the chessboard in between them like a magician. Jesse nodded. Jesse took his pieces and put them into place. He moved his piece across the board first.

They smiled at each other, ignoring the obvious weight of the situation.

"So, why here?" Jesse asked.

Sal stared intently at the board. "When you were a little boy, you were always so nervous. Always so scared of what your father would say if he knew you'd been taking money from me. But even then, you knew it had to be done. You knew you couldn't let the fear of a beating outweigh the fear of going hungry, of not having food on your table." Sal looked at Jesse with resigned pride. "Even then, as a little boy, you knew that this world was for the strong, for those who took what they wanted from it."

Jesse jumped Sal's piece. "You put any animal in a situation where it would starve, it will figure out a way to eat."

"Don't downplay yourself, boy. You're strong. Stronger man than your father, and any other man I'd ever known."

Jesse raised his piece to move, but Sal snatched his wrist with a shaky hand. Sal's anger and sadness bubbled to the surface. "Why? For what? You could've run this city if you wanted to. I could've given you the keys. But for what? Why go against me? To prove some moral code? To be more like the suits in the financial district? For a fucking woman?"

Jesse fought off emotion. "I don't know." He didn't. He could've killed Bobby, been Big Sal's heir, and things would've been easy.

Sal scooted the board away. Jesse's head hung low, his king dangling free in his fingers. "I did fuck up. I tried to go against my nature. My entire life, people tried to tell me what I was: a street rat. Thug. Son of a violent drunkard. But I said no. That wasn't me. I went to college to get that stain wiped from my name." Jesse tipped over one of Sal's pieces with his piece. "But you can't fight your nature. And that was my mistake."

Sal's baggy eyes grew hard with anger. "You're so entitled and stupid. I can't.... this was not a good idea. This game is over. Soon, Hymie will be here, and this will all be done with." He threw his hands at the situation.

Jesse shook his head. "I don't know about that, Sal."

***

Hymie's crew waited in a dive bar on Carrollton Street waiting for their next orders. One of the five men waited by the phone. Hymie would be calling any moment now, but the time rolled by too slow for his liking. His attention was diverted when four unfamiliar men walked in wearing heavy coats with newspapers under their arms. The first man that walked in had devilishly red hair and a slender frame and a demonic smile. The man on the phone nodded his head toward the four newcomers, and the other men in Hymie's crew checked out why they were there. The red-haired newcomer put his hand up defensively and apologized for walking into the wrong place. The man on the phone nodded, then tried to reach out to Hymie. Hymie answered and told them to sit tight until someone got back to them. Hymie then hung up without another word.

The man who was on the phone was bewildered to see the red-haired man still standing there.

"I thought I told you lot to get on." He and his crew all stood at attention.

"So," the red-haired man said. "Is everyone here with Hymie?" He counted with his index finger and mouthed the numbers.

The man who was on the phone was annoyed now. "Who wants to know?"

The red-haired man nodded. "I'll take that as a yes."

Tommy guns appeared from under the newspapers. All of their eyes went wide. Small muzzle flashes and gun fire filled the room. Chips of wood and glass exploded, suspended in the air, all while the bodies of Hymie's hit squad shook and trembled on their feet and lumbered backward with the force of the bullets.

One man survived; the one who was on the phone. His last breaths were leaking from the holes in his body, his energy drained with each inch he attempted to crawl. Laughter from the red-haired man filled the room. Then glass crunched under boots. The crawling man felt the sharp pinch of the wood chips and glass stabbing into his skin through his pants. The collective blood soaked deep into the wood and spread out until a deep red color set in. The crawling man followed an ankle that appeared in front of him all the way up to the face of the devilish looking man with red hair. The man pleaded in small spurts. "Who— why? Who are you?"

The man with the red hair, Joe, pulled out his pistol. "Jesse Pike says hi."

The man's eyes went wide. One bullet crashed through his skull. The other dead men hung sporadically over tables, or rested sideways on chairs, all with their last bit of life seeping through the holes in their bodies. Joe looked to the other shooters and whistled, nodding his head toward the

Tommy gun. "A beaut', ain't it?"

***

Sal sat at the edge of his chair. "What are you talking about?"

"The game isn't over for me." Jesse sat back and crossed his legs, then brushed his jacket sleeve down. "You always used to brag about how you were the most protected man in New Orleans, which you were." Jesse began counting off fingers. "But that was because of your political power, and your hired guns. Which, now, both of those are gone. Now you're an old man near death. There's no backup coming, Sal."

Sal was speechless.

"One thing you always did, Sal, was overestimate exactly how much I really needed you. I've made friends of my own now."

***

Hymie slammed the phone down and groaned. He was getting too old for this shit. His son scampered on the floor with a hand full of crayons, then eyed the wall like a blank canvas. But Hymie ignored it. He was busy waiting for Big Sal or Junior to call. If the little shit was gonna scribble on the walls, his wife could deal with it. She was up cleaning already anyway. The vacuum whirred loudly and agitated the shit out of him. He waved at his wife to get out the living room. She smirked then let the vacuum fall where it was. Hymie shook his head.

A knock at the door. He waited for her to get it, but she was busy giving him the long-distance cold shoulder in the kitchen. He rocked to his feet and eyed his son as he made a long squiggly line against the wall. Outside the door were uniformed officers. Hymie rubbed his jowls and put on his best friendly voice. "What can I help with today, officers?"

"Sir, you're under arrest for the murder of DA Cameron Mulligan."

Hymie's beady eyes zig-zagged around to look for a way out of this, contemplating whether or not he should kill the cops, run away with his family... or maybe leave his family there, and go and get them later. His wife and son walked behind him.

"What's the meaning of this?" his wife asked.

Hymie decided to play it cool.

He planted a soft kiss on his wife's cheek and rubbed his son's head. "I'll be alright. This'll get cleared right up."

Hymie was carted off and his son and wife held onto each other in the doorway.

The officers drove in silence for the entire ride. Hymie watched familiar landmarks zoom by him. The district precinct was passed up miles back, then they passed through another one, until they ended up in the Warehouse District on a side-street with no other cars on it. Hymie looked around; nothing other than trash blowing up the cobblestone road and a door to the warehouse on the right. Hymie chuckled. "You boys ain't cops, are ya?"

The cops said nothing.

Hymie threw his shoulder into the backdoor and rocked the car side-to-side. The cops hopped out and tried to yank him out of the back seat, but he kicked and wiggled away the best he could with his hands cuffed behind his back. The cops got his legs eventually and dragged him to his feet. Hymie screamed for help. It fell on deaf ears.

They pushed him through the door, into the warehouse, past a mountain of crates, and into the center where he saw Rory, Clyde, and Twitch standing next to open crates of booze.

Anger, fear, and anxiety manifested as a taut grin on Hymie's pallid flesh. He laughed. "You fucking boys, eh?" He eyed the booze curiously. The fake cops pushed him to the ground. One of the cops spoke in a silky Irish brogue. "He's all yours."

Hymie turned at the waist to look at the officers. "Oh, the little shoe shines made some friends, I see." Clyde's arm was stuck in a sling with a patch of blood at the top of the shoulder. Hymie snickered. "I see my guy got you good, eh?"

Silence.

Hymie said, "Clyde, look at you, you sick, sick, bastard. You think your brothers are gonna ever respect you? You're sick in the head; a degenerate. Not even man enough to do what you wanted me to do."

Clyde clenched his fist at Hymie's words.

"But don't worry; you'll end up on the end of that noose one way or another," Hymie said. He looked at the crates of liquor once again, then it finally sunk in what their plans were. He appreciated it. He figured Sal would appreciate it, as well. Hymie cackled and rocked back and forth manically. "Do it if you're going to do it! Come on! Right in the face."

Clyde took a gun from his waistband with his free hand and held it out. Rory stepped up. He took it from Clyde and held his arm out as stiff as a rod but his knees trembled. Hymie scooted closer and pressed his head to the barrel. "Just like that, that way, not even my family can have an open casket."

Rory bit his lips and held his gaze on Hymie as much as he could, but Hymie's intense, sociopathic glare never wavered or broke or lost its intensity.

Clyde stood right at Rory's side and whispered in his ear. "Just one squeeze. It ain't that hard. Just a little pressure." He spoke soft and even, almost like a father teaching his son how to hit a baseball. Another second went by, the tremble in Rory's knees worsened, and he lowered the gun. He hung his head, then handed Clyde the gun.

Clyde closed his eyes and rotated his head a little like he was trying to loosen the tension in his neck. "It's fine," he said. "It's fine."

He stepped up and placed the barrel to Hymie's head and in that moment, it set in to Hymie that he was the one on the other side of the gun for once. He wouldn't break though. He wouldn't cry like a ninny bitch like most of the fucks he'd put down. He closed his eyes, felt the cool steel against his head, then waited for that tell-tale boom of lead slamming through cranium.

The gun clicked.

Strength drained from Hymie's body and he shook like he'd just come in from the cold; warm piss stained his pants legs, and he hyperventilated. He opened his eyes to see

Clyde staring at him with a deranged smirk that rivaled his own. Clyde chuckled. "In the bakery, when you laughed? I get it now."

A tear ran down Hymie's face and his mouth curved into an O, but Clyde pulled the trigger but before he could even begin to plead for his life. An echo thundered throughout the warehouse and Hymie's body plopped to the ground. Tiny dots of blood splashed against Clyde's loafers. He took his foot and swiped the stray chunk of Hymie's brain matter onto Hymie's suit. He wouldn't need it anymore.

He turned around, handed the gun to Twitch, and placed his hand on Rory's shoulder.

Rory's eyes stayed locked on Hymie's body and he spoke in a whisper. "You— you knew there was no bullet in that first chamber. Why? Why would you do that?"

Clyde shrugged. "I just wanted to see that fat fuck lose that stupid grin, and I wanted you to be the one to make him lose it."

Rory's mouth hung open but no words came out. Clyde patted him on the back. "You ain't a kid no more, baby boy. Next time that chamber won't be empty."

Twitch and Clyde walked away, but Rory stayed a second longer, eyes lingering on Hymie's body, and his hands shaking at his side.

***

The weight of realization pushed Sal back in his chair. Jesse was calm and still. Sal's eyes became angry slits. He looked over Jesse's shoulders toward Junior. Junior shook where he stood, eyes staring holes into the ground. "You sold me out, son. You served up your own dad. And for what?"

A single tear slid down Junior's cheek. "For everything." Junior walked over and handed Jesse his gun. He exited the room.

"I gave him a simple offer: be your punching bag for another year or two, or he could be the man now. No Big Sal loyalists, no oversight telling him how dumb he is, and I'd stay out of whatever assets he's in control of." Jesse stood. "It wasn't a long conversation."

Sal squeezed the top of his cane. He looked so small now. "And, what? You just going to shoot me and get away with it?"

Jesse pressed the barrel to the side of Sal's head.

Sal chuckled. "I bet you have a plan for that, as well. I always knew... knew my demise would come from the inside. But I never expected this."

Jesse inhaled, exhaled. Inhaled, exhaled. Thought about how easy it would be. He just had to simply press the trigger and it would be over. Big Sal didn't bother to fight. He put his hand on Jesse's. It was the touch you gave a man who'd gotten a terminal diagnosis.

Sal nodded with a pained grin. "Jesse, wait, you were always like a so—"

The muzzle flashed, then Sal's body slumped sideways in the chair, then tumbled over. Jesse wrapped Sal's hand around the gun and left.

Chapter 35

New Beginnings

Every inch and crevice of St. Patrick's Church swelled with people who wanted to catch one final glimpse of Cameron Mulligan's body. His body was front and center, where the sun's light gave the multi-color stained glass windows a warm glow. The backdrop was a golden tabernacle glinting from rows of candlelight. Light shone down through the roof. It beamed over Cameron's body, like the lights of heaven were calling his soul home. The organ music and the low prayers of the people filling the rows and lining the walls worked in tandem to stir an emotion Jesse couldn't allow himself to feel until then: remorse. He was angry after Cameron was shot, in shock, even. But at the funeral, the tidal waves of sadness broke through his dam of anger. He stood in line to view the body.

Two rows ahead of him was Rose. His gut sank for her.

He wanted to go sit by her, assure her it would all be ok. Death is a stain that's scrubbed clean in time, is what he would say. She'd see through the lie. She spent many nights waking him from his father's ghost when they were in college.

Jesse was at the front now. He couldn't take his eyes off of the hollowed corpse. It... he looked peaceful. Unlike when he last saw him, his eyes wide, pleading for salvation, then the lull of realization when there would be none. Jesse held back tears. He strained his eyes to keep a single drop from rolling out. He leaned close to the casket, placing a steadying hand on the smooth wooden surface.

"You won, Cameron," Jesse paused for composure. "The Reform Party won." Tears blurred his vision. Andrew McCabe, Cameron's pick for Deputy Mayor, was voted-in in his place.

The bloodshed had caused an uproar in the citizens. Everyone wanted change. The ORD did their best to slow down the black and Italian vote with "literacy tests," but even staunch supporters of the ORD couldn't ignore that they were incubators for criminal factions.

The papers came up with a name for the gangland violence centering on the election period: "Bloody November." Cameron's death was pinned on Hymie. The connecting factor: Hymie, a career thug with a history of violence, killed Cameron Mulligan out of anger over the probes into the Thompson Co. Liquor hijacking. Hymie's body was found with the remaining missing crates of booze. Nobody cared to look deep into his death; he was a dirtbag killed in a deal gone wrong. Hymie's wife claimed two uniformed cops picked him up. No one believed her. Last Jesse checked, Hymie's family left town.

The city would be different now; it only took the sacrifice of a respected young man and philanthropist to make a change. And maybe that's what the city was built upon, Jesse figured; the bodies of those who bothered to give a fuck.

The funeral director coughed to let Jesse know his time had run out. He stopped to tell Andrew McCabe congratulations for his win. "Cameron would be proud to see how you will change the city." Andrew McCabe clasped Jesse's hands and gave a solemn nod. Jesse looked at Cameron's father. His head was slack on his shoulders, but his eyes were open. The lights were on, but no one was home. Then he stopped at Rose. She stood to hug him. She grabbed him like he could fly away, and he needed her to weigh him down; he held her like he wanted to absorb her pain. He whispered in her ear, "I'm so sorry." She stepped back and mouthed, "It's ok." Tears streamed down her face. He realized their hands dangled in one another's, hooked by the index and pointer fingers. They both let go. She walked past Jesse and whispered in a low, soft voice, "Take care of yourself." A loud sob erupted from her mouth.

Big Sal's funeral was no different than Cameron's. It was as packed and emotionally heavy. Jesse stood smushed in between a cluster of people off in the corner. He couldn't make it in time to get closer. The crowd was full of local celebrities, immigrants, a few politicians past and present, a few decrepit gangsters, small-time business owners, and the members of the East Coast Bianchi family. Everyone else sobbed, but their faces were stone. The clan was comprised of a woman and three men about Jesse's age, maybe a little older. They looked like they wouldn't let Sal's murder go. Jesse prayed Junior could hold up his end of the bargain, and make sure they wouldn't pry too deeply. The people went up and told stories about Salvatore's philanthropy, his love of the community, and his good-spirited nature. About half true. But then again, death absolved all sins.

Big Sal died a hero in some people's eyes, but a villain in others. Scandals marked the end of his life and tarnished his name. Plus, he was in bad health. It made sense he'd off himself. That's what the papers said, and what Junior was feeding to the out-of-state people who Big Sal worked with. The investigation was also handled by Detectives Nedley and Rodgers. The entire affair was wrapped up nice and tight, or so Jesse thought. But the scowls on the faces of the East Coast family said otherwise.

The service ended with a convoy to Lafayette Cemetery No. 1. About a dozen close friends and family stood around the mausoleum. The trees hung overhead and provided shade for Jesse to play the background while the family and close friends paid their last respects and put roses on top of the casket. Mrs. Bianchi, who wore a black hat with a black veil draped over her face, turned to Jesse and waved him over. He protested, but she walked over with a rose in her hand and guided him closer. She placed a hand on his shoulder. "You were like a son to him."

Jesse saw a faint smile through the thin veil. He walked slowly up to the casket, people parting to let him through, and laid the rose gently on top. He felt nothing. Absolutely nothing. It was disarming for him. He knew the grief would hit him twice as hard later down the line. Everybody formed a prayer circle around the casket as the groundskeeper began to push it into the giant marble slab. Jesse held hands with Junior on his left and Mrs. Bianchi on his right, her frail hand trembling in his, and he still felt nothing.

***

Jesse lumbered up the steps of the Rising Sun. Each step upwards felt like a mile high rise in altitude. He stopped at the double-doors, because once he walked through those doors, he would be a different man, and he needed time to catch his breath before that change came.

Inside the building was slow. Somber music played on the gramophone and drifted in from the east parlor, where Clyde, Rory, Twitch, Catherine, Davy, Rudy, and Joe sat spread out around the room. No one chatted or even looked at each other, but all were confused as to the nature of the meeting. All eyes fell on Jesse when he strode in and pulled a chair up to the center of the room. "Hello, everyone. This is going to be quick, so please save the questions for afterward. Today, I am taking back leadership of the Rising Sun, and all interests that entails."

Low confused chatter rose.

"Not only that," Jesse said. "We'll be working with Joe and his crew." Jesse motioned his arms toward the grinning, red-haired man. "He and his men helped us in our time of need, so I find it beneficial to strike up a continuing partnership. He's going to help us get access to fine, Irish whiskey," Jesse pointed to Rudy. "Which will come in via ships granted access with Mr. Thompson's connections in the Coast Guard." Rudy didn't look up from the floor once. Jesse had called Rudy beforehand and told him he needed to speak with him. Rudy had tried the defiant act, but Jesse reminded him that Twitch could shoot a tick off a dog's ass, and that Rudy should probably consider moving somewhere with no windows if he wanted to keep his petty games going.

Jesse smirked. "Thanks for that, by the way, Rudy."

Rudy muttered under his breath. "Yes, happy to help."

Jesse pointed at Davy now. "Davy, we're going to need you to play middleman again. There are some points in it for you." Davy tipped his hat and smiled. "And Catherine, I heard you really helped Clyde out a lot around here, so you can continue to work here." Catherine nodded. "Well, that's all, everyone." Everyone filed out slowly. All except for Joe. Rudy shuffled behind the line, but Jesse pressed a hand into his chest. "My friend Joe wants to talk some business with you. Is that ok?" The venom in his words let Rudy know it wasn't a request. Rudy turned to see Joe playfully waving at him.

Clyde waited for Jesse in the foyer. "What the hell was that? What happened to quitting?"

Jesse snickered. "No one ever really quits, do they? We either die or end up in the clink." Visions of his happy ending with Rose eroded to ash. "I'll run the restaurant and do this. I talked to Melvin. He's over the mop-up with Albert."

Clyde stepped in front of his stride. "No, you can't. We had a deal."

Jesse got close to Clyde's ear. "You almost got me killed, brother."

Clyde's eyes went wide. "Wh... what the hell are you talking about? I didn't—"

Jesse gripped his shoulder and stared into his eyes. "Yes, yes you did. Don't talk. Listen. When you were high, you went and told Hymie what I told you about Bobby. The hitman said so when Twitch got it out of him." Jesse's lips quivered from anger. "You don't even remember do you?" Jesse shook his head. "You almost got all of us killed because you're a junky, brother. A fucking junky." He gripped the back of Clyde's neck and held his face close to his and could see Clyde searching through the haze of his booze and drug-clouded memories, and saw when the truth emerged slowly, like a light through dense fog. "Jesse..."

Jesse let him go. "This is how you repay me. You never question me again. I point, and you follow. On top of that, if I ever see you shooting-up, over-drinking, or anything like that ever again, I'll..." Jesse stopped his sentence short. "Clyde, do you understand? I'm running the show; I have nothing else other than this. You might as well leave me this." Jesse left Clyde standing like a sentry in the foyer. He was going to let him sulk for a while.

The day went on as usual: the girls filed in and lounged

around the various rooms of the house. Then the guests arrived. They greeted Jesse with a smile and a handshake. Then the west parlor came alive. The music swelled through the room, smoke drifted to the ceiling, guests who were too sober and timid to approach a girl hours earlier were now too drunk to be able to speak. Madam Eve pulled money folds from her bosom and handed them to Jesse, who then handed them to Mickey to put in the safe.

Jesse sat on his stool by the bar and watched life around him go on as if nothing extraordinary had happened recently. Two men died grisly deaths; Cindy left, probably on a train out west or maybe to New York; Rose was gone. She was still in the city, but lost to him emotionally. He'd heard rumblings she'd taken a leading role in Mulligan's foundation.

Clyde was broken as much as the day he was released from prison. Jesse felt grief and resentment for him. Rory experienced death up close and personal several times in the past months, and he acted like it didn't bother him. He watched Rory move around the brothel and crack jokes like nothing happened, a big smile on his face and hearty laughs from him and whoever listened to him. But behind his charm and energy and that all-engrossing aura that sucked everyone closer to him like a vortex, something had cracked. Strangers couldn't notice it, but Jesse could. His brother, who wasn't made for the world Jesse and Clyde grew up in, who had held onto his humanity for as long as he could, was losing it. He was mostly numb for now, but one day, it would hit him. And it would hit him hard.

And Jesse, well, he was back here like he'd never left, sitting on his stool by his bar, shaking his customers' hands and ordering shots on the house. Everything mended back together like a jagged, healed scar. It made Jesse laugh. This was the beauty and the ugliness of New Orleans: she always eventually went back to normal. Whether it was the Spanish flu, the lynchings of the early 1900s, or Bloody November, she never strayed too far from what's normal. Life here always popped back into place like a rubber-band. And she never let you forget who you really were.

Epilogue

God's Wrath

The New Orleans Customs House was a giant four-story slab of gray granite and cast iron resting on the rounded corner of Canal and North Peters Street. Outside of it, a man in a thick black coat and bowler hat leaned against his walking stick and admired the Greek and Egyptian revival architecture, every square inch of its beauty and grace, with the observation of a true connoisseur. The inside was even more illustrious, a home meant for the Greek Pantheon; vaulted ceilings, thick columns that stretched to the heavens, with an open skylight over the stairs. But this also saddened him; this was also home to a bunch of incompetent fucking suits. That's what the man thought. One of the greatest feats of architecture and it's wasted on a cesspool like New Orleans—like a huge diamond found in a plop of shit.

He eyed everyone walking around like they were vermin. Nothing but bureaucrats, sodomites, and harlots lived in New Orleans, in his opinion, and he tried to figure out which were which. But that could wait. The big clock on the wall indicated he was late for his first day at his new job, and he couldn't afford to make a bad first impression.

He click-clacked his way up to the 3rd floor where the Treasury Department had set up an office for the Prohibition Bureau, and entered the chatty office with a wide grin.

"Good evenin'," he said, his southern drawl hearty yet tender, strong yet endearing, smoother than a drip of honey fresh off the comb. "I'm terribly sorry for my late arrival." All ten agents' heads perked up from paperwork and from by the water cooler, but none of them stopped gabbing to acknowledge him. He sighed. This level of attention to detail allowed the whole city to spill over with liquid sin.

He hobbled over to a desk where an agent had his legs up and fingers laced across his stomach. The chatty agent recounted a trip he'd taken to a local brothel with pride and gusto and the confidence of a stage performer. The agent stopped talking, assessed the older man, and raised an eyebrow. "Call the number if you have a tip, sir. We're hard at work here."

The older man grinned. He picked up the biggest book near him, raised it above his head with both hands and slammed it down with the might of a lumberjack dropping an ax. The explosion boomed around the room and caused all conversations to stop, and all movement to cease. Nothing could be heard in the room save for the phones ringing off the hook.

The older man removed his hat. Then tossed it on the chatty agent's desk.

"Hello, everyone. I am R.J. Harris." He paused. All eyes were glued to him. "And I am your new boss."

He eyed each and every one in their faces, and it revealed without a single word that they knew who he was. They all stood and straightened out their sleeves and shirts and ties and scampered back to their desks, but it was too late. He'd seen enough. He pointed his stick at the chatty agent in front of him. "You. You're terminated."

The agent didn't try to protest. He walked out after a few moments, completely neutered, his pride and gusto shattered on the floor.

R.J. walked over to the secretary's desk and asked where the Director's office was.

She pointed down the hall. He nodded his head and curled a smirk under his thick white mustache. A young agent jumped in his face as he was walking and stammered like a child gearing up to ask a parent for an expensive toy. "Pleasant weather we're having today, aren't we sir?"

R.J. snickered. "Yes. Proof that even God's light shines on Hell every now and again."

The chatter of R.J.'s legend passed back and forth amongst the agents as he walked up the hallway. Some say he'd taken the scalps of over a thousand Indian men. Others say he took down several moonshiners all by himself. R.J.

would never state what was true or false. He wanted his underlings to fear him, and his colleagues to revere him.

R.J. made his way down to his new office. The Director was huddled over a box filled with his belongings; family pictures, badge, his notebooks.

"Ah, ah, ah." R.J. waved his cane. The Director turned with a frown. "I'll be keeping anything pertaining to investigations, past and current."

The Director flung the thin books back on the desk. He made sure to bump R.J. on the way out.

"I heard the north is quite pleasant, Director. Erm, sorry, ex-director. And, oh, did your men have time to do what I asked before your... untimely... transfer?"

The ex-director said over his shoulder, "She's in the interrogation room."

R.J. followed the subtle cries and made it to the bare office the bureau was using as an interrogation room.

"My, my," he said. "Aren't you a pretty little thing?"

The woman said nothing. Black streaks ran under her eyes.

"Now, now," he pulled a handkerchief from his front pocket. "No need to cry." He handed her the handkerchief, but she ignored it. He let it fall to the floor right by her foot.

"Well, that'll be there if you need it." He dropped a folder on the desk in between him and her, and hummed as he combed through the page after page. He moved slow and deliberate, letting the woman stew in her anxiety until she was ripe for the kill. He read through the text, but oh, he also watched her squirm and fidget her way through several emotions: fear, contempt, sadness, then outright anger, all with her face and without saying a word. Her fear pulsated from her in waves like a tide, and he soaked it up.

She turned to hide the fact she was crying again. *Almost there,* thought R.J.

She said, "Please, I want to speak to a lawyer."

He snickered. *Got her.*

"When I was told that things down here were going to Hell in a handbasket, I didn't think it was almost literal." R.J. licked his finger and flipped to the next page. "So, I'm on the train—leaving from West Virginia. My God; those Godless, moon-shining, inbred mongrels. Forgive me; I'm working on my foul tongue." He smiled. "I'm on the train heading back home to Baton Rouge. Heard of it? Your files, yes, I read up on you, says you're not from here originally. And I know girls like you typically don't travel much." He paused and looked her up and down. Pretty young thing, she was. Her glare was full of pure hate. "But anyway, I'm coming down to Baton Rouge and I remember my nephew had something big coming up." He tries to snap to remember what the big thing was. "Oh. He was running for Mayor."

The woman's eyes drifted to the floor.

R.J. stood and undid his tie and unfastened his cufflinks, then took his coat off and folded it over the chair. "Then I find out, because I have a lot of friends in high places in this state, that he was killed. Assassinated by Godless, gangster bastards. And then I think to myself, maybe this is God's will. Maybe a good man like my nephew dying will make these sick, weak-minded souls see the error of their ways." His voice veered into veiled anger. "But no, no, more killings happen days after. More Godless, deranged bastards spill blood across this city."

The woman wanted to crawl out of her own body just to get away from him. "None of that has anything to do with me."

"Oh, no, it doesn't. But then yes, it does. You're the beautiful little spider nestled up in this here web. You were caught, let's see. Ah, yes; seeking to terminate a pregnancy." He shook his head. "Blasphemous whore."

He walked behind the woman and placed his hands gently on her delicate shoulders. He imagined how easy it would be to grind them into dust, right in between his fingers, and leave her to stew and rot like Cameron was left to stew and rot. But feeling her shudder underneath his grip would have to sate this hunger.

"Now, now," he squeezed tighter. "Don't you begin to cry again. I'll get to it: my nephew got gunned down by gangster scoundrels like a dog, and my research since I've been here has merited that a Jesse Pike was hysterically holding my nephew's body." His grip grew tighter. "People said he said he was the one responsible for my dear sweet nephew's death." His eyes turned menacing and his thumb began to graze the back of the woman's neck. She moved away from his touch like oil from water.

Her whimpering stopped and she shot up. "Let me go!"

R.J. went blind; her chair tumbled across the room, the desk flung over, the pages once on the desk fluttered in the air and fell slow to the earth like delicate snowflakes. The woman backed away slowly. R.J.'s hair was a mess over his face, but his demonic eyes could be seen between the strands.

"Oh, if I let you go, it'll be to jail. So you're going to tell me everything you know about the Pike Brothers and this Jesse Pike. And any of his other associates." His smile was like a predator baring its teeth. He backed away, muttered low to himself with his eyes closed. "'For the wrath of God is revealed from Heaven against all ungodliness and unrighteousness of men, who by their unrighteousness suppress the truth.' The good Lord remade the world when he wiped it away with water, then he gave a rainbow and said 'fire next time.' I am the fire. I am God's wrath."

Words were stuck in the woman's throat now; her face was void of any expression. That's the ripe state he wanted her in: unable to think, talk, articulate or believe that there was a world outside those four walls. He for now was her judge, jury, and executioner, and the only rights she had were the ones he gave her.

R.J. licked his lips and brushed his hair back. Then he picked up the table and the chair then motioned for her to sit, which she did. "Now, let's continue this chat," he said. "Starting with, Ms. Cindy: does Jesse know you're carrying his child?"

About the Author

By day Danny Cherry Jr. is a Customer Service Representative and caffeine-addled office-drone with an MBA. But by night, he writes political and personal essays; op-eds; novels; narrative nonfiction; and short stories. He has written for Buzzfeed News, Politico, The Daily Beast, Truly*Adventurous, Transformation Magazine, X- ray Lit Mag, Fiyah Lit Mag, Ploughshares, Antigravity Magazine, Apex Magazine, and Hexagon Magazine, as well as a few dozen blog posts on Medium.com. His short story, "Brief Life Story of Lila," was shortlisted for Best American Sci-fi and Fantasy 2023, and was added to Locus Magazine's "recommended reading list" for 2022.

You can follow him on twitter (or X, I guess) @ Deecherrywriter, where he posts every single thought he has in the moment without even a second thought. Oh, he's also reluctantly on Tiktok, Instagram, and BlueSky under the same handle.

www.bigeasypress.com

Acknowledgments

The last people I want to acknowledge are my readers. Without you, my words would just fade into a void.

Thanks for reading! Please add a review and rating on Goodreads and wherever you purchased the book, and let me know what you thought! Reviews and ratings help out indie authors a lot, and doesn't take very long to do. Also, if you want to keep up with my magazine writing, or want to know when other novels are released, please subscribe to my newsletter: Bigeasypress.substack.com

Go here to get to Goodreads (as well as see some other links)